FINDING LOVE AT HEDGEHOG HOLLOW

HEDGEHOG HOLLOW BOOK 1

JESSICA REDLAND

B
Boldwood

First published in Great Britain in 2020 by Boldwood Books Ltd.

1

Every effort has been made to obtain the necessary permissions with reference to copyright material, both illustrative and quoted. We apologise for any omissions in this respect and will be pleased to make the appropriate acknowledgements in any future edition.

A CIP catalogue record for this book is available from the British Library.

Paperback ISBN: 978-1-80048-561-7

Ebook ISBN: 978-1-83889-115-2

Kindle ISBN: 978-1-83889-116-9

Audio CD ISBN: 978-1-83889-230-2

Digital audio download ISBN: 978-1-83889-113-8

Large Print ISBN: 978-1-80048-319-4

Boldwood Books Ltd.

23 Bowerdean Street, London, SW6 3TN

www.boldwoodbooks.com

For my Auntie Gwen, a real life 'hedgehog lady'
With lots of love xxx

'Would I be right in thinking that wasn't easy for you?' Dad whispered to me shortly after we exited the church behind the newlyweds.

My stomach did somersaults. Had he guessed the truth? 'It was really easy,' I said quietly, hoping to deflect him. 'All I needed to do was smile, hold the bouquet, arrange her train and smile some more. My cheeks are aching.'

'And I bet your heart is too. Mine would be if my cousin had just married the love of my life.'

'Dad! Shhh!' Even though he'd spoken softly, I still felt the need to grab his arm and lead him down the church path away from prying ears – like Great-Aunt Agnes's. Mum's auntie already hated me for some unfathomable reason so it was best not to provide her with more ammunition.

'James is *not* the love of my life,' I insisted, very much aware of the shake in my voice. 'We just... well, he... it was...' Looking up into Dad's warm brown eyes, I crumbled. There was no point denying it. 'No, it wasn't easy. If I was to compile a list of the worst days ever, losing Gramps would be top but today wouldn't be far behind.' My voice cracked on the final words.

Dad pulled me into a hug, instantly comforting me with his

warmth and strength. At six foot four, there was a lot to hold onto and I didn't think I'd ever grow too old for a hug from him, especially on a day like today.

'Thanks, Dad,' I said as we separated. 'I needed that.'

'Can everyone except the bride and groom move away from the church entrance please?' called the wedding photographer.

I lifted up the skirts of my bridesmaid dress as Dad and I moved further down the church path. With a heavy heart, I turned and watched Chloe and James gaze adoringly at each other under an archway of pink and cream roses while the photographer snapped photos and tried to shoo away the paparazzi of friends and relatives thrusting mobile phones into his shot. The mid-August sun warmed my bare arms and I closed my eyes for a moment, head tilted upwards, as the gentlest of breezes kissed my face, comforting and relaxing me.

Dad and I stood in silence for a few minutes, watching the photographer issue instructions to Chloe and James to stand side by side, hold hands, face each other, kiss. I couldn't help fantasising that I was the one in the ivory dress instead of my cousin, starting my happy ever after with the man with whom I'd been hopelessly in love for nearly two years.

Unable to bear watching them any longer, I drew my eyes away but they rested on the equally unsettling sight of Mum smiling proudly and hugging Auntie Louise, mother of the bride. A familiar wave of sadness swept over me. I completely understood that their sisterly closeness was multiplied several-fold by being identical twins but what I'd never understood was why that warmth and affection couldn't be shared with Dad and me. I actually couldn't remember the last time she'd hugged me. Some people aren't tactile but she didn't fall into that camp, frequently hugging Auntie Louise and Chloe. I'd always had a difficult relationship with her and had often wondered if part of it was her envy of how close I was to Dad. Yet she was so close to her twin that surely it couldn't be a surprise that Dad and I, left on the periphery, had forged such a strong bond. *Stop it, Sam. Not today. Today is challenging enough without going down that road.*

'Mum looks nice,' I said. In keeping with the colour scheme, she wore a pale-pink floaty dress, a matching pink waterfall jacket and a fascinator.

'Your mum looks beautiful,' Dad said, a wistful tone to his voice. 'It's good to see her in something that isn't black for once.'

I couldn't remember seeing Mum wear anything but dark, drab colours. Auntie Louise, by contrast, usually wore bright colours although she'd opted for a muted palette today. Her mother-of-the-bride outfit was really classy – a fitted dusky pink shift dress with an ivory lacy bodice, pink jacket and matching wide-brimmed hat.

'And you look very smart,' I added. Dad was a vet so I was used to seeing him in a shirt and trousers but he'd invested in a charcoal three-piece suit and new shoes for the wedding and he looked very distinguished.

Looking towards the bride and groom once more, I sighed. What a strikingly beautiful couple they were. With his muscular physique, dark blond hair, immaculately coiffed beard and piercing blue eyes, James could have been a model – and so could Chloe. The off-the-shoulder bodice and the bottom of her ivory dress were covered in intricate pink and cream embroidery. Her waist-length blonde hair was piled in loose curls on the back of her head, pinned back with sparkly flowers, while two delicate plaits criss-crossed over the top of her head like a headband. Absolutely stunning. Although Chloe could have worn a binbag and still looked incredible. Her dad, my Uncle Simon, had Danish roots and those genes had blessed Chloe with straight pale-blonde hair, ice-blue eyes and chiselled cheekbones.

Chloe attracted male attention wherever she went and, once we hit our teens, was never without a boyfriend. As we got older, she became a magnet for men who used her like a beautiful trophy on their arm. None of them appreciated her. She was cheated on several times, put down or made to feel stupid. I remembered one particular ex ridiculing her for her job as a pre-school assistant, calling it, 'playing with children all day because you're too thick to teach them'. She was no pushover so wouldn't take it for long before ending it and moving on, yet she never seemed to learn, picking the same alpha-male bad-boy type each time.

She also struggled with female friendships, being on the receiving end of jealous accusations of flirting with their boyfriends or trying to outshine them all the time, so she clung to me – the one person who'd always been there for her.

It saddened me that, as a result of so many negative experiences, Chloe was insecure about her looks when she absolutely had no need to be, whereas I – the one who blended into the crowd – was really comfortable in my own skin most of the time. I was five foot eight and slim, same as Chloe, but the complete opposite in colouring. My hair was thick and brown like Mum's and Auntie Louise's. For years, Chloe had tried to persuade me to get it thinned out or highlighted 'to attract the men' but I resisted. If I needed an expensive haircut for a man to notice me then they weren't worthy of my time, and no amount of toning or shading was going to make me the sort of woman who'd get a second glance when Chloe was around anyway, although that wasn't necessarily a bad thing.

My favourite feature was my eyes, which were hazel with amber and green flecks and a dark rim. When I wasn't with Chloe, and therefore not invisible, they were the first thing anyone noticed.

'Chloe looks stunning, doesn't she?' I said.

'She certainly does,' Dad agreed, 'and so do you. Lovely to see you in a dress for once.'

I curled my lip. 'Even a pink one?' I loved the style – full-length A-line tulle skirt with a ruched off-the-shoulder bodice, satin waist ribbon and corset-style detailing at the back. But the colour?

Dad laughed. 'It suits you. Although, being the only bridesmaid, I'd have thought Chloe could have given you some say in the colour.'

'She gave a few other options – very unenthusiastically – and you know how it is. What Chloe wants...'

'...Chloe gets,' we chorused together, smiling at each other.

'Which was one thing when you were kids and it was one of your

Barbies or dresses,' Dad continued. 'But you do know you can say no, don't you?'

'I know, but it was obvious how much she wanted pink and it's her big day, not mine.' My voice caught as I said the words. *No, definitely not mine. If only...* I cleared my throat as I continued. 'Her excitement far outweighed my objection so I was happy to go with the flow.'

Dad looked down at me earnestly. 'I love that you've always been so kind and thoughtful, Sammie, but I worry about it too. You're not kids anymore. You don't have to keep giving her what's yours.'

'I know, but James was never mine to hold onto.' A lump constricted my throat and I had to blink back my tears.

He shook his head, frowning. 'I know I only saw you together a few times but I thought you two were happy. Next thing I know, he's with Chloe and you're a bridesmaid at their wedding.'

'Sucks doesn't it? If it had been up to me, I'd have married James, had his children, and we'd have grown old together. But he wasn't feeling the love. Then one day, he finally was. Except it wasn't for me.'

'Oh, Sammie,' he said gently, his eyes full of sympathy and his shoulders slumped. 'I'm so sorry.'

'Please don't be nice to me. You'll set me off again.' I took a deep breath. 'I know it's not ideal that he chose someone in my family but, if it hadn't been Chloe, I'd have lost him to someone else. It was never going to last much longer, no matter how much I wanted it to. But it *was* Chloe he fell for and it is what it is. And look how happy she is. She deserved to find a good guy after all the bad ones.'

How could I begrudge her happiness with someone who I knew to be a genuinely lovely person whose only flaw, from what I'd seen, was that he hadn't fallen helplessly in love with me like I had with him?

'Can I have the bridesmaid and best man?' the photographer called. 'And can the immediate family be standing by please?'

'That's our cue.' Dad squeezed my hand as we stepped forward. 'You know I'm here for you if you ever want to talk about it.'

'Thanks, Dad. I know and I love you for it.'

As we posed for what seemed like hundreds of photos, I pushed my heartache aside and focused on Chloe's happiness. She wasn't just my cousin, she was my lifelong best friend. With only a six-month age difference, we'd been in the same class at school and had attended many of the same after-school clubs. We lived a couple of streets apart and our families holidayed together so every aspect of our lives had always been inextricably linked. And now we were linked by James, and I just had to learn to live with that or risk losing Chloe.

Two Years Earlier

As I drove through the picture-postcard pretty North Yorkshire village of North Emmerby towards Hannah and Toby's cottage, butterflies stirred in my stomach. Tonight I would finally meet Toby's best friend, James Turner – the man whom they were both convinced would be perfect for me.

I'd been best friends with Hannah for eight years, having met her at Liverpool University where we'd studied our degrees in adult nursing. She'd met her fiancé, Toby, a few years after graduation and, over the years, I'd spent many evenings or weekends in their company. The subject of James and I getting together had frequently arisen but we'd never been single at the same time so it hadn't been an option. Until now.

The butterflies intensified as I passed The Fox and Badger where Toby's thirtieth birthday celebrations would be taking place tonight. *Deep breath. Calm down. You can't spend the next four hours stressing about it.*

James and Toby were playing golf and James had strict instructions to return to the pub at 6 p.m. where Toby was expecting to join

Hannah and me for a birthday meal. What he wasn't expecting was the fifty friends and family members who'd be waiting to surprise him.

I parked in the lane outside their home, Fuchsia Cottage. The front door opened and Hannah rushed out for a hug. 'Thanks so much for coming early.'

'Couldn't leave you to put up all the decorations on your own,' I said, squeezing her tightly. 'Do you think he suspects anything yet?'

'Not a thing. Or, if he does, he's doing a brilliant job of acting like he doesn't.'

* * *

Twenty minutes later, we'd carried everything into The Fox and Badger's function room and were attaching thirtieth birthday banners to the walls.

'Are you excited about tonight?' Hannah asked. The mischievous twinkle in her eyes accompanied by a cheeky wink left no doubt as to what she meant, sending the butterflies soaring again.

'A little bit excited and very nervous. I feel like there's a massive expectation on us meeting and fireworks exploding. What if he doesn't like me?'

She placed her hands on her hips and raised her eyebrows at me. 'What's not to like? Besides, you might not like him either, although I don't think that will be the case. I still maintain that you're perfect for each other.'

As we continued to decorate the room, Hannah enthused about how much James and I supposedly had in common – same taste in music, films, books, sense of humour, outlook on life. If – or rather when – Hannah and Toby abandoned us together, at least we'd have plenty to talk about.

'Does he know you're trying to set us up?' I asked, positioning a balloon bouquet in one corner of the room while Hannah placed one in the adjacent corner.

She twisted a highlighted lock of hair round her middle finger and gave me a coy look. 'I've dropped a few hints. Subtle. Understated.'

I laughed. 'By which you mean unsubtle and overstated.'

Hannah looked at me with mock offence. 'What would make you say something like that?'

I shook my head at her, smiling. 'Ooh, maybe the unsubtle approach you've used on me. What was it you said? Oh yeah. "Toby's best mate James is a hottie and the perfect way to get over Harry would be to get under James". I think those were your *exact* words.'

She had the decency to look embarrassed. 'It's a good idea. It's been over two years since it ended with Harry and how many dates have you been on during that time?'

I sighed. 'None.'

'Exactly. It's time to get out there again.'

I knew she was right but my experience with Harry had massively knocked my confidence. He'd been my first long-term boyfriend and I'd thought it was going well. I thought we were in love and heading for old age together. Apparently not.

Harry was a junior doctor at the surgery where I worked after graduating. We were friends for a couple of years but it developed into something more. Relationships at work were frowned upon so I transferred to Whitsborough Bay's district nursing team. On our one-year anniversary, Harry invited me to move in with him but, two years later, he casually told me over breakfast one Saturday that it wasn't working and I needed to move out. Immediately. It seemed to come from nowhere. He claimed the relationship wasn't going anywhere, it had only ever been a bit of fun and surely it was better to end it now with happy memories rather than let it deteriorate until we ended up hating each other. I packed my belongings, feeling too shocked to cry and too confused to debate it further. If he didn't want to be with me, I wasn't going to humiliate myself by begging him.

I was carrying the last couple of bags out to my car when a woman showed up with a car full of suitcases and boxes. Turned out they'd been seeing each other for four years but she was married and unwilling to leave her husband. Presumably Harry's relationship with me was an attempt to make her jealous and coax her into action and it had finally worked. I didn't stick around to find out for certain.

After that, I hadn't felt ready to trust again so I'd avoided men, but the idea of being with someone two of my closest friends vouched for was appealing. There was no way they'd push us together if he was a player.

'We've confirmed a date for the wedding,' Hannah said, bringing my focus back to her. '3rd March next year.'

'Oh my gosh! That's brilliant news.'

'You'll be chief bridesmaid and James will be best man, which will be so fabulous if the two of you are an item.'

'And maybe a tad awkward if we're not.'

She winked at me. 'You will be. I'm convinced of it.'

* * *

'Surprise!'

Party poppers exploded and streamers were hurled as Toby stepped into the function room that evening. From the astonished expression on his face, Hannah had been right and he genuinely hadn't suspected a thing.

Toby hugged and kissed Hannah. I hung back in the crowd and took a moment to check out James while he greeted Toby's parents. Hannah's 'hottie' description was bang on. I hoped he had an amazing personality to match his good looks because first impressions were setting off serious fireworks.

I felt so nervous, I was shaking by the time Hannah appeared by my side with James in tow.

'The famous best friend! We meet at last.' He gave me a huge smile. 'I've heard so much about you, I feel like I've known you for years already.'

Relaxing my shoulders, I laughed. 'Same here. Your ears were probably burning on the golf course because someone's been singing your praises all afternoon.'

'How funny because Toby was doing the same about you.' James gave Hannah a gentle nudge in the ribs. 'You two are about as subtle as a sledgehammer.'

She raised her hands in surrender and tried to look innocent. 'No idea what you could possibly mean. Toby and I just wanted our best man and chief bridesmaid to get acquainted. And I'll leave you both to do just that.'

Without waiting for a response, she turned and made her way across the room, no doubt grinning to herself.

'Would you like a drink?' James asked.

'I'd love one, thank you.' I followed him to the bar.

'I wouldn't let on to those two, but I've been really looking forward to meeting you. I couldn't wait for six o'clock to arrive.'

My stomach did a back flip.

He fixed those intense blue eyes on mine and smiled. 'What are you drinking?'

While he ordered our drinks, the butterflies took flight. They continued to soar as he led me to a dark corner so we could talk. They swooped when he wrapped his arms round me and held me close on the dance floor later that evening and they went crazy when he took my hand as we walked back to Fuchsia Cottage after the party ended.

'I knew you two were perfect for each other,' Hannah slurred, clinging onto Toby as they staggered along the lane beside us. 'Didn't I call it?'

'You one hundred per cent called it, Hannah,' James said. He rolled his eyes at me and we laughed at the state of the pair of them, ricocheting off each other.

We all piled into the kitchen to make coffee but Hannah only got as far as filling the kettle before declaring she had no space for any more liquid and needed sleep. Toby followed her upstairs, leaving James and me alone.

'Did you mean it when you said Hannah had called it?' I asked, the several glasses of wine consumed across the evening making me feel brave.

James took my hands in his and drew me closer to him then gently kissed me. His lips were warm and his beard was soft as he moved his kiss across my cheek to my ear and then back to my lips.

'I hope that answers your question,' he said.

'It does.'

'Can I take you out for dinner one night this week?' he whispered. 'Are you free on Tuesday?'

'I am and yes please.'

* * *

I lay in my bed an hour or so later smiling, the feel of James's tender kisses still on my lips. Hannah and Toby genuinely had called it. He made me laugh, I made him laugh, we shared so much in common and, when we kissed, it felt as though we'd been designed to fit together. Knowing that he was in the room next door meant drifting off was not going to be easy but I eventually slipped into happy dreams.

On Sunday morning, I awoke a little after seven to the sound of the front door closing. Peeking through the blinds, I saw James heading towards his car with his overnight bag in his hand and my stomach sank. He'd clearly woken up full of regret and was making a swift escape to avoid any discomfort. Maybe not the perfect fit after all.

* * *

Half an hour later, I opened the front door to leave.

'Going without saying goodbye?'

I jumped and turned to face James, leaning against the kitchen door frame, looking a little unsure of himself.

'I thought you'd gone,' I said.

'Not yet. I wanted to see you first. Make sure everything's okay between us after last night.'

My stomach sank for the second time that morning. Did that mean he regretted last night and wanted to make sure there'd be no awkwardness at the wedding next year? 'We're fine. Last night was great but, don't worry, I won't hold you to dinner this week.' I was going for casual but my voice sounded strained.

'You don't want to go out with me?' He looked hurt.

'Erm... yes, I do, but I'm handing you a get out of jail free card.'

'What if I don't want a get out of jail free card?' he said, his lips curling into a smile as he took a step closer to me.

I smiled shyly and placed my bag on the floor. 'Then it looks like we're going out to dinner on Tuesday.'

'And what happens if I can't wait that long?' He took another step closer so that our bodies were almost touching.

'I'm free tomorrow night too.'

'And what if I can't wait that long either?'

'I don't need to rush off now,' I whispered, gazing into his eyes.

'In that case, would you like to spend the day with me?'

'I'd love to.'

He wrapped his arms round me and gently kissed me.

'I was worried you might have slept on it and changed your mind,' he said when we broke apart.

I saw the uncertainty and felt his vulnerability – just like my own – and, at that moment, I fell a little bit in love with James Turner.

3

Six months later, Hannah and Toby said 'I do'. I felt all gooey inside as they smiled tenderly at each other and kissed for the first time as husband and wife. I stole a glance across to James, looking delectable as best man in a light-grey three-piece suit with a coral tie and pocket handkerchief, but he was looking straight ahead and didn't catch my eye. I smoothed down my coral bridesmaid dress, smiling to myself. Could that be James and me in the next year or so? I hoped so.

They turned to face their friends and family, huge smiles on their face, then walked down the aisle to rapturous applause. James joined me as we walked behind them, followed by Hannah's two young nieces. He squeezed my hand and gave me one of his warmest smiles, sending the butterflies soaring in my stomach. Could the wedding put him in the right romantic mood to declare his true feelings? James hadn't said he loved me yet, but I knew he was cautious and keen to take things slowly after a previous long-term relationship ended badly. I was determined not to be the first to say it after realising that Harry had only ever responded with a non-committal 'me too' each time I said those words to him.

With James living and working in York and me based an hour away in Whitsborough Bay, there wasn't much opportunity for spontaneity in our relationship but we made it work. We spent most week-ends together and tried to meet up one evening during the week.

James travelled over to Whitsborough Bay a couple of times in the early days and met my parents, but Mum did nothing to make him feel welcome. So it made more sense for me to drive to York instead, especially as James owned his own place.

Living back at home wasn't ideal but it made financial sense for me. After the Harry disaster, Dad had insisted I move back into my childhood bedroom while I saved a deposit for a place of my own, much to Mum's disgust.

James and I spent a lot of time with Hannah and Toby and I loved that closeness we had as a unit of four. I imagined years stretching ahead of us with joint holidays and, down the line, perhaps joint family holidays.

Our time together was always filled with chatter and laughter which made me realise how perfunctory my relationship had been with Harry. He'd been very wrong for me and I'd been too inexperi-enced to realise it, but James couldn't be more right.

* * *

'Could you see yourself doing this?' I asked James as we sat at an empty table, watching the newlyweds shuffling to their first dance that evening. Five, maybe six, glasses of champagne had made me feel brave, but not quite brave enough to add 'with me'.

'One day,' James responded. 'When I meet...'

My stomach plummeted to my feet as he faltered, biting his lip, squirming on his chair, avoiding eye contact with me. And that was it. That was the moment of absolute shocking clarity. The reason he hadn't said he loved me was not because he'd been hurt before or because he didn't want to rush things. It was quite simply because he didn't feel that way. How could I have been so blind? Had my experi-ence with Harry taught me nothing?

'When you meet the right person?' I finished for him, hoping the music would prevent him from hearing the wobble in my voice. Willing myself not to cry and swallowing hard on the lump blocking my throat, I added, 'But that person isn't me, is it?'

James slowly shook his head then turned to face me. 'I'm so sorry, Sam. I do love you—' he shook his head again '—but not in that way. I wish I did, but you can't control who you fall in love with. I love being with you but there's something missing between us.'

'Like what?'

'Some sort of spark. I felt it when we first met but I think it was the excitement of something new and... I'm so sorry... it faded.' His voice was thick with regret and I knew he was telling the truth. He'd tried but, for him, love hadn't grown.

Twiddling with a strand of hair, I forced out the words, 'Is there someone else?'

'No! I'd never do that to you.'

'So what are you saying?' I asked. 'You want us to split up?'

He took my hand in his. 'No. That's the thing. I really care about you, we have fun together, and there's nobody I'd rather be with.' He reached out with his other hand and stroked the side of my face. I nuzzled against his soft palm, my heart thumping. All was not lost. Then he added that fatal word. 'Yet.' One tiny word with only three letters, but oh so powerful. Yet. He hadn't met anyone he'd rather be with *yet*. He was biding his time until someone better came along.

'Okay,' I said, because what else could I say? It was far from okay. It would *never* be okay.

'I just don't see us together for the long run,' James continued. 'I really wish I did but I don't. How do you feel?'

How do I feel? I love you and I want to marry you! But of course I didn't say that. I don't know what got into me – probably a combination of self-preservation, humiliation-avoidance and the desire to hold onto him for as long as I could – but I opened my mouth and out it tumbled. 'I feel exactly the same although I didn't realise it until I watched Hannah and Toby saying their vows. I started picturing my wedding day but I couldn't imagine you being the groom. I don't want to lose you, though. I'm happy to continue with this, whatever this is.'

I expected him to laugh and call me out on my lies. Surely me stumbling over my words and fidgeting with the tablecloth were a dead giveaway? Instead, his eyes lit up. 'Really? I was worried about hurting you.'

I smiled. 'If I'd been madly in love with you, we'd be picking up pieces of my broken heart off the floor right now, but seeing as I'm not...'

James hugged me. 'You're the best, Sam.'

He believed me. How could he believe such rubbish?

'So are you,' I said, squeezing him back. 'Will you promise me something? If you meet anyone who gives you that spark you're looking for, will you tell me? I mean immediately. Don't let me find out later or hear it from someone else. I couldn't cope with that again after what happened with Harry.'

James pulled away from me and nodded solemnly. 'And you promise me too?'

I nodded and crossed my fingers beneath my seat. I'd already found the one and I just had to hope the spark he'd initially felt towards me ignited once more because the one I had for him had never extinguished.

4

Nothing changed between James and me over the next three months. Or rather nothing changed outwardly. We still saw each other just as regularly. We still talked incessantly. We still laughed a lot. But, inwardly, *everything* had changed for me. I was falling apart, my heart breaking every day, knowing that the man I loved didn't love me back and never would. I knew I was kidding myself that he'd wake up one day and suddenly realise that he felt more than affectionate friendship.

I couldn't bring myself to confide in Hannah or Chloe – the two people I normally turned to when anything troubled me. I hated that I was keeping something so important from them but I knew why. They'd tell me to end it because that was the advice I'd give if either of them presented the same situation to me. Why waste time investing in something completely one-sided? But I wasn't ready to face that so I lied. I repeated James's words to them – we were having fun but neither of us saw it lasting long-term because we didn't have that spark.

Hannah challenged me on it after she returned from her honeymoon.

'You've been together for nearly seven months now,' she said, frowning. 'That's a long time if the relationship's going nowhere. What's the point in staying together?'

'What did you say was the best way to get over Harry? I'm taking your advice and I'm enjoying it very much, thank you. Does every relationship need to be heading towards something?'

She shrugged. 'No, but be careful, won't you? I'd hate to see you getting hurt again.'

'I could only get hurt if I was hopelessly in love with him, which I'm not. Sooner or later, one of us will meet someone else and it will end. For now, we're great friends—'

'With benefits,' she finished.

'No! Don't say that. It makes it sound tacky.'

'What else would you call it? Look, if it works for you both, then go for it and have fun. But if you feel more than friendship—'

'I don't.' I realised I'd probably said that too quickly and sharply so I smiled and hoped I could lie convincingly. 'I'll admit that I was pretty smitten at first and thought James could be the one, but there's something missing. He's not my forever.'

'You're sure?'

'I'm sure. So are you looking forward to getting back to work?'

She narrowed her eyes at me again but I gave her my most dazzling smile which must have convinced her because she sat back in the armchair and chatted about her return to work.

Chloe was more accepting of the casual nature of our relationship. She hadn't yet met him and James didn't do social media but I'd posted a few images of him on Facebook and Instagram.

'Good on you,' she said as we walked arm in arm along the promenade at North Bay one calm evening in late March. 'If I had a friend who looked like your James, I'd be more than happy to indulge in a bit of no-strings shagging.'

'It's not quite no-strings,' I said. 'We're not allowed to see other people and, if one of us meets someone, we have to tell the other one.'

'Sounds like the perfect arrangement. Where can I get me a James?'

'No idea. Aisle ten at the supermarket?'

She laughed. 'If only. So when am I going to get to meet him? You've been together forever.'

'Hardly forever and you know it's not intentional. Mum won't let him stay over so it's easier for me to go to York.'

She squeezed my arm tighter. 'Try not to let her get to you,' she said gently. There wasn't much else she could say. My mum adored Chloe and hated me. Chloe had claimed I was imagining things when we were younger but, as we'd moved into our twenties, she'd had to admit that she could see how differently Mum acted towards us both.

'You know me,' I said. 'Always trying to keep the peace and go with the flow.'

'I wish you didn't have to.'

'Me too.' I sighed. 'Anyway, back to more cheery subjects. I've pencilled James in for Gramps's seventy-fifth in June so you'll get to meet him then, if not before.'

'About time too.'

* * *

Mum and I weren't close but her dad – my Gramps – and I were. I sometimes wondered if he'd originally gone out of his way to shower me with love to compensate for his daughter's indifference towards me but, whatever the reason, I absolutely adored him and the special bond we shared.

Throughout childhood, I frequently visited Nanna and Gramps at Meadowcroft, a large bungalow set in two acres of land in a village called Little Tilbury about forty minutes south of Whitsborough Bay. I often stayed during the school holidays, baking with Nanna or helping Gramps in the garden. Gramps was a keen ornithologist and his sprawling back garden – which included a copse – was a haven for birds. He taught me all their names, food preferences and nesting choices. The garden backed onto open fields and attracted a multitude of other wildlife, especially at night.

Hedgehogs, rabbits, foxes and even badgers were regular visitors, exploring the hedgerows, the copse, and seeking out the treats Gramps left for them. My grandparents would let me stay up late, and we'd all hide in the conservatory with the lights off, watching the nocturnal activities. Sometimes Chloe stayed but nature seemed to bore her so it was usually just me and I loved the undivided attention.

Nanna and Gramps were the most adorable couple, always laughing together and holding hands whenever they went out. It was obvious their love was deep and lasting, but Nanna was taken from us too soon. Five years ago, when she was only sixty-nine, she needed a routine operation. Nobody was worried about it and we were all looking forward to three big celebrations after she recovered: Gramps's seventieth, their golden wedding anniversary and then Nanna's seventieth. But she caught an infection which turned into sepsis. None of us could quite believe she'd gone, especially Gramps. It was like someone had turned the lights off behind his eyes and I feared I'd never see him smile again.

After Nanna died, I spent as much time with Gramps as I could. I'd drive over to Meadowcroft most evenings after work and spend at least one day there each weekend. He was so lost without Nanna, struggling to find a reason to exist. It broke my heart to see him like that. He even lost interest in the birds and wildlife but slowly I coaxed him back outside, reminding him how many living things relied on him and trying to show him a reason to go on. Gradually the colour returned to his cheeks and he started to smile again. I could still feel the weariness, the loneliness, and the understandable disinterest in a life without Nanna, but the melancholy became less frequent. He started spending time with another widower in the village and slowly, surely, he built a life without Nanna.

We began going out for walks together and, each time, he'd share something new with me about Nanna. I think it was his way of keeping her alive, sharing his precious memories with me, but it made me feel so much closer to them both too.

At the start of the new year, we took a stroll through the village and I mooted the idea of a party to celebrate his seventy-fifth birthday.

Gramps paused then smiled. 'I think your nanna would have wanted that. We never got to celebrate those three special occasions the year we lost her. I think she'd like us to celebrate the next milestone.'

'So it's a yes?'

'It's a yes. As long as you help me organise it.'

I hugged him. 'I'd be delighted to.'

5

'You've done me proud, Sammie,' Gramps said as we stepped into the function room at Sanderslea House Hotel, a few miles from Meadow-croft. 'It's wonderful.'

He wandered round, studying the various photos I'd had blown up of him from being a baby through to present day. Tears pricked my eyes as he lightly stroked an image I'd taken of Nanna and him in the garden a few days before her op, looking happy and healthy. We could never have guessed it would be the last ever photo taken of her. I took a deep breath and busied myself rearranging some flowers in one of the table centrepieces.

'Thank you,' he said, returning to my side.

'My pleasure, Gramps.' I watched him glancing across at the photo again. 'I bet Nanna's here in spirit.'

He turned and gave me a gentle smile. 'I guarantee it. She'd be so proud of you, you know. I certainly am.'

'I miss her.'

'I know. She was the best,' he said, his voice cracking.

We stood side by side for a moment, lost in our thoughts.

'Why don't you take one of those selfies of us before anyone else arrives?' Gramps suggested, his voice sounding stronger.

Gramps loved a selfie and I had a wonderful collection of the two of us together, smiling or pulling silly faces. We wandered over to the balloons and I took a few photos of us in front of them, feeling a warm glow inside as he looked through them, smiling. 'Will you print me some of these off for our collage?'

'Of course.' We'd created a fabulous selfies collage on one of the spare bedroom walls at Meadowcroft. If Nanna's absence hit him too hard, he loved to sit on the bed and look at it. He said it instantly cheered him up and reminded him of how much he still had to live for.

'What time is your young man expected?' he asked.

'Not till about eight but he's looking forward to seeing you again.'

'Good. It's been ages. I need to make sure he's still good enough for my favourite grandchild.' He winked at me and I nudged him gently.

'Ssh! You can't show favouritism like that.'

'Why not? You, Sammie, are truly special. I've always known it and, if it hadn't been for the care and attention you gave me after we lost your nanna, I don't think I'd be here today celebrating my seventy-fifth. I hope you know how much I love you, my angel, and I'm only sorry that certain people in your life don't see you the way I do.'

'Aw, Gramps. I love you too.' I hugged him tightly, pushing back the tears once more. I knew it broke his heart how Mum treated me but little did he know that his words could be applied to my relationship with James too.

'Happy birthday!' The loud greeting broke us apart and we turned to see Auntie Louise, Uncle Simon and Chloe making their way towards us with bags of gifts. Mum and Dad followed a few minutes later and soon the room was full of friends and family, handing out hugs and gifts, chatting and laughing.

It warmed my heart to see Gramps looking so happy. I glanced over at Nanna's image on the wall and smiled at her. She was definitely with us celebrating.

I wondered whether Gramps would see through James and me tonight. I'd kept finding excuses not to take James to Meadowcroft because Gramps noticed everything about me and, if there were only the three of us together, his suspicions would definitely be aroused. He wouldn't rest until he'd got to the bottom of it and he'd give me the advice I didn't want to hear. I figured that the party would provide safety in numbers and enough distractions for Gramps. I was wrong.

* * *

Shortly before 8 p.m., I nipped into the ladies in the back corner of the function room to freshen up before James arrived. When I came out, Gramps was waiting nearby with a large glass of rosé wine for me.

'I meant to get you one earlier but guests kept appearing.'

'Thank you, Gramps.' I reached for it and gratefully took a few sips. I'd been too busy playing hostess to grab myself a drink. 'Are you enjoying yourself?'

'Having a wonderful time, my angel. No sign of James yet?'

'He should be here soon.' I nodded towards the other side of the room where Chloe was chatting to one of Gramps's neighbours. 'Chloe looks amazing tonight.' She wore a soft peach halter-neck dress and her hair was styled into loose curls.

'And so do you,' Gramps said.

'Thank you.'

Chloe turned towards the door and stared for a moment before giving a toss of her hair.

'Oh aye, who's she got her eye on now?' Gramps muttered.

We both turned our gaze towards the door and my stomach plummeted to the floor. James had arrived but he wasn't scanning the room in search of me. Someone else had already caught his attention. His mouth opened and he ran his fingers across his facial hair, seemingly completely mesmerised. I hardly dared follow his eyeline but I had to be sure.

Eyes locked, Chloe and James crossed the room, like magnets pulling together. And, at that moment, I knew I'd lost him. The physical attraction was obvious and, as soon as they spoke, there was no way they wouldn't gel.

'Is that your James?' Gramps asked, adjusting his glasses as they started to speak.

I nodded slowly.

'Then I need to play host and welcome him,' he said, a defensive note to his tone. I knew he'd seen what I'd just seen.

He grabbed my hand and pulled me out of the shadows and across the room.

'Sammie's boyfriend,' Gramps declared loudly. 'So pleased you could make it.'

My cousin and boyfriend both seemed to snap out of their trance and realise they weren't alone anymore.

'Erm yes... Sorry I'm late, William. Happy birthday!' He shook Gramps's hand then turned to me and gave me an awkward peck on the cheek, almost as though we were strangers.

'I see you've met my cousin, Chloe,' I said, trying hard to keep the tightness out of my voice.

'Yes, just this second. I... er... I was just asking her where you were and here you are.'

'Here I am.'

Silence. It was excruciating. I could feel Gramps willing me to say something, to stake my claim, but what could I say? All I could think of was, *Should Gramps and I just leave the two of you alone?*

'How was work?' I asked.

'What do you do?' Chloe asked before he could respond.

'I'm Director of Marketing for Denleigh Insurance in York.'

'Director? Wow! You must be *brilliant* at your job,' Chloe touched his arm as she said it. My heart raced as I watched her in full flirt mode right in front of me. Was she even aware she was doing it?

'I'm feeling quite warm, Sammie.' Gramps slipped his hand into mine. 'Would you accompany me outside for some fresh air?'

'Of course. Excuse us a moment.'

I swear they didn't notice us leave. I gulped down the rest of my wine and abandoned the empty glass on a nearby table as I followed Gramps out of a side door.

A gentle breeze cooled my blazing cheeks as I sat beside him on a wooden bench round the corner, out of sight of the function room windows.

'That was the first time Chloe and James have met?' Gramps asked.

'Yes.'

'And you've kept them apart deliberately?'

I shrugged. 'No. Or at least I don't think so. Maybe I did subconsciously.'

Gramps put his arm round me and I rested my head on his shoulders. 'Tell me I was imagining the fireworks just now.'

'I wish I could.'

He squeezed my shoulder and we sat in silence for several minutes until the coolness of the evening became too much and I shivered, goose bumps covering my arms.

'It's too cold out here,' Gramps said, standing and offering me his hand. 'Do you have plans for tomorrow?'

'James is driving back to York tonight for a stag weekend so I was planning to go into Whitsborough Bay for a mooch round the shops. I don't have to, though.'

'Let's spend the day together. Come to Meadowcroft and we'll talk.'

* * *

Back inside, Chloe and James were still talking animatedly, laughing and leaning closer to each other as they spoke.

'I'll just nip to the ladies,' I told Gramps.

'Are you alright?' His soft grey eyes were full of concern.

I nodded and smiled reassuringly but I didn't trust myself to speak in case it all tumbled out. We'd talk tomorrow. He'd seen it. I'd seen it. The whole room had probably seen it.

To my relief, there was nobody in the toilets. I paced up and down a few times, taking deep breaths, willing myself not to cry. When I felt back in control, I leaned over one of the sinks and splashed some cold water over my face. As I dabbed myself dry with a paper towel, I shook my head at the woman looking back at me from the mirror. Why hadn't I made more effort? There I was in jeans, a loose white top and flip flops, minimal make-up, with my hair pulled back into a low ponytail, not much different to how I wore it for work. And there was Chloe... being Chloe. All it had taken was one look across a crowded room and the sparks had flown. The thing James was missing with me, he'd just found with my cousin. Of all the women in all the world...

I pushed the door open and stepped back into the function room. Warmth and laughter engulfed me and I pushed my shoulders back. *Mingle. Enjoy yourself. He'll come and find you soon and you can act like everything's fine. You're used to that.*

* * *

The following morning, I picked up Gramps and drove to Great Tilbury. We managed to walk the full length of the village and back again, including a pause to feed the ducks, without either of us mentioning Chloe and James but, as soon as he suggested elevenses in April's Tea Parlour, I knew we couldn't put it off any longer.

'You and James,' he said as soon as our drinks were delivered. 'Talk to me.'

'There's not much to talk about. I love James and he doesn't love me. Simple as that.'

'He told you this?'

'Three months ago at Hannah and Toby's wedding.'

'Does he know how you feel about him?'

I twiddled with my ponytail. 'No. We're only together until he finds the missing spark with someone else.'

Gramps exhaled slowly and shook his head as he poured milk into his cup. 'You know that phrase your nanna used to say? If you love something, you have to set it free.'

My shoulders drooped. 'Yes. The thing is, I know the rest of that saying and I *know* he won't come back.'

'Then he was never yours, was he?'

A tear slipped down my cheek and I quickly swiped it away. 'I've always known that.'

'Your nanna also said that the fragrance always stays in the hand that gives the rose.'

I frowned at him. 'I've *never* heard that phrase in my life. What does it mean?'

'It means that an act of kindness – like the one that you already know you're about to do – will benefit the giver too.' He put his hand over mine. 'It might take a while for you to feel the benefit but everything—'

'—happens for a reason,' I finished. 'I know. And thanks for noticing what happened last night.'

'I've always noticed everything about you. I've noticed how you always step into the shadows and let your cousin shine. I've noticed how a harsh word or look from your mum hurts you yet you don't rise to it. I've noticed how you talk down your accomplishments and make a fuss of everyone else's, as though nothing you do is important. But I want you to know that you shine like a diamond, my angel. Don't let anyone make you believe that you don't.'

'Thank you. That's so lovely of you, Gramps.' I poured the tea into both our cups and sighed. 'I don't know if I can bear to see James and Chloe together.'

'You don't know that will happen. Yes, something was there last night, but a successful relationship is so much more than physical attraction. They might not get together or, if they do, it might not last. Then he'll be out of both your lives and you can move on.'

'I know. I mustn't assume the worst.'

Gramps added half a spoonful of sugar to his tea and stirred it slowly. 'When will you end it?'

I released a slow, steady breath. 'We're meeting up for dinner on Tuesday. I'll do it then.'

'It will be hard but you know it's the right thing, don't you?'

'I know, Gramps.' My head told me it should have happened months ago, but my heart still wanted to cling on.

'Promise me you'll let him go.' He fixed his kind grey eyes on mine and squeezed my hand. 'Find your forever instead.'

'I will, Gramps. I promise.'

* * *

When I got back home, I sent James a short text saying I'd had a lovely day with Gramps, I hoped the stag do was going well, and that I looked forward to seeing him on Tuesday. He responded with the thumbs up, pint of beer and zany face emojis. I lay on my bed, the phone resting on my chest, a feeling of loss enveloping me. Next time I saw James, I'd be ending it. Would that be goodbye or would I see him again... as Chloe's boyfriend? I did an involuntary shudder at the thought.

6

The following morning, I awoke feeling empty, knowing I was a day closer to saying goodbye to James.

From the minute I went downstairs to make a cup of tea, my very presence seemed to irritate Mum.

'Thanks for putting the washing on yesterday,' she said, her voice dripping with sarcasm as she sorted through the laundry basket.

'You told me to leave it because you wanted to wash the trousers you were wearing yesterday.'

'You could have done the lights.'

There was no point responding. It was a classic no-win scenario with which I was all too familiar. If I'd done the light wash, I'd have been told off for ignoring her instructions not to do the washing.

'Would you like a cup of tea?' I asked.

'Do I look like I have time for tea?'

Stay calm. Count to three... 'Is there anything you'd like me to do?'

'I'd like you to get out of my kitchen so I can get on with the washing.'

'Is there anything else I can do to help? Shopping? Cleaning?'

'If I have to ask you to do it, then it's not really helping, is it?'

I hated that meaningless phrase. Every time I showed the initiative to do something without being asked, she bit my head off for not doing it to her exacting standards. If I went shopping, I was always accused of buying the wrong brand or the wrong size. If I cleaned, I allegedly missed a bit so she had to do it all again.

I hated letting Mum see that she'd upset me so I showered and dressed then nipped into Whitsborough Bay to print off the photos from Gramps's party.

Sitting in my car, I flicked through the photos, my heart racing at an image of Chloe and James together. I lightly stroked James's face and sighed, the loss already stabbing at my heart, then gently placed the photos back in my bag and set off towards Meadowcroft.

* * *

There was no answer when I rang the bell so I unlocked the door and let myself in. Gramps had given me a key after Nanna died, saying he spent more time in the garden than the house and would never see me if I relied on him hearing the bell.

I called his name as I stepped into the hall. It was unusually dark and an uneasiness clawed at me when I pushed open the lounge door. Why weren't the curtains open?

'Gramps?' I called.

No answer.

'Gramps? It's after eleven. Are you still in bed?'

I tentatively pushed open his bedroom door but he wasn't there. The curtains were open and the bed was made. I took a few deep breaths to still my racing heart.

'Gramps? Where are you?' I stepped back into the hall. Maybe he'd taken advantage of the blue skies and sunshine and gone straight out to the garden.

I pushed open the back bedroom, planning to look out the window, and screamed.

Wearing the same clothes as yesterday, Gramps was positioned against the headboard, opposite the collage of selfies. An invite to his seventy-fifth birthday rested on his knee and a half-eaten piece of birthday cake lay on a plate on the bedside table.

'Oh, Gramps.' My lip wobbled and tears pooled in my eyes as I stared at him.

I slowly shuffled towards him and gently closed his eyes. There was no need to check his pulse. I'd seen death many times and he'd obviously joined Nanna last night.

'Send my love to Nanna,' I whispered before kissing his cool cheek and removing his glasses. 'Give her a big hug from me and thank her for letting me keep you for another five years.'

A shuddering sob shook my body and tears dripped down my cheeks. With shaking hands, I removed my phone from my pocket. I wanted Dad but I knew I needed to try Mum first. Gramps was, after all, her father. Mum barely ever answered the phone to me and today was no exception. I tried Dad.

'Hi Sammie.'

'Dad? Gramps is dead. I'm at Meadowcroft and he's dead. Can you tell Mum and Auntie Louise?' The words tumbled out between sobs.

'No! Oh, Sammie. Are you okay?'

'Not really. Can you drive over?'

* * *

Losing Gramps was unbearable. I'd never known pain like it. Instead of uniting us in our loss, it drove a further wedge between Mum and me. She was understandably distraught at the loss of her remaining parent but she accused me of not trying to save him. Why hadn't I called an ambulance sooner? Why hadn't I attempted CPR? How dare I call myself a nurse? Even when the coroner confirmed that a massive heart attack had taken him the previous evening, there was no reasoning with her.

At work, I couldn't stop crying. Worried about my emotional state, my manager insisted I take some time off until after the funeral. While that was undoubtedly the right thing for my patients, it wasn't ideal for me because it gave me too much time to think.

Mum took bereavement leave and made it clear that she hated me being under her feet. I couldn't say or do anything right. I offered to help organise the funeral or wake but was accused of interfering. I suggested going to Meadowcroft to feed the wildlife and keep on top of the weeding but was accused of trying to make it my home. Dad tried to keep the peace but it only resulted in more arguments so, not wanting to drag Auntie Louise, Uncle Simon and Chloe into our battle, I spent the next week or so between Hannah's and James's.

James was brilliant. He let me cry, he let me vent and he had a ready supply of hugs and comforting words. I knew I had to end it but not right then; not when my heart was already broken.

I returned to Whitsborough Bay on the Tuesday, a couple of days before the funeral. Mum had thankfully calmed down, her anger replaced by the silent treatment, which was mildly preferable.

Chloe and I prepared a eulogy which Dad offered to read out on our behalf as we knew we wouldn't be able to get beyond a few sentences without breaking down. The only way to get Mum's buy-in was for Chloe to present it as her idea with a few contributions from me rather than the other way round. Not that it really mattered. The important thing was for that wonderful man to be appropriately remembered.

At the funeral service, I huddled close to James but, as I listened to Dad reading out the words that Chloe and I had prepared, all I could think about was my final day with Gramps and his last request. I couldn't keep putting it off. I'd focus on saying goodbye to Gramps but then I needed to say goodbye to James. Soon.

I hadn't expected 'soon' to be that very evening.

7

Present Day

After the group photographs outside the church were complete, there was time to mingle while Chloe and James had some photos taken at the other end of the churchyard in front of a beautiful willow tree.

Surveying the guests, I spotted Hannah sitting on a shady bench. She was eight months' pregnant and probably relieved at the opportunity to escape the sunshine and rest her feet.

I waved then picked up my skirts and started to make my way towards her when a cold hand on my arm froze me to the spot. Spindly fingers. Lily of the Valley eau de toilette. I shuddered.

'Great-Aunt Agnes.' *Smile. Be nice.* 'How lovely to see you.'

'And you, my dear,' she said through gritted teeth. Such a lie.

'Lovely service,' I said when she showed no sign of moving away.

'Indeed. It's so wonderful to see our little Chloe so happy. But I'm somewhat confused. Wasn't that young man your boyfriend, dear?'

And there it was. The jugular. 'Yes, he was, but it was never serious. James and Chloe make a much better couple than James and I ever did.'

'Yes, well, I suppose beautiful people do tend to gravitate towards each other.'

Ouch!

She patted my arm again, making the hairs stand on end. 'Still, there's plenty more fish in the sea, as they say. I'm sure you'll find someone more on your level eventually.' I swear she was chuckling to herself when she sidled away.

'Who was that?' Hannah asked when I flung myself down beside her and released an exasperated growl.

'My Great-Aunt Agnes,' I muttered, curling my lip up and exaggerating a shudder.

'Oh. I wondered if it might be her. I take it from your reaction that she was being her usual delightful self?'

'Of course. Straight in there with a comment about James being my ex and out of my league.'

Hannah winced. 'I hope you ignored her.'

'If only. She always seems to have some killer insult which she hurls at me like a grenade before walking off leaving me picking up the pieces. I wish I could think of a good comeback but I always go blank.'

'You don't need one. Rise above it. If she gets her kicks out of making other people feel small, that's her problem, not yours. She's clearly full of crap.'

'I know she is, but she manages to get to me every time. It probably wouldn't bother me if she was like that with everyone but she isn't. Chloe's always been the golden girl and I've been the one she can't stand but I don't know why.'

'Families, eh?' She rubbed her hands in circular motions over her baby bump as she rolled her eyes. 'So, how are you holding up?'

'I'm good. It was a lovely service.'

'It was, but that's not what I asked you.' Her tone softened and she gave me a sympathetic look. 'Your heart was breaking all the way through it, wasn't it?'

I looked down and brushed some imaginary fluff off my dress. 'I'm fine. It's ancient history and, like I said to you before, it was never serious anyway.'

Hannah linked her arm through mine and gently pulled me to her side. 'Don't insult our friendship by pretending you were never in love with him and, if I'm not mistaken, still are.'

I relaxed against her and sighed. 'I've just had this conversation with my dad. Is it that obvious?'

'Only to the people who love you as much as we do. I was never convinced by that friends having a bit of fun crap but you were so adamant that's all it was that I thought it was maybe just wishful thinking on my part, wanting to keep you together as this happy couple we could double-date with. Then I saw you watching them saying their vows earlier and I knew. I'm so sorry it didn't work out.'

I pressed my fingers to my lips and shook my head. 'Do you think Chloe knows?'

'No. Don't panic. I think she's so smitten with James that she wouldn't notice if you grew horns and danced the fandango.'

'She sent me a "HOT TIP" this morning. Look.' I handed Hannah my phone. Chloe and I didn't speak every day but we kept in touch by text and social media. Something we'd done for years was to send each other texts starting with the words 'HOT TIP' when we came across something the other would like. It could be anything – a book, a film, an advert, a fragrance or an item of clothing. We knew each other so well that the recommendation was invariably spot on. Sometimes the tip would be advice or something funny.

✉ From Chloe

HOT TIP! Samantha Wishaw. The unicorn of best friends. Rare, precious, and kind. Guaranteed to add sparkle to your world. Most claim they don't exist but I know they do because I'm lucky enough to have one xx

'I feel so guilty,' I said as Hannah returned my phone. 'I doubt she'd have sent me that if she knew the truth.'

Hannah shook her head. 'You can't think like that, Sam. You let him go so he could be with Chloe and I'd say that *does* make you the unicorn of best friends. Not many people would do that. Oh, hang on, she's coming over.'

'Hi you two,' Chloe said.

'Congratulations,' Hannah said, heaving herself up and kissing Chloe on both cheeks. 'You look beautiful, Chloe. Will you give us a twirl?'

While Chloe picked up her skirts and turned round so we could see the detailing on the back of the bodice, Hannah turned to me, her expression sorrowful. I gave her a weak smile and nodded to assure her I was okay.

'Such a stunning dress on a stunning bride,' Hannah said when Chloe was facing us again. 'James is a very lucky man.'

'I'm the lucky one.' Chloe reached for my hand. 'And I'm so grateful to Sammie for encouraging us to get together.'

'That's Sam for you,' Hannah said, a slight edge to her tone. 'Always doing what's best for others.'

I shrugged. 'I'm a hopeless romantic, that's all. I could see they were perfect together.' How I managed to keep smiling, I'll never know.

'The photographer's going to do a confetti shot in about five minutes,' James said, joining us. His proximity to me made my heart race. Would it ever stop?

'Excellent,' Chloe said. 'I love confetti.'

He smiled at her so tenderly that the butterflies in my stomach swooped and soared, making me feel quite nauseous. He'd never looked at me that way. It was right that they'd both found their matching heart and I genuinely was thrilled for Chloe because, alongside Hannah, she was my best friend and I loved her very deeply.

'Did you ask Sam?' James said.

'I was just about to.'

'Ask me what?'

'I'm just going to track down Toby,' Hannah said, leaving the three of us alone.

'We've messed up,' Chloe said as soon as Hannah was out of earshot. 'Are you still insured to drive anyone's car?'

'Yes. Why?'

'After we've done the confetti shot, we have a huge favour to ask you...'

8

'This is ridiculous.' Releasing a frustrated squeal, I smacked the palm of my hand against the steering wheel of James's car several times until it was red and sore.

Taking a deep breath, I executed yet another three-point turn. Although, in the narrow country lane, it was more like a seven-point turn. Maybe nine.

'You have passed your destination. Please turn round at the next available exit.'

'And you can shut up too.' I stabbed at the sat nav button. 'You have lied to me three times, you useless piece of...' I took another deep breath. 'None of those destinations were anything resembling a country manor, were they?'

So far, I'd been directed to a riding stables, a dead-end lane and now my final disaster – a tumbledown barn in the middle of nowhere. Seriously, nowhere. There were no houses, no vehicles, no animals; just green fields and hedges as far as the eye could see.

I glanced at the clock on the dashboard and grimaced. I was already an hour and a quarter late. I'd missed the drinks reception and the photos which was hardly ideal considering I was the only bridesmaid. The meal would have started fifteen minutes ago and, if I didn't find my way back to civilisation soon, I was going to miss all the food and the speeches too. Even though it was hardly my fault, Chloe was going to be so mad with me for disrupting her plans for a perfect wedding day.

Stopping the car, I fished my mobile phone out of the door pocket. Still no signal. What on earth had possessed me to agree to Chloe's request? Dad was right; I was too kind to her and it was always my downfall. They'd mistakenly left a plant – one of their thank-you gifts for those who'd helped make the day special – at Auntie Louise and Uncle Simon's. So, of course, I'd agreed to drive James's car back to Whitsborough Bay to get it for them, figuring I'd only be half an hour at most behind everyone else; no problem. Apologising for the inconvenience and calling me a 'life-saver', James programmed his sat nav with the postcode for Aversford Manor, their reception venue, and showed me how to activate the route when I left Whitsborough Bay. It all seemed pretty simple. Then he hugged me and kissed me on the cheek, and the touch of his lips against mine, his warm breath against my ear and the woody aroma of his body spray sent me back to the island of unrequited love all over again. I'd tried so hard in the run-up to the wedding to convince myself that I wasn't still in love with him but my heart betrayed my head every time. Could life be any more complicated?

I glowered at the plant, secured between towels in the passenger side footwell. 'Whoever your new owner is, I hope they're flipping well grateful.'

Leaning back in my seat, I exhaled loudly, then put the car back into gear and set off down the lane again. I paused at the junction, trying to decide which way to go next. Why didn't I know this area at all? I'd lived in Whitsborough Bay all my life and the Yorkshire Wolds started less than ten miles to the south west of the town, yet it was an area I'd never explored. Gramps had lived there but I'd never ventured beyond the village next to his. When he lived somewhere so beautiful and peaceful, there'd never been any need to explore. I was going to have to get used to it, though. Next month, I'd be starting a new job in the area and would move here as soon as I'd settled in.

Leaving my friends on the Whitsborough Bay district nursing team had never been part of my plan, but nothing over the past few years had turned out as I'd hoped so I shouldn't have been surprised when Chloe excitedly announced that she and James had changed their mind about starting married life in York. By the end of last year, he'd sold his house, they'd bought and moved into a new-build on a small development close to her parents and mine, and James began commuting to work by train.

I could psych myself up and put a brave face on for the planned family events but it was too much having James living only a ten-minute walk away. I felt constantly on edge, worried about bumping into him at any minute and finding myself back at square one. If I was going to have any chance of getting over James, I needed distance and the only way to get that was to leave Whitsborough Bay.

Relocating to the Wolds appealed – far enough away to warrant a move but close enough to home to regularly see my family. Hannah was a district nurse there and joining her team would have been ideal but there were no vacancies.

For several months, I blew hot and cold about returning to nursing in a surgery but ultimately couldn't bring myself to apply for any of the vacancies. I was beginning to wonder whether I needed to consider a complete career change when I spotted an advert for a Health and Social Care Tutor at Reddfield TEC. I'd never seriously considered teaching before but I was always the one who got new starters up to speed and I loved it – so I filled in an application form, convinced they wouldn't offer the job to someone with no teaching experience or teaching qualifications. But they did. I was joining the college in early September at the start of the new academic year. It was going to be very different but I was excited about the fresh start and if it wasn't for me, there was nothing to stop me returning to district nursing after a year or two. At least I'd have put the physical distance between James and me that I desperately needed.

* * *

Twenty minutes later, I fought back screams of frustration as the sat nav directed me to a farm and the robotic voice declared once more that I'd reached my destination.

'No! I haven't. Does this look like Aversford Manor to you?' I reached for my mobile again. Still no signal. Glancing up the farm track, I couldn't see any buildings. A tatty wooden sign hung from a rusty pole with the name 'HEDGEHOG HOLLOW' written on it in peeling black paint.

'Please let there be someone home who can tell me where the hell I am. Or that they have a landline so I can call Dad. Or both.'

I turned onto the gravel track which inclined towards the horizon. Overgrown green fields flanked the track either side of a rickety wooden fence which had certainly seen better days. A myriad of potholes full of muddy rainwater from the previous day's downpour jostled me from side to side, and made me gasp. James was not going to be impressed at the state of his car but needs must.

After passing a small copse on both sides of the road, the track bent sharply to the left, revealing a large three-storey stone farmhouse smothered in ivy. Surrounding the house were several stone barns and outbuildings in various states of disrepair including a wooden one that looked as though a sneeze in its direction would bring the timbers crashing down.

I stopped in the farmyard in front of one of the more sturdy-looking stone barns and checked I wasn't about to step out into a cowpat or puddle before I exited the car. Ruining my shoes and dress would be par for the course in my current living nightmare.

Standing in the yard, rolling my stiff shoulders, I shielded my eyes from the sun as I took in the stunning location. All around me fields rose and fell across the Wolds – assuming that's where I still was – with the occasional building interrupting the greenery. Birds chirped and crickets sang in the long grass. But birds and insects appeared to be the only signs of life. No other animals, no people, no vehicles. I inhaled. No farmyard smells either. This definitely wasn't a working farm and, judging from the sorry state of it, it could well be abandoned. Wouldn't that just be the cherry on the top of a perfect day?

Hitching up my skirts, I made my way towards the double-fronted farmhouse, pressed the doorbell, and listened for the ring. Nothing. I rapped on the knocker and waited. No answer. Feeling very much like I was casing the joint and that a beefy farmer might clamp his hand on my arm at any moment and yell, 'Get off my land!', I cautiously made my way towards one of the large paned windows to the left. The glass looked as though it hadn't been washed for the past decade, adding to my suspicions that the place had long since been abandoned. Grimacing, I rubbed some of the dirt away with my fingers and peered through one of the glass panes into what looked to be an enormous kitchen-diner. Unless the occupants had left in a hurry mid-task, someone *definitely* lived there because there was washing up piled in the sink, an open box of cereal and an open carton of milk on the worktop.

Returning to the door, I knocked again, then opened the letterbox and shouted, 'Hello? Anyone home?' I stood up and waited for a minute or so, then crouched down and shouted through the letterbox again. 'Hello?'

Nothing. Damn! Stepping back from the house, I scanned the first floor windows and the dormers on the top floor for signs of life but I couldn't see anything. I'd try one of the other windows at the front and then I'd have to accept that nobody was home and hope to stumble across another farm – an inhabited one this time.

Making my way towards the house again, I stopped and looked down as something wet slapped against my ankles.

'*Noooo!*'

I'd only gone and let go of my dress at some point and it had been dragging through the muddy puddles, a steady band of muck rising up from the hem. My pink shoes were streaked with mud too. Chloe was going to flip. Seriously, could the day get any worse?

Picking up my skirts again – a bit pointless considering the state they were in now – I stepped up to one of the windows to the right of the front door. I rubbed one of the panes before shading my eyes and looking into the lounge. Again, there were signs of life like a mug and a newspaper on the coffee table. *Wait. Is that a woman standing near the door?* A crow cawing momentarily drew my attention away and, when I looked back, my breath caught. *Oh no!*

Dashing to the front door, I tried the handle, relief flowing through me as the door opened.

'Hello?' I called running down the hall. 'Can you hear me?'

A white-haired man who looked to be in his eighties was slumped against the lounge wall, his face grey and his eyes closed. Blood trickled from cuts on his head and cheek. My heart thudded. *Please don't let me be too late!*

'Hello? My name's Sam and I'm a nurse.'

I lifted the man's wrist and felt for his pulse. It was weak, but it was definitely there. *Thank goodness.*

'Hang in there. I'm here to help you.'

I spotted a landline phone on a large dresser and lifted the receiver. Relieved to hear a dialling tone, I called 999.

With the ambulance on its way, there was nothing I could do without my medical bag except try to make him comfortable and reassure him. There was a blanket draped over the back of the sofa.

'Stay with me,' I urged the man, tucking the blanket round him and straightening his large dark-framed glasses. 'Help is on its way.'

His eyes flickered and he murmured something unintelligible.

'Don't try to speak. You're safe now. An ambulance is coming.' I checked his pulse once more. 'You're doing great. You gave me a scare, though. I only stopped by to get some directions. I'm on my way to my cousin's wedding reception, you see...'

As I jabbered to him, regularly checking his pulse, I couldn't help picturing Gramps slumped against his headboard that heart breaking Sunday morning. I'd been too late to save him but hopefully I was just in time to save this man.

9

'Here's my phone number,' I said to Rich, one of the paramedics, while his colleague secured the patient inside the vehicle. 'I know it's not always easy to find out information but, if you can, I'd love to know how he's doing.'

Rich took the piece of paper and smiled. 'I'll do my best. You do realise that, by getting lost, you've probably saved his life?'

I nodded. 'If the sat nav hadn't been so useless, I'd never have been here. He'd have—' I couldn't bring myself to finish the sentence.

'Well, you were here and he's alive right now because of it. Lucky for him you're a nurse.' Rich closed the back doors then clambered into the driver's seat. 'You know where you're going now?' It turned out I was in an area called Huggleswick, only a couple of miles away from Aversford Manor.

'Yes, thanks. I'll check for any pets then lock up and get myself to the wedding.'

Rich started the engine. 'I'll be in touch.'

I watched the ambulance move slowly and steadily down the farm track, then went back into the house. Closing the door front behind me, I leaned against it, suddenly feeling quite shaky, tearful and nauseous. Dealing with scenarios like that had been part of my day job for seven years. Regular. Normal. But today was anything but a normal day for me. I was in a bridesmaid dress with no medical equipment, I hadn't eaten or drunk anything since breakfast, I was hopelessly lost and the man I loved had just married my cousin.

Get it together, Sam. Focus on the pet hunt. I made my way into the kitchen but couldn't see any dog or cat bowls in there although that didn't mean there weren't any pets.

I wandered round the rest of the ground floor, opening and closing doors, an air of sadness engulfing me. The rooms were huge and each had oversized windows with stunning views. The place oozed with potential to be an amazing family home but it felt tired and unloved. The décor was dated and the whole place was in desperate need of a good clean. In my years as a district nurse, I'd seen homes like this so often: once loving-family abodes full of love and life, which were now prisons to one surviving spouse who didn't have the energy, enthusiasm or perhaps the good health to keep on top of everything.

The lounge at Hedgehog Hollow told a tale of TV dinners for two, except one of them was only present in photographs rather than in person. Opposite a green lumpy sofa stood a Welsh dresser – the only surface not thick with dust – covered in photos in gleaming silver frames. They showed what appeared to be the same woman develop from a fresh-faced twenty-something brunette to a woman probably in her late fifties with greying hair.

A black and white wedding photo took pride of place in the middle of the dresser. They'd certainly been a handsome couple back then. The style of her wedding dress was very similar to Nanna's so they'd likely wed in the early or mid-sixties.

There weren't any children in the photos but animals featured heavily – dogs, cats, horses, sheep and several hedgehogs. I smiled as I peered more closely at a triple frame showing a picture of the woman holding three tiny hoglets in the palms of her hands, another of her holding a large hedgehog curled into a ball, and one of her feeding an injured hedgehog.

'Was the farm named Hedgehog Hollow especially for you?' I whispered. 'I love hedgehogs. Looks like you did too.'

It wasn't just hedgehogs I loved. Any animals did it for me – probably unsurprising with Dad being a vet and Gramps being so passionate about wildlife. While I was growing up, Mum refused to let me have any pets. She always said that if she let Dad bring one waif or stray home, it would open the floodgates for them all and the house would be 'over-run with moggies, mongrels and one-legged rabbits.' Between the garden at Meadowcroft and helping out with cage-cleaning and odd jobs in the veterinary practice where Dad worked, I managed to get my animal fix.

Straightening up from the photos, I scanned round the rest of the lounge, shaking my head. I toyed with the idea of using the landline to call Dad but the state of the farm suggested money was tight and I didn't want to add to the phone bill without permission. I needed to get going. I'd do the washing up, dispose of that milk on the side and empty the bins so at least he wouldn't return home to an infestation if he was in hospital for some time. Assuming he ever returned home.

I was just about to leave the house when my ears pricked up. Was that a cat mewing? I put the binbag down and listened again. Definitely mewing and coming from the back of the house.

Opening the door to a large cloak and boot room, I looked down at the most stunning grey striped tabby cat. Greyish-green eyes fixed on mine and its head tilted to one side as if trying to work out who I was and whether I had food.

'Hello, Tabby,' I said. 'Where did you appear from? You weren't in here earlier.' I shifted aside a coat dangling from the external door to reveal a cat flap. I hung the coat on one of the hooks. 'You won't be able to get out again if that stays there.'

I bent down and offered my fingers for a sniff. Tabby weaved round my legs, purring loudly, tail high in the air revealing that she was a girl.

I found an empty water bowl hidden by some wellington boots that had toppled over. I filled it with fresh water from a Belfast sink and lay it down on the floor. She must have been thirsty as she instantly lapped from it.

'Food,' I muttered, opening and closing cupboards. Inside the third one were several boxes of wet and dry cat food and a couple of bowls. 'I'll put this out for you and then I'm going to have to leave you but I'll come back tomorrow to feed you if I can find a spare key. I'll leave food outside if I can't. Hopefully your owner will be home soon but I promise I won't let you starve.'

When I'd filled the bowls and put them down, Tabby tucked in, still purring.

The cloakroom door had been closed when I arrived so she was obviously an outdoor cat who came in for sustenance. She'd be fine at the farm providing I dropped by occasionally and I was more than happy to do that until her owner returned. *Please let him return.*

10

Glancing at my watch, my stomach churned as I dashed across the car park at Aversford Manor some time later, clutching that damn plant. Four hours. I'd missed four hours of the reception and here I was turning up in a dress and shoes caked in mud, with dishevelled hair, and handing back a car that looked like it had been off-roading in a mudslide. Yet I'd hopefully saved someone's life. And I'd delivered the plant intact. Would Chloe be able to focus on those positives and not be too mad that her only bridesmaid had gone missing in action?

'Dad!'

He was pacing up and down in the hotel reception. I'd discovered a mobile signal in a corner of the farmyard so had been able to ring him just before setting off.

Dad opened his arms and I rushed into them gratefully, holding the plant out to the side.

'Sounds like you've had quite an ordeal,' he said, when I pulled away.

'You could say that. I'll tell you all about it over a large drink.'

'You might want to clean up a bit first,' he suggested, wrinkling his nose.

I reached up and touched my hair which was rapidly escaping

from the beautifully styled up-do. 'I can probably salvage the hair.' I looked down at my dress and shoes. 'Not so sure about the outfit. Chloe's going to go mad, isn't she? I bet she's livid with me already.'

Dad's grimace told me the answer to that. 'I'm sure she'll understand when she hears it from you. Besides, it was her fault. What was she thinking, sending her only bridesmaid back for a plant, of all things?'

My natural reaction was always one of being protective towards my cousin. 'She wasn't to know that the sat nav would mess things up and get me hopelessly lost.'

'Even so, any of the other guests could have done it. What were we saying earlier about you being too kind for your own good?' Dad sighed. 'You go and get yourself ready. I'll find Chloe, let her know you're here, give her the plant then meet you in the bar with a large glass of wine.' He reached into his pocket and handed me a key card. 'I've already checked you into your room and taken your bag up.'

I accepted the card in exchange for the plant. 'Thanks, Dad. What would I do without you?' Blowing him a kiss, I headed up the stairs towards the bedrooms.

'Did Chloe tell you who the plant was for?' he called.

'No. Who?'

'Who insisted on organising the flowers?' he asked, ruefully.

'No! So I went through all that for Great-Aunt Agnes?'

'But you saved someone's life. That's an amazing thing.'

I sighed and shook my head. 'I'll be back down soon.'

* * *

The mirror in my hotel room revealed a sorry sight. My hair was sticking out in all directions, with large chunks hanging limply round my shoulders. There was a smear of mud on my left cheek, mascara smudges below my eyes, and my cheeks were red and blotchy. As for my dress? Disaster. There was mud and grime smeared across the bodice and on other parts of the skirt – not just the bottom as I'd originally thought – and was that blood? I deliberately hadn't cleaned up the man's wounds because I hadn't wanted to leave him alone while I found a cloth, but I must have brushed against him.

I had nothing else to wear. All I'd brought was jeans and a T-shirt for the morning and I could hardly join the evening do at a posh country hotel wearing those. I'd have to sort out my hair and make-up and leave the dress as it was. If nothing else, it would be a talking point and anything to steer the conversation away from, 'Wasn't James your boyfriend, dear?' was most welcome. Plus, there was a disco so it would be dark. I might be able to get away with it. Hopefully nobody would spot the blood.

* * *

Fifteen minutes later, with my hair and make-up sorted and some of the mud sponged off my shoes, I was about to go downstairs when my phone beeped with a message:

✉ From Rich
Thomas came to earlier and they think he's had a
mild stroke but he has low blood pressure so he's
definitely in overnight, maybe longer. Would you
like me to let you know if I find anything else
out? Rich

His name was Thomas, was it? He looked like a Thomas.

✉ To Rich
Thank you so much. Yes please to keeping me
posted. I found a gorgeous tabby cat. There was a
spare key so I'll feed her again tomorrow on my
way home. I didn't get a chance to say earlier but
I'm starting a teaching job at Reddfield TEC next

month so will be moving to the area. Any local
knowledge gratefully received

✉ From Rich
Great news about the cat and congrats on the new
job! You'll love it here … once you find your way
round. I'd invest in a better sat nav, if I was
you! If you need a tour guide, just shout. My
partner, Dave, and I have lived here all our lives
so we know all the back roads … and the best pubs

I smiled at his comment about his partner. Rich obviously liked to
get his cards on the table from the very start. It had crossed my mind
that he was attractive – athletic build with broad shoulders and dark
hair – but I hadn't been remotely attracted to him. How could I be
when James still held my heart tightly?

✉ To Rich
I'll take you both up on that! Thanks. Better haul
my muddy backside down to this wedding and throw
some shapes on the dance floor … if my cousin is
still speaking to me, that is!

There were several missed calls showing on my phone from Chloe,
Dad and Hannah, alongside a dozen or so 'where are you' texts from
Chloe and Dad. Hannah had also sent a longer text:

✉ From Hannah
You've either bottled it or you've got hideously
lost. Whichever it is, I'm hoping you're OK. Chloe
had a scary bridezilla moment when you weren't
here for the photos. She was convinced I knew
where you were but I pleaded ignorance and, of
course, didn't say anything about our earlier

conversation and never will. My back is killing me
and I'm shattered so I drove home after the meal.
Toby's getting a taxi home later. You know where I
am if you want to talk. Big hugs xx

I wasn't surprised to hear about Chloe's reaction. She was prone to
being overly dramatic in high-stress situations and I completely
understood why my absence would not have been appreciated.

✉ To Hannah
Got hideously lost. Arrived safely now but covered
in mud! Long story which I'll tell you tomorrow.
Thanks for the concern. Hope you're feeling better
after putting your feet up xx

My heart raced as I made my way down the stairs and my legs
actually felt quite wobbly. Grabbing the handrail to steady myself, I
took a deep breath, pushed back my shoulders and continued my
descent. It was fine. Everything was fine. My dress was muddy but it
wasn't ripped. The love of my life was now my cousin-in-law, if such a
title existed, but he made Chloe happy which made me happy. I'd get
over him eventually and a little physical distance would help that.
Once I'd settled into my new role, I'd find somewhere to rent and fully
start afresh.

'Where's the wedding reception, please?' I asked the woman
behind the check-in desk.

'Go down that long corridor and you'll find the lounge and bar on
your left
and The Arundel Room on your right a little further down.'

Thanking her, I headed down a dark, wide, stone-flagged corridor,
the sounds of laughter and the baseline of the music hitting me as I
got closer to the end. *You can do this. You're only late and muddy. It's not
the end of the world.*

I peeked into the bar as I passed. It was busy but there was no sign of the bride or groom. I needed to seek out Chloe first, apologise for missing everything, then I'd find Dad and down that much-needed glass of wine.

I'd almost reached the end of the corridor when Great-Aunt Agnes's voice pierced through me. 'Not so fast, young lady.' Damn! She must have been in the bar and seen me sneaking past.

Turning to face her, I braced myself for a lecture.

'Where do you think you've been all afternoon?'

'I got a bit lost and—'

'A bit lost? A bit? We left the church five hours ago, Samantha. Where on earth did you go? Via Manchester?' Her shrill tone cut through me.

'I really need to find Chloe and explain it to her.' I started to turn.

'I hope it's a good excuse. You've certainly had plenty of time to dream one up.'

'What's that supposed to mean?' I turned back to fully face her, hands planted on my hips.

'You know *exactly* what it means. Can't say I blame you for running out, though.'

'I didn't run out. I was sent to get something – for you, as it happens – and I got lost on my way here. Several times.'

'Probably because you were so distracted. Can't be easy pretending to be the doting bridesmaid while your cousin marries the man you love.' She raised her voice on that last sentence and, from the way she nodded her head as she looked past me, I knew why. What a cow.

'You're in love with James?' Chloe cried.

Heart thudding, legs shaking, I turned round to face the bride, standing near the entrance to the function room. Her eyes were wide and her mouth open.

'Of course not.' I hoped I sounded convincing.

Great-Aunt Agnes sidled past me and stood next to her favourite great-niece. They both stared at me and I could feel my burning cheeks betraying me. I couldn't keep eye contact and my hands seemed to have taken on a life of their own, plucking imaginary threads from my dress.

Chloe took a few steps closer to me. 'Look me in the eye and tell me that you're *not* in love with *my* husband.'

A crowd had gathered round us, no doubt drawn out of the bar and function room by the raised voices. I could feel everyone staring at me as though they were watching a real-life soap opera unfold. And among them was my hero: my dad.

'Chloe, sweetheart,' he said, moving to my side. 'What sort of question is that to be asking on your wedding day?'

'A question I want to hear the answer to,' she said through gritted teeth. 'So, I'll ask you again. Samantha Wishaw, are you in love with my husband?'

A wave of nausea rising in me, I gulped. Why couldn't I just look her in the eye and say: *No, Chloe, I do not love your husband.*

'And I want you to swear it on our Gramps's life,' she added.

Never good with confrontation, my legs were shaking so much, I feared they might give way. 'Chloe, let's not do this now.'

A shocked murmur rippled round the growing audience.

'So you lied when you told me it wasn't serious between you both.' Her voice was loud and pitchy.

'Not exactly.'

'Stop lying,' she cried, stamping her foot.

'I'm not lying.' I took a step closer to her and lowered my voice. 'You want the truth? The truth is that it wasn't serious between us because...'

'Because what?' she demanded when I tailed off and lowered my eyes.

'Because James wasn't serious about me,' I muttered.

'Which means *you* were serious about him.'

'Does it matter? He's with you. He loves you, not me. Never me.' I could hear the desperation in my voice.

Chloe looked at me with big, sad eyes and, for a moment, I thought she was going to hug me and maybe say sorry that I was hurting. But then she straightened up, narrowed her eyes and shook her head at me. 'I think you should leave,' she hissed.

'What?'

'You heard me. Go. Now.' She hitched up her skirts and turned away.

'Chloe!' I dived forward and grabbed her arm but she snatched it away and spun round again.

'I mean it. You're not welcome at our wedding and, given that you're in love with my husband, I'm not sure you're welcome in our lives either.'

'You can't mean that.'

'I can and I do. Goodbye, Samantha.'

Picking up her skirts again, she flounced back down the corridor and into The Arundel Room, the crowd turning and following her like rats being led by the Pied Piper. Great-Aunt Agnes looked me up and down, an unmistakable sneer on her face.

'What?' I cried. 'What did I ever do to make you hate me so much?'

'Ask your father,' she snarled, then turned and strutted away.

Dad put his arm round me. 'Come on. Let's get you back to your room,' he whispered, and I let him lead me back towards reception, the murmurs and giggles of the wedding guests becoming more muffled with each step.

But we didn't get far. 'Samantha!'

I turned to see Mum marching down the corridor towards us.

'What the hell are you playing at?' she snapped, her face flushed with anger.

'I've done nothing wrong.'

She planted her hands on her hips and glared at me. 'Have you heard yourself? Being in love with Chloe's husband is hardly nothing.'

'Debs, I don't—' Dad began.

'Did I ask your opinion?' she shouted, turning on him. 'I should have known you'd be on her side, as always.'

'It's not about taking sides,' Dad muttered.

'No, it's about your precious daughter being up to her usual tricks.'

I winced. 'What tricks?'

'You've always been jealous of Chloe and you'll do anything to stop her being happy. Sabotaging her wedding day is a new low, even for you.'

'I love Chloe,' I cried, astonished at Mum's accusations. 'I walked away from James for her.'

'And now you resent her for it and you're trying to get him back.'

'I'm not.'

'Could have fooled me.' With a final filthy look at both of us, she flounced back down the corridor towards the party.

I turned to Dad. He was staring after her, his brow furrowed, his hand rubbing the back of his neck.

'Why does she hate me so much?' I whispered, tears pooling in my eyes.

Dad turned back to me and his expression softened. 'She doesn't hate you, poppet.'

'We both know she does.'

'Your mum is very...' He paused as though searching for the right word. 'Complex,' he added eventually.

Complex? I could think of a few other choice words for what Mum was but, right now, I had more pressing matters to deal with than yet another confrontation with her.

Taking a deep breath and wiping at my eyes to prevent the tears from falling, I straightened up. 'I'm going to order a taxi then get out of here. You might as well go back to the party. There's no point in you falling out with everyone as well.'

Dad put his arms out and pulled me into a hug. 'I'm not going anywhere.'

11

Despite the hotel receptionist's best attempts, there were no taxis available until past midnight. Dad had been drinking so he couldn't drive me, and Hannah had already left. With limited choices, I booked a taxi for 7 a.m. so I could hopefully make my escape before anyone else arose. I'd get the driver to detour via Hedgehog Hollow so I could feed Tabby.

Dad wanted to accompany me to my room but I was adamant that he should return to the party, reassuring him I would be fine staying watching TV. Reluctantly, he agreed, but only after I let him arrange for room service for me.

Saying goodbye to Dad and retreating to my room, I felt confused and numb. I kept trying to put myself in Chloe's shoes but I was struggling to comprehend her reaction. Yes, I'd lied, but it had been to make her happy. Yes, I held a torch for James, but he'd been my boyfriend for nearly a year first so she knew I cared about him. What difference did it make that I still loved him when the feelings clearly weren't reciprocated? James and I weren't even close friends anymore – more like acquaintances. I wasn't any sort of threat so her reaction made no sense.

A plate of sandwiches and savouries were delivered after thirty minutes. Despite barely eating all day, my appetite had vanished and the food remained untouched.

An hour later, Dad checked on me. Sitting on the edge of the bed beside me, he reported that everything seemed normal, Chloe was happy being centre of attention on the dance floor, and nobody was talking about me.

'I believe everything but the last point,' I said. 'But I won't ask you what they're saying. I'd rather not know.'

'I'm so sorry,' he said, squeezing my hand.

'Me too.'

'Do you want to talk about you and James?'

I shook my head and sighed. 'Not tonight, but I would like to know about Great-Aunt Agnes. What she did tonight was bang out of order.'

'What do you want to know about her?'

'Why does she have it in for me? She said to ask you.'

His shoulders slumped wearily and he shook his head slowly. 'Haven't you had enough negativity for one evening?'

I shrugged. 'I can't feel any worse than I do already.'

Dad shifted position so he could see me better. 'It's not you. It's me she hates but she's a small-minded, bitter woman and I imagine she feels powerful taking it out on you.' He shook his head. 'The reason's so stupid and I can't believe she's still holding it against me. I thought Bella had sorted things years ago.'

I frowned. 'Sorted what?' Bella – Great-Aunt Agnes's only child – was Mum's cousin and they were close, often calling and emailing each other. I'd never actually met her because she lived in Florida with her partner, Chanise.

'I knew Bella from college,' Dad said. 'There were rumours circulating round Bella's family about her sexuality. Agnes, being Agnes, hated that and you can imagine the sort of homophobic tripe she spouted at Bella.'

I nodded. Hateful woman.

'Bella hadn't come out back then although she knew she was gay. We were coming up to our A levels and Bella was desperate for good grades so she could go to university and get away from her mum. Agnes kept going on at her about dating boys and it was getting Bella really anxious. I wasn't seeing anyone and had no desire to get into a relationship before leaving for university so I agreed to be her fake boyfriend to give her a break.'

'That was sweet of you,' I said, smiling at him. 'Although you shouldn't have had to do that.'

'I know. I felt really sorry for her. I still do, having a mum like Agnes. Anyway, there was a family wedding for another cousin. Bella asked me if I'd be her plus one so I went along. And, much to Agnes's disgust—'

'That's where you met Mum.' I remembered him telling me they'd met at her cousin's wedding.

'Exactly. Even though I didn't want any ties back home, I fell for your mum and, while I was studying to be a vet, we made the distance work. Bella also headed off to university, found her freedom, found a girlfriend and never returned home. They moved to Florida but split up after a year or so, then Bella met Chanise and they've been together ever since.'

'I don't understand what this has to do with you, though, and why she hates me.'

Dad raised his eyebrows. 'Because I supposedly broke Bella's heart by running off with your mum, which made her hate men and seek solace with another woman.'

'No way! She thinks you turned her?'

'I told you it was stupid.'

'Wow! This day gets stranger and stranger. So you're really saying that Great-Aunt Agnes hates me because she blames you for her own prejudices in not being able to accept a gay daughter?'

'That's about the size of it.'

'Well, no wonder Bella was desperate to escape and no wonder she's barely spoken to her mother since.' I shook my head and sighed. 'Thanks for filling me in, Dad, but I think it's time you went back to the party.'

'I don't like to leave you.'

'Go. I'll be fine.'

He slowly stood up and glanced towards the untouched food on the dressing table, the drop of his shoulders telling me exactly how devastated he was that I was hurting. 'I'll check on you in another hour,' he said.

'I might go to bed so I'll see you at home at some point tomorrow.'

'I'm sorry,' he said as he opened the door.

'I know. Good night.' I slipped off the bed and locked the door behind him, pulled the chain across, then leaned against it, shaking my head. Poor Bella. And what a fool Great-Aunt Agnes was for behaving like that. Her husband – Bella's father – had died when Bella was fourteen so Great-Aunt Agnes had no other immediate family. Couldn't she have found a way to work beyond her prejudices to stay in Bella's life? But people were often like that: quick to make decisions or jump to conclusions and too stubborn to say sorry and ask for forgiveness. Would Chloe be like that?

I sat on the edge of the bed, replaying the evening over and over. I'd get over James one day, hopefully, but I wouldn't get over the loss of my cousin. Why had Great-Aunt Agnes done that? She'd lashed out at me, but she'd also hurt her favourite in the process.

Ten minutes passed. Fifteen, perhaps. I didn't even have the energy to remove my dress. Sighing, I lay back, staring at the deep pink roses on the wallpaper, wondering how it had come to this: me banished to my room on my cousin's wedding day. I was her only bridesmaid, I was her best friend and we'd been through so much together. We should be on the dance floor right now, giggling, hugging, toasting her future. I'd have been thrilled to do that for my cousin, even though her future was the one I'd hoped for myself.

12

Fourteen Months Earlier

Gramps left detailed written instructions with Auntie Louise – the oldest daughter by twelve minutes – about what he wanted for his funeral. He'd insisted the envelope only be opened on his death so neither Auntie Louise nor Mum knew what to expect. Most of his requests were fairly traditional including a service at Whitsborough Bay crematorium and for his ashes to be scattered among the trees at Meadowcroft, just like Nanna's had been. He listed the songs to be played before and after the service and provided a poem to be read out, but his overriding wish was a surprise. He wanted those he loved to celebrate his life rather than mourn his death and he therefore banned black, asking that everyone wear his favourite colour blue instead, in a shade or quantity of their choosing.

I bought a cornflower-blue calf-length wraparound dress especially for the occasion.

'What the hell are you wearing?' Mum cried, eyes widening as I walked into the kitchen ten minutes before the funeral car was due.

I misinterpreted her tone as shock at seeing me out of jeans. 'A dress. I know. It's been a long time...'

Her jaw tightened. 'I can see that it's a dress. What I'm questioning is the colour.'

'It's blue like Gramps wanted.'

'Where's your respect, Samantha? It's a funeral.'

Dressed all in black, she stormed past me and into the lounge, slamming the door shut behind her.

'What was that all about?' Dad asked pulling on his navy suit jacket as he stepped into the kitchen.

'I'm wearing the wrong colour,' I muttered.

He frowned. 'But the dress code is blue and any shade goes.'

'Not this one, it seems.'

* * *

When the funeral limousine arrived, the three of us piled in and sat in uncomfortable silence.

A few minutes later, we picked up Auntie Louise, Uncle Simon and Chloe, all of whom were wearing blue.

'You look amazing, Chloe,' Mum gushed as Chloe sat beside her wearing a short, lacy powder blue dress. 'That dress is so pretty. Your Gramps would be so proud of you.'

'I miss him so much,' Chloe said.

'So do I, sweetheart.' Mum took her hand and held it all the way to Whitsborough Bay Crematorium. Swallowing hard on the constriction in my throat, I turned to look out the window. I would not let her make me cry. It was a celebration for Gramps. No tears.

* * *

James met us at the crematorium. He shook hands with Dad and Uncle Simon, then kissed Mum and Auntie Louise on the cheek, expressing his condolences for their loss. He did the same to Chloe and I didn't miss him lingering a little longer than necessary, or her looking at him with longing in her eyes when he stepped away and took hold of my hand.

When I shuffled into the front row pew beside James, I didn't miss how closely Chloe sat against his other side, despite there being plenty of room to spread out.

I didn't miss how, when he handed her a tissue, their fingers brushed and they exchanged gentle smiles.

And I didn't miss the sparks flying between them throughout the wake. The smouldering looks across the room. The discreet touches. The whispers. The laughter.

Gramps's final words to me echoed round my mind. I had to let James go. Today.

'Can I have a quick word?' I said to James a few hours into the wake. 'Somewhere quiet.'

'Are you okay?' he asked as he followed me out the back of the pub and through the beer garden.

I perched on the edge of the furthest picnic bench, confident that nobody was close enough to overhear us. James sat down opposite me.

I steepled my fingers against my lips as I mustered the strength to say the words. 'Remember what we agreed at Hannah and Toby's wedding? That we weren't each other's forever but we were happy to continue until our forever came along?'

'You've met someone else?' The hopeful expression in his eyes was crushing, yet it also spurred me on.

I shook my head and placed my hands on the table. 'No. Bit preoccupied at the moment.'

'Of course. Sorry. I wasn't thinking.' He placed his hand over one of mine but I retracted mine. Too intimate.

'Anyway, it's been great but I think it's time we called it a day.'

'You want to break up?'

No, James, I want you to love me the way I love you! 'I think it's for the best. Don't you?'

He shrugged. 'If it's what you really want...'

Of course it isn't! But I don't exactly have a choice here. 'I think it's what we both need. Give us both a chance to find someone who *is* our forever. Although I think you might have already found yours.'

Colour flushed his cheeks. 'Who?'

I rolled my eyes. 'Chloe. I'm not blind. I saw the instant attraction at Gramps's birthday party and I've seen the way you've both been looking at each other today.'

He twiddled with an abandoned beermat, the colour in his cheeks deepening.

'Maybe you could ask her out?' I suggested, somehow managing to sound light and casual even though the words were like razor blades slicing my throat.

'I can't do that.' He didn't raise his eyes. 'She's your cousin.'

'And I want her to be happy.' I stood up and brushed down the back of my dress. 'I'm going to say the same to her but maybe it's more appropriate for tomorrow. I'm going home now.'

'Sam!' James called as I headed back towards the pub.

I turned to face him, longing for him to beg me to stay with him yet knowing full well there was no way it would happen.

'Thanks,' he said. 'And you were right. It has been great.'

I nodded and smiled weakly, then turned. Taking a deep calming breath, I stepped back into the pub. 'I did it, Gramps,' I whispered. 'I fulfilled my promise.'

* * *

Chloe and I walked arm in arm along the promenade the following morning.

'I can't believe you ended it with James yesterday,' she said, gently squeezing my arm. 'I thought you two were having fun.'

'We were, but that was the problem. It was great but it wasn't going anywhere.'

'But I thought you were happy with it that way.'

You have no idea! 'I was but it wasn't fair on either of us. One of us was going to have to let go sooner or later. I was actually going to end things last month but I couldn't face the thought of being at Gramps's birthday party without a plus one. You know what Great-Aunt Agnes is like with me. It would have been all, "No boyfriend again, dear? What's wrong with you? Can't hang onto a man?" and you know how much that winds me up. And then Gramps died and, to be honest, I really appreciated James's support.'

We sat down on a bench overlooking the sea. It was the back end of June and there'd been a warm spell all week. Intermittent wispy clouds painted a dotted line across an otherwise deep blue sky and the sea lapped gently onto the beach below us.

'I've told James he should ask you out.'

'What? Why would you say that?' Although Chloe was clearly trying to look and sound surprised, I knew her well enough to know it was fake. James had likely already spoken to her.

'I've seen you together. There's an attraction between you that's worth exploring.'

We both sat in silence, looking out at a lone paddle-boarder.

'I couldn't take your boyfriend,' she said eventually, her tone pleading for me to convince her.

'You wouldn't be. He'd be my *ex*-boyfriend. You have my blessing to go out with him if that's what you both really want.'

'If it was – and I'm not saying it is – but, if it was, you promise we won't fall out over it?'

'I promise.'

'Pinkie promise?' she asked.

I laughed. 'It's years since we've done this but, yes, I pinkie promise.' We wrapped our little fingers together and took turns in kissing them.

'Thanks, Sammie,' she said, resting her head against my shoulder. 'You're the best. I'd hate it if anything ever came between us. I couldn't bear you not being in my life.'

'Same here.'

13

Present Day

I must have finally dozed off in my hotel room at Chloe's wedding because a knock on the door woke me with a start. The digital clock by the bed informed me that it was 23:52. *Who on earth?* I unlocked the door and edged it open a few inches. My stomach did a backflip at the sight of James propped up against the opposite wall with a half-drunk pint in his hand.

'Can I come in?' he asked, his speech slurred.

'I don't think that's a good idea.'

'Probably right.' He wagged his finger at me. 'You're right about lots of things, aren't you?'

I wasn't sure whether that was a compliment or an insult so I shrugged. 'Is Chloe okay?'

'She's amazing,' he said. 'So beautiful and funny and lovely and—'

'I meant after the incident earlier. Presumably you know what happened.'

'Ah. Of course. Yes. She's fine 'bout it.'

'Good. So is there something you wanted?' I cringed at the

haughty tone in my voice, especially as I sounded just like Great-Aunt Agnes.

He nodded and tried to take a slurp on his pint but missed his mouth. 'Oops.' He wiped at his damp beard and neck.

'So what did you want?' I prompted.

'Open the door. I can't see you properly.'

I could do without this but hopefully he would say his piece and go. 'Okay but you're *not* coming in.'

'S'fine. Just want to talk.'

Reluctantly pushing the door open, I half-stepped into the corridor. 'I'm waiting. Talk.'

'Oh yes. I wanted to say... It's just...' He took a deep breath and stood up straight. I could sense him telling himself to sober up. 'I wanted to say I'm really sorry that I didn't love you back and I'm sorry if I hurt you because of that.'

I gulped. 'That's very nice of you. Thank you.'

'You're amazing and beautiful and funny and lovely too, you know. Just not the one for—'

'I know. I get it,' I held up my hand to indicate that he needed to stop talking. 'You'd better get back to the party before you're missed.'

'Will you be okay?' He looked so sad and I knew him well enough to know that his concern was genuine.

'I'll be fine.' My voice softened. This wasn't his fault. It was my mess. My lies. 'Thanks for coming to find me. It was kind of you.'

'It was the least I could do. I didn't know how you felt. You said... If I'd known, maybe I'd have...'

'Maybe you'd have what?' I asked gently when he tailed off. 'You'd have stayed with me and made yourself love me in return? We both know that's not how it works. You and Chloe were made for each other. I think you were meant to meet me so that you could meet her.' I'd always believed in fate and destiny and this made sense to me. The universe had been cruel to me to be kind to two of the people I loved the most.

'I'm sorry,' James said.

'Me too. But I'm sorrier for the way the truth came out. Seriously, how is Chloe?'

He necked the rest of his drink and swayed for a moment before steadying himself against the wall. 'Pretty upset. Putting a brave face on it. I'm sure she'll come round. Be better in the morning.'

'I hope so. You will try to get her to see reason, won't you?'

James nodded. 'Have to. All my fault.'

'It's nobody's fault. It's just...' I shrugged. I wasn't sure what it was anymore. 'Thanks for checking on me. It means a lot. Now get back to your wife and your guests and let me get some sleep.'

James smiled tenderly at me. 'You'll find someone else and he'll be so much better for you than I ever was.'

My heart raced. Someone else? Better than James? He really had no idea, did he? I smiled weakly.

Then he winked. 'Well, better than me might not be possible. Nobody else could have my charm, good looks or witty repartee.' He pulled a comical face at me.

'You always did know how to make me laugh,' I said, smiling.

'A hug to say how sorry I am?' he suggested, looking at me with sad puppy dog eyes as he stretched out his arms. 'Please?'

'Go on, then.' I stepped into his hug and lightly kissed him on the cheek. 'Congratulations, James. You two are going to be so happy together.'

'Oh my God! You just can't help yourself.'

Dropping my arms to my side, I twisted round to face Chloe.

She tightened her fists into balls, clenched her jaw and glowered at me. 'I missed you tonight. I decided I might have overreacted so I came to say sorry, but it seems I wasn't overreacting at all.' The coldness in her voice made me shudder.

I glanced at James, willing him to support me, but he was leaning against the opposite wall once more, head hanging. Begging him to tell the truth – that he'd come to find me – wasn't going to do their marriage any favours.

'It was just a congratulations hug.' I held out my hands towards her, beseeching her to believe me.

She pressed her fingers to her temples and clenched her teeth before shouting at me, every single word drawn out for emphasis. 'You were kissing. I saw you.'

'It was on the cheek. It was a congratulations kiss. That's all.' I kept my voice low, hoping to calm her. It didn't work.

'And if I hadn't appeared, it'd just have been a congratulations kiss on the mouth, and then a congratulations fumble…'

'Chloe! I'm telling the truth.' I took a step closer to her but she put her hand up to stop me.

'I don't think you know what the truth is anymore, Samantha.'

I winced at her full use of my full name for the second time that evening.

'Thanks for ruining my wedding day.' With a final withering look, she grabbed James's arm and stormed down the corridor with him.

14

There were thankfully no wedding guests around when I left the hotel at seven the following morning. Huddled in the back of the taxi with my overnight bag on the seat beside me, I felt like a criminal fleeing the scene of the crime.

The driver waited for me in the farmyard at Hedgehog Hollow while I let myself in with the spare key I'd found hidden under a stone hedgehog. There was no sign of Tabby in the cloakroom but the moment I ripped open a food pouch, she dived through the cat flap, purring.

'I wish you could tell me your name,' I said, watching her gobbling her food.

It was so quiet in the house and so far away from the people who were angry with me that I could happily have stayed there all day. Sighing, I left Tabby, locked up, hid the key, and instructed my driver to take me to Whitsborough Bay.

* * *

I knew it would be coming but it still hurt when Mum tore a strip off me as soon as she and Dad arrived home late that morning. Apparently I was a jealous homewrecker. I sat at the breakfast bar in the kitchen while she vented, trying not to react. I'd learned it was easier just to sit there and take it.

Dad repeatedly attempted to intervene but she screamed him down each time. Eventually she ran out of steam and insults, grabbed her bag and stormed out, presumably to Auntie Louise's.

'I should never have moved back home,' I said to Dad. 'I'm sorry.'

He leaned against the wall, his face pale and drawn. 'Please don't ever say that. This is your home. You're *always* welcome here.'

'By you, but not by Mum. She seems to get a little angrier and more detached every day and I don't know how to make it better.' I stood up and loaded my mug into the dishwasher. 'What are you going to do this afternoon?'

'I need to mow the lawn.' Dad looked beyond me towards the back garden. 'What about you?'

'Reddfield Hospital to see Thomas, the man from yesterday, then Hannah's. I'll probably be back early evening.'

'Don't feel you have to go out all day because of your mum.'

'It's fine. I'd already decided it before you got home.' I hadn't. The idea had only popped into my head while Mum was yelling at me, but Dad didn't need to know that.

* * *

A couple of hours later, armed with a bag of grapes and a bunch of bananas, I made my way across the car park at Reddfield Hospital.

I followed the signs to ward three with butterflies in my stomach. If I'd met Thomas during my daily work, I'd have had no qualms about turning up at hospital to check on him, but this felt strange. We had no professional relationship so I didn't have a reason to be there yet something compelled me to visit him.

There were six beds in the ward and they all contained elderly men. Thomas was on the far right, the top half of his bed partially elevated. His eyes were closed so I hesitated by the foot of his bed. The bruising on his face was deep purple and there was an egg-size lump on his head. He'd clearly taken a heck of a tumble. It looked like his cheek had been glued back together but he had Steri-Strips across the cut on his forehead.

As I stepped closer, the bag of fruit crinkled and Thomas opened his eyes.

'Hi. You probably don't remember me,' I declared brightly. 'My name's Samantha Wishaw and—'

His eyes closed and he drifted off.

I placed the bag of fruit on the over-bed table, sat in the bedside chair and took my course textbook and a highlighter out of my bag. Might as well continue preparing for my new job while I was waiting.

After roughly twenty minutes, I became aware of being watched and looked up from my reading.

'Hi! You're awake.'

Thomas reached for his glasses and frowned after he put them on. 'Who are you?' His voice was low and gruff.

'I'm Samantha Wishaw. I'm a district nurse but—'

'Where's your uniform?'

'I'm not working today but—'

'Then why are you here?'

There was clear irritation in his voice and I felt like I was being interrogated. 'I wanted to see you because...' I hesitated, wondering if this had been a bad idea.

'Come on. Spit it out!'

'I'm the one who found you yesterday.'

He stared at me for a moment, eyes wide. 'You're the one who called the ambulance?'

I smiled. 'Yes.'

His eyes narrowed. 'And I suppose you expect me to thank you for that?'

The anger in his voice took me aback. 'No. That's not why I'm here.'

'Good, because you won't get any thanks from me. Exactly the opposite. What gave you the right? If it hadn't been for you, I could have joined my Gwendoline and now you've ruined it. Twenty years I've been without her. Twenty hideously miserable years but it was nearly at an end. Then you bloody barged in where you weren't wanted and tried to make it all better. Well, it isn't better. It'll never be better until I join my wife.'

His voice had risen to a shout and I was conscious of the other patients and visitors glancing in our direction and whispering. I also felt sick at his words. He'd wanted to die. He hated me for stopping it. How could I even begin to respond to that?

I lowered my voice. 'I'm so sorry to hear you've lost your wife but I couldn't just leave you there. It would go against everything I'm trained for.'

'What were you doing in my house anyway?' He still sounded angry but at least he'd reduced the volume.

'I got lost, stopped to ask for directions, looked through the window and saw you'd collapsed.'

'So you broke into my house and meddled?'

'I didn't break in. The door was open.' I bit my lip. 'I let myself in again this morning, though, to—'

'What?' He tried to sit upright but was clearly too exhausted and slumped back against the pillows.

'To feed your cat,' I said. 'She's beautiful. Does she have a name?'

His face softened. 'You found Misty-Blue?'

I smiled. 'That's a lovely name. Really suits her.'

'I thought she'd wandered off. Haven't seen her for a few days. Thought she'd been taken from me too.'

'Well, she's fine and she's had a couple of good meals. That's kind of why I'm here. Would you be happy for me to keep feeding her until you're discharged?'

'So you can snoop around my house? How do I know you're not a burglar?'

'If I was a burglar, do you really think I'd be sitting here asking for permission to feed your cat? I'd be looting your house right now.'

He pursed his lips. 'Did you put the key back where you found it?'

'Yes.'

'Good. You can leave now.'

'You don't want me to feed Misty-Blue?'

He fixed me with a hard stare. 'She's fine fending for herself.'

'I really don't mind doing it.'

'But I do. Nobody asked you to call an ambulance and nobody asked you to feed my cat. I don't need anybody's help. Goodbye, Nurse Wishaw.'

'Okay. It's your choice. I'm really sorry for upsetting you.' I placed my textbook and pen back in my bag and hitched it onto my shoulder. 'Take care of yourself, Thomas.'

'It's Mr Mickleby,' he snapped.

'I brought you some fruit.' I indicated the bag on the table then made a swift exit before he could hurl any more insults – or perhaps the fruit – at me. I'd already taken enough stick this weekend to last a lifetime.

* * *

'I don't know why you want my approval,' Hannah said later that day, rubbing her back and adjusting her position on the sofa at Fuchsia Cottage. I'd filled her in on everything that had happened since I last saw her at the church. 'You're going to feed that cat whatever I say.'

I smiled. 'You know me too well. Do you think I should visit Mr Mickleby in hospital tomorrow?'

She raised her eyebrows and I laughed.

'You can't blame me for wanting some reassurance,' I said. 'I seem to be doing everything wrong at the moment and Mr Mickleby was far from ecstatic about me saving him.'

Hannah sighed. 'Poor man on his own for twenty years. He's obviously very lonely, but it's a common story, especially in remote locations. You must have seen it before.'

'Unfortunately, yes. Too many times.'

Hannah fixed her eyes on mine. 'Be careful, Sam. He sounds like an angry and bitter man, perhaps understandably, but he's going to take out his frustrations on you and you're not his nurse. You don't need to be part of his life. I know you'll accept whatever he throws at you because you're used to doing that with your mum but we both know it brings you down, no matter how much you try to brush it off.'

'I'll be careful. I promise. I just feel drawn to him. I don't know why.' I shrugged. 'Anyway, let's move onto cheerier subjects. You were going to show me the nursery.'

I stayed at Hannah's for another hour, looking at the nursery and everything they'd purchased ready for the baby's arrival. Gushing over cute clothes and soft toys was a welcome distraction from the situation at home and with Mr Mickleby.

* * *

At Hedgehog Hollow later, Misty-Blue appeared for food once more. I wanted to play with her but, as I was there against Mr Mickleby's wishes, I wasn't going to risk sticking around longer than necessary.

Driving back to Whitsborough Bay, I felt on edge. Mr Mickleby's reaction had really thrown me and it wasn't like me to be so affected by an angry patient, not that he was actually one of my patients. Could it be because I felt guilty? Guilty that I'd saved a man when all he wanted was to escape his lonely existence and be with his wife. Guilty that he could still have years ahead of him, all alone, while the home that had presumably once been filled with love and laughter gradually fell into further ruin. Guilty that I hadn't been there to save Gramps who, despite also grieving for his lost love, had found a way forward without her and, in the same circumstances, would have wanted to live.

15

The house was in darkness when I got back to Whitsborough Bay. Dad had left a note to say he'd gone out for a drink with one of his colleagues. Mum was presumably still at Auntie Louise's.

I'd phoned Chloe several times across the day but it rang once each time then went to voicemail. I wondered if she'd blocked me and a quick search online suggested she probably had. Had it really come to that? Bridesmaid to blocked in the space of one day.

Chloe and James would be heading to Mauritius for their honeymoon tomorrow and I couldn't let them go without trying to sort things out with Chloe. After making myself some dinner, I walked round to their house, hoping the face-to-face approach would work.

My heart raced as I rang the bell. *Please let her hear me out.*

Auntie Louise answered the door, laughing at something, but the smile immediately slipped from her face when she saw me.

'Hi, Auntie Louise. Could I speak to Chloe, please?'

'She doesn't want to speak to you, Sam.' It was a very matter-of-fact statement, completely lacking in emotion.

'I know. She wouldn't answer my calls and—'

'And that should have been a big clue to just leave it.'

'But she's my cousin and best friend. I want to make things right. I'd really like to speak to her.'

She shook her head.

'Please?'

Her eyes flashed at me and I knew I'd pushed it too far. 'Are you incapable of listening? Chloe said no. I said no. Haven't you done enough damage already? Why can't you just leave her and James alone?' Auntie Louise had always been kind to me so I certainly hadn't expected such an angry outburst.

'I'm sorry.' The words barely came out as a whisper.

'And so you should be. This should be the happiest time of their lives but, thanks to you, we've had tears and arguments all day. This is about them, not you. Just go away, Sam. Leave it alone.' Then she slammed the door. That was me well and truly put in my place.

I slowly made my way home, pulled on my PJs and crawled under my duvet with the TV on low. What a day! It seemed like the whole world was angry with me. I was going to have to accept that there was no chance of making peace with Chloe before she went abroad and I needed to let that one go. Hopefully she'd have a relaxing time and come back willing to talk. Surely James would manage to convince her that the hug and kiss on the cheek were innocent and that he'd been the one seeking me out.

Mum's anger was the norm so there was nothing I could do about that.

As for Mr Mickleby, I wasn't prepared to let that one go. Most of my family didn't want or need me but maybe he did. Maybe a few small acts of kindness could ease that loneliness and ease my guilty conscience. It was worth a try.

16

✉ To Rich
Is the offer to be my tour guide still open? I'm
not working this week so I'm free any day that
suits but no worries if you have too much on.
Thanks

✉ From Rich
I have a day off on Thursday and no plans so
consider me your guide for the day. I'm also free
for lunch today before my shift starts if that's
any good x

I drove across to Hedgehog Hollow to feed Misty-Blue – a quick in and
out again – then across to the village of Umplesthorpe to meet Rich in
his local, The Black Swan.

Rich must have arrived moments before me as he was at the bar
ordering a drink. He turned round and gave me a huge smile. 'Perfect
timing. What can I get you?'

'An orange juice, please.'

He placed the order.

'Do you live close by?' I asked.

'Three minutes' walk in that direction.' He pointed to his right.

'Very handy.'

He grinned. 'A bit too handy sometimes.'

We took our drinks over to a table by the window.

'Lucky you having a week off,' he said.

'It's actually three weeks off. I finished as a district nurse last Thursday and will start at the TEC next month. Because I've never taught before, I wanted some time to get my head round the syllabus, read the course text and be as prepared as possible.'

'Good idea. So what promoted the career change?'

Over paninis I briefly explained the situation at home. Rich told me more about his job and we chatted about Dave, his partner of five years. We also talked about Mr Mickleby and Rich admitted that he'd keep persisting if he was in my position.

All too soon, it was time for Rich to leave for his shift but I was excited about the friendship I could see forming. He was so easy to talk to and it was refreshing to start building a friendship with a man after years of working in a female-dominated environment.

'Looking forward to Thursday already,' he said as we left the pub. 'And good luck with Mr Mickleby. Hope he's a bit more forgiving today.'

'Oh gosh, so do I.' I opened my car door. 'Time to go and find out. I'll see you later.'

* * *

Thomas Mickleby was sitting up in bed when I arrived fifteen minutes into visiting time, his head turned towards the window at the end of the ward.

'Hello again,' I said, approaching his bed.

He turned from the window, clear surprise on his face. 'What are you doing here?'

'I came to see you.'

'You've seen me.' He paused then added in a more hostile tone, 'Now you can go.'

'Are you expecting any other visitors today?'

'Yes. Her Majesty the Queen said she'd call in.'

I smiled. So Mr Mickleby had a sense of humour. That was a good sign. I ignored his sarcasm and sat down. 'I fed Misty-Blue this morning. She sends her love and hopes you're home soon.'

'I told you not to feed her.'

'And I decided to overrule you. My dad's a vet and I'm a nurse so caring for animals and people is part of my DNA.' I nodded towards his over-bed table where the bunch of grapes had been massively depleted. 'Did you enjoy the grapes?'

'They were okay, I suppose,' he muttered.

I leaned over, picked one off the bunch and popped it in my mouth. 'Mmm. Delicious.' I gave him a cheeky grin. 'So how are you feeling?'

'Are you asking me that because you have to or because you actually give a damn?'

'The latter. I'm not your nurse so I don't *have* to show any interest in you, but I am a human being and I *want* to.'

Silence. He stared at the ceiling and I sneakily popped another grape into my mouth.

'I'm old, I'm creaky, my eyesight's fading, my balance is iffy, I've had a mild stroke and I have gout. How do you think I'm feeling?' He sounded weary and that was hardly surprising.

He turned and fixed his gaze on mine, as though challenging me to turn his ailments into positives; something I'd never do. Old age could be cruel, especially when the body started to give up but the mind was so active, as his clearly was given the steadily flow of sharp comments.

'Could be worse. You could have an annoying do-gooder plying you with grapes and feeding your cat.' I smiled and winked at him.

I swear his lips twitched but he didn't say anything.

'Your farm's in a stunning setting,' I continued. 'Have you always lived there?'

'No.'

I waited a few moments but he didn't expand. 'My grandparents had a bungalow with some land and trees. I used to stay there a lot when I was a little girl and I loved it. It was so tranquil. I always thought of it as my happy place. I get that same feeling at your farm.'

'It's too bloody quiet,' he grumbled.

'Could you not sell up and move somewhere a little less remote?'

'I can't leave my Gwendoline.'

I frowned. 'I thought you said she'd died.'

'She was taken from me twenty long years ago. I scattered her ashes there. She loved that place.'

'What happened to her?'

He removed his glasses and placed them on the bedside cabinet. 'I'm tired. You need to leave.'

I stood up. 'Okay. You get some rest and I'll be back tomorrow.'

'Don't bother.'

I'd only taken a few paces when he called out. 'Nurse Wishaw?'

'Yes?' I returned to his bed.

'If you do come back, maybe you could bring some more of those grapes with you. Not that you're welcome back. I don't want to see you but if you're going to insist on this pointless charade, it might as well be worth my while.'

I smiled. 'Grapes it is. Anything else?'

'I like blackcurrant juice.'

'Grapes and blackcurrant juice? Consider it done.'

'And if you're going to break into my house again, you might as well bring me my pyjamas, slippers and dressing gown. Can't bear these damn hospital gowns. And my toothbrush and paste. I don't like the flavour of the one they've given me. Doesn't mean I want to see you. I'd just like my own things.'

'I understand. You get some sleep and I'll see you tomorrow.'

'Second door on the right,' he called. 'No snooping elsewhere.'

'I promise.'

I smiled as I walked off the ward and down the corridor. Had I just taken a baby step with Mr Mickleby? I hoped so.

* * *

Back home, there was no chance of making any steps forward, baby-sized or otherwise. As soon as I opened the door late that afternoon, I could hear the roar of the vacuum cleaner from the lounge and steeled myself. Mum vacuuming was a sign of her being in a foul mood – fouler than normal – and it was bound to be my fault.

The lounge door flung open. 'I don't know how you dare show your face around here.' Spittle flew from her mouth as she spoke and her eyes bore into me, conveying her displeasure. 'They nearly didn't make it onto the plane because of you. I hope you're proud of yourself.'

With a final withering look, she slammed the door, and the roar of the vacuum echoed round the house one more.

I sat down on the stairs with my head in my hands. This thing with Chloe would blow over eventually. It had to. Not that it would make much difference to my relationship with Mum because she'd find something else to have a go at me for and, every so often, she'd throw this one back at me, making me feel like I was a horrible, vindictive person with an agenda to ruin everyone's lives. Occasionally, when I was feeling low and her words cut a little too deep, I wondered if I was that person. You hear the bad things enough times, you start to wonder if they're true.

17

The following morning, I awoke early with a fresh determination. There was nothing I could do to change what had happened with Chloe or how Mum felt about me so the best tactic was avoidance. I *could* do something to help Mr Mickleby.

I showered and dressed but remained in my room, listening out for my parents leaving for work.

With the coast clear, I made my way down to the kitchen to prepare a casserole. I programmed the slow cooker to be ready for when they returned from work, set the dishwasher away and carefully wiped down every surface. I even emptied the kitchen bin so that I couldn't be accused of leaving the place smelling of onions.

I left a note against the slow cooker:

Enjoy! Going to the library for the day then having dinner at Hannah and Toby's so back late x

One last look round the kitchen reassured me that there was nothing Mum could be angry about. I grabbed my bag, locked up and drove to Hedgehog Hollow.

* * *

I stood in the farmyard beside my car and closed my eyes for a moment, breathing in the fresh air, feeling the gentle kiss of the sun on my arms, listening to the sounds of nature. So peaceful. I could imagine myself back in the garden at Meadowcroft with the smell of chocolate cake or scones wafting out the kitchen window while Gramps tested me on the names of birds and plants.

'What is it about this place?' I whispered, looking up to the sky. 'I feel so close to you here, Gramps.'

A mewing made me look down. 'Misty-Blue! Good morning.' I bent down and stroked her. 'Do you like being picked up?' I gently scooped her into my arms and she nuzzled her head into my hair, purring.

I opened my car door and removed my mobile from my bag. 'Should we take a selfie for Mr Mickleby?' I asked. 'Aw, that's a lovely one. Come on, then, let's get you some food.'

* * *

'Good afternoon, Mr Mickleby,' I said, smiling warmly. 'Did you have a good sleep?

'Worst ever. Bloke in bed three died.'

'Oh no. Had you become friends?'

He sneered at me. 'Have you heard yourself? Friends? It's not the first day at school, you know.'

'You know what I meant. I thought you'd maybe chatted to him.'

'It's not a night down the pub either.'

'Grapes,' I said, placing them on Mr Mickleby's over-bed table. I lifted up the bag I was carrying. 'PJs, slippers and dressing gown.'

Without a word, he pushed back the covers, took the bag from me, rummaged in it for his slippers, then shuffled down the ward wearing them.

Sighing, I sat down and dug out my textbook again. A thank you would have been nice.

When Mr Mickleby returned, he thrust the empty bag at me and lowered himself onto the bed without a word.

'Misty-Blue asked me to take a selfie this morning,' I said, taking out my phone. 'She's very photogenic.'

Placing my phone in his eyeline, I scrolled through several pictures.

'She doesn't normally like being picked up,' he said. 'She must like you.'

'I'm glad someone does.' Realising that could sound like a dig and undo any progress I'd made, I swiftly added, 'I'm not very popular at home right now.'

He stared at me and I wondered for a moment whether he was going to ask me to expand.

'Thanks for getting my things and for feeding Misty-Blue.'

'You're welcome.'

Silence.

'They're letting me go back to the farm tomorrow,' he said after a couple of minutes.

'And how do you feel about that?'

'I'm thrilled. Leaving one prison to return to another.' His voice dripped with sarcasm.

'Misty-Blue will be pleased to see you. How are you getting home?'

He shrugged. 'They said something about an ambulance if I didn't have someone to pick me up.'

'Do you have anyone?'

He stared past me and out of the window. 'Not a single soul since my Gwendoline was taken.'

My heart broke for him. Never had one sentence been filled with so much meaning. No wonder he was angry at me for saving him. I knew he'd lost his wife but had he been completely alone for twenty years? It didn't bear thinking about. I hoped it was an exaggeration but the look in his eyes and the sadness in his voice suggested not.

'I'll collect you tomorrow,' I said.

He turned to me, frowning. 'You'll do no such thing. Why are you here anyway? I don't understand. What's in it for you?'

'Why should there be something in it for me?'

'Because nobody does anything for a complete stranger without an ulterior motive.'

'Some people do.'

'And you're one of those people?'

'I told you before, caring for people and animals is part of who I am.'

'Then it's time to find yourself another person and another animal to care for. Thanks for bringing my things in, thanks for the fruit, and thanks for feeding the cat but it ends here.' The aggression was back. 'I didn't ask you to save me on Saturday and I don't want you to try to save me now. I just want to go back to my farm tomorrow and be left alone to...' He rolled onto his side, facing away from me.

Die. He wanted to be left alone to die.

'What would happen to Misty-Blue if you returned to Hedgehog Hollow and simply waited to die?' I asked.

His shoulders tensed, as though I'd hit a nerve. 'She'd be fine.' His voice was strong and confident. 'She was a stray so she'll go back to being a stray. She doesn't need me.'

The slight hesitation in his tone as he said that gave me hope. He had one reason to live and I needed to keep pushing it.

I stood up. 'I'll see you tomorrow.'

'Weren't you listening?'

'I was listening. I chose not to hear.'

* * *

When I arrived back from Hannah's late that evening, I could hear the TV on in the lounge.

'Hi, Dad,' I said, poking my head round the door.

He smiled at me. 'How was your day?'

I sat down beside him on the sofa and updated him on my visit to Mr Mickleby. He'd expressed the same caution as Hannah when I'd told him about my visit on Sunday and he repeated his concerns now.

'I know what I'm doing. Don't worry about me.'

'I'm your dad. It's my job to worry about you. By the way, thanks for the casserole. It was delicious.'

The door opened. 'Hi, Mum,' I said.

'What are you watching?' she asked Dad, barely glancing at me.

'Nothing. Feel free to change channel.'

He handed her the remote and she flicked over.

'Did you enjoy your dinner?' I asked.

'Could have done with more seasoning,' she said, her eyes focused on the TV. 'And I didn't appreciate you leaving me with the dishwasher to empty.'

I couldn't win. Ever.

18

'Oh, it's you.' Mr Mickleby didn't exactly look thrilled to see me when he opened the door at Hedgehog Hollow late the following morning. 'You found me.'

I'd driven to hospital only to discover he'd discharged himself last night.

'Can I come in?' I asked.

'Do I have a choice?'

'You always have a choice but—'

Misty-Blue ran down the hall and weaved round my legs.

'But Misty-Blue invited me round for a playdate and she'll be ever so disappointed if you send me away.'

I swear his lips twitched again. With an exaggerated sigh, he turned and shuffled back down the hall, leaving the door wide open, which I took as my invitation to step inside. Closing the door behind me, I picked up the cat to give her a scratch behind the ears.

'Are you my new best friend?' I whispered to her. 'Are you going to help me with your owner?'

Thomas stared at me, wide-eyed, as I stepped into the lounge with Misty-Blue draped over my shoulder. 'Either you've drugged her or you're a cat whisperer,' he said.

'Just someone who knows how to handle animals. You said she was a stray?'

'Sort of. Found her in one of the barns six years back. Her mum had presumably died having the litter. Awful sight. Two kittens were dead and the other three were barely alive. I did my best but I couldn't save one of them. Misty-Blue and her brother, Smokey, were fighters but he wandered off a couple of years back so it's been just the two of us since then.'

Misty-Blue jumped down from my shoulder and up onto Thomas's knee. He looked at me in surprise again. 'You really do have a gift. She's never done that to me before.'

The look of love and the way he stroked her so tenderly brought tears to my eyes. 'She's probably realised she took you for granted and has missed you while you've been away.'

'Aye. Perhaps.'

'They told me at the hospital that you got a taxi home last night.'

'Couldn't face another night on that ward. Far too noisy.'

'I can imagine. Especially after sleeping somewhere as peaceful as this.' I smiled at him. 'Can I make myself useful and make you a cup of tea or coffee?'

'You might struggle. No milk, no teabags and no coffee.'

'Did you have a meal at the hospital last night?' I couldn't help myself. The nurse in me kicked into action.

Silence.

'Breakfast?'

Silence.

'Why aren't you eating? Are you struggling to keep food down?'

Mr Mickleby sighed as he picked at a loose thread on the arm of the chair. 'I don't know.'

'How can you not know?'

'Because...' Pick, pick, pick.

'You haven't been trying to eat, have you?'

He stopped picking and looked up, but not at me. I followed his gaze towards the dresser and the photos of his wife and I understood.

Wounds could be cleaned and dressed, medication could be prescribed, and comforting words could be given to a patient facing terminal illness. But there was no bandage for loneliness. No prescription. No words of comfort. Yet it was a growing epidemic and just as destructive as any diagnosed illness. Thomas Mickleby was so lonely that he wanted to die.

'Mr Mickleby, I know you want to be with your wife but, believe me, starvation is *not* the way forward. It's a slow and extremely painful way to go and I can't let you do that to yourself.'

He didn't respond, which I took as confirmation that starvation was where his head was. I had to change his mind. 'Is that what your wife would have wanted for you?' I asked, injecting into my voice every ounce of empathy and understanding I possessed.

Mr Mickleby stared at the photos for a moment longer, then lowered his eyes. 'No. She'd hate that.'

'So you're not going to starve yourself?'

He fixed his grey eyes on mine. 'No, Nurse Wishaw, I'm not.'

'Good. Now I have a very important question. Do you like tuna mayonnaise?'

'Yes. Why?'

I stood up. 'You'll soon find out.'

I left him and marched outside to my car where my lunch was sitting in a small cool bag in the boot: tuna mayonnaise sandwiches, a yogurt, a banana and some fresh orange juice.

Back in the kitchen, I placed the sandwiches on a plate, grabbed a teaspoon for the yogurt, poured the juice into a glass, and carried them through to Mr Mickleby on a small tray with a cartoon hedgehog on it.

'I know it's not quite lunchtime but you need food.'

'Where did that come from?' Although he was frowning, there was no mistaking the hunger in his eyes.

'It was my packed lunch but, erm, I had a huge breakfast this morning and I'm not hungry.'

He was too busy staring at the sandwiches to notice my shuffling and lack of eye contact. 'If you're sure...?'

'It'll only go to waste otherwise. Enjoy.' I hoped my stomach wouldn't grumble and betray me. I'd skipped breakfast that morning but I could easily buy some more lunch later.

I sat down on the uncomfortable sofa and flicked through my textbook, trying to look busy, but barely registering any of the words. There was no need for Mr Mickleby to keep letting me into his home. If I was going to help him like I'd helped Gramps, I needed to tread carefully and not appear as though I was trying to take over his life so I was best to stay quiet for now.

When he'd finished eating – every last scrap – I took the tray from him and washed and dried the few items used.

'Do you have any food in the house?' I asked as I returned to the lounge.

He sighed. 'A few out-of-date herbs and spices. Can't make much from them.'

'What did you do about food before the stroke?'

'I rubbed a magic lamp and a genie delivered it for me.' He rolled his eyes. 'What do you think I did? I drove to the shops and bought it.'

'But you can't do that now?'

'You're not going to shut up until you have a full answer, are you?'

'Sorry, but no. I know I'm not here as your nurse but I can't help myself.'

He removed his glasses, wiped them on his blue cotton shirt, then replaced them. 'I used to drive so I managed a weekly shop at one of the supermarkets in Reddfield but I ran into the back of someone's car at the start of the year. It was a young lass from over Addlington way. She'd only been driving a few weeks and she admitted it was her fault for stopping suddenly but it didn't matter. I'm the one who went into her so I had to do a sight test and I failed. My driving days were over.'

He sounded resigned to it rather than angry.

'Her mum was a passenger and they both felt bad. The mum

offered to shop for me each week and it worked fine but they moved away at the end of July which left me stuck.'

It was the most I'd heard him say and my heart went out to him for losing what I suspected was the only company he'd had for a long time, not to mention his valuable food supply. His voice had softened as he spoke; he'd obviously appreciated the assistance which suggested he wasn't completely closed off to someone being there for him, despite the protests in hospital.

'Did you tell them at the hospital that you were stuck for getting food?'

'It's none of their damn business and I'm *not* a charity case.' His raised voice made Misty-Blue leap off his lap and bolt it out of the lounge. He stared at me defiantly. 'I paid that lass's mother and it was their way of saying sorry for causing an accident.'

'I appreciate that but this isn't about "charity" either. It's about helping out someone in need. The hospital could have made a referral to Social Services who could talk you through your options.'

'What options? I'm not withering away in some crumbling old care home. I'd rather do that here, thank you very much.'

'Nobody's going to send you away. As long as you've got the capacity to think for yourself and make your own decisions, they'll do whatever they can to help you stay in your own home.'

'Good, because next time I leave here, they'll be carrying me out in a box. Hopefully very soon.'

'Would you like me to get some shopping for you?'

'No. I'd like you to go away and leave me alone.'

'And how are you going to manage this week?'

'I don't know. Bill Davis runs the farm next door and rents my fields. I'll maybe ring him.'

'You know him well?'

He shrugged. 'Not spoken for years. The rent money comes in every month so there's no need to get in touch.'

'Mr Mickleby! That's no good. What if I leave here today and you can't sort out anyone to shop for you? I'll be so worried about you.'

He frowned. 'Why?'

'Because that's who I am. I sometimes wish I didn't care so much about people...' I tailed off and shook my head. Now was not the time to be thinking about Chloe or Mum.

'I'm not your responsibility so you can stop worrying about me,' he cried, then his tone softened. 'You're obviously a good lass with a big heart but you're not my nurse, you're not a friend and you're not a relative so thank you for the lunch and everything but this has to be goodbye.'

I rummaged in my bag for a notepad and pen and scribbled down my details. 'If you change your mind or you need anything, this is my number. Please call me.' I marched over to the dresser and placed it under the phone. 'Take care of yourself.'

He inclined his head but didn't speak. With a heavy heart, I left the farmhouse and made my way to the car. He was right. I had no connection to him and therefore he wasn't my responsibility, yet somehow he felt like it.

19

'Your house is gorgeous,' I said the following morning after Rich had given me a tour of Brook Cottage – the home he shared with Dave.

'Thank you. It was a wreck but Dave's a builder so we gutted it and turned it into what we wanted. We've got planning permission to extend the kitchen and create a third bedroom but we need to save up.'

'At least the labour's free.'

Rich grinned. 'He has his uses. Shall we go?'

It made more sense for Rich to drive so I could look out the window and take in my surroundings. By lunchtime, I'd ruled out the area south of Reddfield. There were lots of pretty villages but it was a bit too far from Whitsborough Bay. I wanted distance from James but didn't want to be quite so far from Dad.

'Would you be better off looking for somewhere to buy instead?' Rich asked. I'd told him that Gramps's will had divided his estate equally between his daughters and granddaughters so I had a good deposit to put down when I was ready to buy. Mum had *not* been impressed by that.

'It's too risky. If teaching doesn't work out, I might have to move again to return to district nursing so I need to keep that flexibility.'

Most of the area was unknown to me but Rich, Hannah, Hedgehog Hollow and Gramps's village were all on the north side, bringing some familiar areas and more of a feeling of home.

Rich was the perfect tour guide. He seemed to know everyone and, as we drove past farms, hamlets and through villages, he maintained a running commentary of gossip. The Wolds might look like a sleepy place where nothing much happened but, if even half the things he told me were true, it was rife with scandal. It sounded like a great community, though, and I looked forward to becoming part of it.

It was great getting to know Rich better. We talked about our careers and I talked about the situation with Chloe and James in much greater detail than I'd managed over lunch on Monday.

'My sympathies,' he said. 'It's not easy. My ex, Craig, and my best mate, Matt, got together. That would have been tough enough if it had happened at the end of our relationship but it happened shortly after Craig and I met.'

'Oh, Rich, that's awful. How long were you with Craig?'

'Two years. I was living with him but apparently Matt came round every time I was on night shift. When I found out, I moved out and Matt moved in. He wanted to stay friends but there was no way. I couldn't forgive him for seeing my boyfriend for the whole time we were together. Mates don't do that.'

'No, they don't. Poor you.'

'It was horrendous at the time but I met Dave five months later and he's the best thing that's ever happened to me.'

'Everything happens for a reason,' I said, smiling at him.

As we drove through the village next to Hannah's, my phone started ringing with an unfamiliar number.

'Hello?' I said.

Silence.

'Hello? Is anyone there?'

'Is that Nurse Wishaw?'

'Mr Mickleby? Is that you?' My heart started to thump.

'Yes. You left your number.' He sounded out of breath.

'Are you alright?'

'I fell. Don't call an ambulance. I'm not hurt but I can't get up. Can you help me?'

'I'll be there in about twenty minutes. Do you want me to—'

He'd already hung up.

'Trouble?' Rich asked, casting me a concerned glance.

'We need to get to Hedgehog Hollow. Mr Mickleby has had another fall.'

* * *

'Hello? Mr Mickleby?' I called out, pushing open his front door.

'I'm in here.'

I ran towards the lounge. He was lying on the floor near the dresser with the phone on its side next to him.

'What happened?' I asked, crouching beside him.

'I fell.'

'Fell or fainted?' I checked his pulse.

He sighed. 'Fainted.'

I raised my eyebrows at him. 'Lack of food?'

'Might have been,' he muttered.

Rich appeared by my side with his first aid kit.

'I told you not to call an ambulance,' Mr Mickleby shouted. 'Why don't you listen?'

'I do listen and I didn't call an ambulance. This is my friend, Rich. We were out in *his* car when I got your call. He's a paramedic and he's got a first aid kit.'

I moved aside while Rich ran through various checks then we both eased Mr Mickleby to his feet and helped him over to the armchair. Even though he was all skin and bones, he was a tall man and I'd have struggled on my own so it was just as well Rich had been with me.

Rich went into the kitchen to get Thomas a glass of water.

'Where were you when you started to feel faint?' I asked.

'Coming down the stairs. I thought I was going to fall down them but I made it to the bottom then keeled over in the lounge. Like I told your friend, I didn't hit my head or anything.'

Rich re-appeared and handed over the water, instructing Mr Mickleby to only take small sips.

'When I woke up, I didn't have the strength in my arms to get up but I managed to crawl to the dresser and pull the phone off. Your number fell down with it.'

He looked quite shaken up. Feeling faint on the stairs had probably done it. There could have been a much more painful outcome.

'Will you let me get you some food now?'

He nodded slowly.

'Good. Glad we've got that sorted.'

'I don't have any cash in the house but I've got a cheque book.'

'A cheque works for me. Will you excuse me a moment? I just want a quick word with Rich.'

We stepped into the hall. 'I'm not sure about leaving him but he needs to eat.'

Rich nodded. 'There's a local store in the next village. How about I get him some basic provisions for dinner and breakfast and you can do a proper shop tomorrow?'

'Thanks, Rich. You're a star.'

Rich left and I returned to the lounge and sat down on the sofa. It would have been easy to sit there and say, 'I told you so' but who would that benefit? He'd learned his lesson the hard way and, by calling me, had finally accepted he needed help.

'Are you warm enough?' I asked.

'A bit chilly.'

'What can I get you?'

'There's a blue cardigan in the kitchen.'

Moments later, I helped him into his cardigan and also passed him the blanket off the back of the sofa.

'Your friend looked familiar. Does he live round here?'

'Umplesthorpe, but you probably recognise him from Saturday.

He's one of the paramedics who attended to you. I asked him to let me know how you were and we stayed in touch.'

'Your boyfriend?'

I smiled. 'No. Just a friend. He's been showing me round the area today so I can narrow down where I'd like to move to.'

He nodded slowly as though taking it all in. 'You're not from round here yourself?'

'No. I'm starting a new job in Reddfield next month, hence the move. I'm Whitsborough Bay born and bred.'

'My Gwendoline loved Whitsborough Bay,' he said. 'Especially the north side.'

I smiled. 'That's my favourite part. I love walking along the promenade in front of the beach huts or a walk round Hearnshaw Park.'

He stared at me, his expression unreadable, before his eyelids started drooping. Reassured from Rich's checks that he hadn't hit his head, I let him drift off and dug out my textbook again.

* * *

Rich returned with a bag of basics and a takeaway carton containing a jacket potato with cheese and beans from a café near the mini-market. I plated it up but Mr Mickleby insisted we didn't stick around to watch him eat. He'd moved from the lounge to the kitchen with reasonable ease so, after feeding Misty-Blue, we bid him goodnight and I made him promise he'd call me again if he had any further incidents.

I felt drained as we pulled away from the farm and could happily have gone home but Rich had arranged for his partner, Dave, to join us for dinner at their local and I could hardly refuse after Rich had been so helpful all day.

As it turns out, I was glad I stayed. A giant bear of a man with shaggy hair, a bushy beard and a voice like honey, Dave couldn't have done more to make me feel at ease. The pair of them were like a comedy act together, outdoing each other with hilarious anecdotes about people they'd encountered through work or those who lived locally.

By the end of a laughter-filled evening, I knew that I'd found two fabulous new friends and some of the fear I had for my new start dissipated. I also knew I'd made huge progress with Mr Mickleby. I'd sleep well tonight.

20

'Food delivery,' I said, holding up a bag for life late the following morning.

Without a word, Mr Mickleby stepped back to allow me inside, then closed the door and followed me into the kitchen.

'It's just a few basics for starters.' I placed the bag on the table. 'I've got some fresh soup and a roll for your lunch and a ready meal for your tea. I thought we'd better discuss what you like and what you can cook before I do a full shop.'

'What flavour soup?' he asked.

I lifted out the two soup cartons and held one in each hand. 'Pea and ham or leek and potato.'

'Leek and potato,' he said after a slight pause. 'It was my Gwendoline's favourite.'

'She had good taste, then. It's my favourite too. You want it now?'

He nodded. 'Seems a long time since breakfast.'

I emptied the contents into a bowl and placed it in the microwave.

'Nice Aga,' I observed while the soup heated.

He shrugged. 'No idea how to use it. My Gwendoline was the chef. I'd have helped her, mind, but she loved cooking and baking and would always shoo me out of the kitchen.' He took a spoon from the drawer by the sink. 'There were two reasons we bought this place and the kitchen was one of them.'

'What was the other one?'

'The hedgehogs.'

The microwave pinged so I gave the soup a stir then set it going again.

'The hedgehogs?' I asked.

'Yes, the hedgehogs.'

Hmm. I was glad we'd cleared that one up. 'Would you like your roll buttered?'

'Yes, please.' He passed me a knife and a side plate.

By the time I'd finished buttering, the microwave had pinged again. He took the bowl out and sat at the battered wooden table with it.

'I'll put these away while you eat,' I said, taking a carton of milk and some cheese out of one of the bags. I wanted to ask about the hedgehogs but I could tell from the way Mr Mickleby was scooping up his soup that he was ravenous and, now that he'd accepted that eating was a good idea, I didn't want to put him off his stride.

Unpacking gave me a good chance to check out his cupboards which were, quite literally, bare. I found a shelf of out of date herbs and spices, just as he'd said, accompanying old bottles of vegetable and olive oil. If he didn't cook, I suspected they'd been there since Gwendoline died.

When he'd finished his lunch in silence, Mr Mickleby make himself a cup of tea and retired to the lounge. I was going to leave his dishes – I wasn't his skivvy after all – but it seemed petty when it would take me all of two minutes to wash and dry them. I wasn't going to do without a cup of tea, though.

Mr Mickleby's eyes widened as he watched me sit down with my drink. I prepared for a sarcastic comment about me making myself at home but he surprised me.

'My Gwendoline would be having words with me about my

shocking manners,' he said. 'I never thought to offer you a cuppa. I'm sorry, lass.'

I smiled, relieved that I wasn't on his bad side. 'That's okay.'

He shook his head. 'It's not okay and I'm sorry. It's no excuse but it's been so long since I've had company. I've quite forgotten how to entertain.'

The obvious loneliness was heart-breaking. 'In that case, you can entertain me by telling me about the hedgehogs.'

'The hedgehogs?'

'Yes. You said there were two reasons you bought the farm: the kitchen and the hedgehogs. I'd love to know more about the hedgehogs. I'm assuming that's Mrs Mickleby holding them in those photos on your dresser.'

He smiled and I swear it took years off him, his face lighting up with pure love. 'My Gwendoline adored hedgehogs. She found a litter of abandoned hoglets when she was little, looked after them, and was hooked. We must have looked after hundreds of injured and abandoned hedgehogs after we married and it was always her dream to be able to do more. As soon as I saw this place, I knew I had to buy it for her. She had such big plans. One of the barns – the biggest stone one – was going to be the rescue centre. We bought plastic crates for beds and a stack of other things. She had an agreement set up with the local vet for medicine at cost. It was all coming together. And then...'

'What happened?' I asked when he fell silent.

'She'd had a sore throat for a while but she was never one to kick up a fuss. Turned out it was a bit more serious than a sore throat. By the time I convinced her to see a doctor, because the weight was dropping off her, it was too late. Cancer of the oesophagus. Advanced. Two months later, she was taken from me.'

'I'm so sorry.'

'Me too, lass. I know you judge me for wanting to join her...'

I shook my head vigorously. 'I don't judge anyone for anything. But it's my job to preserve lives so I've only been doing what comes naturally.'

'I know.' He sighed. 'It's just that, since my Gwendoline was taken from me, I haven't known a single day of joy.'

'But she died twenty years ago.'

'Exactly. So do you understand why I wanted to...?'

I nodded. Yes, I understood. I got it. Life without James had been unbearable and we'd been together for a tiny fraction of the time that Thomas and Gwendoline had been so how I felt must have been magnified a thousand times over for poor Mr Mickleby. I couldn't blame him if he hated me for saving him when he could have been at the end of his pain and loss.

21

The next few days passed in a blur of visits to Hedgehog Hollow, studying, and searching for properties to rent. Sadly, studying was the only success story. The content of the syllabus was familiar and I felt more prepared for my new role with each passing day.

Finding somewhere to live wasn't so successful. I'd never lived on my own before and decided that now wasn't the right time to make that big step so I'd been looking for a room in a shared house. The first house smelled so strongly of cigarette smoke that my eyes watered, despite the advert declaring it was a no-smoking property. The second one was a stereotypical dirty student house with overflowing bins, pots piled up in the sink and mess everywhere. The third house would have been perfect if it hadn't been for the owner repeatedly telling me how much she resented needing a lodger to make ends meet after her boyfriend dumped her and moved out. Not exactly welcoming.

As for Mr Mickleby, hostilities resumed. I left the farm on Friday with a list of his favourite foods and battled my way round the supermarket on Saturday morning to get what he needed. To give him his due, he thanked me and even smiled as he watched me fill his fridge and stock his cupboards. He had his cheque book ready and it all went smoothly. Until I returned on Monday morning to check on him and found myself back at square one. Why was I there? Why was I bothering with an old man? Did I have nothing better to do? Why couldn't I just leave him in peace?

On Wednesday morning, I drove over to Hedgehog Hollow with some fresh milk, bread and fruit. It was blowing a gale and lashing with rain so he let me into the hall and instructed me to wait there. Moments later, he returned with a cheque and opened the door for me to leave. I got the distinct impression that I wouldn't have even been permitted to step inside if it hadn't been for the rain. I couldn't engage him in any conversation – not even small talk about the appalling weather – and returned to my car feeling very low.

I hadn't planned to visit Hannah but I felt the need to be with someone who liked me.

'You might have been right about Mr Mickleby,' I said to her over a warming mug of hot chocolate at Fuchsia Cottage. I updated her on my contact with him over the past week.

'What are you going to do?' she asked.

'I honestly don't know. If he was a patient, I'd be pleasant but just get on with my job, accepting he doesn't want to talk. But he's not a patient and I'm out of my depth.'

Hannah paced up and down, rubbing her back and wincing. 'This is really getting to you, isn't it? So why not just end it?'

'I can't do that. He'll starve.'

'He's not your responsibility, Sam.'

'I know, but—'

She stretched then continued pacing. 'But what? What is it about Mr Mickleby? There has to be something that's driving you to put yourself through all this grief.'

I gulped down the last of my drink and put it down. 'I've been asking myself the same and I keep coming back to Gramps. He looks a bit like him and he reminds me so much of how Gramps was after Nanna died. Lost. Lonely. I want to help.'

Hannah sat down and rubbed her bump. 'You know what I think

it is? I think it's because, after everything you've been through over the past year, you're lost and lonely too and you're looking for someone or something to fill that void. Mr Mickleby does just that. He's a project for you to get your teeth into and he's a potential replacement for your Gramps.' Her voice was soft and understanding.

Could that be it? It would certainly explain things. 'I don't mind him not being talkative as long as he's polite. It's the hostility I can't bear. I get enough of that from my mum.'

* * *

I couldn't sleep that night. Mr Mickleby's situation weighed heavily on me. As I'd said to Hannah, he reminded me so much of how Gramps had been in the weeks and months following Nanna's death – a shadow of a man so overcome with grief that he barely functioned. I'd done everything I could to bring Gramps back from the brink and, while he'd never stopped aching for Nanna, he'd found peace and happiness once more. Thomas Mickleby was a stranger and a grumpy one at that so it wasn't going to be easy but I had to try to bring meaning to his lonely existence too. I had to believe that there was a reason why I'd stumbled across Hedgehog Hollow and saved his life otherwise what had it all been for? I'd lost most of my family as a result of being so late to the wedding and I was loathe to accept that something good hadn't come out of that horrendous day.

It was clearly going to take a lot of time and patience to fully crack that rough exterior but I was willing to give it a go. I had patience and I had time. But did Mr Mickleby?

* * *

Rich and Dave invited me to Brook Cottage for dinner on Friday night and said I was very welcome to stay over so I could have a few drinks. I decided to take them up on the offer, saving me a drive back to Whitsborough Bay in the dark and a return the following morning to do Mr Mickleby's shopping.

We had a lovely evening together, full of laughter once more, and it was exactly what I needed to build me up again after a tough week.

'Any success with the second batch of house viewings today?' Dave asked.

'Disaster again.' I'd spoken to Rich earlier in the week and told him about the first three unsuitable viewings. 'Two got cancelled. One of those went to someone else and the other changed their mind about letting out the room. The third one was on a busy main road with no parking. Six-nil so far. You don't want a lodger here, do you?'

They both grinned at me.

'Funny you should say that,' Rich said. 'You remember I told you we want to extend? We figured we could save a lot faster if we rent out the spare bedroom. So we were wondering if, instead of renting from a stranger, you'd like to rent from your two new best friends.'

They both looked at me eagerly, like dogs waiting for walkies, and I felt quite overcome that these two wonderful men had entered my life and were there for me when, as Hannah pointed out, there was a void.

'Oh my gosh! Really?' I looked from one eager face to the other. 'Yes please!'

We laughed as we gathered in a group hug.

'You can move in whenever you want,' Dave said. 'We need to empty a few things out the wardrobe but that won't take long. You could even move in as soon as tomorrow.'

I smiled at them both. 'Chloe and James get back from honeymoon on Monday. If she returns all relaxed, happy and full of forgiveness, I think I'd better stick around for a week or so to make sure we're back on track before I move.'

Rich nodded. 'But if she comes back in a grump and refuses to speak to you...?'

'Then any day from the middle of next week would be perfect. You two are brilliant. Thank you.'

'I think we should drink to our new roomie,' Dave declared, holding up his pint.

As I clinked my glass against theirs, I suspected I'd be moving in imminently. I had a horrible feeling that Chloe was *not* going to return from her honeymoon eager to pick up our friendship again.

22

A pep talk over breakfast from Rich and Dave about how inspiring they found my kindness towards a stranger filled me with positivity as I drove to Hedgehog Hollow on Saturday morning. I could do it. I could get Mr Mickleby onside. I just needed to keep chipping away at that tough shell and not take it to heart when he snapped at me because it wasn't about me. It wasn't personal.

'I wasn't sure if you'd be back,' Mr Mickleby said as soon as he opened the door.

'What makes you say that?'

'I wasn't very well-behaved on Wednesday.'

I gave him a gentle smile. 'I'll be honest with you. I nearly didn't return.'

'Yet here you are.'

'Yes. It's Misty-Blue's fault. She keeps texting me and telling me she wants to play with the cat whisperer. She even demanded I bring toys.' I reached into one of the shopping bags and produced a feathered cat teaser.

Mr Mickleby smiled, calming my remaining nerves, and stepped aside to let me in.

'Misty-Blue!' he called as we headed towards the kitchen. 'Nurse Wishaw's here to see you.'

I placed the bags down on the kitchen table. 'Please call me Sam. Samantha, if you prefer.'

'Samantha, then. I don't like it when people shorten their names.' He didn't offer me his first name in return. Too soon for him, perhaps?

'Ah, there you are!' I bent down to scoop up Misty-Blue and give her a cuddle. 'I have a toy for you, as instructed. Do you want to play?' I dangled the teaser in front of her and she snatched at the feathers.

'Tell you what, Mr Mickleby, why don't you play with her while I unpack this lot?'

Without a word, he took the teaser from me and sat at the other side of the table playing with the cat, his smile widening with each pounce. If I'd have known a simple cat toy could create such magic, I'd have produced one much sooner.

When I finished unpacking, Mr Mickleby surprised me by offering to make a cup of tea.

We sat at the kitchen table with our drinks and he continued to play with the cat.

'Wednesday was a dark day for me,' he offered eventually. 'Exactly twenty years since my Gwendoline was taken.' He looked up and there was such pain in his eyes. 'I'm sorry. I took it out on you.'

That would certainly explain the backwards step. 'I'm the one who's sorry. I wish you'd said.'

'I couldn't. Who's still grieving after twenty years?'

I reached across the table and placed my hand gently over his. 'Someone who loved their wife as much as you clearly loved yours.'

He nodded, tears sparkling in his eyes. 'You're a good lass. Thank you. Do you have a young man?'

'No. I did and I thought he was my forever but it turns out I wasn't his.'

'Your forever? I like that. Gwendoline was my forever, even if she didn't get to stay with me forever. The past two decades without her have been painful but I'd live them again for the thirty-seven years I had with her.'

He turned to the cat and dangled the teaser again. What a love they must have shared. If I ever felt ready to let another man into my life, that was what I wanted.

23

I spent all Monday morning feeling anxious, wondering whether Chloe would be willing to speak to me when she got back from her honeymoon early that evening. My stomach felt like there was a hamster inside it running on a butterfly-filled wheel, making me feel a mixture of nausea and excitement.

She hadn't blocked me on social media... yet. Sitting at the breakfast bar at home having some lunch, I scrolled through her honeymoon photos on Facebook. Tanned and glowing with happiness, it was obvious that she and James had loved Mauritius and who wouldn't? It looked like paradise on earth.

Exactly as it had done pre-wedding, each selfie of them hugging and kissing felt like a punch in the stomach but I was going to have to get used to it and get over him somehow. I couldn't continue like this.

As the afternoon progressed, the nausea strengthened. I tried hard to stay focused on my teaching prep but kept having to read the same thing over and over again.

A walk along the seafront at North Bay did little to calm me down. I kept looking at my watch and counting down the hours till their return.

* * *

'Why won't you believe me that nothing happened at the wedding?' I sat on the stairs at home that evening, watching Mum pull on her jacket ready to accompany Auntie Louise and Uncle Simon round to Chloe and James's house.

'Nothing happened because Chloe appeared.' She wouldn't even look at me.

'It was a hug. Just a friendly hug to say congratulations and thanks for checking on me. Completely innocent. I don't understand why you always want to think the worst of me.'

With an exaggerated sigh, she turned to face me. 'It doesn't change the fact that you're in love with your cousin's husband, does it?'

'But he loves Chloe, not me.' I felt like I was stuck in Groundhog Day, regurgitating the same argument over and over.

'How would you feel if it was the other way round and Chloe was the one in love with *your* husband? I don't imagine you'd be thrilled by it, would you?'

'It wouldn't bother me. If I was confident my husband loved me and I trusted him, there'd be nothing to worry about.'

'Exactly. But this is Chloe we're talking about. Think about it, Samantha.'

The front door opened and Dad stepped into the hall, smiling, but the smile was swiftly replaced by a frown as he looked from Mum standing with her hands on her hips to me, slumped on the stairs. 'What's going on?'

'Ask your daughter. I'm off to see Chloe and James.' Mum pushed past him. 'I'll see you later.'

The door slammed shut and I winced. 'Sorry, Dad. I made the mistake of asking if I could go with her.'

He nodded, the strain of the past fortnight clearly showing in the dark shadows under his eyes and the creases on his forehead. 'How about you pop the kettle on and we'll have a chat. I have to get changed first. I've got cat vomit down my shirt.'

'And I thought I was having a bad day.'

'The joys of being a vet.' He grimaced but I knew he wouldn't have it any other way. He adored animals and he loved his job. It had been touch and go whether I'd follow in his footsteps and become a vet, but I decided to give people a try instead. I sometimes questioned whether I'd made the right decision. People could be very cruel.

Dad patted my shoulder as he squeezed past me on the stairs. Taking a deep breath, I went into the kitchen and put the kettle on.

The fortnight since the wedding had been horrendous at home. Mum had spent most of her time with Auntie Louise, presumably speculating on whether I'd ruined Chloe's marriage. Apparently the 'happy couple' had another bust-up at the airport which nearly resulted in them skipping the honeymoon but James had somehow managed to persuade Chloe to board the plane. My fault, according to Mum. Of course. Mauritius was so romantic and beautiful that Chloe had mellowed after a couple of days and she'd forgiven James. But she hadn't forgiven me and Mum seemed to take great delight in telling me that.

'I don't know what Mum meant when she said, "think about it, Samantha",' I said to Dad after I'd relayed our latest spat. 'Do you?'

He looked thoughtful as he sipped on his coffee. 'She hasn't mentioned anything to me so I'm only speculating here. You said you'd mentioned trust and I think that might be it. I think it's less about you and more about Chloe worrying about history repeating itself after her previous bad relationships.'

'But that's about James, not me. She must know I'd never try to take James from her.'

Dad shrugged. 'I know you wouldn't but she's been cheated on before so trust is a big thing for her.'

Sitting across the breakfast bar from him, I could see that his eyes were bloodshot, as though he'd been crying, or perhaps from sleepless nights. All my fault too. 'I'm sorry you've been caught in the middle. It's not fair of Mum to take it out on you.'

'You mustn't blame yourself for how your mum is with me.' He smiled weakly. 'After thirty-six years together, I'm used to it.'

'Are you and Mum happy?' I asked.

His eyes widened. 'Why do you ask that?'

'I can't remember the last time I saw you laughing with each other and you never go out together, just the two of you.' On the rare occasion they went out for a drink or a meal, it was always with Auntie Louise and Uncle Simon, or with Dad's work colleagues. 'You didn't celebrate your wedding anniversary last month and it was a landmark one.'

'Thirty years isn't that special. People tend to celebrate silver then ruby. Besides, there was too much going on with Chloe's wedding approaching.'

I raised my brow, conveying that I wasn't buying that.

'Despite what the movies might show, marriage isn't easy,' Dad said. 'You have to work at it and some marriages take more work than others.'

'You haven't answered my question.' My heart thumped because I knew the answer. They hadn't been happy together for years. The only time Mum seemed to be happy was when she was with Auntie Louise or Chloe. Dad didn't make her happy and I certainly didn't.

Dad slipped off the stool. 'We're fine.' He bent down to place his mug in the dishwasher. 'Don't worry about us.' Turning round to face me, a fixed smile on his face, he said, 'So, tell me about your day.'

* * *

When Mum arrived back home a little after ten, I was waiting on the stairs. As she stepped into the hall, she was smiling and looked more relaxed than I'd seen her in ages. Then she clocked me as she hung up her jacket and her smile faded, her shoulders stiffening.

'How was she?' I asked.

'They had a wonderful time, no thanks to you.' Her voice was cold and accusing.

'Did she say whether she's willing to see me or even just speak to me?'

'She wants nothing to do with you.'

'Did you try to bring her round?'

Mum narrowed her eyes at me. 'Why would I do that when I think you're in the wrong?'

'Because I'm your daughter. Because Chloe's family.'

'I can't have this conversation again, Samantha,' she snapped. 'I've had a lovely evening then I get home and, surprise, surprise, it's all about you again.' She shook her head and started to walk down the hall.

'Well, it won't be about me for much longer.' I swallowed hard on the lump in my throat, picturing Dad's pained expression as we'd discussed Rich and Dave's proposition earlier. I hadn't wanted to tell him while Mum was there so it had been the first opportunity to discuss it. Moving out again had always been on the cards, even if I hadn't taken the job at Reddfield, but he hadn't expected it to happen so soon. I told him that the final decision as to when I moved out would rest on Mum's reaction towards me when she arrived back from Chloe's and whether Chloe was willing to talk because, if hostilities were going to continue, he was the only reason to stay in Whitsborough Bay. And, deny it as much as he wanted, there was no escaping the fact that my presence wasn't doing his already strained marriage any favours.

Mum stopped and looked up at me through the slats on the banister. 'What's that supposed to mean?'

'I'm moving out.'

'Moving out?'

'My new friends, Rich and Dave, have offered me their spare room.'

'When do you leave?'

'The room's available now so probably Saturday.'

She frowned and, for the briefest of moments, I thought she was going to tell me there was no rush, that she was sorry, that we could work something out. My heart thumped and my palms sweated as I held eye contact and waited for her to give me some sort of indication that we were cracked rather than broken.

'Yes, well, I think that's best for everyone.' Straightening her shoulders, she strode down the hall towards the kitchen. 'Why wait till Saturday?' she added, before closing the door.

I felt like I'd been punched in the gut. Shaking, I clung onto the banister as I fought for air. Why did I do it to myself? Why did I keep believing that she might treat me with anything but indifference or contempt?

Should I chase after her? Tell her I didn't have to go yet? Beg her to talk to me and work out why our relationship had always been so difficult? But what was the point? She'd made a choice and it was the same one as always: Auntie Louise and Chloe instead of Dad and me.

I crept back up the stairs. Sighing, I looked round the large double bedroom – my home for the past twenty-eight years, only broken by my time at university and the two years living with Harry. Time to say goodbye.

✉ To Rich
Chloe refused to see me and Mum can't wait to be rid of me. Can I start moving stuff over tomorrow? xx

✉ From Rich
Dave says he's had a crap day and you've just turned it into a happy one. We've already emptied the wardrobe so you can move in as soon as you're ready. Welcome to Brook Cottage xx

24

I drove into Whitsborough Bay first thing the following morning and treated myself to a set of matching suitcases and several storage boxes. I spent the day packing while my parents were out at work and dropped a car-load off at Brook Cottage at dinnertime.

As soon as I stepped through the front door back at home early that evening, I heard raised voices coming from the kitchen.

'... being unreasonable,' Dad cried. 'You should be trying to make peace between them, not causing more of a rift.'

'Why's that my responsibility?' Mum yelled back. 'She made her bed, she can lie in it.'

'Sammie didn't ask for any of this.'

'And neither did Chloe. Her marriage was nearly over before it started because of *her* jealousy.'

'It has nothing to do with jealousy. It was...'

Stepping back outside, I gently closed the door and sat on the doorstep with my head in my hands. I could still hear the shouting but not the words. A door slammed and, moments later, the driveway illuminated with the light from my parents' bedroom. I counted to three then opened the door again and announced brightly, 'Hello? I'm home!'

Dad stepped out of the kitchen, a fixed smile on his face. 'Hi, poppet. How was your day?'

'Good, but it would be better with a hug from my dad.'

'I can manage that.'

He held me a little more tightly than usual and I had to blink back the tears. What had I done to him? He was always fighting my corner and it had destroyed his marriage. It was destroying him. I was going to miss him so much when I moved out but I couldn't wait to get some distance between Mum and me. Would my absence be enough to fix their relationship? I suspected it was way beyond that.

* * *

'That's the last box,' Dad said, closing the boot of his car the following afternoon.

'You didn't have to finish early, but I really appreciate that you did.'

'There's no way I was going to let you leave home without saying goodbye. Besides, it gives me an excuse to check out your new home and your housemates as well as saving you ten trips in that tiny car of yours.'

The back seat and boot of my car were full and I'd probably have had to do another three trips on top of yesterday's if Dad hadn't offered his removal services. I hadn't originally intended to move all my possessions – just the essentials – but arriving home last night to a warzone made that decision for me. My relationship with Mum had never been good but it had significantly deteriorated since moving back home after the break-up with Harry. I therefore needed to remove every trace of me from the family home so that Mum knew I was gone and never coming back. A fresh start for both of us and hopefully a fresh start for her and Dad.

Mum had completely ignored us while we were packing the car but she stepped out of the house now, pulling a jacket on. 'I'm going to Louise's,' she said to Dad.

'Okay. I'll see you later.'

She looked across at me and I held my breath, waiting to see whether her parting words would be kind or bitter. I hadn't expected there to be no words at all. She straightened her collar, shook her head, then marched down the road.

I rested against my car door, hanging my head and closed my eyes for a moment. *So that's it. I move out for good and she doesn't even say goodbye.* I could feel Dad watching me so I straightened up and smiled. 'Let's get this show on the road.' I flung myself into the car and slammed the door before he could speak. The last thing I wanted right now was sympathy. What I needed was to move on and forget about her. Or try to.

25

Mr Mickleby was waiting with the door open by the time I'd crossed the farmyard the following morning, his expression stony. *Oh no, what now?*

'I've been thinking about the Aga,' he said. 'How much do you think it might cost to get it serviced and have someone show me how to use it?'

'And a good morning to you, Mr Mickleby,' I declared brightly.

His expression softened. 'Sorry. Good morning, Samantha. Did you manage to get moved yesterday?'

So he'd actually listened to me when I told him my plans?

He must have registered my look of surprise. 'I do listen to what you say. I'm just not very good at conversation.'

'If you let me in, I'll tell you about my move and you can tell me about the Aga.'

I followed him into the kitchen and began unpacking the shopping. 'What's prompted you to ask about the Aga?'

'Eggs. You bought a box and I can't eat them but I really fancy a fried egg.'

'You do know you can microwave them?'

He curled up his lip. 'Very funny. I may not be a good cook but even I know that eggs explode if you stick them in the microwave.'

I buried my smirk. 'You don't put the *whole* egg in. Let me put these away and I'll show you. Is that why you want to use the Aga? To poach or fry an egg?'

He nodded.

'I haven't a clue how much a service would cost but I can soon find out.' I bit my lip. 'Is money tight? Would it be better to try and sell it?'

Mr Mickleby pursed his lips and shook his head. 'Parts of my body may be failing me but my eyesight isn't. I see what you see, lass. I know the farm's crumbling around me. I know the barns are dilapidated and the track has craters in it. I know I've neglected the house. I know the place needs a damn good clean. When my Gwendoline was here, the house gleamed and sparkled, just like her. When she was taken from me, it didn't seem to matter how much I ran the hoover round or sprayed the polish, nothing ever gleamed and sparkled again. So I did the bare minimum, if that, and waited to be reunited with her.' He sighed and shook his head again. 'Never happened. I've got the money. I could pay for the barns to be rebuilt, the track resurfaced and the farmhouse refurbished, but what I haven't got is the energy or inclination. We had plans. Great plans. But what was the point in me executing them without my Gwendoline? Do you understand?'

I prided myself on not making assumptions but I'd made a huge one about his finances and it had been very wrong of me. 'Yes. It makes sense. I'm so sorry. I shouldn't have assumed...'

'Aye. Never assume things because you'll usually find you're wrong. I built up a business with a friend of mine and we sold it for a lot of money. But I understand why you'd have assumed. As I say, I have eyes and I see it. I was only asking about the money in case the person who services it doesn't take cheques. I was thinking I might need to write you a cheque in advance so you can get the cash out.'

'How about I get a quote and we take it from there?'

He nodded and silence fell on us.

'Would you like me to show you how to microwave an egg?' I asked.

'Aye, go on. This, I have to see.'

I showed him how to poach an egg in a mug, taking pleasure at the look of astonishment on his face, especially when he took a forkful and admitted it tasted good. He had a go himself and I couldn't stop smiling as I watched the expression of sheer delight as he devoured an egg sandwich.

'Haven't had eggs since my Gwendoline was taken. Thank you.'

'My pleasure.' And it really was. 'What was she like?' I asked gently.

'My Gwendoline?' He shrugged. 'She was the kindest woman you could ever meet. Kind to strangers, to children, to friends and, most of all, to animals. She adored anything and everything to do with nature and she found beauty everywhere.' His eyes shone and his face lit up again as spoke about her. My heart ached at the thought of a love so enduring that two decades apart didn't diminish it.

'She sounds lovely.'

'She was. But folk took advantage. They do that with kind people. Broke my heart to see how her family and some friends treated her.' He shook his head, frowning. 'She was happiest here at the farm but her time was cut far too short. They say the good ones go young, don't they? She was the best of the best. And if you want to know how I felt about her... She was my everything, lass. She made me laugh, she made me cry, she made me feel. That woman brought me so much joy every day. She made me the man I am today ... or rather the man I was before I became the cynical, grumpy, ill-mannered, bad-tempered old duffer you seem to keep subjecting yourself to.'

So much love. So much loneliness. My throat was thick and my eyes blurred with tears. I didn't trust myself to speak as the words would erupt in a muddled, snotty, torrent.

'Can I ask you a question?' he said.

I nodded.

'Why do you bother with me?'

Taking a deep breath, I hoped I could get the words out. 'Because, cheesy as it might sound, I care about what happens to you. You remind me of someone who meant the world to me. You remind me of my Gramps.'

'You say he was taken too?'

'Last summer, two days after his seventy-fifth birthday.'

'I'm sorry to hear that. Was he cynical, grumpy, ill-mannered and bad-tempered, then?'

I smiled as I shook my head. 'Far from it. But he also lost the love of his life too soon and I see that same lost, haunted look in your eyes. He never said anything but I know he wanted to follow her, just like you wanted to follow your wife. It wasn't his time, though. His family needed him. I needed him. And he needed us too.'

Silence. Had I said too much? There was no stopping me now, though.

'I don't know what your beliefs are, Mr Mickleby, but I've always believed in destiny and things happening for a reason. There's a reason I found you that day. There's a reason I'm in your life now. I think you need me, even if that's only for a bit of company and someone to make sure you're eating, but I also think I need you in my life. I'm not sure why just yet, but I'm sure the reasons will present themselves eventually. They usually do.'

His lip wobbled and he took a white handkerchief from his pocket and mopped his eyes.

'I'm sorry. Did I go too far? I didn't mean to upset you. Do you want me to go?'

'No. I...' He sat forward as though he was going to tell me something but, after a pause, he sat back in his chair again. 'Actually, I'm a bit tired. Let me know about the Aga, will you?'

I rose and picked up my bag. 'Can I get you anything before I go?'

'I'm fine. Thank you. You're very kind.'

'I try my best.'

* * *

Standing by my car five minutes later, I paused for a moment, breathing in the fresh air and looking round the farmyard. It truly was a stunning location. Did Mr Mickleby ever explore the farm? We were a few days away from September and the past couple of weeks had mainly been warm and dry. If the good weather held, perhaps I'd see if he fancied a walk round the farm one day. He moved slowly but I wasn't aware of any mobility issues otherwise. It would do him the world of good to get some fresh air. And if he wasn't feeling up to it, then I could roll up my sleeves and get those windows scrubbed so at least he could see his surroundings.

26

Dad drove over to Umplesthorpe to take me out for Sunday lunch at The Black Swan.

'Any news from Chloe?' I asked after we sat down with our drinks.

Colour rushed to his cheeks. 'We all went out for a meal last night and Chloe and James had big news.'

He held my gaze, his eyes sad, his lips set in a thin line and my stomach felt like it was on a spin cycle. 'Big news' could only be one thing.

'They're having a baby?' I struggled to force the words out. 'How far gone?'

'Thirteen weeks. They went for a scan on Friday and everything's looking good.'

I tried to smile, but I suspected it was more of a grimace, and I hated myself for it. I genuinely was thrilled for them. Chloe adored children and had never hidden her desire to have a large family. Being surrounded by under-fours all day in her role as pre-school assistant had been tough on her when she'd flitted from one disastrous relationship to the next, accepting that none of her boyfriends were husband or dad material, but panicking that she'd never meet someone who was. Then James came along and everything fell into place for her and fell apart for me.

'Please say something,' Dad urged, as I stared into my lime and soda, slowly stirring the cordial that had settled on the bottom.

I released the stirrer and slumped against the backrest. 'It's not about them having a baby. I always knew that was going to happen sooner rather than later and, knowing how desperate Chloe was to start a family, I'm not surprised it's sooner. What upsets me is that this is the sort of thing I'd usually hear first, yet she didn't tell me she was pregnant before the wedding and she's not going to tell me now at all because we're not friends anymore.'

Dad sipped on his lemonade. 'Nobody knew before the wedding. Well, James did, obviously, but they wanted to keep the focus on the wedding and not the baby.'

'Did Chloe say you could tell me?'

The pain in his eyes broke my heart. 'I'm sorry, poppet. I agonised over whether to tell you or not but I thought it would be more painful finding out later that everyone had kept it secret.'

'You did the right thing and it's not your fault.' I sighed deeply. 'How did we end up so broken?'

'I don't know, Sammie. I still don't understand Chloe's overreaction to all of this. Give her time. You're her only close friend. She'll soon realise how much she misses and needs you and then she'll come crawling back.'

I wasn't so sure. 'She has James now.'

'A husband is no replacement for the one person you've known and loved your whole life.' His voice was full of defeat.

'Are you talking about Chloe and me or Mum and Auntie Louise?'

'That obvious?'

'To me it is. I take it Mum knows you're here tonight to tell me about the baby. What did she say?'

He hesitated, then smiled. 'No need for you to worry about that.' He picked up a menu and scanned his eyes down it. 'This all looks delicious. What have you tried?'

His enthusiasm wasn't fooling me. The argument would have been horrific. Chloe's relationship with me was not the only thing that was broken.

27

'Welcome to the team, Sam.' My new manager, Lauren, enthusiastically shook my hand on my first day at the TEC. 'Great to have you on board.'

'Great to be here,' I said. Staff training had been scheduled for the first two days of the new academic year, with students returning on Wednesday.

'I was thinking we'll ditch your bag and coat in the department office, have a quick tour, grab some drinks and return to the office to run through a few things. How does that sound?'

'Perfect.'

She opened a door shortly after we started our tour. 'This will be your classroom. I've left up the posters and displays that your predecessor used but feel free to change anything and everything.'

'It looks like a great start. Thank you.' A ripple of nerves ran through me. It was suddenly very real. On Wednesday, I'd be standing at the front of the class and actually teaching. I had the knowledge, I had the practical experience and I'd studied hard but would I cut it as a tutor? Only time would tell.

* * *

'We've got half an hour before the training starts.' Lauren sat back in her chair in the small department office. We'd had a quick tour round the whole building and she'd run through a structure chart and various bits of key information. 'You'll get a proper induction tomorrow afternoon with the other new staff so now's the perfect chance to get to know each other a bit better. Shall I start?'

I smiled. 'Go ahead.'

'My background is nursing, like you. I fell into teaching by accident but I absolutely love it. I'm twice divorced and definitely *not* looking for husband number three. Two was bad enough.' She rolled her eyes at me. 'I'm not saying I'll never have a relationship again but, for now, my fingers are burned. I haven't got kids but I have a twin sister, Connie, and a fabulous nephew. I hate cleaning and cooking but love gardening. I never faff with my hair or nails which is ironic for the person who manages the hair and beauty courses. I love adventure sports and I hit the big five-o next year so I'm doing a tandem skydive to celebrate. Oh, and Connie has somehow talked me into having a joint fiftieth party. What can you do, eh? The team are all coming so I hope you will too. It's Friday 28th February. Pop it in your diary.'

'Thank you. You don't look anywhere near fifty.' And she didn't. With honey-highlighted long blonde hair and a youthful face, I'd have placed her in her early forties.

She beamed at me. 'I knew there was a reason you were my favourite at interview. So, over to you, life history in sixty seconds.'

'I'm from Whitsborough Bay but I'm living in Umplesthorpe now, renting from friends. I'm twenty-eight and single. I split up with my boyfriend in June last year and he married my cousin last month which is one of the reasons I was keen to move away from home.' I cringed. Had I just shared that on my first day with my new boss? There was a warmth about her that made me feel so comfortable talking to her.

She nodded encouragingly so I continued. 'My Gramps died at the same time as Chloe and James got together. Then there was an incident at their wedding which has caused a family rift. It's been a tough year or so but I'm excited for a new start.' I sighed. 'And now my mind has gone completely blank. What else do you want to know?'

Lauren gave me another of her warm smiles. 'That's fine for now. Sorry about your crap year. Shit happens and it's how you deal with it that makes you happy or miserable. You can roll in that shit and stink up your life or you can spray the air freshener and move on. I think you're an air freshener kind of woman, aren't you? Put that man firmly behind you and move on.'

I laughed. 'I'm sure a little distance will help.'

'You do know the best way of getting over an ex? Get yourself a new man.'

'Ooh, no. It's a bit soon for that.' I winced as I said it. We'd split up over fourteen months ago so it was hardly recent.

'A bit soon? He's not dead. He dumped you and married your cousin. There's no time like the present.'

Technically I was the one who did the dumping, not that it really mattered.

'I think I've got enough on my plate settling into a new job without adding a new man onto the scene. And it's not like I can conjure one up just because I feel like it. Decent, single men aren't that easy to find.'

'True, but I can think of several off the top of my head who live round here, including my nephew who's about your age. Mind you, that's one damaged young man so maybe not him, but I can definitely think of others. Just shout when you're ready.'

I was dying to ask about the 'damaged' nephew as that was a very intriguing way of putting it, but I was conscious it was nearly time for the staff training to start. Plus, I didn't want to give Lauren even a sniff of a suggestion that I was interested in meeting someone new. She'd no doubt be straight on the phone and have a date organised for this evening if I did.

'Maybe one day,' I said.

She stood up and winked. 'One day soon. Best get to this training.'

28

'Something's happened to you this week, Samantha,' Mr Mickleby said. It was Saturday afternoon and we were both leaning against the fence that separated his overgrown back garden from a wildflower meadow while the Aga was serviced. 'Your sparkle has faded.'

I raised my eyebrows. 'Does that mean you think I normally sparkle? Is this a compliment, Mr Mickleby?'

'If you're going to be hanging around, you might as well start calling me Thomas.'

I smiled. Another major step forward. 'Thomas it is. I'm glad we've dispensed with the formalities. And I'm fine. It's always tiring starting a new job. So many people to meet and things to remember.'

I turned my gaze back to the sea of flowers and grasses rippling in the gentle breeze. Wild poppies danced beside buttercups and clovers but I had no idea what any of the others were called. The smell of wild garlic reminded me of the walks down the coastal paths in Whitsborough Bay and momentarily transported me back to childhood. I loved the Wolds but I did miss the sea. The meadow sloped gently downwards towards a small copse and, beyond that, there were rolling hills.

'It's so beautiful here,' I said. 'Has this always been a meadow?'

'It was a paddock when we moved in. The previous owners had

horses but my Gwendoline fancied the place as a nature reserve. It took hours to sprinkle the seeds during our first spring here. We added the poppies and a few others that autumn but she was taken before she got to see the full effect.'

'So the two of you created this beautiful wildflower meadow by hand from scratch?'

Thomas nodded.

'I know it's not much of a consolation for your loss but this meadow is part of both of you. You created life together. There must be thousands of insects and animals living in among the flowers thanks to you.'

He rested his chin on his hands and was silent for a moment. 'Aye, lass,' he said eventually. 'You're right. We created life.' He turned to me. 'That's a happy thought. Yet your sparkle has faded even more.'

Damn. It was the talk about creating life, taking me back to the new life that Chloe and James had created and the step further away from reconciliation it took us. I'd messaged Chloe on Facebook to say I'd heard her good news and I was thrilled for them both but her reply was: *I thought I made it clear I wanted no contact with you. Leave me alone.* A little later, she unfollowed me on social media.

'You don't want to hear about my woes,' I said, my grip tightening on the fence.

'You've listened to plenty of mine. And it's not like I've got a load of other pressing priorities.'

'Honestly, I'm fine. But thanks for asking.' I wouldn't dream of burdening him with my worries about my family. Poor man had enough to deal with.

We stood in companionable silence for several more minutes.

'I can't imagine this as a paddock,' I said.

'I've got some photos. Would you like to see them?'

'I'd love to.'

* * *

I'd just finished making tea for Thomas, the Aga-engineer and me when Thomas wandered down the stairs with a cardboard storage box, smiling.

'Found them!'

I followed him into the lounge and sat beside him on the sofa.

'Gwendoline was very organised.' He placed the box on the coffee table and removed the lid.

He wasn't kidding. The box contained dozens of white A5 envelopes, each with a theme and year written on the front.

'This is the one.' He lifted out an envelope, opened it and fanned the photos out across the table.

It was fascinating looking at the series of photos showing the hard work that had gone into transforming the paddock into the meadow. Most of the photos were of the land but there were some of Thomas and Gwendoline digging or sowing seeds, always with a smile on their faces.

'I haven't looked at these since she was taken,' Thomas said, gathering the photos back into a pile once we'd finished looking through them. 'I enjoyed that, though. Thank you.'

'Do you have any more hedgehog pictures?' I asked. 'I love the ones on your dresser.'

'Hundreds of them.' He rummaged in the box and pulled out several envelopes. 'Knock yourself out.'

For the next twenty minutes or so, I worked through an envelope at a time, looking at the photos while Thomas gave a running commentary.

'They're so adorable,' I said. 'I had no idea they varied in colour quite so much.'

'We've got photos of an albino one somewhere. They're extremely rare. Something like one in a hundred thousand but we've had two in our time. Very precious. And we've had blonde ones.'

I picked up another envelope and removed the contents. The first few photos were close-ups of someone holding hogs in their hands followed by some hedgehogs on grass. As I revealed the next image, I gasped and clapped my hand over my mouth.

'What is it?' Thomas asked.

I pointed to the woman in the photo, cuddling a hedgehog to her chest, too astonished to form any words.

Thomas peered at the photo. 'That's Elizabeth Danby. She was a friend of Gwendoline's. You know her?'

I nodded numbly. With shaking hands, I flicked to the next photo – a close-up of the same woman, followed by one of Gwendoline and her laughing together.

'How do you know her?' Thomas persisted.

'She's my nanna.'

It was Thomas's turn to gasp. He grabbed the photos from me and quickly riffled through them, stopping at a photo of Gwendoline lifting up a young girl of about five or six. 'Is that you?'

'Oh my gosh!' I cried, a forgotten memory now vivid in my mind. 'The hedgehog lady. Your wife was the hedgehog lady.' I remembered her visiting Meadowcroft with hedgehogs ready to release in the garden. She'd tell me their names and why she'd rescued them, and let me stroke their bellies. I remembered her bringing me pictures of hedgehogs to colour in and being delighted when I presented them to her on her next visit.

Thomas looked as shocked as I felt. 'You're Sammie?'

I nodded. 'Only a few people have ever called me that.'

'My Gwendoline adored you. I can't believe it.'

'Neither can I. I'd completely forgotten about it until just now because it was so long ago but it's all coming back to me. Does this mean you knew my grandparents?'

He shook his head. 'I was running my business back then, working long hours. I never had the pleasure. They came to Gwendoline's funeral, but that day's a blur. I have no idea who I spoke to or what was said.'

I took the pile of photos back from Thomas and flicked through the rest. I appeared in several more images that had clearly been taken over a few years, from age four to eight.

'I remember Nanna telling me the hedgehog lady had been poorly and we wouldn't see her again but there were lots of hedgehogs around to remind us of how kind she was. I can't believe that was Gwendoline.'

'She used to think of you as the granddaughter she never had, you know. She always come back from Meadowcroft full of tales about what little Sammie had said or done. She thought you were the kindest, most beautiful girl she'd ever met. If she knew you were going to be at your nanna's house, she'd try to visit, even if she had no hedgehogs to release, just to see you.'

'Really? That's so lovely. She was always so kind to me and I remember she gave great hugs.'

He smiled. 'You must have been about seven when I bought the farm. Gwendoline couldn't wait to invite you to visit during our first summer. She was so excited about you seeing the rescue hogs but she fell ill before it could happen.'

'I'd have been eight when she died.' I flicked through the photos again, shaking my head. 'I honestly can't believe it. It's like you and I were meant to meet. Like I was meant to find you that day.' My voice cracked with emotion as I fought back tears.

Thomas nodded, tears glistening in his eyes. 'Aye, Sammie. I think you're right.'

* * *

I rang Dad as soon as I got back to Brook Cottage later that afternoon.

'I remember the hedgehog lady,' he said. 'I don't think I ever knew her real name. What a small world.'

'Isn't it? I tell you what, it certainly changed Thomas's attitude towards me. He'd mellowed last week and seemed happy enough to see me, but it was like we were long-lost friends by the time I left today. I feel like a weight's been lifted.'

'I'm relieved to hear that because I was getting a bit worried about you.'

'There's no need to be. Not anymore. Do you remember any talk about me visiting the farm once they'd set up the rescue centre?'

There was a pause.

'Dad?'

'I do recall it being mentioned but...' He sighed. 'Your mum wasn't too keen.'

'Why not?'

'It was a long time ago. I can't really remember. Does it matter?'

'I guess not.'

'I might even have a photo of Gwendoline somewhere. I'll try to find it before I see you again.'

We said our goodbyes and hung up. Dad had the most amazing memory and he'd definitely have been able to remember why Mum wasn't keen on me going to Hedgehog Hollow but he was trying to be diplomatic as always. It had probably been a ploy on Mum's part to spoil my enjoyment. She'd often done that.

29

My second week as a tutor went smoothly. I knew my way round the buildings, had got to grips with the timetable, and had learned the names of all my students. The preparation time in August had definitely placed me in a strong position to be on top of things. Which was just as well because I had something on every evening that week.

Hannah was increasingly uncomfortable and desperate for Baby Spiers to make an appearance and Toby was working long hours so he could take a fortnight off work when the baby arrived. Keen to help, I prepared them a couple of evening meals. I took Rich and Dave out for a meal to thank them for letting me move in, and Dad came across another evening. Around all that, I spent as much time at Hedgehog Hollow as possible.

Thomas was like a changed man. He'd been through the box of photos and found some more of me and my grandparents with Gwendoline at Meadowcroft. Dad had also found four photos of us all which delighted Thomas.

'She was so beautiful,' he said, gently stroking her image with his thumb after I handed them over.

'She certainly was. You were a very lucky man.'

He smiled. 'That I was. And I told her that every day.'

* * *

Sunday brought great news.

✉ From Toby
It's a girl! Amelia Charlotte Spiers was born at 5.42am with lots of dark hair and a cracking pair of lungs. Only 6lb 6oz and she's already got daddy wrapped round her little finger. Hannah is tired but doing great. Needed c-section xx

Shortly before visiting time started that afternoon, I wandered down the corridor towards the maternity ward, clutching a gift bag and a helium balloon.

'Sam!' Toby looked up from the chair beside Hannah's bed where he was cuddling a sleeping baby.

Hannah turned from him to look at me. 'Hi. We didn't realise you were coming today.'

'I wanted to be one of the first to say congratulations and to welcome Amelia Charlotte to the world. Aw, you two. She's completely adorable. I can't wait to—' Something about the looks they exchanged stopped me in my tracks.

Hannah wrinkled her nose. 'James texted to say that he and Chloe would visit at two and we hadn't heard from you so...'

'It's fine. Completely my fault. I didn't think at all.' I placed the bag on the end of the bed and hastily tied the balloon to the handles. 'I don't want to cause a scene so I'll leave these and skedaddle. I'll catch up with you when you're home.' Keen to show Hannah it wasn't her fault, I leaned over to give my friend a kiss on the cheek. That's when I heard her voice.

'What's *she* doing here?'

My heart thumped and my cheeks burned as I stood up.

'Sam was just leaving,' Toby said. 'See you soon, yeah?'

'Yeah. Congratulations again. I'll look forward to my hug later.'

'You're not choosy, are you?' Chloe said. 'As long as it's someone's husband.'

'Chloe!' James hissed.

I met Chloe's eyes. 'I can't believe you just said that.' My voice caught in my throat. 'You know I meant the baby.'

'Yeah, well, what you say and what you mean are two different things, aren't they?'

I hitched my handbag onto my shoulder and cleared my throat to make my voice stronger. 'You know what, Chloe? I'd have asked if we could talk but there's no talking to you, is there? The Chloe I know and love doesn't make bitchy comments like that so, if she appears again and she wants to talk, she knows where to find me.' I gave a feeble wave to Toby and Hannah. 'See you.'

As I strode past the other beds and out of the ward, I imagined Chloe running up to me, grabbing me in a hug, saying she was sorry. But I knew it wasn't going to happen.

* * *

'Sammie! I wasn't expecting to see you today,' Thomas said an hour later. The ease with which he'd moved to using my pet name filled me with comfort, especially as he'd previously been adamant that he didn't like shortened names. It made me feel special.

I shrugged. 'I wasn't expecting to be here. I can go if it's inconvenient.'

He smiled. 'Of course not. Come in, lass. Are you going to finally tell me what faded your sparkle?'

Over a cup of tea in the lounge, I told him all about the situation with my family, ending with the awkward encounter at hospital and how I didn't recognise my cousin anymore. Thomas apologised that he couldn't offer me any words of advice because the obvious thing to say was to give it time, yet he wasn't convinced that time was a great healer because it certainly hadn't helped him come to terms with life without Gwendoline.

I took the cups into the kitchen. There were some pots waiting to be washed from breakfast and lunch so I filled the sink and did the dishes. When I returned to the lounge, Thomas was lightly snoring. I could have left at that point but there was nothing for me to rush home for. Rich and Dave were away so I'd be on my own, stewing.

I looked towards the grubby windows at either end of the lounge. It would certainly keep me occupied. Would Thomas mind? He'd never objected to me washing up and a bit of energetic scrubbing on the downstairs windows could be just what I needed to burn off my frustration.

* * *

Thomas nodded as we stood at the far end of the lounge, looking out at the overgrown garden, the meadow beyond it, and the rolling fields and hills beyond that.

'Well, I never,' he said. 'I hadn't realised they were quite so mucky. Thank you. Can you sort a window cleaner for the rest?'

'If you've got a ladder, I don't mind doing them. I quite enjoyed it.'

'I've only got an old wooden one and I reckon the rungs will be rotten. Even if they weren't, there's no way I'd let you clamber up a ladder to the top floor. Far too high.' He continued to look out at the garden, then sighed. 'You know the problem I have now?'

'What's that?'

'I can't ignore the state of the garden. Do you think you could find me someone to overhaul it? If I'm going to fully appreciate those views, I think that jungle needs to go.'

'I'll look into it. One of my landlords, Dave, is a builder. He has loads of friends in different trades. I'm sure he'll know a gardener.'

'Thank you.'

'When it's done, you could get a bench put outside,' I suggested. 'It would be lovely for you to sit there and enjoy the meadow, being close to what you and Gwendoline created.'

'Aye, Sammie. That'd be nice. Maybe after the garden's sorted, you can help me pick something out.'

'I'd like that.' I glanced at my watch. It was nearly six. 'I think it's time I left you in peace.'

'You're welcome here anytime. I hope you know that. It's what Gwendoline always hoped for.'

'Is it what you want?' I asked.

'It is. I'm struggling to remember what life was like without an annoying do-gooder plying me with grapes and feeding my cat.' He gave me a warm smile and my heart melted.

'I'll see you next week. Bye, Misty-Blue.' I bent down and gave her a quick stroke. 'Take care, Thomas.'

'And you. Don't let that cousin of yours get to you. Remember all the people in your life who love you instead.'

As he waved me goodbye, I couldn't help wondering if he included himself in that group. Each time I saw him, he seemed more and more like Gramps. That bitter, rough manner had softened no end and I could see more and more of the caring person he clearly was. He had a cheeky sense of humour like Gramps too, and I looked forward to seeing more of it.

30

Over the next few weeks, I settled into a routine. Teaching was completely different to what I was used to but, so far, I loved it. I had a couple of challenging students but most of them were well-behaved and eager to learn. Lauren was extremely supportive, giving me loads of encouragement as well as invaluable tips around responding to difficult students, being organised and dealing with the unexpected.

Rich worked shifts and Dave often worked late but I enjoyed the balance of packed house versus peace and quiet. We enjoyed the same food and could all cook so whoever was home first tended to make a meal for the others, which worked really well.

Thomas was an increasing delight to be around. After discovering my connection to Gwendoline, it was as though he'd adopted me as his long-lost granddaughter. With the Aga now working, we sometimes cooked together and I was fascinated to hear all about his life with Gwendoline before and after buying Hedgehog Hollow, and all the animals they'd cared for over the years.

I met Hannah and Toby's gorgeous daughter, Amelia, and instantly fell in love although I felt tearful back at Brook Cottage afterwards, wondering whether I'd actually be permitted to see Chloe and James's baby when it arrived. The way things were going, it wasn't looking good. Uncle Simon had phoned a couple of times to check I was okay and I spoke to and saw Dad regularly. I knew they were both trying hard on my behalf for a reconciliation but nothing seemed to work.

My twenty-ninth birthday approached and I became obsessed with checking my phone, wondering if Chloe would take it as an opportunity to hold out an olive branch. For as long as I could remember, we'd always taken a day off work to spend our birthdays together then gone out for a family meal in the evening. My teaching role meant a day off wasn't an option but I would be free for an evening meal. Only my extended family clearly weren't talking to me so that wasn't an option either. Dad arranged to take me out for a meal in Great Tilbury – the village next to Gramps's – and astonished me by saying that Mum would join us.

The day itself arrived – 17ᵗʰ October – without so much as a card from Chloe. No call, no text, no message. A card arrived from Auntie Louise and Uncle Simon but in his handwriting rather than hers. Then Dad called to say that Mum had a splitting headache and couldn't make it. Not exactly a shock announcement.

When Dad and I stepped into the pub's restaurant, I nearly burst into tears. Waiting at our table were Rich and Dave, Hannah, Toby and Amelia, and Thomas. And perhaps most surprisingly, Uncle Simon was there.

'Happy birthday,' he said, squeezing me tightly. 'It's been too long. I've tried to—'

'It's fine. Please don't fall out with anyone because of me.'

The food was delicious but the company was amazing with so much laughter. A little over two months earlier, half of the group had been strangers but they'd stepped up and been there for me when my family hadn't. They may not have all been connected to me by blood, but they were my family now and I was so grateful to them for being in my life.

'I'm sorry I couldn't get everyone here,' Dad said as he drove me home later.

'Don't be. Tonight was brilliant. The people who were there mean the world to me.' And they really did.

* * *

Mum and Auntie Louise turned fifty-five in early November which usually meant a family meal for the six of us. There was still a family meal for six ... except the sixth person was James instead of me. Dad had to be the bearer of bad news, telling me Mum was concerned about awkwardness between Chloe, James and me, especially in Chloe's 'delicate state'.

She might have blanked me on my birthday but I couldn't bring myself to completely ignore Mum on hers. I drove across to Whitsborough Bay on the Wednesday evening – the day before – with a card and gift. I'd only visited twice since moving and both times had been short and far from sweet.

'Were we expecting you?' she asked when she answered the door.

'It's a surprise visit to say happy birthday and bring you a gift.'

'You know I don't like surprises, Samantha.'

'I know but—'

'So why would you surprise me when you know I don't like surprises?'

'Because it's a nice surprise.'

'*No* surprise is a nice one.'

She clearly wasn't going to invite me in. Why hadn't I thought it through? What made me think I'd be welcome just because I had a shiny gift bag in my hand?

'Happy birthday, anyway.' I handed her two gift bags. 'The silver one's for you and the pink one's for Auntie Louise.'

'I'll see she gets it.' She took them without a word of thank you.

'Is Dad home?'

She rolled her eyes. 'So much for coming to see me.'

'No. I did. I just thought I'd say hello before I leave.'

'He's not in so you've had a wasted journey.' And she shut the door on me.

Why did I bother? Why did I put myself through this constant cycle of hoping things might be different between us when they never were and every encounter left me feeling destroyed?

31

The first day of December fell on a Sunday and I woke up with a sense of dread. Christmas. The subject of me spending Christmas Day at Whitsborough Bay hadn't yet arisen but with the big day looming ever closer, there was no putting it off. The birthday situation had left me fairly certain that, for the first time ever, I would not be spending Christmas with my family.

Rich and Dave were like excited little boys about Christmas. It had been steadily building up over the past couple of weeks but, as soon as I made my way downstairs for breakfast, it was obvious that the arrival of December had cranked things up a notch.

They weren't going to let the fact that they were jetting off to spend Christmas and New Year in Mexico stop them from decorating the house. As soon as I was dressed, they insisted I accompany them to a nearby Christmas tree farm to select the perfect tree for the lounge and the three of us spent the day decorating the tree and the rest of the house while Hallmark Christmas movies played back-to-back.

Their enthusiasm was infectious and, once again, I thanked my lucky stars that they'd both come into my life. They never made me feel like the lodger or like I'd started to outstay my welcome. As far as they were concerned, it was my home as much as theirs. They'd both been rocks when I'd returned home in tears after delivering Mum's birthday gift and had helped me bounce back to my usual positive self.

* * *

I was getting ready for bed when my phone rang shortly after half ten. Dad never called that late.

'Everything alright?' I asked warily.

'It is now but I just wanted to let you know that Chloe had a scare earlier. They were worried she might be losing the baby but she's been checked over and the baby's fine. It was just some spotting.'

'Is Chloe okay?'

'A bit shaken but she's fine. She's been told to rest up and avoid any more stress.'

I frowned. 'Has she been particularly stressed lately?'

Dad sighed. 'There was a situation over Sunday lunch.'

'What sort of situation?'

'Simon and I decided to tackle the subject of Christmas Day and it didn't go down very well.'

'What happened?'

'It got a bit heated and Chloe stormed out.'

I closed my eyes and silently counted to three. 'Please don't push it any further with any of them about Christmas or about anything else to do with me. I love that you and Uncle Simon have been trying to fight my corner but it really isn't worth it anymore. The message is coming through loud and clear and, to be honest, I'm tired of it all. I need to let it go.'

'I'm so sorry, Sammie. How about I come over to you for Christmas instead?'

'You'll do no such thing. I was thinking about spending the day with Thomas anyway so this has probably worked out for the best.' It hadn't entered my head until now but it actually felt like the perfect solution. He had nobody else. If he wanted to be alone with his thoughts, I'd respect that and not push him, but I'd be honoured to spend the day at Hedgehog Hollow with my favourite octogenarian if he'd let me.

32

'I've brought the boys and we come bearing gifts,' I said to Thomas the following Saturday.

Rich and Dave called their greetings to Thomas then opened the back of Rich's van and lifted out a Christmas tree.

Thomas grabbed my arm. 'Is that a real tree? For me?' The excitement in his voice was unmistakable and reassured me I'd done the right thing. I'd asked him a few days ago if he'd like to spend Christmas Day with me – an offer he gratefully accepted – and the conversation turned to Christmas. He admitted that Christmas barely registered the year he lost Gwendoline and, in subsequent years, he couldn't bring himself to celebrate. I'd told him that, if we were going to have Christmas Day together, he needed a tree. 'Maybe a small artificial one,' he'd conceded.

'A small artificial one would have been lost in that gorgeous new lounge of yours, wouldn't it?' I said as Rich and Dave carried the tree inside.

'I don't think I'll have enough decorations.'

'We thought of that already.' I went to the back of the van and lifted out some bags. 'Let's get decorating.'

Thomas took me up to the first floor to retrieve his old decorations while Rich and Dave set up the tree.

'Most of them can be thrown out,' he said when I'd carried a couple of crates down to the lounge. 'There are some hedgehogs I'd like to put on the tree and there's an angel that my Gwendoline loved.'

He added the decorations he wanted then sat back while the three of us finished the job, a contented smile on his face as he watched us. When we were almost finished, Rich and Dave excused themselves and said they needed something from the van.

'What are they up to now?' Thomas asked.

'You'll find out soon.'

Five minutes later, I stepped back. 'All finished. How does it look?'

'Absolutely beautiful. Just like my new lounge and my hallway and the garden and the outside of the farmhouse. You've been miracle-workers.'

Dave had put me in touch with Rhys Michaels, a landscape gardener from Whitsborough Bay. He'd overhauled Thomas's garden although he said he'd need to return in the spring to plant a few bulbs. He'd also tamed the rampant ivy and the farmhouse was looking so much better for it.

Thomas had then announced that he wanted to give the lounge an overhaul. Apparently me cleaning the windows had made him realise how tired and dated it was so Rich, Dave, and I had stripped the wallpaper one Saturday and taken up the threadbare carpet on the Sunday, discovering stunning Yorkshire flagstones on the floor. Thomas sensibly decided he wanted to have those cleaned up instead of covering them but that made him curious as to whether there were flagstones in the hallway too so we lifted the carpet there to discover Victorian tiles. A few of them were cracked but most had been well preserved. He then wanted the hall and stairs on both floors redecorating so the three of us got the strippers out again and one of Dave's mates skimmed all the walls before we embarked on a massive painting session.

Helping Thomas pick out furniture and fittings for the newly refurbished rooms had been great fun. We procured some shiny new frames for the photos of Gwendoline and I managed to find someone who was able to work on the original prints to restore some of the colour and detail. The expression on Thomas's face was more than worth the small fortune it cost me.

'It's ready,' Rich said, poking his head round the lounge door.

'Brilliant. We'll be out shortly.'

Thomas eyed me suspiciously but I wasn't going to give anything away.

'You need a warm coat and something on your feet.'

Still giving me suspicious looks, he did as he was told and I opened the French doors at the back of the room and stepped out. Rich and Dave were standing by the side of the house. They stepped aside as we approached.

'My bench!' After Rhys had finished the gardens, I'd shown Thomas some images from a local garden centre online and he'd picked out the sort of bench he liked: a sturdy wooden one with thick legs.

'Take a seat,' Dave said.

Thomas sat down and looked towards the meadow. 'Perfect. Absolutely perfect.'

'It's a bit chilly out here today,' I said, 'but on warmer days, you'll be able to sit there with a cup of tea and gaze at your meadow.'

He smiled and nodded. 'You three are amazing, you know. Absolutely bloody amazing.'

He stood up again and shook hands with the boys then he did something he'd never done. He opened his arms and hugged me tightly. That one hug said more than words ever could. I don't know about Rich and Dave, but I was certainly feeling emotional. To anyone else, it was just a bench but, to Thomas, it was the means of bringing him closer to the life he'd created with his wife and where she'd been laid to rest. It was everything.

33

For the first time in my entire life, I woke up on Christmas Day morning in an empty house. I'd never felt so lost and alone. It was shortly after 5 a.m. and, despite there being no rush to get up and start ripping open gifts, there was no chance of me nodding off again. How had it come to this?

I wasn't due at Hedgehog Hollow until ten. That was a lot of hours to kill. I lay there for another hour then reluctantly rolled out of bed and padded downstairs to make a drink.

A text came through from Dad an hour later while I was watching a Christmas film.

✉ From Dad
Happy Christmas to my wonderful daughter. I've been awake for a couple of hours and suspect you might have been too. It breaks my heart that we're not together today for the first time ever. I'll miss you every minute of every hour but can't wait to see you tomorrow xx

✉ To Dad

You know me too well! Yes, been awake since five.
Happy Christmas to you too. I know it's not ideal
but please do try to enjoy yourself. My advice for
the day: don't mention my name! We'll have an
amazing day together tomorrow xx

* * *

'Wow! Mr Thomas Mickleby, you look fantastic.'

He smiled as he ushered me in out of the cold. 'I always used to wear a suit on Christmas Day and my Gwendoline would wear a nice dress so I thought I'd make an effort. She loved dresses. Such a stylish woman.'

'I feel very honoured that you've dressed up for me.' I placed a couple of bags on the floor and removed my coat. 'And I'm glad I put a dress on although I'll admit I went for a slightly casual interpretation.' I'd gone for a muted red woollen dress accompanied with grey leggings and flat boots.

Thomas took my coat and nodded approvingly. 'It suits you, Sammie. Happy Christmas.'

'Happy Christmas, Thomas. Is the oven on?'

'As instructed.'

'Excellent.' I picked up the bags and headed towards the kitchen. 'Let me get the turkey in. Everything else is prepared. I was up ridiculously early this morning so I thought I might as well get the veg peeled and make the pigs-in-blankets.'

Thomas followed me into the kitchen and transferred the vegetables from plastic containers into pans of water while I placed the small turkey in a roasting tin and prepared it for cooking. With a cup of tea – not quite the usual prosecco tradition because I was driving – we moved into the lounge.

'Don't be mad at me,' I said, placing my tea on a side table and heading back towards the hall. 'I know we said we weren't doing presents, but I have something for you. Back in a moment.'

I stepped out into the cold again, retrieved the two presents from my car and returned to the lounge.

'You've been my surrogate granddad and such a good friend over the past few months and I wanted to give you a couple of special gifts to say thank you and happy Christmas.'

'You shouldn't have...'

'But I wanted to so we'll hear no more about it. As you can see, this one is pretty big so you might need to stand up to open it.'

'A new tractor for the farm?' he joked, taking the impossible-to-disguise canvas from me.

I laughed. 'Combine harvester, I think you'll find.'

Grinning, he tore the paper, revealing the back of the canvas. Turning it round, he gasped. 'It's our meadow,' he whispered, pressing his fingers to his lips. 'Oh, lass. How did you do it?'

'I took some pictures of it in September and commissioned a local artist to paint a canvas so that, even when the wildflowers aren't in bloom or it's too cold or wet to sit on your bench, you can still gaze at your meadow.'

Thomas picked up the picture and gently propped it up against the wall. 'I don't know what to say.' He hugged me tightly.

'I've got something else.' I handed him a small, flat giftbox. 'Not quite as big but just as meaningful.'

He undid the ribbon and lifted the lid. His lip wobbled and tears pooled in his eyes as he silently read the poem on the silver plaque which I'd had perfectly sized to fit on his bench:

> *Though seasons have passed and years have flown*
> *You've never really been on your own*
> *For Hedgehog Hollow has held her heart*
> *Her spirit's in the meadow you both did start*
> *Her laughter is in the whispering leaves*
> *Her love is in the air that you breathe*
> *Although you have been broken-hearted*
> *A love so deep can never be parted*

So sit a while, enjoy the view
Because Gwendoline's here, enjoying it too

'Did you write this?' he whispered.

'Yes. I might have gone through a whole box of tissues doing it.'

'It's the most beautiful...' His voice cracked. 'Oh, give us another hug.'

He mopped his cheeks with his handkerchief and blew his nose while I dabbed my eyes with a tissue.

'It's the best thing ever,' he said. 'Will you ask one of the young lads to attach it to my bench when they get back from their holiday?'

'Of course!'

Thomas gently stroked the plaque then wandered over to the fire surround and rested it on the mantlepiece. 'It can keep me company for now. And don't be mad at me either because I've got you gifts. Have a look under the tree.'

'Thomas!'

'Don't you start with me, young lady,' he said in a mock-stern voice. 'You're not the only one who relishes the surrogate granddad and granddaughter friendship, you know.'

'When have you been able to get me gifts?' I asked, pulling out the pile from under the tree.

'Rich and Dave sorted them for me then dropped them off, all wrapped too, so I haven't seen them myself. I hope you like them.'

I loved all my gifts but the best ones were a classy silver chain with a hedgehog on it and a soft toy hedgehog. I took the chain out of the box and fastened it round my neck, feeling the cute little creature with the tips of my fingers. 'I love it. I love them all. Thank you so much.' I picked up the soft hedgehog and cuddled him to me. 'I'll call him Mickleby, after you and Gwendoline.'

Thomas's eyes shone and he nodded. 'She'd have liked that, Sammie.'

I fingered my necklace again.

He stood up. 'I've got something else for you and I don't know if you'll like it or not so I didn't wrap it. Hang on.' He disappeared out of the lounge and, when he came back, he was holding a plastic suit carrier close to his chest. 'This was my Gwendoline's. She never wore it. She always said she was saving it for a special occasion. You're a similar build to her and I thought this would suit you, for a special occasion, like.' He unzipped the carrier and peeled it back to reveal a fifties-style peach-coloured dress covered in black net with tiny flowers. It had capped sleeves and several layers of the net were ruched at the waist and gathered over the skirt.

I moved over to him and lightly touched the fabric. 'It's beautiful. I couldn't accept it, though.'

'My Gwendoline would have liked you to.'

'It's too gorgeous for someone like me.'

'What are you talking about?'

'I could never get away with something like that. It's for someone beautiful and glamorous. Like Chloe.'

'Like you,' he scolded. 'You shine, Sammie. You sparkle like a diamond and don't let anyone ever tell you otherwise.'

My hand dropped to my side and I stared at him, wide-eyed. 'That was one of the last things my Gramps said to me. That exact same thing.'

'Then you'll know that it's true. So do you want the dress or not?'

I smiled. 'Yes, please. I'd love the dress.'

'Good. Glad that's settled. There's a wardrobe full of dresses like this upstairs and she'd have wanted you to have them all.'

Thanking him again, I fastened up the suit carrier and draped it over one of the armchairs. 'I'd better check on the turkey. Do you want another cuppa?'

'Please.'

When I returned to the lounge ten minutes later, Thomas was standing in front of the fireplace, looking at the plaque again. He turned and smiled.

'Is poetry a hobby of yours that you haven't told me about?'

'Gosh, no. I know nothing about poetry. I've never written

anything like that before. I was always planning to get a plaque for the bench but inscriptions are usually from the bereaved party to the one they lost and it felt wrong for me to try and write what you might be thinking. Then that poem popped into my head, pretty much ready-formed. It was almost as though Gwendoline was right beside me, guiding me as to what she wanted to say.' I shook my head. 'That probably sounds really daft.'

Thomas stared at me for a moment and I couldn't read his expression. Had I said too much, suggesting the spirit of his dead wife had guided me?

'Sit down, lass,' he said eventually, returning to his chair. 'I want to tell you something because, from what you've just said, I don't think you'll worry I'm losing my marbles.'

I sat down on the sofa, intrigued. 'Okay. I'm listening.'

'That day I collapsed, I saw... it was...' He shrugged. 'I saw my Gwendoline, as real as you are now. She was standing in the lounge, right over there, smiling at me. I reached out to her but she wouldn't take my hand. I asked if she'd come for me but she said, "I will, but not today. It's not your time yet." And then she told me she was sorry she'd been gone so long but she was going to send me someone who could restore the joy to my life. She said, "We can't be reunited until you've experienced pure joy again".' He picked up his mug and took a sip. 'I thought she meant a new wife so, of course, I protested. Nobody could ever take her place in my heart. She laughed and said no, not a wife, but she was going to send me an angel who was going to need me as much as I needed her.' He put his cup back down. 'And that's what she did. She sent me an angel. I know that I was rude to you many times and said some harsh things, but I want you to know that I'm grateful you saved my life that day. I'd had nearly twenty miserable years without my Gwendoline and, during that time, I existed but I didn't live. Then she sent you to me and, for the past few months, I've remembered what it feels like to be alive. My Gwendoline was right. You have brought me pure joy.'

Tears streamed down my cheeks. Crouching down beside him, I took his hand. 'I believe she was here. I think I saw her that day too.'

Thomas nodded, his eyes filling with tears. 'I knew you were special. And she knew that too.'

'I believe she's always here, Thomas, just like it says on the plaque. And what she said about me needing you just as much was so true. You've been more like family to me than most of my real family have been and I don't know how I'd have got through these last few months without your companionship. We were two lonely souls who both needed company. Remember I said, shortly after we met, that I thought there was a reason I needed you. That was it.'

He squeezed my hand. 'Two lonely souls. Not so lonely anymore.'

34

Considering there were only two of us, Christmas dinner felt as noisy and chaotic as it usually was with my family. Thomas insisted on us pulling a whole box of crackers between us and we laughed uncontrollably at the stupid jokes. Six crackers each meant we had to wear six party hats each which was not easy. There was even the threat of a food fight after I sneaked a sprout onto Thomas's plate when he stepped away from the table to get the salt.

When we'd finished eating, I cleared the dishes over to the sink and we spent an hour or so over coffee and after-dinner chocolate mints, reminiscing about Christmases past. I loved hearing about the traditions Thomas had enjoyed as a child and about the ones he and Gwendoline had created.

'We'd often talk about how we'd celebrate Christmas when we had children,' he said. 'But it wasn't to be.'

'You couldn't have kids?' I'd been curious about it but it's not the sort of thing you just come out and ask someone.

'We lost the first two quite early and we thought it was third time lucky when she fell pregnant again but Andrew was stillborn at eight months. When Olivia was stillborn at seven months, we had to say no more.' He kept his voice strong but I could hear the pain and sadness.

'I'm so sorry. That must have been horrendous.'

'Aye, lass, especially the two bairns who nearly made it. It wasn't to be and I sometimes feel comforted knowing those babies have their mum back.' He straightened up and smiled gently. 'That's why she was so attached to you. You were the closest thing she had to a daughter or granddaughter.'

'She was always kind to me. I wish I'd realised.'

'You were too young. You couldn't have understood.' He smiled. 'Animals became our children, especially hedgehogs. Every single one was precious and we were so lucky to have them.'

I cleared away the cups and the debris from the crackers to give Thomas a moment with his memories.

'You said you had a game for us to play,' he said a few minutes later.

'I don't know if you'll like it so you must say immediately if it's uncomfortable but it's a game called "Speak Out". I retrieved it from one of the bags, opened the box, and handed him a mouthguard. 'The idea is that you put one of these in your mouth and try to say the phrase on the card. I've got to guess it before the timer runs out.'

Thomas raised his eyebrows, shrugged, and put the mouthguard in. He gave me a thumbs up then took it out again. 'Let's do it. Loser does the washing up.'

'You're on.'

I have honestly never laughed so much in my life. I'd never played the game myself but Rich and Dave had insisted I borrow it from them, swearing it was one of the best purchases they'd ever made. I hadn't thought Thomas would be up for it but then again, I hadn't expected him to want to pull six crackers in a row and wear all the party hats. We only managed half an hour of the game but had tears rolling down our cheeks most of the time; happy ones this time. My sides ached from belly laughing and Thomas got the hiccups.

'Well, I never,' Thomas said, handing me his mouthguard to rinse. 'Such a simple idea and so hilarious. I haven't laughed like that since my Gwendoline was taken.'

Somehow I lost. I wasn't sure whether it was because Thomas was rubbish at enunciating or whether I was laughing so much that I couldn't hear him but I had my forfeit. I'd have done the washing up even if he'd lost, though.

'You go through to the lounge and have a nap if you want. I'll get tidied up in here and join you in about twenty minutes.'

He stood up and gave me another hug. 'Thanks, lass, for everything you've done for me. Your dad's so right about you. Besides my Gwendoline, you are the kindest person I've ever met and shame on that Chloe, your mum and your auntie for not wanting you in their lives.'

'Thank you.' I gave him a squeeze then stepped back. 'Maybe we can all start afresh in the New Year.'

'I hope you can. And I think next year will bring you a kind man too. Someone who has a heart as big as yours that he's been saving for you. This James lad wasn't right for you, but I reckon the right one is round the corner and when you find each other, you'll be as strong and everlasting as my Gwendoline and me.'

'That's certainly something to aspire to,' I said. 'Right, you get yourself into the lounge and I'll be through shortly.'

'Bye, Sammie.' He blew me a kiss as he left the kitchen.

I switched on his old radio and the velvety tones of Bing Crosby filled the room. What an emotional day, up and down, up and down. But, surprisingly, one of the best Christmas Days ever. Not surprising because I was with Thomas, but surprising because I wasn't with my family. Then I smiled. I *was* with family. He might not have been connected to me by blood but Thomas was now my family and I cherished every single moment with him. Hopefully the rest of them would get their act together in the New Year and, if not, I'd stop wasting my energy worrying about it and focus on those who did want me around.

* * *

Forty minutes later, the washing up was done and I'd placed the left-overs into plastic tubs in the fridge for Thomas to eat on Boxing Day.

As I boiled the kettle to make us another cup of tea each, I watched a robin bobbing around on the path outside the kitchen window. It flitted up to the window ledge and cocked its head to one side as though watching me. Another robin joined it and they hopped along the ledge together. I watched, mesmerised. Robins were solitary birds so it was a rare and beautiful sight.

The kettle clicked off and a feeling of warmth enveloped me, as though I was being hugged. I turned round, half-expecting to see Thomas, but there was nobody there.

Making our drinks, I crept into the lounge, not wanting to disturb Thomas if he was napping. Sure enough, he was asleep in his armchair. Placing the cups and saucers on the coffee table, I looked up at him again. He'd taken the plaque off the mantlepiece and was hugging it to his chest along with one of the framed photos from the dresser. Through the dim glow emitting from the lights on the Christmas tree, I could see a smile on his face.

I flicked on a side lamp and glanced across at Thomas to check it hadn't woken him up. His eyes were open and he was still smiling.

'Good nap?' I asked, giving him a warm smile, which slipped when he didn't turn towards me.

'Thomas!' I cried, running towards and grabbing his wrist. The plaque and the photo frame slid off his knee and rested against the arm of the chair and all I could hear was his voice in my head saying, 'I saw my Gwendoline, as real as you are now... She said, "We can't be reunited until you've experienced pure joy again" ... Then she sent you to me ... You have brought me pure joy.'

'No! Don't leave me! Thomas!' I thumped my palm against the arm of the chair. 'I need you! I need you!'

I fell to my knees, deep, anguished sobs shaking my body. 'Stay with me.' My pleas were fruitless. That wonderful man had gone.

I rested my head on his knee, silent tears raining onto the fabric of his best suit. 'You're together now,' I whispered. 'You've got your wish. Give the hedgehog lady my love.'

Wrapping my arms round his legs, I hugged him, gulping back my pain. 'I'm going to miss you so much. You brought me joy too. I love you, Thomas. Rest in peace, my friend, reunited with your forever.'

35

On the afternoon of Friday 10th January, Dad led a procession of three cars up the bumpy gravel track at Hedgehog Hollow. I sat in the passenger seat next to him, the box containing Thomas's ashes resting on my knee, still warm from the crematorium.

Dad gave me a sideways glance. 'How are you holding up?'

'Still finding it hard to believe he's gone.'

We pulled up in the farmyard. Hannah parked on one side and Rich and Dave on the other. Rich helped Hannah with Amelia's buggy then, in a small huddle, we made our way slowly towards the meadow. The gravel crunched under our feet, the grass whispered in the gentle breeze and great tits chirped on the bare branches of the trees, but we remained silent.

The day had dawned dark and grey with the threat of rain. During the short service at Reddfield crematorium, the room darkened and rain pounded on the roof for ten minutes, then we emerged to a pale blue sky and weak sunshine.

We took a walk along the river then celebrated Thomas's life over a long pub lunch until it was time to collect Thomas's ashes and reunite him with Gwendoline.

Back at Hedgehog Hollow, we stood in a semi-circle by the edge of the meadow. There were very few flowers in bloom but the grasses and buds swayed gently with the promise of an explosion of colour in the coming months.

A mewing made me look down. Misty-Blue rubbed against my legs. I'd been up to the farmhouse every day to feed and play with her but I needed to make a big decision about a longer-term home for her. Rich was allergic to cats so Brook Cottage wasn't an option, but I didn't want to say goodbye to her. Maybe it was time to look for somewhere to rent on my own – somewhere that allowed pets.

I swallowed on the lump in my throat and looked round at my Dad and friends. 'I can't thank you enough for being here with me on this sad day. When I met him, Thomas Mickleby was a prickly man who'd given up on life but a little bit of kindness and a lot of persistence can lead to great things. I find it hard to believe that I only knew him for four-and-a-half-months. It feels like a lifetime. He helped me as much, if not more, than I helped him and I'm truly devastated that we didn't get longer together.'

I paused to wipe my cheeks then opened the gate and took several steps into the meadow, leaving the others resting against the fence.

'Thank you for letting me be part of your life. I'll never forget you.'

I eased the lid off the box then tipped out the ashes in a wide arc. They swirled and danced on the breeze then settled. How poignant that Thomas and Gwendoline's final resting place was in the midst of the life they'd lovingly created.

'Look after him for me, hedgehog lady.' I kissed my fingers and blew my kiss into the meadow. 'Goodbye. Thomas.'

36

'That can't be right.' I stared at the solicitor first thing on the morning after Thomas's funeral, shaking my head.

Mr Jeffreys, an officious-looking man in his late fifties steepled his hands under his chin. 'I can assure you that it is, Ms Wishaw. Are you ready to hear the condition, now?'

Was I ready? I had no idea what I was right now. Dazed, confused, stunned.

'Thomas has really left me everything?'

'That's correct.'

'When did he do this? He never left the farm.'

'I made a home visit in November.'

'But why me?'

'Thomas Mickleby had no family, or at least no relatives he's been in contact with for the best part of forty or fifty years. As far as he's concerned, you've been like the daughter and granddaughter he never had and he wanted you to be his sole beneficiary.'

When Mr Jeffreys had asked to see me, I'd assumed Thomas had left me a keepsake. The bench, perhaps, or some photographs to remember him by. The last thing I'd expected was to inherit

Hedgehog Hollow, consisting of the farmhouse, outbuildings and sixty acres, along with a very hefty bank balance.

'Ms Wishaw...?' Mr Jeffreys prompted. 'The condition?'

'Sorry. It's such a lot to take in.'

'I take it that Mr Mickleby didn't discuss his bequest with you?'

'He didn't breathe a word.'

'Then you definitely weren't aware of the condition.'

Condition? He kept saying that. What did that even mean? 'No. This is all unexpected news today.'

'So I see. The condition is that you can only inherit if you finish what Mr and Mrs Mickleby started. He wants you to run Hedgehog Hollow as a hedgehog rescue centre.'

'What? But I know nothing about rescuing hedgehogs.'

'Then I suggest you either need to learn quickly. Or you walk away.'

'Walk away?'

'If you choose not to accept the condition, Hedgehog Hollow will be sold and the proceeds from the sale, along with Mr Mickleby's savings, will predominantly go to the British Hedgehog Preservation Society with a smaller amount divided up among other local animal sanctuaries. This amuses you?'

I hadn't realised I was even smiling. Feeling thoroughly chastised, I pursed my lips. 'No. I'm just smiling at Thomas's condition. It's very him.'

'Do I take it you accept the condition?'

My heart raced. I adored hedgehogs but the only knowledge I had was gleaned from watching their nocturnal activities in Gramps's garden. I knew what they ate, when they hibernated and when they mated but that was about it. Was that enough to turn Gwendoline's dream into reality? It was such a big responsibility. Was it something I could run alongside teaching or would it be a full-time commitment? The barn they'd intended to use would need repairing. It wasn't in the same state of disrepair as some of the others but it definitely needed work.

I looked up at Mr Jeffreys. 'It's a big decision.'

'I'd have thought it was an easy one. Do you have any idea how much a farm like Hedgehog Hollow is worth? All you have to do is run the rescue centre for five years then you can sell up and you'll be a very rich young woman.'

My jaw tightened. 'Do you like hedgehogs, Mr Jeffreys?'

'I beg your pardon.'

'I said do you like hedgehogs?'

'Not particularly. Flea-carrying vermin with no road sense.' He laughed at his own joke but my best unimpressed expression soon stopped him. 'Sorry. Inappropriate.'

'Thomas loved hedgehogs and his late wife loved them even more. It was her dream to run a rescue centre at the farm and that's why he bought it. She died before they could get it up and running and Thomas was devastated he never fulfilled her wishes. This is his way of achieving her dream. For me, it's not about inheriting a property or money. It's about whether I'm the right person to finish what they started. If I accept, I wouldn't be making a half-hearted effort with the aim of shutting it down in five years so I can grab the money and run. If I accept, it will be about Thomas, Gwendoline and the hedgehogs. The easy route is *not* to accept and the animals they love will still benefit. But that wasn't their dream. The inheritance is neither here nor there. My ability to achieve their vision is the only issue here.'

He nodded slowly. 'I can see why Mr Mickleby chose you.'

'Could I have some time to think about it?' I was keen to talk it over with Dad and to get Dave's input on the time and cost for a project like this.

'Mr Mickleby thought you might say that. This is for you.' He slipped a pale blue envelope across the table with my name on the front in spidery ink. 'I was instructed to give this to you if you wanted some thinking time. I have another appointment now so I suggest you read the letter and come back to me as soon as you have a decision, the sooner the better so you can either move in and get started, or we can take action to get the property on the market.'

* * *

There was only one place I could go to read the letter. I pulled my coat tightly round me and adjusted the scarf Thomas had bought me for Christmas as I sat on the bench in his back garden. The sky was cornflower-blue but a frost lay on the ground, the January sun not carrying any heat to melt it.

Taking a deep breath, I took the letter out of my coat pocket and opened it. Misty-Blue jumped up onto the bench beside me and I snuggled her to my side.

My dear Sammie,

If you're reading this… we've shared our last moments together and I have finally joined my Gwendoline. I hope and pray I had the opportunity to tell you what you mean to me. In case I didn't, I wanted to say thank you for saving me. I don't just mean the day you stumbled across me after my stroke. I mean every minute of every day ever since. You've brought light and joy back to my bleak existence and I've been more alive since I met you than I've felt since my Gwendoline was with me. She told me she was going to send me an angel and that's exactly what she did.

If you're reading this… you'll know about your inheritance and the condition I place on this.

If you're reading this… it's because you are exactly who I think you are: a kind-hearted woman who desperately wants to say yes because you want to be the one to achieve our dream, but you're worried you can't do it. Am I right?

If you're reading this… it's because it isn't about the farmhouse, the land or the money. You're not that kind of person. I knew exactly who you were that day you gave me your lunch. My Gwendoline always used to say that those small acts of kindness reveal a person's true character.

You may be wondering why I've asked you to do this and the answer is because I know you can. I know you love animals. It was one of the reasons my Gwendoline loved you so much. I've seen your caring and nurturing nature firsthand. Does it matter whether it's people or hedgehogs? The same skills are needed and you have them.

You'll need to learn how to run a business but I believe you have those skills already too. When you helped me refurbish the lounge and hall, it was like a military operation on the tightest of budgets.

I believe in you, Sammie. I know you can fulfil our dreams and take Hedgehog Hollow beyond what we could have done.

You told me shortly after we met that you believed we'd met for a reason. You said you thought you might need me and you weren't yet sure why. That was the moment when I fully understood why you'd been sent to me. It wasn't just about bringing back my joy; it was about making my Gwendoline's dream happen and giving you your moment in the spotlight. Always remember that you shine. Those who try to take away your sparkle aren't worthy of it.

I've written down everything I can remember about caring for hedgehogs although I'm sure some of the thinking will have changed over the years. I've also written down the name of a local vet. Gwendoline made an arrangement for medication at cost and discounted consultations but I don't know if the practice still exists or, if it does, if the vet will even remember the arrangement after all this time.

We'll both be watching over you. We love you and believe in you. Please believe in yourself. Look after Misty-Blue for me.

Yours fondly

Thomas

P.S. As well as opening the rescue centre, I have another unfinished project for you. Do NOT live in a mausoleum. I want you to clear out my belongings without any guilt and turn the farmhouse into your home – not a shrine to me. Please continue the work we started together. I insist!

I read the letter over and over, tears chilling my cheeks, then took my phone out of my pocket. I'd changed mobile provider and now had much better coverage in the area. It was still patchy but it worked in the house and there were several hotspots in the grounds.

'Hi Mr Jeffreys. It's Samantha Wishaw. I've read the letter and I accept the condition. I'd like to make this work.'

'Very good,' he said. 'I'll have my assistant prepare the paperwork. If you could make an appointment for Monday or Tuesday, I'll run through some other information with you, get your signature, and arrange the transfer. In the meantime, I understand that you already have access to a spare key. Is that right?'

'Yes.'

'In that case, you're very welcome to enter the property. Just don't go changing anything until the transfer is official.'

* * *

I sat down on the sofa in Thomas's lounge. *My* lounge. Would I be able to get used to that? *My lounge in my house.* It didn't feel real. I had no idea how many bedrooms there were. I'd been up to the first floor to get Thomas's PJs when he was in hospital and again to get the Christmas decorations. I'd stripped the hall and stairs wallpaper but I hadn't paid any attention to how many doors there were on either floor or what was behind them.

Feeling a little like an intruder, despite what Thomas had written about it being my home, I made my way upstairs, my hand running up the banister that Dave had painstakingly stripped back to the original wood, Misty-Blue trotting beside me.

On the first floor, I counted two bathrooms and five large bedrooms, two of which were completely empty. The top floor had a further two enormous bedrooms which were also empty. Brown, beige, green and orange floral or geometric designs on the wallpaper clashed with what could only be described as bus-upholstery-chic carpet designs. I felt like I'd stepped back in time to the seventies or eighties. Of the three used bedrooms, one appeared to be an office with a large desk by the window playing host to an ancient dusty word processor. Shelves lined the other walls, filled with books, ring binders and storage boxes. Another bedroom was used for storage – the one we'd been into for the decorations. It contained several over-flowing cardboard boxes but no furniture. In Thomas's bedroom, the bed was neatly made with a pair of folded grey pyjamas resting on one of the pillows. A plush hedgehog sat on the other, making me think of Mickleby, the soft hedgehog Thomas had given me the morning he died. I'd cuddled it every night since then. Had he known he was going to leave me that same afternoon or had his death been sooner than expected?

Feeling quite overwhelmed as I closed the door, I sat on the top stair of the first floor, hands hanging limply between my legs, gazing down the staircase at the beautiful tiled floor in the entrance hall. And that's when it struck me. The refurbishment of the lounge, hall and stairs had never been about Thomas; it had always been about me. He'd known his days were numbered and he'd wanted to get the farm-house ready for me. He'd wanted my opinion on every paint colour, every piece of furniture, every fixture and fitting. Pulling myself to my feet on the banister, I ran down the stairs and into the lounge. Wow! How had I not realised it before? It was all my taste; exactly what I'd have chosen for my own home, right down to the chrome light switches.

'Oh, Thomas,' I whispered. 'I can't believe you did that.'

37

'You're being very mysterious,' I said to Dave as he returned from the bar in The Black Swan with a round of drinks on Tuesday evening. He'd arrived back at the cottage after work and instructed Rich and me to get ready because we were going to the pub as soon as he'd showered and changed. We'd protested that we'd been there last night to celebrate me signing the paperwork on my unexpected inheritance but Dave insisted he had important news and we'd want another celebratory drink. I'd looked at Rich when Dave headed upstairs but he was clearly as bewildered as me.

'A toast,' Dave said, ignoring my comment. 'To Thomas Mickleby. Gentleman, philanthropist and fairy godfather.'

Rich and I clinked glasses with him, exchanging confused looks.

'Mysterious and perhaps a little bit weird,' Rich said.

'Sorry. Couldn't resist. So it would appear that, as well as being a man of property, our departed friend had a very healthy bank balance.'

'We already know that. He left me fifty grand.'

Dave stroked his beard. He was clearly enjoying the suspense. 'He actually had quite a bit more than that to spare. I had a phone call from that Jeffreys bloke this morning asking if I could drop by his office so I did. It seems that Thomas left instructions that, if you took on the farm, me and the lads were to finish the downstairs, gut the upstairs, re-fit the kitchen, sort the barn, fix the fencing and get the track and farmyard resurfaced. If there's money left, which I'm certain there will be, we're to repair the other outbuildings.'

I stared at him. 'Are you serious? Thomas commissioned you?'

He held up his hands. 'Honest. I was gobsmacked. We'll be kept in work for months doing all that.'

I put my hand over my mouth. 'Oh my gosh, Dave. I can't believe he did that.'

'That man is like the gift that keeps on giving,' Rich said, raising his glass again.

'There's no need to spend anything on the house,' I said. 'Those funds can be directed to work on the rescue centre instead.'

Dave shook his head. 'Not an option. The instructions were very specific.' He reached into the back pocket of his jeans and passed me a folded sheet of blue paper.

'He wrote you a letter too?'

'You might as well read it.'

Dear Dave

If you're reading this, I'm gone and Sammie has agreed to set up a hedgehog rescue centre at Hedgehog Hollow. I was so impressed with the work that you and your friends did in the lounge and hall that I want to engage your services for three major projects:

1. Refurbish the rest of the farmhouse. It needs gutting. Both floors upstairs have never been decorated, the kitchen needs ripping out and replacing and the rest of the downstairs needs attention. The gardener you recommended – Rhys Michaels – has tamed the ivy but please check there's no damage to the farmhouse. I've left enough money to work on the gutters, windows and roof if you believe that work is needed now or in the foreseeable future.

2. Repair the barn to be used for the hedgehog rescue centre. There's a hole in the roof and the walls need patching. There's heat,

*light and water, but they'll all need checking before fitting it out to
Sammie's requirements.*

*3. The farm track and farmyard need resurfacing and the fence
alongside it needs repairing. If there's any money left, please use it
to repair or dismantle the other outbuildings, depending on what
Sammie wants.*

*You need to pay yourselves properly too; no discounts or 'mates-
rates'. I insist. There's plenty of money for you to make a hefty profit
and get that home extension done.*

*My solicitor will contact Rhys and arrange for him to keep the
gardens and ivy in check.*

*You might wonder why I've kept the money aside for you instead
of giving it to Sammie. That's because she'd invest it all in the
rescue centre and not spend a penny on the house. She never puts
herself first. I want the farmhouse to feel like her home, not mine,
which means a fresh start. Don't let her cut corners and order the
cheapest kitchen units or leave rooms unfurnished. I insist on a
quality, thorough re-fit because that wonderful young lass deserves
the best. I know I can trust you and your friends to do that for her.*

*Sammie brought joy to my life and I know you've brought joy to
hers. Take care of her for me.*

Kindest regards,

Your friend, Thomas

'Wow!' I said, tears rushing to my eyes. 'He thought of everything,
didn't he?' All I'd shown him was a bit of kindness and he'd done all of
this for me. In a short time, he'd come to know me so well. I'd definitely have directed the funds away from the farmhouse yet he'd
made sure it was in writing that I couldn't. I didn't know how to feel. I
was astonished, grateful and excited, yet I'd have given it all up in an
instant for more time with Thomas.

'I was going to say that they broke the mould after they made
Thomas,' Rich said, looking at me. 'But that would be a lie. You're
made from the same mould. No wonder you two bonded.'

'I agree.' Dave stroked his beard again. 'So when do you want us to get started?'

'Yesterday?'

* * *

We only stayed in the pub for one drink as Dave wanted to look at his diary to see where he had flexibility. My mobile rang while I was in the kitchen boiling the kettle. Withheld Number.

'Hello?' I said.

Silence.

'Hello. Anyone there?'

There was definitely someone at the end of the phone but they remained silent after a further prompt so I hung up.

I'd no sooner settled in front of the TV with a hot chocolate than it rang again.

'Hello.'

Silence again.

'Chloe? Is that you?' Was that a sob? I pressed the phone closer to my ear. 'Talk to me, Chloe. I'm here for you.'

The call disconnected. I shook my head and sighed. I wasn't going to try to make contact with her, not that I could after she'd blocked me. If she really wanted me, she could try again. What was it that Thomas and Gramps had said about me shining? Thomas had given me an amazing opportunity to step into the spotlight and make a difference on a project that was all mine and nothing to do with Chloe. I was going to grab that opportunity with both hands and make it happen. I'd show Mum, Chloe and Auntie Louise that I may not be the sort of person who could make relationships work but I was the sort of person who could make dreams come true, even without their support.

38

I opened my bedroom curtains on Sunday morning and took a step backwards. Wow! Complete whiteout. There'd been sporadic flutters of flakes across Saturday afternoon and into the evening but, looking at the front garden wall, roughly ten centimetres had settled overnight.

There was a knock on my door. 'Are you decent?' called Dave.

'Yes. Come in.' I smiled as the door opened and he stepped into the room with a mug of tea and a plate of toast.

'I heard your alarm so I figured you were up. Have you seen the snow?'

'I was just looking at it.'

'I don't think you're going to make it up to the farm today.'

'Why not?'

'What do you drive?'

'Oh gosh. I'm going to have to change my car, aren't I?' I absolutely loved my mint-green Fiat 500, even though Thomas used to take the mickey out of it and call it a Mint Imperial. It was going to be no good for bad winters in the Wolds, though. 'Do you think I'll need a van?'

Dave pondered for a moment. 'I don't think so. I'd suggest a 4x4 with decent boot space. You're only going to be transporting a few hedgehogs around. They're not exactly enormous.'

'Maybe I can get one of those jeeps and be like the proper country set.'

'Ooh. Wait here. We've got something for you. They arrived yesterday but I wanted Rich to see them before I gave them to you.'

Dave scooted out the room and thundered down the stairs. Moments later, he reappeared and handed me a large white box. 'Consider it a housewarming gift. Perfect for joining the country set.'

I lifted the lid and grinned at the contents: a pair of wellington boots in a hedgehog design. 'Aw. I love them. Thank you. You realise I'm going to need to test these. Let me get washed and dressed, then do you wanna build a snowman?'

'I thought you'd never ask.'

* * *

Thirty minutes later, we stepped back to admire our efforts.

'His body's a bit wonky,' Dave said. 'Like a spud.'

'Then we'll have to call him Spud. It must be about fifteen years since I built a snowman.'

'And were you always this bad at it?'

I gave him a playful shove. 'If he's rubbish, that's your influence. I'll have you know, my dad was a brilliant teacher. Our snowmen survived way longer than any of the others on the street.'

'You didn't build snowmen with Chloe, then?' Dave adjusted Spud's lopsided bobble hat.

'Chloe was always more of an indoors person. She hated the snow. I don't think she ever built a snowman, had a snowball fight or made snow angels.'

'Seriously? That's part of growing up.' He pushed Spud's carrot nose in a little further. 'I take it you still haven't heard from her?'

'No, but somebody keeps calling me. They don't speak but I'm certain it's Chloe.'

'What will you do if it is her and she wants to be friends again?'

'I'll be friends again.'

He frowned. 'Really? Why?'

'Because she's my family.'

I shrugged as Dave raised his eyebrows.

'There should probably be a better reason than that, shouldn't there?' I said. 'Come on. I'm getting cold. It's my turn to make you a drink.'

* * *

'What was she like as a kid, then?' Dave asked when I handed him a mug of coffee.

'Chloe?' I curled up on the other end of the sofa from him. 'Cousin, sister and best friend rolled into one.'

'I mean personality-wise. First three words that come into your head. Go!'

'Fun, insecure, spoilt.' I blew on my coffee. 'That didn't sound too good, did it?'

Dave gave me a weak smile, his eyes full of sympathy. 'I don't think anything about your relationship with her sounds too good. Look, it's none of my business and I get that she's family so it's a little more complicated than your average toxic friendship but—'

'You think our relationship's toxic?'

'From the snippets you've told me, yes. Sorry. Of course, I've only known you since she cut you off so it could—' Dave's phone rang, stopping him mid-flow. 'It's my mum.'

'You get it. We'll talk later.' I took my coffee and headed up to my bedroom to give Dave some privacy.

It had started snowing again. The grass we'd exposed by rolling the balls for Spud's head and body was no longer visible and the coating over Spud's scarf made him look like he had an extreme case of dandruff. Wrapping my hands round my mug, I watched the snow, sipped on my drink, and considered what Dave had said about Chloe.

Was he right? Did we have a toxic relationship? Obviously things were sour at the moment but had there always been problems?

Pulling out a plastic crate from under my bed, I lifted out a photo album. Dad had created it for me when I moved in with Harry. He'd had tears in his eyes as he handed it over, telling me that it was from him and Mum as a reminder of the first chapter in my life. I could tell from the disinterested look on Mum's face that she'd had nothing to do with it.

I plumped my pillows, plonked myself down on my bed, and opened up the album. The first few pages were baby photos of me on my own, then with Chloe when she was born six months later in April. Baby photos became toddler photos, then first day at school, the pair of us standing outside the school gates in our grey pinafores and royal blue cardigans, holding hands. Christmases, birthdays, holidays... Nearly every photo included Chloe and every single one contained happy memories. The pair of us used to have such fun together. She made me laugh so much. I only had to flick through the photos to see that.

But there was no denying she *was* spoilt and it was mainly Mum who spoilt her. Auntie Louise and Uncle Simon's income was tight so Mum would compensate by regularly buying Chloe gifts or, more often than that, giving her something that Dad had bought for me. The minute Chloe's eyes lit up at the sight of a new doll or book or packet of pencil crayons, Mum would hand it over with a promise to buy me a replacement, which never materialised. If Dad bought me a dress, Mum would say how much prettier Chloe would look in it and it would disappear from my wardrobe. I told Dad I preferred jeans and T-shirts, convinced Chloe wouldn't be as interested in them.

Every time Mum snapped at me or acted indifferently to a good grade from school or an award from any of my out of school clubs, Chloe would appear by my side with a smile and a hug and soon take my mind off it and I immediately forgave her for taking my things. After all, it wasn't her fault. She never asked for them; Mum just gave them to her, setting an expectation that she could have whatever she wanted.

What else had I said to Dave? Insecure. Yes, she was extremely insecure and clingy. We'd barely been apart until university and Chloe worked herself up into an anxious state about me leaving, convinced I'd make loads of friends and no longer want her in my life. She insisted on joining Dad as he drove me to Liverpool and she clung onto me, sobbing, when it was time to leave me in my room in the halls of residence. She made me pinkie promise I'd never replace her as my best friend. I'd laughed and hugged her tightly, assuring her that she was irreplaceable but I remembered having to play down my friendship with Hannah because any mention of new friends seemed to upset her.

And nobody listened like Chloe. As teenagers, we'd walk up and down the beach for hours, talking about anything and everything. I was there to pick up the pieces after her many relationship disasters but she built me up again after it ended with Harry. She was the person I turned to when Mum hurt me and she always knew what to say to make me feel positive.

So, yes, she was spoilt but Mum had created that. She was insecure but that was a direct result of how others treated her. But she was so much fun and that was her through and through. That was the real Chloe. That was the person I loved and missed.

39

When I left for work on Wednesday morning, the snow had cleared and Spud the snowman was a shadow of his former self. I retrieved the soggy hat and scarf, feeling that same sadness I'd felt as a child when the snow melted away the snowmen that Dad and I had lovingly created. By Thursday morning, Spud was nothing more than a lump of snow, a couple of twigs and a handful of stones. The wildlife had obviously helped themselves to the carrot.

Rich and Dave had done some asking around and discovered someone in the next village with a red Land Rover Defender for sale. Rich knew quite a bit about cars and assured me it was in great condition so I dipped into my inheritance from Gramps.

One of the lads Dave worked with had been looking for a small car for his wife so I reluctantly said goodbye to my beautiful Fiat 500. As I handed over the keys on Saturday morning, it struck me that this was it: I was *never* going to live back in Whitsborough Bay. My home, job, business venture and all my friends were now on the Wolds. I'd always imagined Whitsborough Bay being the place I'd settle, yet the Wolds already felt like my home. I missed the sea but I could still visit. I didn't miss living there, though, because what was there left for me? Dad. That was all.

* * *

'Nice jeep,' Hannah said when she opened the door to Fuchsia Cottage an hour later. 'It suits you. And I *love* the wellies.'

'Thank you. Housewarming gift from the boys.' I slipped off my wellies in the hall. 'How's the beautiful Amelia?'

'Still very cute and still very loud. She's asleep at the moment but she should be awake soon. Kettle's just boiled.'

She made us drinks and we sat down at the kitchen table.

'Has it sunk in yet?' she asked.

I'd told her about Thomas's will over the phone but this was our first opportunity to catch up in person. 'No. I don't know if it ever will.'

'I bet you miss him.'

I nodded. 'Nearly as much as I miss Gramps which is ridiculous given how short a time he was in my life.'

She smiled gently. 'It's not the time someone's in our lives but the impact they have on us. You saved Thomas's life so you had a pretty intense connection from the start and the two of you had such a huge impact on each other.'

'Waaaahhhhh!!!!!!'

'I knew that was going to happen.' Hannah stood up. 'Back in a moment.'

Ten minutes later, Hannah re-appeared with Amelia. She was dressed in a cute grey pinafore with a cat's face on the bib, a long-sleeved pink top, and striped woolly tights. Her cheeks were rosy and her dark hair was all fuzzy on one side of her head and squashed flat on the other.

'Hey cutie,' I said, lightly stroking one of her pudgy cheeks.

Hannah kissed her daughter's head. 'Any progress with your family?'

'No. Dad told them about Thomas but only Auntie Louise acted on it. She sent me a sympathy card which was lovely of her so I texted to say thank you. Nothing since then.'

'I'm so disappointed with them all, especially Chloe. I've always liked her but the more time I spend in her company, the more I want to give her a slap across the chops because of how she's treating you.'

'Have you seen a lot of her?' It was inevitable that they would with their husbands being best friends, but the idea didn't sit comfortably with me.

Hannah curled up her lip. 'A bit. James seems to think that, just because he's Toby's best mate, Chloe and I should be besties too, especially now that she's pregnant and we therefore have "loads in common".' She did air quotes to emphasise the point.

'As long as you don't break friends with me and become besties with her,' I said, in an intentionally childish tone.

'Never. I tolerate her because of Toby and James but that's it. You've done nothing wrong and I'm livid that she won't accept that.'

Amelia wriggled in Hannah's arms and looked across at me.

'I think it might be cuddle time.' Hannah passed her over.

I kissed Amelia's cheek and stroked her soft hair. 'So adorable. I might be in love.'

Hannah smiled. 'That's good to hear because I have a very special question to ask you. We want to get Amelia christened and wondered if you'd like you to be one of her godparents.'

I gasped. 'Really? Oh, Hannah, I'd love to. Thank you.' I looked into Amelia's big brown eyes and felt quite choked up. What an honour. 'You've made my day.'

'What are you like, you big softy?' Hannah squeezed my hand. 'I have to warn you that Toby will be asking James to be godfather.'

'And Chloe...?'

'... will be a guest at the christening but the godparents will be you, my sister, Toby's brother and James.'

I cuddled my goddaughter to my chest. 'When's the christening?'

'Not till around her first birthday so we're way ahead of ourselves with this.'

We chatted for another hour or so about the christening and my plans for Hedgehog Hollow.

'I'd better head off,' I said, passing Amelia back to Hannah. 'Dave's having a parcel delivered shortly after one and I promised to be back for it.'

'It's been so lovely to see you,' Hannah said. 'And we're very excited about a proper tour round your new farm, aren't we Amelia?'

'I'm not moving in until the work's done which will be a few months yet, but you're welcome to visit any time. In fact, if you haven't got any plans next weekend, maybe you could drop by?'

'I *never* have plans these days but I'll check with Toby and let you know.'

Giving them both a hug, I opened the door and tutted. I'd parked right outside Fuchsia Cottage, quite close to the car in front of me. There'd been plenty of space behind me but now some idiot had parked their 4x4 right up to my back bumper. There was no way I was going to be able to get out of the space.

'Something wrong?' Hannah asked.

'Look.'

She tutted too. 'The one in front is next door's but they're on holiday. The one behind belongs to the man who lives next door but one in that direction.' She pointed to my left. 'Do you want me to give him a knock?'

'It's okay. I'll do it. Does this man have a name?'

She shrugged. 'I don't really know him. He's not lived there very long. Renting. Tends to keep himself to himself.' She screwed up her nose. 'Maybe a bit grumpy?'

I rolled my eyes. 'I'll brave it. See you later.'

Taking a deep breath, I knocked on the door of Wisteria Cottage and I cringed as I heard someone shouting inside. I knocked again, a bit louder this time. The door flung open and I was faced with an unshaven man in his early thirties with dark hair, dark eyes and broad shoulders. He had a striking resemblance to the actor Chris Pratt. Rich and Dave were huge fans of Marvel films and we must have watched the *Guardians of the Galaxy* films at least four times since I'd moved in with them.

'Yes?'

I realised I was staring at him and it would probably be a good idea to speak. 'Er, hi. Sorry to bother you. I was wondering—'

'Not interested.' He closed the door.

Damn! He obviously thought I was trying to sell something. The shouting resumed but I was going to have to knock again.

'What?' he cried, yanking the door open once more.

My first instinct was to run away from the angry man, but what good would that do me? I needed to get home and he was going to have to move his vehicle for that to happen. I straightened up taller.

'You've parked right behind my car and I can't get out. I wondered if you'd mind moving.'

'I'm on the phone.'

I hadn't even registered that he had a mobile in his hand.

'I'm really sorry but I need to be somewhere.' Why was I apologising? He was the one who'd parked inconsiderately.

'I'll move my car when I've finished my call.' He moved to close the door and I saw red. For years I'd put what I wanted aside to please other people and I wasn't going to do it now. I'd promised Dave I'd be home for the delivery and I wasn't going to let him down.

'No. You'll move it now.' I sounded so confident. Didn't feel it.

He looked a bit taken aback but I was on a roll.

'You've parked right up to my bumper and I can't get out. I need to be somewhere urgently. It's your fault so you can put it right. Now.'

He stared at me for a moment, eyes wide, and I waited for him to protest but, instead, he sighed. 'This isn't finished,' he snapped into the phone. 'I'll call you back.'

If I hadn't stepped aside, I swear he'd have barged me out the way.

'You shouldn't have parked so close to the car in front,' he grumbled. 'Only an idiot would do that.'

Rude! The looks of Chris Pratt and the personality of a prat.

'And only an idiot would have parked so close behind me without checking I had space at the front.'

I was so flustered that I stalled twice as I was trying to manoeuvre out of the space and I swear Hannah's grumpy neighbour laughed at me. Who behaved like that?

I was still seething by the time I pulled up outside Brook Cottage. The courier arrived as I was unlocking the door so I'd only just made it. Sometimes it paid to stand up for yourself.

40

Dad drove over to Umplesthorpe for an early Sunday lunch at The Black Swan the following day, then we both drove over to Hedgehog Hollow.

'It's very you,' he said, when I'd given him the grand tour.

'You think so?'

'I do. There's a sort of contentment about you here that I never saw back home.'

I led Dad back into the kitchen and put the kettle on while I pondered on his words. He was right. Even though I still thought of the farmhouse as Thomas's home, Hedgehog Hollow had started to feel like my home too and I did feel content there. I always had.

'How are things at home?' I asked, handing him his drink.

'Same as always.' The half-smile suggested he was trying to sound buoyant but I wasn't fooled. The situation had emotionally and mentally drained him.

'I hoped things would improve when I moved out.'

Dad shrugged. 'I'm sure they will. With a bit more time.'

How much more time did they need before one of them finally said the words out loud? It was obvious to me that their marriage was over and had been for a long time but who was I to criticise? I knew all about waiting and hoping.

* * *

I spent Wednesday lunchtime in the department office, catching up on some paperwork. My mobile rang with an unknown number and the same thing happened as before: nobody speaking but definitely someone breathing.

'If that's you, Chloe, and I'm sure it is, talk to me,' I said, in my best gentle nursing voice. 'I'm listening.'

There was something that sounded like a sob, then the phone went dead.

'Bad news?' Lauren asked, dropping a file on my desk.

I put my mobile down. 'No. I keep getting silent calls and I'm convinced it's my cousin but she never speaks. I'm worried about her.'

Lauren perched on the corner of my desk. 'I thought you'd decided she wasn't worth bothering with after the way she'd treated you.'

'I had. But she *is* family and we have history. If she's upset and reaching out, I'm not going to push her away, but I'm not going to be the best of friends with her either. Can't keep pushing on a closed door.'

'Too right. And speaking of friendships or perhaps a little something more, are you ready to let me set up you up on a date yet? I still think my nephew would be perfect for you.'

'Do you ever let up?'

'My love life is non-existent and that's how I want it to stay. Doesn't mean I can't vicariously have one, though. Stunning girl like you would be snapped up.'

'Stunning? I think your eyes need testing.'

Lauren reeled back. 'You, Sam Wishaw, are a very attractive woman and I don't want to hear another word suggesting otherwise. So, can I set you up?'

'No! I've got so much to do with work and the farm, the timing couldn't be worse.'

She slipped off the desk, shaking her head. 'If you ask me, the timing couldn't be better. If I know you as well as I think I do, you'll work every single evening and every weekend which isn't good for anyone. The odd date here and there will give you the perfect break.'

'I get breaks. I visit Hannah and Amelia and nip to the pub with Rich and Dave.'

'Not the same as a hot date,' she said, heading for the door.

'But much less stressful,' I called. 'And heartbreak-free.'

* * *

After five months in the area, I'd sussed my way around but remained clueless when it came to the more remote areas. One of my best students couldn't get to college because her mum had a broken leg and couldn't drive her. She was eager not to fall behind so I'd offered to drop off the course textbook at Thursday lunchtime.

I knew she lived in a hamlet called Addlington Row but my sat nav wasn't recognising the postcode. I found myself in a mobile signal black spot and it felt like the day of the wedding all over again.

Pulling back onto the B-road after another dead end, I set off slowly down the narrow country lane and willed the next turning to be the right one. I flicked through the radio channels until I found something cheerful that I could sing along to. I was building up to the resounding chorus when I spotted the top of a vehicle hurtling towards me round the next bend. The road wasn't wide enough for the two of us.

I slammed on my brakes and yanked my steering wheel to the left, mounting the bank just in time as the vehicle sped past with millimetres to spare. Heart racing, I thumped down on the horn and held it for several seconds. *Bloody idiot!* In my rear-view mirror, I could see the driver stopping further down the lane.

I jumped out of the jeep and quickly checked there was no

damage from mounting the bank. There was nothing obvious on the bodywork but I was livid. Slamming my door shut, I stormed down the lane to where the green jeep was reversing back towards me.

'What the hell do you think you're doing?' I yelled as it stopped and the driver's door was pushed opened. 'You could have killed us both.'

I had no idea who I was confronting and I didn't care. Nothing could be that urgent to justify such reckless driving and they were about to feel my wrath.

A man jumped out of the driver's seat and my eyes widened. Of all the people. It was the Chris Pratt lookalike – Hannah's mysterious grumpy neighbour who'd boxed me in.

'You,' I spat. 'What is it with you? Do you think you own the roads?'

He narrowed his eyes at me, as though trying to place me.

'Saturday in North Emmerby? You blocked my car in. So where's the fire?'

'What fire?'

'I assumed there must be some sort of emergency if you needed to race along at about eighty miles an hour.'

'There *was* an emergency. There still is. Are you hurt?' There was an urgency in his voice that riled me. Where was the apology? Where was the regret?

'Luckily not.'

'And your car?'

'It's not hurt either, but only because I was going slowly and spotted you in time.'

'Then I commend you on your brilliant driving skills.' He stepped back into his jeep and reached for the door handle.

'Is that it?' I darted towards the door and grabbed it. 'No apology?'

He looked taken aback. Obviously not used to being confronted. Good-looking guys like him probably got away with murder. Quick cheeky grin and a wink and all was forgiven. 'I'm sorry,' he muttered. 'I won't do it again but I genuinely do have an emergency to get to so if you could let go of my door...'

'One more thing,' I said.

'Jesus! What?'

'I'm lost,' I said, in a gentler tone. 'I need to get to Addlington Row. Do you know it, please?'

'Turn round, head in the direction I'm going, first left, first right, and it's on your left. Got it?'

'Got it. Thank you.'

'Can I go now?'

'Yes. You go and deal with your *big* emergency.'

'Thank you. So can you let go of the door?'

I hadn't realised I was still clinging onto it. Letting go, I stepped back so he could set off.

Legs shaking, I walked back to my jeep. Did I just think of him as good-looking? 'No. It's because Chris Pratt is easy on the eye and he reminds me of him but green-jeep prat is a grumpy, inconsiderate, reckless idiot.' I chuckled to myself. 'Jeep Prat. That's what I'll call him from now on.'

As I turned the car round, I wondered if he might have deliberately given me the wrong directions as revenge for shouting at him. Thankfully I pulled up in front of Addlington Row five minutes later. He wasn't 100 per cent idiot, then. Maybe just 99 per cent.

41

I spent Saturday at Hedgehog Hollow, throwing myself into what Rich had christened 'Project Prickles'.

Scaffolding had been erected so, while Dave and his team made a start on repairing the roof and gutters, I spent the day in the barn, sorting through the supplies that Thomas and Gwendoline had purchased before her illness.

There were fifty or so plastic crates which, with breathing holes, would make perfect hedgehog homes. They needed a thorough hosing down but they'd be good as new once clean. I found a crate filled with round plastic plant trays, presumably for food and water, which were also filthy but undamaged. Roughly thirty rolls of blue paper towel seemed to have survived the years thanks to being swathed in several layers of thick cellophane. Unfortunately, several fleecy blankets were covered in mould and three industrial sized packets of washing powder had clumped into solid lumps from the damp. It seemed a shame to chuck so much out but two decades was a long time in a cold, damp barn. It was a miracle we'd been able to salvage anything.

I spent Sunday at Brook Cottage. After filling in the forms online to register Hedgehog Hollow Rescue Centre as a charity, I split my time between teaching prep and hedgehog research. There was so much to learn about hedgehogs and it excited yet scared me. I was desperate not to let the Micklebys down.

* * *

Dave called in a favour from an architect friend, Justin, who'd visited the farm last week to measure up for a freestanding mezzanine. Ideally we'd have had a second storey installed to make best use of the double-height space but I couldn't justify the time and money needed to reinforce the barn.

I arranged to meet Justin at the farm immediately after lessons on Tuesday.

'You've missed him,' Dave said when I got out the car. 'He came early and I didn't feel I could ask him to wait with it being a freebie. He's left the plans, though, and I think you're going to be pleased.'

'Wow! I wasn't expecting this,' I said a few minutes later as I studied the drawings laid out on a trestle table in the barn.

'Me neither. I assumed he'd have done a mezzanine at one end. I never even thought about one wrapping all the way round but it gives you so much more space.'

'I love it. Thanks for sorting it out.'

Dave smiled. 'Any time. And speaking of sorting things out, I want to show you something.'

It was almost dark so he grabbed a torch and I followed him round to the back of the farmhouse. He switched the torch on and focused the beam on Thomas's bench.

I felt a warm tingle inside. 'Oh, Dave. You screwed the plaque onto it. It looks brilliant. I wish Thomas could have seen it.'

'At least he got to read the poem before he went. I got a bit choked up reading it myself. I can't believe you wrote it.'

'Neither can I.' I ran my fingers across the plaque, picturing Thomas's delighted expression when I gave him it. I missed him so much. 'I think I'll sit here with Thomas and Gwendoline for a bit. Tell them about the plans.'

'I'll leave the torch with you.'

I sat down on the bench to the side of the plaque, smiling as the torchlight caught the silver and sparkled. A light breeze teased the strands of hair that had broken loose from my ponytail, tickling my face. I tucked them behind my ear and, taking a tissue out of my pocket, gently rubbed a thumbprint off the plaque before turning to face the meadow. The grasses were silhouetted against the rapidly darkening sky.

'I'm doing what you wanted,' I said. 'It's going to look fabulous. Five-star luxury accommodation, I reckon. We've cleared the barn and the roof's getting fixed right now. I've traded my Mint Imperial for a 4x4 and the boys bought me some wellies covered in hedgehogs. You'd love them.' My lip started to wobble and my eyes filled with tears. 'But I'm scared, Thomas. I know you said in your letter that you believed in me, but this is huge. What if I mess it up?'

The breeze stilled for a moment and I swear I felt someone squeezing my hand. Standing up, I blew a kiss towards the meadow, before making my way round to the barn to return the torch.

With some unexpected time back, it was the perfect opportunity to visit the veterinary practice with which Gwendoline had made arrangements. I probably had an hour before it closed.

* * *

Alderson & Son's Veterinary Practice was easy to find. Set back from one of the A-roads, it was only about five miles from Hedgehog Hollow which was probably why Gwendoline and Thomas had chosen it. There were several vehicles in the well-lit large car park, suggesting a popular practice. I stood at the back of my jeep, taking it all in. The building itself looked like it might have started life as a bungalow but had been extended and converted into a business. A gate to the left led to a house, set back behind the surgery which was presumably where the owner lived.

I hated how nervous I felt but negotiating something for free or reduced cost was out of my comfort zone. My best-case scenario was that the vet remembered the arrangement he'd made with Gwendoline and was happy to still honour it but, after twenty years, how realistic was that? My worst-case scenario was that he couldn't remember it and wasn't willing to make a fresh arrangement with me. *Deep breath. You can do this. You're going to be friendly and confident and not accept no for an answer.*

The reception area was bright and modern, opening out into a comfortable waiting area; quite a contrast to the practice where Dad worked which was dark, dingy and desperately in need of a fresh lick of paint at the very minimum. We jokingly called the owners the Brothers Grim because of how grim and depressing the place had always looked.

'Can I help you?' asked a young woman behind the reception. I noticed that all the staff were wearing royal blue polo shirts with the name of the surgery embroidered on the left side. Very smart. A name badge clipped to the other side told me I was speaking to Sadie.

'Hi, yes, I don't actually have an appointment, but I'm not here with an animal.'

If Sadie thought I was a little odd, she didn't let it show. She just continued to smile encouragingly.

'Slightly strange one,' I continued. 'A friend of mine died recently and left me his farm in Huggleswick on the condition that I do what he and his wife always dreamed of doing which is opening a hedgehog rescue centre.'

'Aw, how lovely,' Sadie gushed. 'I adore hedgehogs. So how can we help?'

'My friends made an arrangement with this practice to have any hedgehogs they rescued treated at cost. They made the arrangement with Mr Alderson but they never used the service because my friend's wife died.'

She wrinkled her nose. 'It's not an arrangement I'm aware of.'

'I wondered if Mr Alderson's free or whether I can make an appointment to see him another day about it.'

Sadie tapped a couple of buttons on her computer. 'You're in luck. We've had a cancellation but let me just nip down and have a word with him in case he's taking the opportunity to catch up on things. Won't be a moment.'

An elderly couple came in with a golden retriever wearing a plastic cone round its neck. I gave it a stroke while another receptionist booked them in, by which time Sadie had returned.

'He doesn't recall anything about it but he's happy to have a brief chat if you want to go down. It's the fourth door on the left.'

'Thank you. I really appreciate it.'

'Anything for the hedgehogs.' She gave me a beaming smile.

A male voice called, 'Come in,' soon after I knocked.

Stepping into the office, I was about to speak but Mr Alderson had his back to me and raised a finger, presumably to silence me. I realised he was on the phone.

'Yeah, yeah. No, I'm looking at them now... Not what we thought but that's a good thing...'

I could only see the back of his head but the colour and style of his hair suggested someone quite young. If Thomas and Gwendoline had made the arrangement with the owner twenty years ago, then this couldn't be the owner. Unless... Alderson and *Son*.

'Okay. I've got a visitor so I need to go but keep your eye on things and we'll catch up tomorrow. Bye.' He hung up and spun round to face me. 'Sorry about... You! Are you stalking me?'

My stomach sank to my boots. No! The universe had to be having a laugh. Of all the people in all the world, why did it have to be Jeep Prat?

'I... er...' I was genuinely lost for words. I needed a huge favour from him, or his dad, yet our two encounters so far had been hostile.

'Come to have a go at me again?' he asked, a hard edge to his voice.

'Thanks to you delaying me last week, a good friend of mine nearly lost a horse and foal.'

Anger surged through me. 'How was I supposed to know that? You ran me off the road.' So he really had been racing to an emergency. It had never entered my head that he could be a vet.

'And I stopped to check you weren't hurt but you weren't content with that. Had to keep going on and on.'

We stared at each other, jaws tense, teeth clenched. This was ridiculous. I sighed and dropped my shoulders. 'Can we start over? I didn't come here to have a go at you and I'm not stalking you. I genuinely didn't know you worked here. I came because I've inherited a farm that I need to turn into a hedgehog rescue centre and the friends I inherited it from said they had arrangements with you to treat the hedgehogs at cost and I was hoping to discuss whether that arrangement could still stand.'

'What's the name of the farm?' His tone had softened.

'Hedgehog Hollow in Huggleswick. The owners were Thomas and Gwendoline Mickleby.'

He shook his head. 'I know the farm but Mickleby...? It's not familiar. When was this?'

I grimaced. 'That's the problem. It was quite a long time ago and I think the arrangement might have been with your dad rather than with you.'

Jeep Prat stiffened and his eyes narrowed. 'Did Beth send you?'

'Who's Beth?'

'It doesn't matter.' He straightened up and shook his head. 'I'm sorry, but my father no longer works here and he never will again. I'm not prepared to honour any arrangements that man put in place. Anything he ever said or did has got *nothing* to do with me or this practice anymore. I think you should leave.'

I turned to go but a sudden surge of confidence flowed through me. I'd vowed not to accept no for an answer and I wasn't going to let someone tell me what to do again. I turned back round.

'I'm sorry I shouted at you last week and I'm sorry for whatever bad blood there is between you and your d… Mr Alderson Senior. I'm not expecting you to honour the same arrangement but I wondered if we could discuss something.'

'I don't think so.'

'Please. Maybe another time?'

'You can close the door on your way out.'

The last vestige of strength drained from me. I couldn't do this. I couldn't fight. I felt completely and utterly defeated. 'Okay. Well, thanks anyway. Bye.'

He didn't respond so I closed the door and slowly made my way back towards reception. I'd failed Thomas and Gwendoline already.

'How did it go?' Sadie gushed as I stepped back into the reception area. 'Are we going to be treating lots of adorable hoglets?'

'It'll take me a while to get up and running,' I said, too professional to bad-mouth her boss. 'Thanks for your help. Bye.'

I released a shaky breath as soon as I closed my car door. That honestly couldn't have gone worse. My throat felt tight and my eyes were itchy but I refused to cry. Mr Alderson Junior aka Jeep Prat had already been held in low esteem and now he'd plummeted even further. If he was that grumpy and aggressive, I wasn't sure I wanted to do business with him anyway. There were plenty of other vets in the area. They might be further away from the farm but I could explore opportunities with them instead.

Perhaps when I was feeling a bit braver.

42

The forecast indicated that we were in for a storm at the start of next week so it needed to be all hands on deck at Hedgehog Hollow across the weekend to get the barn watertight. Dave and Pete – a roofing specialist – had worked tirelessly all week. They'd finished the roof, and most of the damaged stonework round the top of the barn had been repaired. The objectives for the weekend were to put the guttering up and replace the large broken window at the back.

I drove across first thing on Saturday morning. There wasn't much I could do to help as it was specialist work but I wanted to feel useful. Spotting a hose mounted in a spiral on the side of the farmhouse, opposite the barn, I tested the tap to make sure the water was connected and decided to give the plastic crates a hosing down. I spread out the first stack and turned on the hose but the pressure wasn't strong enough. I turned the tap up just a notch and screamed as the trickle turned into a torrent and the hose took on a life of its own, like a snake, wriggling out of my hands. The water wasn't just flowing out of the end either; holes all along the pipe spurted icy jets in my direction. Squealing, I dived for the tap and frantically turned it but the top came off in my hands.

'Here, let me.' A man grabbed it from me, clamped it down on the tap and must have managed to turn it because the torrent of water finally ceased. I shook my arms, slicked back my hair, and turned to thank my knight in shining armour.

Only he was more a prat in a shining jeep.

'What are *you* doing here?' I cried.

'Saving you from drowning by the looks of it,' he quipped, wiping his wet hands down his jeans.

'I had it under control.'

'I could tell.'

We stared at each other. Water dripped down my face and I wiped it away. One of us was going to have to bend. 'Thank you,' I muttered. 'I would have managed, though. It just took me by surprise.'

'Hoses are known for that. Devious little buggers. Like to take their victims completely unaware.' Although his face remained deadpan, his eyes twinkled. Was there a sense of humour lurking under that gruff exterior?

I shivered, my clothes clinging to me. 'I need to get changed. Was there something you wanted?'

He looked towards the farmhouse. 'I can wait here while you change.'

I shook my head. 'That's not my home. Well, it is, but I don't live there yet. My clothes are in Umplesthorpe where I'm staying.'

'Right. I won't keep you then. I was passing and thought I'd drop in and say sorry about the other day at the practice. I might have been a bit rude.'

'You were. *Very* rude.'

'I'm sorry.'

'Apology accepted. Was that everything?'

'No. I, er... if you want to make an appointment to talk about the hedgehogs, I suppose I'd be willing to hear you out.'

Suppose. If it hadn't been for that one word, I'd probably have shaken his hand and made a deal there and then, but it changed the whole sentiment of his offer. He supposed he'd be willing? How very magnanimous. It was like he was doing me a massive favour. Well, he was, but that wasn't the point. It was the way he said it that set me on edge. I clenched my teeth. There was no way I could work with the smug-faced, condescending Mr Alderson Junior.

'No thanks,' I said. 'You made your views very clear so I'll look for a vet who genuinely wants to help.' I wasn't sure whether I was still shaking from the cold or from anger. It was so tempting to add, 'Now get off my land,' but I managed to restrain myself.

'I'm sorry. It was just that you mentioned my father and... it's...' He ran his fingers through his hair and sighed loudly. 'Forget it. You wouldn't understand. You'd better get home and get changed. You're shivering. Maybe see you around.'

He stomped back to his jeep shaking his head and sped off down the track. I released the breath I'd been holding. Why had I just done that? I had never acted stubborn in my whole life yet the one time when it was really important, I'd dug my heels in and made things harder for myself. He'd been willing to talk. I could have had an arrangement in place by the end of the week. But, if he wasn't passionate about hedgehog rescue, what was the point? He had to *want* to do it and that tone of voice indicated a man who definitely didn't want any part of it. Or had I just assumed that because I wanted to see the worst in him?

I sighed again. He wasn't worth any more of my time. I stacked the crates back together and mentally added fixing the tap and buying a new hose to the ever-growing Project Prickles list, then went to tell Dave I was nipping home for dry clothes.

As I drove down the track, sitting on a towel, I found myself replaying my conversation with... I didn't even know his first name. I felt stupid referring to him as Mr Alderson Junior but I also felt pretty mean referring to him as Jeep Prat. He'd reached out an olive branch, albeit seemingly reluctantly, and I'd batted it away. And that hurt look in his eyes when he'd mentioned his father. There was clearly very bad blood between them. He said I wouldn't understand. Given my relationship with Mum, I would probably understand it better than anyone. I knew the pain a parent could cause only too well.

43

My heart leapt as I drove back up the track in fresh, dry clothes and spotted Dad's car in the farmyard. I knew it was his Saturday off but I hadn't been expecting to see him. He was over by the barn talking to Dave.

'Dad!' I cried, rushing over and hugging him. 'What a lovely surprise.'

'I've got another surprise for you.' He took my arm and led me into the barn where a man was standing looking up at the beamed ceiling.

'Uncle Simon!'

'Surprise!' he said, hugging me tightly. 'I'm sorry I haven't made it over sooner.'

'That's okay. You're here now and it's great to see you. How's everyone?'

'They're fine. Chloe, Louise and your Mum have gone to Hull, shopping for baby stuff so I thought it was the perfect opportunity to check out your new estate.'

'Estate?' I rolled my eyes at him. 'What are you like?'

* * *

It was so good to spend some time with Uncle Simon and it turned out to be unexpectedly reassuring too. Over tea and biscuits, he was eager to know all about hedgehogs and what I'd need to do to look after them which made me realise how much I'd taken in from the research I'd undertaken since accepting Thomas's gift. I knew all about feeding, nesting, and breeding. I could list all the hazards that hedgehogs regularly faced and talk about the ailments I was most likely to deal with like strimmer injuries, fleas, starvation, dehydration, or problems caused by eating or getting tangled in litter.

'Did you know that hedgehogs can swim?' I asked them both. 'But they often drown in ponds because they can't get out again. It's the same with cattle grids. They fall into them and they're trapped without food and water. The man who set up the British Hedgehog Preservation Society campaigned to have escape ramps in all cattle grids. Most county councils make this mandatory now.'

'You sound so knowledgeable,' Uncle Simon said, smiling.

'You know what? I didn't realise I was until just now. I was panicking that I didn't know enough.' The construction work hadn't fazed me thanks to Dave and his skilled, reliable friends and contacts, but the idea of running the rescue centre had been making me nervous. My priority had to be marking assignments and teaching preparation but I'd devoted every other spare hour to hedgehog homework.

'You know loads,' Dad reassured me. 'And I suspect you might have found a new love.'

I smiled. 'I can't help it. They're so gorgeous but so vulnerable. It breaks my heart that their numbers are in such serious decline. I just want to gather them all up and protect them forever.'

'You can't do that but you're certainly doing your bit,' Dad said. 'I'm so proud of you.'

'We all are,' Uncle Simon added. He must have seen my face fall because he added, 'And that includes your Auntie Louise.'

'She's barely spoken to me since the wedding.'

'I know but she's in a difficult position. You have to appreciate that.'

I did, but the whole thing was still stupid. The punishment didn't fit the crime. What had I really done, after all? I'd let go of the man I loved so he and Chloe could live happily ever after.

'They're going to stop by on their way back from Hull,' Uncle Simon said.

'Very funny,' I quipped, not believing him for a moment.

'I'm serious. They've got the directions and they're coming here.'

My eyes widened. 'And Mum and Chloe have agreed to this plan?'

'No, but they'll come round. I told Louise that enough is enough. I want this family fixing and this is the part she needs to play.'

I stood up and gathered the mugs, sighing. 'Thanks, Uncle Simon. I appreciate the effort but I can guarantee they *won't* call in on their way home.'

'Louise promised.'

'And I'm sure she had every intention of keeping that promise. But you know how persuasive Chloe can be and she has the pregnancy as her ace card. She just needs to hint at being tired or stressed and they'll go straight back to Whitsborough Bay instead.'

'They won't have a choice,' Uncle Simon said. 'Louise will be telling them that Jonathan's staying for dinner with you and she needs to pick me up.'

'Simon!' Dad cried. 'You didn't tell me that. They'll be mad at me for bringing you here, especially when you've just done a night shift and should be sleeping. And they'll be mad at Sammie for making me stay.'

'No, they won't.'

'I agree with Dad,' I said, heading towards the door. 'I appreciate the sentiment though.'

Holding onto the kitchen sink moments later, I took a few deep breaths. He meant well and I loved him for it, but there was no way this wasn't going to all backfire on Dad and me.

* * *

By mid-afternoon, I could tell that Uncle Simon's night shift had caught up on him and he needed a nap, even though he insisted he was fine.

'Who's the nurse here?' I asked, fixing my sternest look on him. 'You need your sleep.'

'Okay. I submit. A nap might be nice.'

Dad and I bundled up in our coats and boots and headed back out to the barn, leaving Uncle Simon stretched out on the sofa.

'How are things at home?' I asked, as we sat down on a pair of deckchairs in the barn with another mug of tea. 'And don't fob me off with "fine" because I know they're not.'

He sighed and shook his head slowly. 'It's not too good, Sammie. Right now, it feels like we're two strangers who happen to live in the same house.'

'Me moving out hasn't made any difference?'

'No.'

'So what are you going to do?'

'I don't know. It's not working, but actually ending it...' He shook his head. 'It's easier said than done.'

I stood up. 'Come on. Let's have a walk and talk about something nice. You can tell me all about the animals you've met this week. We haven't done that for a while.'

'Sounds good.' Dad stood up and smiled at me. 'I'm so proud of you too, you know.'

'Thank you. It means a lot.' And it really did. There was no saying whether Uncle Simon's attempts to fix the family would go anywhere but at least I could rely on the men in my life. Dad, Uncle Simon, Rich and Dave, Dave's mates, Thomas and... I shook my head as an image of Jeep Prat popped into my head, his eyes twinkling like they'd done when he'd joked about dangerous hoses. Where had that come from? That was one man I definitely could *not* rely on and one who I hopefully would never encounter again.

'I've got to tell you about this vet I met...' I said, linking Dad's arm. 'Rudest man ever.'

44

'Oh my gosh! They're here.' My heart raced at the sight of Auntie Louise's and Uncle Simon's car emerging from the track just as Dad and I finished our walk. 'Do you think they'll speak to me?'

'They can hardly ignore you,' Dad said.

Louise stopped the car next to Dad's. An excruciating couple of minutes passed with no movement while Dad and I hung back near the barn. They were facing the other way and probably hadn't even seen us. Then three doors opened and they all exited. Good start. Dad and I stepped forward.

'Sam!' To my astonishment, Auntie Louise rushed towards me and gave me a hug. It was an awkward one, but at least it was a hug and that was a huge step forward. 'What a stunning location.'

'Thank you.' I looked towards Mum. 'Hi, Mum.'

'Samantha.' Just a nod of the head; no smile and definitely no sign of a hug.

'Hi, Chloe.'

She glowered at me. I tried not to stare at her bump. Last time I'd seen her was at the hospital in September when Amelia was born and it was too early for her to be showing. Now she was almost at term and I'd missed the whole thing.

'How are you fe—?'

'Where's your toilet?' Chloe interrupted.

'In the farmhouse, under the stairs. Front door's open.'

With an almost imperceptible nod of her head, she waddled towards the house.

'Would you like a tea or coffee?' I asked.

'We're not staying,' Mum said, coldly. 'Chloe's shattered and I've got a headache. We're only here to pick up Simon although why you two couldn't have cancelled your dinner plans so Jonathan could drive him back is beyond me.'

'Debs!' Auntie Louise snapped. 'It's not Jonathan's or Sam's fault. They had plans, Simon wanted to get out the house, and he insisted they didn't change their plans for him. And he wanted us to see the farm.'

'There you go.' Mum swept her hand round the yard. 'Seen it. Can we get Simon and go?'

Auntie Louise shook her head. 'No. I want a tour.'

I swear it was the first time I'd ever seen Mum give her sister a dirty look. I'd be blamed for it, of course. 'Fine,' Mum snapped. 'But my feet are aching from traipsing round the shops so I'll wait in the car.'

Auntie Louise pressed the key fob to lock the car. 'No. You'll look round your daughter's new home.'

Wow! Go Auntie Louise! Very feisty. I needed to take assertive lessons from her.

'Okay, then.' I took a deep breath. 'So, the farm is sixty acres but another farmer rents and farms most of it so really it's just the immediate area, a garden and a meadow. This is the barn where the rescue centre will be...'

Auntie Louise asked lots of questions and either was genuinely interested or was doing an excellent job of pretending she was. I felt the ice thawing between us. We'd always had a good relationship before the wedding, despite Mum no doubt poisoning her mind against me over the years, and hopefully we were on our way to it being restored.

Mum, on the other hand, acted like a small child being dragged out on a hike when they really wanted to stay inside playing computer games. She hung back, looking disinterested and saying nothing. And it still hurt. I still longed for her approval.

Chloe didn't join us, although she was probably exhausted from shopping and needed the rest. She'd have likely stayed inside even if we'd still been friends.

When I'd finished showing them round inside the farmhouse, Chloe appeared in the hall and announced that she was tired and wanted to go home. She didn't even look at me. Maybe she was waiting for me to make the first move and engage in conversation.

'Did you get what you needed in Hull?' I asked her.

'Yes.'

'How long is there left now?'

'Four weeks.'

'And are you and James excited?'

She gave me a withering look. 'I wondered how long it would be before you mentioned him.'

'Chloe, that's not fair,' Auntie Louise said. 'It was a perfectly natural question.'

'Not when you're in love with my husband, it isn't.'

'It's been six months,' I said, my eyes pleading with her. 'Can't we just drop it?'

'Just like that? You nearly ruined my wedding, you nearly ruined my marriage and you think it's something that can just be dropped because a few months have passed?'

My hand tightened on the banister. 'Chloe! I didn't ruin anything. If it hadn't been for Great-Aunt Agnes stirring things, you'd never have known about it.'

She gave a derisive snort. 'Oh yes, because *secretly* being in love with my husband is so much better.'

My whole body tensed and I couldn't stay calm any longer. 'For goodness' sake, Chloe,' I snapped. 'Grow up and change the record. James loves you, not me. Never me. So this jealousy thing you've got going on is pathetic. I'm no threat to you and your happy little family and I never was.'

'But you lied to me.'

'Yes, I did, but so what? Who would the truth have helped? I loved James who I will remind you was *my* boyfriend before he saw you. I saw your connection so I let him go and kept quiet because it wouldn't have benefited anyone to admit the truth. I don't love him anymore, though, so you can all untwist your knickers. I've met someone new.' I knew my cheeks were already burning from the confrontation so they couldn't darken any more from the lie.

'Yeah, right. You're just saying that,' Chloe muttered, sneering at me.

'It's the truth,' Dad said, stepping out of the lounge with Uncle Simon by his side. 'Sammie was telling me all about him earlier on our walk, weren't you, poppet?'

'Yes, that's right.' *What? Eek!*

Dad widened his eyes and nodded encouragingly. 'He's a vet at a practice near here.'

'That's great news,' Auntie Louise said. 'Does he have a name?'

Argh! Think! I could hardly say Mr Alderson Junior or Jeep Prat. 'It's Chris,' I said, thinking of his doppelganger.

'Well, I hope it works out for you and Chris.' She turned round and addressed Uncle Simon. 'Are you set? Right, let's head off then.'

I stepped down into the hall. 'Thank you for stopping by.'

Auntie Louise hugged me and this time there was genuine warmth in her embrace. 'It's been good to see you. I've been really silly. I'm sorry.'

'Forget it,' I whispered. 'Fresh start from now. Thanks again for the card after Thomas died. It meant a lot.'

She squeezed me tightly and kissed me on the cheek. 'You're a good lass. We'll talk soon.'

'This place is amazing and what you're doing is so impressive,'

Uncle Simon said, stepping forward and giving me a bear hug. 'I'll be back soon to check on progress.'

'You're welcome any time,' I said.

I noticed Auntie Louise gesturing to Mum and I got the impression she was trying to push her into giving me a hug too. As if that was ever going to happen. But at least she spoke, even if it was an unenthusiastic mumble. 'Good luck with the rest of the refurbishment.'

'Thank you.'

They all turned to go and my heart sank. Chloe wasn't going to speak.

'Can I send the baby a gift when it arrives?' I asked, following them to the door.

'He,' she corrected.

'You're having a boy?' Her face clearly suggested she hadn't meant to reveal that.

'I might be. As for a gift, you can do what you like. You usually do.'

Enough was enough. Fire coursed through my veins. 'No, Chloe. That's your approach to life, not mine.'

She looked surprised for a moment then shook her head and walked away.

'I shouldn't have said that,' I said to Dad when they'd gone.

He put his arm round my shoulders and cuddled me to his side. 'Yes, you should. She needed to hear it.'

45

'How did it go?' Rich asked when I finally made it home on Monday after an open evening at the TEC.

'I feel like I've talked non-stop for two hours but it was good.'

'Dave made lasagne and there's a plate with your name on it,' he said after I'd told him about a few of the students I'd met and some of the funny questions I'd been asked.

'What am I going to do without you two? Do you want to move into the farm with me?'

Rich laughed. 'Don't go making offers like that because we might just take you up on it. Let me go and heat your food up.'

He returned a few minutes later with a plate of lasagne and salad. 'Tuck in.'

'You're a star. How's your day been?'

'High body count today. We lost three.'

'No! That's tough. How are you holding up?'

Rich talked to me while I ate and I'd almost finished my meal when my mobile rang. Unknown number again. I shovelled in the last mouthful. 'Hello?'

Silence. Again.

'Look, Chloe, if that's you and you want to speak, just speak because this is completely pointless.'

There was a definite sob.

'I'm hanging up now...'

'No, don't,' she said. 'I need to see you.' Her voice was weak and shaky. 'There's something I need to ask you but not over the phone.'

'You saw me on Saturday. Why didn't you speak to me then?'

'I wasn't expecting to see you. Mum didn't tell us where we were going until we'd pulled onto the farm track.'

That would certainly explain the few minutes that passed before they exited the car. They'd probably both been having a go at Auntie Louise.

'Are you free on Thursday night at about half six?' she asked.

I was tempted to be churlish and put her off but my curiosity was piqued. 'I can be.'

'Can I meet you at the farm? I should be able to find it again.'

'I thought you were meant to be resting.'

'Like you care.'

'Chloe! That's ridiculous and you know it.'

'Can you do Thursday at the farm or not?' she snapped.

I sighed 'Yes. See you then.'

'What does *she* want?' Rich asked after the call ended.

'Not a clue.' I really wasn't in the mood for another confrontation with Chloe. But she hadn't said she wanted to talk; she'd specifically said she wanted to ask me something. What could that be? It certainly wasn't going to be asking me to be a birthing partner or a godmother to their baby.

As I lay in bed that night, I couldn't stop thinking about Chloe. Our angry exchange of words from Saturday raced through my mind, particularly the part where I'd said I wasn't in love with James anymore. As the words came out, I'd realised they were true. The first couple of months after the wedding had been hard but I'd soon realised I missed Chloe way more than I missed James. That ache had gone. I'd barely spared him a second thought for months. He'd stopped being the man I loved and he'd started being the cause of a huge family rift and I resented him for it.

I smiled to myself. It was completely over. I definitely didn't love him but I definitely wasn't looking for a new relationship, no matter how much Lauren kept nagging me about setting me up. Romantic attachments brought hurt and complications and I didn't have the time or energy for them. My one and only priority was getting Hedgehog Hollow Rescue Centre up and running, fulfilling Thomas and Gwendoline's dreams.

46

Half six came and went at the farm on Thursday evening. Then quarter to. Then seven. I could understand ten to fifteen minutes late but half an hour wasn't like Chloe. Unless she'd got lost.

Dad rang ten minutes later. 'Thought I'd better let you know that they thought Chloe was in labour earlier so James took her to hospital. It was Braxton-Hicks and she's home again now.'

'I take it everything's fine with the baby?'

'Yes. He's doing well.'

'That's good. And is Chloe okay?'

'A bit stressed. I don't think pregnancy has suited our Chloe. She never did like doing anything difficult.'

I couldn't help smiling at Dad's harsh but accurate summation. 'Thanks for letting me know. She'd asked to meet me at the farm tonight so that explains the no-show.'

'She wanted to see you? Do you think she's seen the light and decided to put all the silliness aside?'

'I've no idea and now I'll have to wait even longer to find out. Don't say anything to Chloe or anyone else, though. I got the impression it was all a bit cloak and dagger.'

'My lips are sealed.'

'Thanks, Dad. So, how's your week been?'

'Not so good. We got some shock news at work today.' His voice was strained. 'The Brothers Grim are selling up and I'm going to be out of a job in a fortnight's time.'

'What? How come? I thought they were a few years off retiring.'

'They were but a building contractor made them an offer that was apparently too good to turn down. It's going to be retirement flats.'

'Oh no!' I slumped back against the cushions. 'I'm so sorry. Why only a fortnight's notice?'

'The contractors are pushing to start with the renovations. They'll pay us our full notice so at least that's something.'

'Are there any jobs going at other practices?'

'I haven't had a chance to look yet but I'll get onto it at the weekend. Oh. That's your mum back. I'd better go. Don't worry about me. I'll soon find another job.'

'Okay. Call me over the weekend.'

Poor Dad. It seemed to be one thing after another but a brilliant vet like him would soon find a new practice so I wasn't too concerned.

Looking at my watch, I hesitated. I could go back to Brook Cottage or I could go upstairs and make a start on sorting through Thomas's belongings.

I'd brought some instant hot chocolate and a packet of chocolate biscuits with me – Chloe's favourites – so I made a drink, helped myself to a few biscuits and then grabbed a roll of binbags. I'd tackle the bedroom that Thomas had used as an office first. I suspected that nearly everything would go straight in the bin or recycling but I felt I should sort through it rather than just ditch it, just in case.

* * *

Two hours later, I stretched my arms out, releasing the tension from my back and shoulders. There'd been boxes and files full of paperwork, receipts and bank statements dating back to the sixties. It appeared that Thomas and Gwendoline had been meticulous about keeping records. I found a box file containing information about the history of the farmhouse and old photos. I could easily have spent an hour or so going through them so I put them aside to take back to Brook Cottage. One more box then I'd call it an evening.

Removing the lid of a cardboard box, expecting to find more paperwork, I discovered bundles of letters instead; coloured envelopes in assorted sizes tied together with ribbons. Love letters perhaps? Would it be wrong to read them? But surely it would be just as wrong to throw them out. Replacing the lid, I decided to take them away for further inspection when I had a spare moment.

When I went to retrieve my bag from the lounge, I spotted a text:

✉ From Chloe

Sorry for not coming. Thought baby was on his way but just Braxton-Hicks. Couldn't call you because James would have overheard. I still need to ask you something but not over the phone. James will be out on Wednesday from 7pm. Can you come to me for 7.30?

'James would have overheard... James will be out', I muttered. What was going on? It had to be connected to him if she was being so mysterious about it.

The absence of the word 'please' made me feel like I was being summoned. She'd said sorry for not showing so that was at least something, although I felt the absence of kisses and emojis. It saddened but didn't surprise me that cold, formal texts symbolised our relationship now.

✉ To Chloe

Thanks for letting me know. Braxton-Hicks are very common and it can be difficult to distinguish from actual labour. Yes, I'll see you on Wednesday at 7.30pm. Any clue as to what you want to ask me?

✉ From Chloe
No. I can't go into it now

✉ To Chloe
OK. See you later. Take care x

The timing worked well for me as I could stop by on my way back from Whitby. Dad had put me in contact with Pauline Redcliffe, the owner of Redcliffe Rescue, a centre situated between Whitsborough Bay and Whitby. She took in hedgehogs, foxes, birds, badgers, rabbits and any other wild animals that needed care. I'd arranged to spend the first three days of the half-term break as a volunteer there. She'd even offered me her spare room to save me the ninety-minute commute each way.

I re-read Chloe's texts and sighed. I could have said no, but my curiosity was still piqued. And, of course, what Chloe wants...

On Saturday, Hannah helped me bag up Thomas's and Gwendoline's bedroom; a task I'd been dreading doing on my own. I recognised various items in Thomas's wardrobe and could remember the last time he'd worn them, so I felt quite tearful going through his clothes.

'Wow!' Hannah exclaimed, holding up one of Gwendoline's many fifties prom-style dresses in each hand. 'These dresses are stunning. Was it something like this that Thomas gave you for Christmas?'

I nodded. 'She had good taste, didn't she?'

'Are you going to keep them?'

'Thomas said I could but I don't know. It doesn't feel right. And when would I wear them?'

'I'm sure you'd find an opportunity,' Hannah said. 'But it's up to you. Why don't you hang onto them for now and make a decision later?'

Even harder than sorting through clothes was sorting through their personal possessions. I decided to keep their wedding and engagement rings and a silver bangle with a hedgehog etched onto it but I put the rest of her jewellery aside, unsure whether or not it was valuable. If it was, it might provide valuable funds for the centre down the line. I was sure that's what Gwendoline would have wanted.

* * *

When Hannah left, I finished sorting the office and, on Sunday morning, I started on the storage room. Dad spent Sunday afternoon with me, helping me finish that before moving onto the kitchen. I felt guilty about packing up their life together but I kept reminding myself that it was what Thomas had wanted; he'd specifically said so in his letter.

'Have you had a chance to look for jobs?' I asked Dad during a much-needed coffee break.

'A quick look online but nothing in Whitsborough Bay at the moment. I really need to phone round but there's no immediate panic. I'm getting paid for three months and only have to work for two weeks of that so time is on my side.'

* * *

On Sunday night, Dave and I finalised plans for the interior of the barn and ordered the materials for it. Construction of the mezzanine would likely start on Friday, which was exciting.

I packed, ready for my trip to Whitby. Rich and Dave kept joking about me going on 'work experience' and it actually felt like I was, except this was the most important work experience of my life. I had three days and two nights to lap up as much knowledge as I possibly could because, next time I handled a hedgehog, I'd be the one solely responsible for its wellbeing. Scary thought!

48

'Welcome to Redcliffe Rescue!' Pauline Redcliffe shook my hand vigorously the following morning. A petite woman with a stylish grey pixie crop and bright blue eyes, emphasised by red-framed glasses, she had a warm smile and a gentle, soothing voice.

'Thanks for letting me pick your brains and for letting me stay here.'

'I will *never* turn down assistance so more than happy to make it reciprocal. I'll show you round but, first things first, coffee.'

She led me into a staffroom and busied herself making drinks. 'It's not the busiest time of the year for hedgehogs because it's hibernation season but we've got four autumn juveniles and an injured hog – Elvis – who I'm treating with painkillers and antibiotics at the moment so you'll be able to see what that involves.'

I knew what she meant by autumn juveniles. The summer months saw most births and those hoglets had plenty of time to fatten up ready for hibernation but autumn babies had a fight against time and often ended up in rescue centres over the winter, needing help to gain weight, or sadly didn't make it.

'What happened to Elvis?' I asked.

'He was hibernating but a dog got to him. He has a couple of puncture wounds but they're healing well and he'll be fine.'

'Aw, poor thing. Do you name all the hogs?'

She grinned. 'We name all our animals. We tend to pick a theme and exhaust it and, because we've been open for so long, we're on revisits of old themes. Elvis was the start of our current singers' theme but our autumn juveniles are Fred, Wilma, Barney and Betty.'

'The Flintstones? I love it.'

* * *

The amount of information I absorbed over the next few days was phenomenal. Pauline explained the thinking behind the whole set-up from the size and layout of the 'beds' where the animals stayed to the information gathered on their charts. She shared the things that hadn't quite worked and where she thought there was still room for improvement. There was so much about the practical set-up of the centre that I'd never have even considered.

Her passion for wildlife was obvious and her team of eager volunteers shared the same passion and vision for preserving all species. It was inspiring.

The variety of animals and birds they'd treated over the years was astonishing. The treatment room contained a large whiteboard showing the numbers of successful releases for the year to date and across the centre's lifetime.

'I call it my happy board,' she said. 'Most days are wonderful but we can't save them all. Some come to us too late to help, some seem to be making great progress but rapidly go downhill, and sometimes we have tough decisions to make. If an otherwise healthy hog has lost its legs for whatever reason, it can't survive in the wild and the kindest thing is to say goodbye.' Her voice cracked and her eyes sparkled with tears as she shook her head. 'It affects me every time – even talking about it – but I come in here and I look at those numbers on my happy board and I can't feel sad anymore because we save so many more than we lose.'

I hadn't held a hedgehog since childhood. Holding a partially curled-up Elvis brought back so many forgotten memories and, with them, such a rush of love for those beautiful creatures.

'He likes it when his belly's stroked,' Pauline said. 'He'll unfurl even more if you do that.'

I gently ran my thumb over Elvis's soft belly and, sure enough, he opened out for more attention. 'Oh my gosh. That's amazing.'

Pauline smiled. 'One of the many perks of the job. Who wouldn't love getting to play with animals every day?'

* * *

I was exhausted by the time I said goodbye. The days had been long and physically demanding, especially as some of her patients were very heavy to move around like Whitney the badger who we released into the wild on my second night there. What a special moment that was, watching her sniffing the air before scurrying into the undergrowth.

With all the doom and gloom in the news, it was reassuring to know that there were selfless people out there who cared so much and I felt honoured that Thomas had chosen me to play a part.

My three days at Redcliffe Rescue had been invaluable. The amount of work was a little overwhelming but I kept reminding myself that I would only be taking in hedgehogs so the set-up would be much smaller than Pauline's, and it would start small and grow. I could do it. I was ready. What I wasn't ready for was seeing Chloe again.

49

My heart thumped as I hit the outskirts of Whitsborough Bay twenty minutes later and I felt quite nauseous as I drove towards Chloe and James's house. Pulling up outside, it struck me that the last time I'd been inside was a few days before the wedding. James had been out with Toby and Chloe invited me round for a 'final girly night' before the big day. I didn't do 'girly' but it was what Chloe wanted so I didn't object. We'd tried on our dresses, painted our toenails, applied mudpacks and curled up on the sofa with a bottle of wine. It had been such a lovely evening because I'd spent it with the Chloe I loved: the sweet young woman who could chatter incessantly about nothing in particular yet remain fun and interesting. She was definitely at her best when it was just the two of us and she was relaxed. Unfortunately, the evening ahead of us now was going to be anything but relaxing.

Chloe must have been watching for me because the door opened as soon as I stepped onto the drive. She didn't smile. For a moment, I wasn't sure she was even going to speak but, as I reached the step, she muttered, 'Thanks for coming.'

Smile. Be pleasant. 'You're welcome. I know I'm fifteen minutes early but you said James was going out at seven so I figured he'd have long gone.'

'Yeah, he's out. Come in.' Still hostile. It was going to be a fun evening.

Chloe directed me into the lounge while she made drinks. It looked the same as it had done before the wedding except for a couple of wedding photos in matching silver frames on the shelving unit. I wandered over for a closer look. There was a formal one of them standing under the arch of roses in the church entrance and an informal one of them laughing hysterically next to the cake, both clutching a piece of iced sponge in their hands and wearing an icing splodge on their faces. It saddened me that I'd missed out on that moment. Turning round, I sat down on the sofa and picked up a cushion to cuddle.

'Here,' Chloe said, handing me a mug of tea. She winced and clutched her stomach.

'Are you okay?'

'Stupid Braxton-Hicks again,' she muttered, sitting down on the armchair. We used to always sit on the sofa together. Maybe the chair was more supportive for her bump, though. I needed to stop assuming that everything she did was a slight against me.

'You're sure they're Braxton-Hicks rather than actual labour?' I asked.

'Yes, Nurse Wishaw. I'm sure. I don't need a diagnosis from you, thank you very much.'

I blew on my tea and braved a sip; anything to keep me from looking at Chloe's disgusted expression or opening my mouth and telling her what I thought of her attitude.

'You said you wanted to ask me something?' I prompted. If she was going to be short with me, we might as well get this over with so I could get back to people who did want to spend time in my company.

Chloe nodded. 'Yes. Are you having an affair with my husband?

'What?' I nearly slopped my drink. 'Are you serious?'

'I'm deadly serious.' Her stony expression confirmed it.

'No! What is this obsession with James and me?' I put my mug down and picked up the cushion again. 'No, Chloe, I'm *not* having an affair with him and I'd *never* do that to you. The last time I saw James was at the hospital after Amelia was born and the time before that was your wedding. And, before you ask, I'm not in touch with him via phone, text or email. I cut all ties with him after the wedding.'

Her eyes flicked to my lap where I was crushing the poor cushion. I exhaled and released my grip.

'I believe you,' she said eventually.

'How very noble of you.'

'So, my next question is do you think James was ever unfaithful to you?'

'Of course not. What sort of question is that?'

She stared at me intently. 'What makes you so certain?'

'Because he experienced how horrendous it is when it happens. He swore he'd never treat anyone like that and I believed him.'

'Yeah, well, people sometimes lie to protect themselves.' She raised an eyebrow at me knowingly.

I sighed. 'If we're going to rake over all that again, I might as well go.' I leaned forward to get up.

'No. Sorry. That's not what this is about.'

I bit my lip to stop me asking if she was okay when she winced and clutched her stomach again.

Moments later, she settled back in the chair. 'I'm convinced that James is seeing someone else.'

I widened my eyes, stunned at what I was hearing. He wouldn't. He had such strong views on the subject. 'I can't believe he'd do that,' I said, gently. 'What would make you think it?'

'He's been distant for the past few months. There've been mysterious phone calls and I know he's taken time off work without telling me. One time he got the train to work like normal and came home like normal but he hadn't been to the office because I phoned and they said he was on a day's leave. Then another time he made out he'd been to work but I heard on the radio that the trains had been cancelled.'

'There could be a logical explanation for both of those times.'

'Like what?'

I shrugged. 'I don't know off the top of my head but I'm sure there's something.'

'He's gone completely off...' She paused.

'Off sex?' I suggested.

She nodded. 'I know I look like a whale at the moment—'

'No, you don't. You're pregnant and that's a beautiful thing.'

'Well, I feel like a whale so I'm not exactly in the mood myself and I understand that James might be worried about hurting the baby, even though I know that sex doesn't do that. He flinches if I touch him and he's started getting changed in the en-suite, which is weird. He swears he still loves me and thinks I look beautiful so the only reason I can think of for him avoiding sex with me is because he's getting it elsewhere. And I thought it might be with you.'

'Well, it isn't,' I snapped, furious that she thought so little of me that she'd even contemplate that.

Tears trickled down her cheeks then she gasped and grasped her stomach again. 'Bloody fake contractions. I'm so sick of them.'

'How long have they...?'

She widened her eyes at me again. 'Are you not listening to me? It's Braxton-Hicks.'

I held my hands up in surrender. 'Sorry. Just trying to help.'

'Then focus on the problem in hand. James. Infidelity. It's not you and, as I said, I believe you. But you're absolutely sure he never saw anyone else while you were together? It would have been easy for him, living and working an hour away. You'd never have known.'

'True, but I trusted him. He wasn't the sort. James would never cross that line.'

A sound resembling a humph escaped from her and I got a niggling feeling in the pit of my stomach. 'Is there something you're not telling me?'

'No.' She wouldn't meet my eyes.

'Chloe! What is it?'

She fiddled with the diamond on her engagement ring but still wouldn't look at me. 'James was unfaithful to you.'

My stomach churned and I clung more tightly to the cushion. 'Who with?'

She didn't answer and, considering she'd already hit me with the infidelity blow, there was only one reason she wouldn't tell me who it was with. 'When?' I spat. 'You hadn't even met until Gramps's party.' My breath came short and fast as Chloe's cheeks flushed. 'No way! Was it then?'

'We didn't mean to hurt you,' she cried. 'It just happened.'

'It just happened? That's absolute bull. Having sex with someone else's boyfriend does not *just happen*.'

'It did. We couldn't help ourselves.'

Shaking with rage, I leapt to my feet and grabbed my bag, unable to bear the sight of her.

'Where are you going?'

'Leaving.'

'But I need your advice about James.'

'Well, you're not getting it,' I yelled. 'All my life, I've bent over backwards to give you everything you've wanted. *Everything!*' I started counting the instances on my fingers. 'You wanted my toys, you got them. You wanted my clothes, you got them. You wanted my mother's love, you got it all. Oh, and you wanted my boyfriend and guess what? You got him too. And what did I get? Absolutely nothing. With you, it's always been all take, take, take and absolutely nothing given in return.' I knew I sounded hysterical but I couldn't help it.

'Sammie! Don't. It wasn't like that.'

'It wasn't? Tell me, Chloe, how was it, because as far I can see, what Chloe wants, Chloe gets.'

She shrugged and gave an exasperated squeal. 'Okay, so it was like that but you can't play the complete innocent in all this. You're just as much to blame. You handed everything over without protest so what do you expect? You never once said, "That's my Barbie or my dress or my boyfriend and you can't have it." So don't lump all the blame on me. You were a pushover and always have been so don't act all surprised and hurt when people let that work to their advantage.'

'Manipulative people just like you?'

'I'm *not* manipulative. It's your fault. You're a pushover.'

'I'd rather be a pushover than use people like you do.' I stormed towards the lounge door and yanked it open, hardening myself to her clenching over her stomach again. 'You were meant to be my best friend. We were practically sisters. Yet you had sex with my boyfriend the minute you met him. Who does that?'

'I didn't know you loved him.'

'It shouldn't have made any difference. He was still *my* boyfriend.'

'I know but you said it was just a bit of fun so I figured you'd soon get bored like you always do.'

'When have I done that?'

'You did it with Harry.'

I shook my head at her. 'I didn't get bored or fall out of love with Harry or James. Neither of them ever loved me. They were both biding their time for someone better, which is the story of my life.'

'Because you don't fight for them,' she yelled.

'Why should I? If you have to fight to get someone to stay with you, that's not a relationship worth hanging on to.'

'It's not just men, though. You moan about your relationship with your mum and with Great-Aunt Agnes but have you ever tried to find out why you don't get on or tried to build bridges with either of them?'

I planted my hands on my hips, shaking with rage. 'You know I've tried a million times to make peace with Mum but she barely gives me the time of day. As for Great-Aunt Agnes, I know *exactly* why she hates me and it's pathetic. After what she did at your wedding, that woman is so completely off my radar that I don't care if I never see her again.'

I hoisted my bag onto my shoulder and opened the lounge door, then stopped and turned to face her.

'I've got a question for you, Chloe, and you might as well answer this because, whatever you say, you can't go any further down in my estimation. Between Gramps's birthday and his funeral, were you and James in touch?'

Silence.

'You might as well tell me.'

She sighed. 'Yes.'

'And did you actually see each other?'

'Yes.'

'When?'

'He didn't go to the stag do that weekend. We checked into a B&B on Ocean Ravine.'

Her face was now bright red and beads of sweat were trickling down her forehead but I couldn't bring myself to ask if she was okay again. I felt sick. He'd texted me from the stag do yet he'd been with her. When I'd phoned him on the Sunday, distraught after finding Gramps dead and he'd been all caring and kind, he'd been in bed with my cousin.

'How could you?' I said slowly, bitterness dripping from every word. 'How could you both do that to me? And then you had the audacity to throw me out of your wedding and turn our family on me when, all the time, it was you who was in the wrong.'

'I knew I'd overreacted by throwing you out but I was embarrassed,' she cried. 'I had to do something. Great-Aunt Agnes had created a scene and I was hardly going to hug you and say it was alright, was I?'

'You could have done. Everyone knew James was my boyfriend first so they'd have understood if I still had feelings for him.'

'Yeah, and they'd have all judged me for taking him away from you. It would have been all "Poor Sammie" and "What a bitch that Chloe is". You'd have been the centre of attention and everyone would have hated me. At *my* wedding. I had to do something. And then, when I caught you kissing him, I thought it was karma. I thought you'd worked out that we'd got it together at Gramps's do and you'd decided to get your own back.'

I shook my head. 'That's where we're different. I'd *never* have behaved like that. *Ever.* I'm glad I saw you tonight. Hard as it was to hear, I've finally got something from you – the truth – and, for once, I haven't had to give you anything in return. I could have spent the evening reassuring you that James wasn't being unfaithful but, do you know what, I can't do that because you've just proved that I never knew him. After all his promises and reassurances that he'd never be unfaithful, he cheated on me with you. Maybe now you're getting that karma you just mentioned.'

'I bet you hope I am.'

'No, Chloe, you're mistaking me with you again.' I softened my voice. 'I hope James *isn't* cheating on you, and not just because you have a baby on the way, but because it's horrendous being on the receiving end of infidelity. I wouldn't wish that feeling on anyone. So I hope it turns out to be innocent, and I hope the pair of you live happily ever after, but I also hope you've learned a lesson from this experience about how to treat the people who love you. Good luck with the baby and good luck with sorting things out with James.' I stepped into the hall.

'Don't go!' she screamed.

I poked my head round the door to see her doubled over. 'Why? We've said all we need to say to each other. What possible reason could there be for me to stay any longer?'

She looked up at me, her face sweaty, tears streaming down her cheeks. 'This isn't Braxton-Hicks.'

50

'Help me!' Chloe cried, her face contorted with pain as she clutched onto the arm of the sofa.

'Are you serious? It's not Braxton-Hicks?'

'My waters broke before you got here,' she gasped.

'Chloe! Why didn't you tell me?'

'I was going to but I wanted to ask you about James first.'

She gripped the sofa again and cried out. I wasn't a midwife but I knew enough about childbirth to know that, with contractions so close together, time was not on our side.

'Where's your hospital bag? Is it fully packed?'

'Yes. Nursery.'

I ran upstairs and grabbed a pink sports bag from the doorway of one of the rooms.

'I'll drive you there.'

'No! I can't walk.' The high pitch of her voice verged on hysteria.

'Of course you can. Come on. I'll help you.' I was so livid with her for her revelation and now for putting herself and her baby at risk that it was hard not to sound frustrated.

'No! Baby's coming. Do something!'

'I need to call an ambulance. Don't push.'

'I want to push.' Chloe sank down onto all fours on the rug, breathing heavily.

'Don't. Not yet. I'm going to dial 999 but I'm right here with you. We'll do this together.'

'James!' Chloe cried as I dialled. 'Call James.'

I shook my head at her. 'Ambulance, please,' I said to the emergency operator.

* * *

Clutching Chloe's hand as we blue-lighted it to Whitsborough Bay General in the back of an ambulance was certainly an unexpected turn of events. Fortunately Chloe lived the same side of town as the hospital so it was all very quick.

I tried James's mobile, Auntie Louise's, Uncle Simon's, Mum's and Dad's but they were all on voicemail.

'Who's James out with?' I asked Chloe. 'Do you have a number for them?' But she was sobbing hysterically and either unwilling or unable to answer. All I could do was leave a message on everyone's voicemail and keep trying.

Baby Turner was born by emergency caesarean at 8.37 p.m. He was breech and the cord was wrapped round his neck. If Chloe had given birth naturally, he was unlikely to have survived. She cuddled him to her with one hand and reached out to me with the other. 'You saved him.'

I shrugged. 'All I did was call an ambulance.'

'You spotted he was breech and you stopped me from pushing.' She shook her head. 'After what I'd told you, you'd have had every right to drive off and never see me again.' Tears trickled down her cheeks as she stroked her sleeping son's head then looked back at me. 'I don't know what's wrong with me. I don't know why I keep trying to hurt you.'

'That's not what you do.' Oh my gosh. Was it? I released her hand and pressed my fingers to my lips, taking a few deep breaths. 'Please, Chloe, tell me that you really do love James.'

She looked down at her son again and gently kissed the top of his head. 'I promise you I do love James. I love him so much it actually hurts but I knew you loved him too. Even when you let him go and tried to pretend you didn't care, I knew, but I was lost already and I couldn't have stopped it even if I'd tried which, of course, I didn't. But there have been times when I wanted to hurt you.'

'Why? I thought we were best friends.'

'We were but... I don't know. Everything seemed to be so easy for you. You found school easy and walked out with straight As, you have a great career, you have loads of friends and you're never bothered about how you look or what people think of you. I've found everything a struggle so I took from you whenever I could.'

'You were jealous?' I'd never in a million years have predicted that.

'It was more than that. I wanted to be you. You were always so comfortable with who you are. You were always kind and genuine and people naturally gravitated towards you. I wanted that.'

I smiled wryly. 'And I wanted to be you. Not because of your looks or your boyfriends but because Mum loved you. You could have had everything I owned if I could have had a hug or a few kind words from her. She never—'

The door burst open and James rushed towards the bed. 'Are you okay? I can't believe I missed it.'

'Where the hell have you been?' Chloe snapped.

James didn't answer. His eyes were on the baby boy cradled against Chloe.

'I'll leave you to it,' I muttered.

'You're not leaving?' Chloe asked, urgency in her voice.

'I'll be outside.'

I took a deep lungful of air as I stepped into the waiting room.

'Sam! I wondered if you'd still be here.'

I spun round to see Toby sprawled out on one of the chairs. 'What are you doing here?'

'I came across for drinks with James. He's pretty low because of... er, because of a few problems he's been having at work. Stupid git had his phone on silent. He'd had a few by the time he picked up your message so I said I'd drive him over and hang out for a bit.' He grinned. 'Definitely a boy, then?'

'Definitely.' I sat beside him. 'Mum and baby are doing well.'

'I thought you two weren't speaking. James had no idea you were seeing Chloe tonight.'

I paused for a moment while I found the right words. 'She wanted to ask me a few things so she invited me over for a chat.'

'You're all sorted now, then? Back to how it was before?'

I hesitated. 'It'll never go back to how it was before. Too much has happened.'

'You want a coffee?' he asked after a moment's silence. 'I spotted a machine near the entrance.'

'That would be great, thanks. Make it a strong one.'

'Will do. Back soon.'

I rubbed my tired eyes and rolled my shoulders before taking my phone out my bag to try Auntie Louise and Uncle Simon again. Still no answer and it was pointless leaving another message. Where were they? I tried Dad and Mum but had no answer from them either.

Sitting back on the plastic seat, I closed my eyes for a moment. At least Toby's presence proved one thing: James hadn't been seeing another woman that evening. Could he really be having an affair? What Chloe said about his lack of libido didn't concern me; I'd come across it before during pregnancy. What she said about the days off work were more worrying but that didn't necessarily indicate an affair. Being distant? Avoiding any sort of intimacy? Taking time off work without telling Chloe? Getting changed in the en-suite? It all seemed very familiar. I remembered a very similar conversation with a pregnant patient a couple of years back. I wouldn't have jumped to conclusions if it hadn't been for Toby's expression when he said James had been down, as though he'd been about to reveal something he wasn't meant to. I was 99 per cent certain I knew what was going on and it definitely wasn't another woman. I just hoped the implications weren't as serious.

51

'Has James got testicular cancer?' I asked after Toby handed me a coffee and sat down beside me.

'Erm, no. What would make you think that?'

'Toby Spiers, you're a terrible liar. Hannah always says so.'

He screwed up his nose. 'He swore me to secrecy, even from Hannah. I'm the only one who knows.'

'How serious is it?'

'They reckon they caught it in time to stop any spread but he's lost one of his little fellas.'

I sighed. Poor James. Thank goodness he'd confided in Toby because going through something like that on his own was unthinkable.

Toby grabbed my arm. 'Chloe doesn't know, does she?'

'No. But he's going to need to tell her. She thinks he's having an affair.'

'She never does.' He shook his head. 'James would never even look at another woman if he was in a relationship.'

'Yeah, well, that's what I thought and that's what I told Chloe but apparently it's not true. He was unfaithful to me.'

'What? When?'

'He had sex with Chloe pretty much as soon as they met and spent the weekend with her, even though we were still together.'

Toby's eyes were wide and his mouth open which filled me with relief. He hadn't known which meant Hannah hadn't either although, if she had, I was certain she'd have told me.

'He never said a word.' Toby sighed. 'I knew it was love at first sight for them both but I didn't know they'd acted on it. I'm sorry, Sam. That must hurt.'

'It does. I never thought...' I shook my head. 'Never mind. Going back to the cancer, why didn't he tell Chloe?'

'He found the lump and made an appointment to get it checked out. He was going to tell her but she started bleeding. She was told to avoid stress after that and he couldn't do it to her. He knows how much having a big family means to her and he wasn't prepared to risk anything happening to the baby, especially if it was cancer and he had to lose both balls. I'm not sure how the news is going to go down with Chloe now, though. That big family might not happen.'

I looked at Toby's worried expression. He'd obviously been shouldering a lot of the burden. 'I bet you've been a rock for James during all of this. I'm sure he'll be fine now but please do what you can to push him to tell Chloe about this sooner rather than later because she needs to know and she needs to be there for him. She won't hear it from me.'

Loud voices filled the corridor outside and then the waiting room door burst open. The nurse on duty had to ask for silence and for only Chloe's parents to go in rather than everyone together. Mum clearly wasn't impressed by that.

'I suppose you've already seen him,' she snarled.

'Yes. I was with her when he was born.'

'Why you instead of James? It makes no sense.'

I didn't have the energy to explain. She could have the facts instead. 'He's a healthy baby boy, 6lb 3oz, born at 8.37 p.m. by emergency caesarean because he was breech. His cord was also round his neck. Chloe's tired but fine. James is with her now. He was out with

Toby and hadn't realised his phone was on silent otherwise he'd have been there for the birth.'

Mum's expression softened, but then she ruined it by saying, 'That still doesn't explain why you're here.'

'It wasn't meant to.'

'Can I get anyone a coffee?' Toby asked, jumping up, no doubt desperate to escape from the tense atmosphere.

Mum shook her head and Dad thanked him but declined.

'I'll just phone Hannah, then,' Toby said. 'Check on Amelia.' If he could have turned and sprinted, I think he would have.

'Are you okay, poppet?' Dad asked, sitting beside me.

'Of course she is. She hasn't just been under the knife like our poor Chloe.'

'Debs! There's no need to—'

'Forget it, Dad.' I stood up and faced Mum. 'You know *nothing* about me or what I've been through this evening so you can keep your unhelpful comments to yourself.'

She looked too astonished at me standing up to her to respond.

The door to Chloe's room opened and Uncle Simon poked his head round it. 'Can we borrow you for a moment, Sam?' He looked across to the nurse. 'Is that okay? We promise to be quick.'

The nurse smiled. 'Very quick, please.'

Feeling Mum's eyes boring into me, I followed Uncle Simon back into the room. James was sitting on the bed next to Chloe, holding the baby. It was a scene that could have floored me, wishing it was our baby he was cradling, yet I felt nothing. If there'd been even a fraction of doubt as to whether I was over him, it evaporated.

Auntie Louise was in a chair beside the bed. She stood up and rushed to me, arms outstretched. 'Chloe says you saved his life.'

'Not really. If Chloe had been alone, she'd have called an ambulance.'

'You're too modest,' she said, releasing me.

Uncle Simon hugged me too and simply whispered, 'Thank you.'

James gave a grateful smile, his eyes glistening.

'Toby's still outside,' I said. 'He sends his best.'

Standing near the foot of the bed, I felt uncomfortable encroaching on this precious family moment, especially when I didn't feel part of the family. Couldn't someone just tell me why I'd been summoned? Maybe it was just to say thank you. Well, they'd done that, or at least Chloe's parents had.

'Was that it? Because I might head back home now that everyone's here.'

'Do you want to hold Samuel William?' Chloe asked.

I was very aware of them all staring at me as I repeated the name. 'Samuel?'

She nodded. 'Samuel as a nod to the woman who has always been there for me even though I've not deserved it and who even saved his life, and William after Gramps, of course. But we'll call him Sam for short. What do you think?'

I opened my mouth but no words came out. Gramps would have loved the tribute to him. As for the tribute to me – another thing I'd never have predicted. The evening just got stranger and stranger.

'Here.' James stood up and handed his son to me.

As I stroked Samuel's soft head, he opened his eyes for a moment and peeped at me, then smacked his lips and drifted off again. I cuddled him close, willing the tears clouding my eyes not to fall because I feared that, if I let them, they'd never stop. It had been a difficult evening, revealing hurtful secrets but, gazing into Samuel's beautiful face, the pain lifted. This new life was a new beginning for Chloe and James and, because of James's cancer, Samuel could be their first and last child, which would be an unexpected and devastating change of plan for them both. Whatever happened, they had Samuel and what a precious gift he was.

I looked up at the eager faces of the two new parents. 'He's gorgeous and I'm honoured that you've sort of named him after me. Thank you.' They both nodded. 'So, who gets the next cuddles because I really must make tracks now or I'll fall asleep at the wheel?'

'Couldn't you stay with your mum?' Auntie Louise asked.

I shook my head as I handed Samuel to Uncle Simon. 'We both know I'm not welcome.' I didn't manage to keep the bitterness out of my voice.

'You'll come back and visit soon, won't you?' Chloe asked.

'Give me a shout when you're home and settled and we'll sort something out.'

I gave out hugs then returned to the waiting room. Toby had returned from his wander and was staring into an empty cup.

The door to Chloe's room opened again. 'Toby, do you want to come in and meet Samuel?' James asked.

Mum gasped. 'Samuel? Like Samantha?'

James nodded. 'Yes. Named after her.'

It was hard not to smirk. She certainly hadn't seen that coming and she definitely didn't like it.

'That's so lovely,' Dad said, smiling.

'Are you sure I'm okay to go next?' Toby asked, nodding towards my parents.

'It's fine, mate,' James said. 'I know you need to get home and Chloe says Sam's car's at our place so I thought you could see the baby then drop her off.'

'I can get a taxi,' I said.

'No. Chloe's insistent. Toby next so you can both head home, then she's keen for her final visitors to meet Samuel.'

Without a word, Mum plonked herself down in Toby's vacated seat and seemed very interested in scraping something invisible from her nails.

I didn't have the energy or the inclination to try and engage with her. 'I could do with some air. Toby, I'll meet you in the entrance.'

Toby nodded and went in to see the new arrival.

Retrieving my bag from under the seats, I hugged Dad who said he'd call me tomorrow.

James followed me into the corridor and we walked several paces in uncomfortable silence.

I stopped and turned to him. 'I know what happened at Gramps's party.'

He gasped. 'Chloe told you?'

Feeling weary, I rested my back against the corridor wall. 'It's been quite a revealing evening.'

'I'm so sorry. We never meant it to happen.'

I wasn't going to say it was fine because it wasn't, but I wasn't going to rake over it again. 'You promised me you'd let me know if you met someone. If I hadn't ended it with you after the funeral, were you going to have the decency to end it with me?'

He sighed as he rested against the wall beside me. 'We had plans to meet for dinner on the Tuesday. I was going to tell you then but your Gramps died on the Sunday and...'

'Yeah, I know. Timing.'

'I'm so sorry. I hated myself for what we did. It's not who I am.'

I lightly touched his arm. 'I know.'

'You didn't get very far,' Toby said, joining us in the corridor. 'Ah. I can guess what you're talking about. I didn't tell her about the cancer, mate.'

James shot upright. 'She knows?'

I cringed. 'We weren't talking about that, Toby. But, yes, I know. Are you okay, James?'

'Yes, but how do you know?'

'Long story and you need to get back to your family but you've got to tell Chloe and soon,' I urged.

'I agree,' Toby said. 'Not tonight, obviously, but she needs to know.'

'What if I can't have any more kids?' James sounded devastated.

'Then you'll cross that bridge together,' I said. 'And let's face it, she's just been cut open and had a person lifted out of her after a difficult pregnancy, so she's not going to be thinking of having another baby right now. It's as good a time as any to talk about it.'

James nodded. 'Thank you for everything. You really are one in a million.'

As he hugged me, I was very much aware once more of having no reaction. No heart racing, no butterflies, no sweaty palms.

'Go back to your family. They need you and they need the truth. Always.'

* * *

As for me, I thought about my conversation with Lauren on my first day when I told her about the wedding: 'Shit happens and it's how you deal with it that makes you happy or miserable. You can roll in that shit and stink up your life or you can spray the air freshener and move on. I think you're an air freshener kind of woman, aren't you?' Yes, I was an air freshener kind of woman. It sucked that James never loved me but I had no control over that. It hurt that the woman he fell for was my cousin but I'd done what I could to control that; I'd let him go. The fact that they'd had sex as soon as they met was perhaps testament to how they felt about each other. What must it be like to be attracted to someone so strongly that you just had to have them there and then? I'd never experienced anything close to that, yet I wanted to believe that one day in the far future when I felt ready to trust again, I would find someone who made me feel that way. As for Chloe and James, I certainly couldn't forget what they'd done and how Chloe had continued to punish me for her crime. Could I forgive? I wasn't so sure. It was a huge ask. But for now, there was a new life to celebrate.

52

Dad phoned on Sunday morning and asked if he could come over to take me out for lunch at The Black Swan.

'I have something to tell you and I didn't want to do it over the phone,' he said as we sat down with our drinks. 'Your mum and I are getting divorced.'

Even though I'd expected it to happen, hearing those words still shocked me. 'I'm so sorry. Are you okay?' He looked exhausted with several days' growth on his face and dark circles beneath his eyes.

He ran his fingers through his hair. 'I will be. I know it's for the best for us both but it feels a bit alien at the moment.' He shrugged.

'Why now? You've been unhappy for ages but didn't seem to want to take that final step.'

'How she was with you at the hospital last week was awful to see. She was so nasty to you.'

'True, but she's always been like that.'

Dad's shoulders slumped. 'I know. I sat in that waiting room trying to think of the last time I'd seen her be nice to you and I couldn't think of a single occasion. Never a kind word. Never a compliment. Always attacking. Always angry. I tried to think of the last time she'd been pleasant to me and there was nothing either. At that moment, I knew I couldn't do it anymore. I couldn't stay married to her. Then I got so mad with myself for not doing something sooner. I shouldn't have let you go through all that.'

'You can't blame yourself, Dad. And you can't say you didn't try because you did. So many times. She just didn't want to change.'

Dad nodded, his eyes full of sadness. 'Thanks, poppet. Anyway, I needed to calm down before I confronted her and it took me till yesterday for that to happen, otherwise I'd have slapped her with a divorce in the hospital car park that very night.'

'How did she take it?'

'Surprisingly well. We're selling the house. Too many memories. They're building another small development near Chloe's so we looked round it yesterday and your mum's picked one.'

'Oh my gosh! That was quick.'

'We've both known it was over for a long time so I think it was a relief that someone finally said it aloud. I've moved into your old room for the moment and we'll both instruct solicitors tomorrow.'

'To new beginnings?' I suggested, raising my glass.

'New beginnings,' Dad said, clinking his glass against mine.

He'd finally done it and I felt relieved for him but also sad. He'd tried so hard to make their marriage work but how can you when one party no longer cares?

As we ate our meal, an idea popped into my head. If Dad had no marriage and no job to keep him in Whitsborough Bay, did he need to stay there?

'Why don't you take some time out and help me set up Hedgehog Hollow?' I asked after our plates had been cleared away. 'You could live at the farm with me and we could get it off the ground together. It would buy you some time to look for a new practice or even set up your own.'

'You mean that?' he asked.

'Of course. I'd love your help but it's completely up to you. No obligation and no rush to make a decision.'

There was silence for a moment but I could tell from the sparkle in his eyes that it wasn't because he was trying to find a way to politely say no.

'I like that idea,' he said eventually, enthusiasm in his voice. 'I need to think it through properly, but I like that idea a lot. Stops me panicking and rushing into the first job that comes along.'

'More new beginnings?' I suggested, raising my glass. 'Or the possibility of them?'

Dad smiled and clinked his glass against mine. 'To Hedgehog Hollow.'

53

Chloe and I had exchanged a few texts since Samuel's birth but we hadn't spoken. I justified to myself that I hadn't phoned her because I didn't want to catch her sleeping or feeding, but I knew it was really because I wanted to avoid an awkward, stilted conversation. I was invited over on Wednesday evening and felt anxious as I drove across after work.

Turning up with a bag full of gifts for Samuel proved to be the perfect ice-breaker. I got to cuddle him while Chloe unwrapped each item and cooed over it. After that, it was the expected conversation with new parents about sleeping and feeding and how it felt to have a baby completely change life as they knew it.

As soon as James left the room to change Samuel's nappy, I knew the conversation was going to take a serious turn.

'I know about the cancer,' Chloe said. 'I feel really stupid for thinking he was seeing someone else, especially you. You wouldn't do that to me. You're too nice. You wouldn't do that to anyone.'

I shrugged. 'I'd like to think not, but nobody knows how they'll react to anything until they're in that situation.'

'I'm sorry I called you a pushover.'

'I'm sorry I called you manipulative.' She had been but I was sorry

I'd yelled it in anger. I'd been thinking a lot about her accusation and she was half-right. I had strong opinions on what was right and wrong and, in a work environment, I voiced them all the time. When it came to family, I did what I could to make everyone happy and keep the peace, like I'd done all my life. Like I'd had to in order to get any sort of attention from Mum. Giving my belongings to Chloe seemed to make Mum happy so that became habit and I learned that the part that hurt was not losing my belongings; it was that the brief smile that lit Mum's face would soon fade and I'd be ignored or resented once more. But it was worth it for that ever so brief moment when I could pretend she cared about me.

James reappeared and handed Samuel back to me then excused himself saying he needed to do some paperwork.

'Do you think we'll get back to how it was before?' Chloe asked when the door closed.

Oh gosh. What a question. I stroked Samuel's tiny hand, trying to find the right words.

'I'll take that as a no, then,' she said.

'No, it's not a no, but it's not a yes either. So much has happened. We've both said and done some things that can't be unsaid or undone...'

'*I've* said and done some things, you mean.'

I shook my head. 'Not just you. I gave you a mouthful last week.'

'Nothing I didn't deserve and I gave as good as I got.'

'Fair point.' I adjusted Samuel's position. 'We can't change the past and we can't pretend our relationship isn't affected by it. For me, the big issue isn't that you and James did the dirty before our relationship ended. I'd be lying if I said that didn't hurt but it is what it is. What I'm struggling with more is the fall-out from what happened at your wedding. You turned on me in front of our family and you turned everyone against me, making out that I'd done something unforgivable when it was you who was in the wrong. I've been ostracised for the past six months, Chloe. I spent my first ever Christmas without my family thanks to you. As it happens, I wouldn't change that because it was my final day with Thomas, but I shouldn't have been pushed away like that. I *do* want to find a way to move forward, but do you see how it can never be how it was before?'

Chloe nodded. 'I really messed up, didn't I?'

'You did what you thought was right at the time.'

'But that's just the thing. I knew what I was doing was wrong – with James, with the wedding, with cutting you off – yet I did it anyway.'

'That's because you're impulsive and you're used to having your own way.' I said it in a gentle voice so she knew I wasn't lecturing her. 'I know I haven't helped with that and neither has my mum or your parents, but you're an adult now with a child of your own. It's time to make decisions about the sort of person you want this little one to become because a lot of his behaviours will be learned from you and James.'

I swear I could see the lightbulb going on in Chloe's mind. 'I hear you. You know what? Gramps was right about you and me.'

'In what way?'

'I used to roll my eyes when he spouted yet another quote. He used to say to me, "Be kind whenever possible. It is always possible." It was apparently something the Dalai Lama said.' She gave me a weak smile. 'He said that, if I wanted to know what it meant, I only needed to look at you.'

'Gramps really said that about me?'

'You were his favourite and don't try to deny it.'

'Perhaps, but who's Great-Aunt Agnes's favourite?' I winked at Chloe and we both started giggling and the more we giggled, the more the hurt slipped away.

When we said goodbye a little later, it felt as though we'd reached a new understanding. We'd return to being a family but our friendship would never be quite the same because that trust was gone. But if we could draw a line in the sand and tentatively move forward, rebuilding the trust gradually, that was fine by me.

54

'Why so glum?' Lauren asked, striding across the department office towards the printer during Friday's afternoon break.

'Rich has to work tonight so I've lost my plus one for your party.' When Lauren had asked me, in my first week at the TEC, to put her fiftieth birthday party in my diary, it had seemed so far away. Now it was here and I was dreading it, especially now that Rich couldn't make it.

Lauren grabbed her papers from the printer then perched on my desk. 'It's not too late for me to set you up with a hot date.'

'Oh my goodness, do you ever let up?'

'I told you. I'm done with men so I need to date vicariously.'

'And I'm done with men too. Not necessarily forever but certainly for the foreseeable future.'

'You're such a spoilsport. Won't you let me matchmake for you just this one time? Call it my birthday gift.'

'Stop it!'

She laughed. 'Can't blame a woman for trying. Right, I'm done for the day. I've got to go and put myself through the humiliating ritual of hair and nails courtesy of my darling twin sister. Apparently, jeans and wellies aren't acceptable tonight either.'

'What are you wearing?'

'A dress and heels. Heels, I tell you. I suggest you have a good gawp and take photos because it's a once in a lifetime never to be seen again moment and I might have to be very drunk to get through the ordeal.'

'Any excuse...'

She laughed. 'I can't believe I let her talk me into this. Must have been half asleep or very hormonal that day.'

Five minutes later, she'd gone and I was all alone in the office. I was in awe of Lauren. She was so funny and down to earth. I valued her opinion and, although I probably wouldn't admit it to her in case I offended her, I saw her as a mother figure in my life. How different might my life have been if my mum had been more like Lauren? I sighed and shook my head. It was pointless pondering on what ifs. Dad had more than made up for the absence of a caring mother and I'd be eternally grateful for that.

* * *

I showered after work and stood in my bedroom at Brook Cottage with a towel wrapped round me, hair dripping onto my shoulders, scowling at the top I'd planned to wear with my smartest jeans for Lauren's party. There was a greasy stain on it which hadn't come out in the wash. I twisted it left and right. It wasn't massively noticeable but I'd not be able to relax knowing it was there.

What to wear? My eyes rested on Gwendoline's dresses, still in their bags from the dry cleaner. I unzipped the one containing the dress Thomas had given me at Christmas and stroked my fingers down the black net. Dare I? He'd said to wear it for a special occasion and this was the closest thing I'd come to that all year.

I applied my make-up a little heavier than usual. After drying my hair, I pulled it into a loose messy bun on the top of my head, securing it with a sparkly clip, then releasing a couple of tendrils at each side.

Pulling on the dress, I looked in the mirror and barely recognised myself. Was it too much? I hoped not. I added a black shrug cardigan and a pair of black ballet pumps because I didn't actually own a pair of heels.

* * *

The taxi driver pulled up outside Aversford Manor and I closed my eyes for a moment. Of all the hotels she could have chosen, why did Lauren have to be having her party at the same venue as the wedding? She'd apologised for it as soon as she gave me my invite and I said it didn't matter but, now that I was here, the bad memories were flooding back. It was just as well Chloe and I had talked and agreed to move forward or I might have instructed the driver to turn round and take me straight back home.

'You alright, love?' he asked.

'Sorry. Just thinking. How much did you say?'

'£8.70, please.'

I handed him a tenner and exited the car, smoothing down my dress.

I'd deliberately arrived half an hour late which didn't sit comfortably with my desire to be punctual but it was that or sit on my own nursing a glass of wine if my colleagues arrived after me, and I didn't relish the thought of doing that. I was really worried about them as it was. We spent so much time in lessons that, despite me being at the TEC for six months now, my relationship with most of the department didn't extend beyond exchanging pleasantries. It would be fine. And if it wasn't, I could smile for an hour or so then make my excuses. The main thing was putting in an appearance.

As I made my way towards the Arundel Room – the same room where Chloe's evening do had taken place – I half expected to be confronted by Great-Aunt Agnes and a furious Chloe, but the coast was clear. Standing in the entrance of the room, my eyes adjusting to the darkness punctuated by flashing lights, it struck me that I hadn't actually made it as far as the function room that night. It was a large room with a parquet dance floor, round tables and chairs up each side, a bar at the far end, and a laden buffet table near the entrance.

I didn't recognise anyone at first and had to fight the flight urge. Then I spotted Lauren at the far end. She looked so different with her hair curled and, as promised, wearing a dress and heels. She looked up and waved me over when the woman she was talking to wandered away.

'Wow! You look incredible,' I said, giving her a kiss on each cheek.

'I feel ridiculous.'

'Well, you don't look it.'

'Apparently I have to do this.' Lauren picked up the edges of her dress and stomped round in a circle.

'Despite the clumpy ballerina moves, you still look incredible.'

'You're too kind. Let's look at you.' She stepped back and I felt obligated to do a twirl too, feeling pretty ridiculous myself.

'That dress is gorgeous. Is it vintage?'

'I think so. It was one of Gwendoline's.'

'That style really suits you. You should wear dresses more often.'

'Ditto. And I love your hair too.'

'You watch me later. It'll be scraped back into a ponytail and I'll have kicked my shoes off and probably ripped my dress.'

The woman she'd been talking to when I arrived reappeared and handed her a drink. 'Let me introduce you to my sister,' Lauren said. 'This is Connie.'

Even though I knew they were non-identical twins, the differences were only subtle. 'Happy birthday,' I said, smiling at her.

'Thank you.'

'And this is my newest star tutor, Sam.'

'Ah! I've heard a lot about you,' Connie said. 'I've been looking forward to meeting you.'

'Thank you. I've heard good things about you too.'

'Except this afternoon when I was slagging you off for making me do girly things and wear a dress,' Lauren added. 'I bet your ears were burning then.'

'They're always burning,' Connie said, laughing.

'Ooh, I've got to say hello to my neighbours,' Lauren said. 'Some of the team are over there, hiding behind that pillar if you want to grab a drink and join them.'

'Thanks. I'll do that.'

'Nice to meet you,' Connie said, patting my arm then heading off to greet someone else.

I looked over to where my colleagues were sitting with their partners. They'd pulled their chairs close together and were laughing over something and I had another rare attack of nerves. What if I wandered over, said hello, and they smiled politely then resumed their conversations? Argh! Maybe I could have a couple of drinks first – a bit of courage juice.

Unfortunately there appeared to be nobody serving at the bar but, if I loitered long enough, surely somebody would materialise. I hoisted my backside onto a bar stool, preparing for a wait.

'Lost any fights with hoses recently?' said a voice.

I snapped my head round to face Jeep Prat. Great. 'What are you doing here?'

'Charming. I was passing and I heard the dulcet tones of the "Cha Cha Slide" and felt compelled to stop and strut my stuff.'

'Don't let me stop you.'

'I won't. But the "Cha Cha Slide" is thirsty work so I need a pint.'

'You'll be lucky. I've been waiting ages and there's no sign of anyone.'

'Looks like I'll have to help myself, then.' Before I could say anything, he made his way behind the bar, grabbed a glass, and started pulling himself a pint. 'What can I get you?'

'You can't do that,' I cried. 'It's not self-service, you know.'

'Isn't it? Oh well, I'll leave some money. Do you think a quid will do it?'

I couldn't decide whether he was joking or not.

'Pint? Half? Gin and tonic? Wine?'

'Large dry white wine, please,' I muttered.

'Coming right up.' He left his pint on the bar to settle and poured me a measure of wine. 'This is my favourite of the dry whites,' he said. 'Fresh and citrusy. Enjoy.'

I took a sip. It was delicious. 'Thank you.' I took my purse out of my clutch and frowned. 'How do I pay? I've only got a twenty-pound note.'

'Coincidentally, a large white wine is exactly twenty pounds.' He smiled and his eyes twinkled. He was definitely joking this time.

'Hilarious.'

'Forget it. The drink's on me. And before you panic, I *will* settle up later and I *am* meant to be serving for the moment. My best mate's the bar manager and a couple of staff failed to show. I worked here when I was younger so I offered to help until reinforcements arrive.'

To the rescue again? Maybe he wasn't as bad as my first few encounters with him would suggest. 'Hope you aren't trapped behind the bar for too long. Well, thanks...' I slipped off the stool and reached for my clutch and drink.

'Wait. Are you in a rush to get back to someone?'

Not at all. I glanced across at my colleagues, still deep in conversation, then turned back to Jeep Prat and shrugged. 'No. I don't know anyone well except one of the birthday girls. I was meant to be bringing a friend but they had to work.'

'Perfect. Well, not perfect that your friend bailed on you, obviously, but perfect because you can keep me company.'

'And why would I want to do that?'

'Because I feel like we got off on a bad foot and the next couple of encounters weren't the most successful either. I'm not the person you probably think I am.'

I fixed him with a hard stare. 'Oh yeah? And what sort of person is that?'

He bit his lip and wrinkled his forehead. 'I'm guessing grumpy, rude, aggressive and a bad driver?'

'Pretty much. That's impressive self-awareness.' I mentally kicked myself. What was it about him that brought out a feisty side in me? And, let's be fair, I hadn't exactly endeared myself to him, had I? I'd shouted at him and I'd lectured him. His assessment of me was likely to be equally as negative as mine of him and I wasn't in the mood for hearing it.

'Sit down. Please,' he said. 'We're practically neighbours and we're bound to keep running into each other so I think it would be good to start over. Don't you?'

I shrugged again.

'How's things going at the farm?'

I put my clutch and drink back on the bar. While I didn't particularly relish time in his company, small talk with him was better than being on my own. And he was being surprisingly pleasant this evening. I heaved myself back onto the stool. 'It's going well but it'll be a while before we're ready for any hedgehogs.'

'And you secured which vet practice?'

My cheeks burned as I took a gulp of my wine. He likely knew all the vets in the area and I suspected he knew I hadn't spoken to any of them. Might as well be honest about it. 'None. I shouldn't have lied. But my dad's a vet and his practice has just closed. He and my mum are getting a divorce, not a moment too soon, so he's going to help out initially which will be amazingly helpful because I work full-time.' Where had all that information come from? That was certainly more than small talk.

'I need to get this customer a drink... hang on. What can I get you, Lesley?'

'A pint of lager and a diet coke please, Josh,' said the woman who'd appeared at the bar.

Josh. So that was his name. At least I could stop calling him Jeep Prat or Mr Alderson Junior. Or my imaginary boyfriend, Chris. I blushed as I thought about that conversation with my family.

He served Lesley, telling her to pop back and settle up later, then scribbled her name and an amount on a pad that he whipped out from under the bar. 'Where were we? Your dad. You say he's a vet?'

'Yes but the owners of his practice have sold it to a property developer so he's out of work as of today but he's really upbeat about it. It's perfect timing, really. Not that losing a job is ever good timing but it's good for the setting up of the centre.' *Wow! Verbal diarrhoea!*

'Sorry. Customer.' Josh moved to the end of the bar again and served up several drinks.

I watched him, sipping on my wine. He seemed to know everyone and I realised I hadn't found out how he knew Lauren although he hadn't asked me how I knew her either. Must find out. I glanced down at my empty glass. How had I finished it already? My head already felt fuzzy – the downside of drinking on an empty stomach – and it had certainly loosened my tongue.

Josh topped up my glass.

'You'd better add me to your list and let me get one for you too,' I said.

'It's fine. It's on me. And thanks but no thanks. I'm driving later so it's just the one for me. So, is your dad a good vet?'

'He's brilliant. I know I might seem biased because he's my dad but the practice would probably have folded years ago if it wasn't for him. The customers loved him, the animals loved him and the staff loved him. They're all out for goodbye drinks right now.' I paused and smiled at Josh. 'Although I'm not sure the animals will be allowed in the pub. There's this one Alsatian who does Elvis impressions when he's drunk and his party trick is to pee at the bullseye on the dartboard. It ricochets everywhere so he's been barred.'

Josh laughed. 'That's funny. I wish it was true.'

'Who says it isn't?'

He laughed again and I frowned, struggling to reconcile this person with the haughty individual I'd met before.

'So, tell me about the hedgehogs,' Josh said, picking up a cloth and wiping the bar.

'What do you want to know?'

He shrugged. 'Anything you want to tell me.'

For the next twenty minutes or so, in-between Josh serving drinks, I told him about how I'd found Thomas collapsed, how we became friends, and Thomas's final wishes for me to fulfil their dream.

'I love that story.' He looked genuinely impressed. 'That's such an amazing thing to do for them.'

'I only hope I can do it justice.'

'I'm sure you'll do them proud. I was thinking about—'

'Joshy-boy!' A man in his early twenties stepped behind the bar, interrupting him. They did a weird fist-bump man-hug kind of thing. 'Our lad said you'd stepped in. You legend.'

'No worries. Happy to help.'

The new arrival glanced up at me. 'Sorry. Were you waiting to be served?'

I smiled politely. 'I'm fine thanks. Josh has been looking after me.' I wasn't sure why I said it like that, although it was true. He'd managed to eradicate my anxieties about being back at Aversford Manor.

Zoning out while Josh brought his friend up to speed, I turned to survey the party. Lauren was standing near the entrance, talking to a small group of guests, arms gesticulating wildly, no doubt spilling her drink everywhere. My colleagues were lined up along the buffet and my stomach clenched. When had I become so anti-social? I could have at least said hello to them. It wasn't their fault that they knew each other well and I was the newbie. They'd never made me feel unwelcome and tonight would actually be the ideal opportunity to get to know them.

'So, how do you know our hosts?'

I jumped at the sound of Josh's voice. I hadn't even registered that he'd finished his conversation and moved round to my side of the bar. As he sat down on the stool beside mine, his leg touched mine and I felt butterflies take flight in my stomach. *Oh-oh. What was that?*

'Are you okay?' Josh asked, looking concerned. 'You look a bit flushed.'

My heart was racing and I knew my cheeks were on fire. *Stop it! I might no longer dislike Josh but I certainly don't fancy him. It's just being in close proximity to a man for the first time since James.* 'I'm fine. I don't drink very often so it's gone straight to my cheeks.'

He smiled and I was drawn to his eyes again. I'd never known anyone have such twinkly eyes each time they smiled, as though the very act of smiling gave power to a string of fairy lights in his irises. *Good grief. Stop it right now!*

'Same here,' he said. 'I'm on call so often, especially after... erm... after one of our vets left unexpectedly, so I rarely get the chance to drink. In fact...' He turned to the lad behind the bar and handed over his half-drunk pint. 'Can you top me up with lemonade?' He turned back to me. 'Where were we? Oh yeah, how do you know—?'

'Ah, there you are, Josh. I thought you must be running late but your mum said you were helping behind the bar.'

'Staffing crisis,' he answered, slipping off the stool and giving my boss a hug. 'Happy birthday, Auntie Lauren.'

Auntie Lauren? Auntie? Seriously? That had to make Josh the 'damaged' nephew she'd mentioned on my first day. Wow! I hadn't seen that one coming.

'Sam!' She rested her hand on my shoulder. 'I was hoping to introduce you to my fabulous nephew tonight and it seems you've already found each other without my intervention.' I could smell the alcohol on her breath as she spoke. She hadn't been lying when she'd said she'd need to be drunk tonight. Her speech was slurred and loud. 'And sitting so cosy together. I knew you two would be perfect for each other. Didn't I say that to you, Sam? I said you two would be perfect together.'

The twinkle vanished from Josh's eyes and was replaced with... I wasn't sure what it was. Sadness? Hurt? Maybe I was just thinking that because she'd told me he was 'damaged' and I could feel empathy for that. Oh my gosh, what if it was me? I was all dressed up but what if my heavier make-up made me look like a clown or a drag queen?

What if it did nothing to hide how plain I was and the thought of me being perfect for him was laughable?

'Auntie Lauren! We're only talking and we could hardly do that if we were at opposite ends of the bar. That's the only reason we're sat so close.' Ouch. It *was* me.

'And talking can lead to—'

'You don't seem to have a drink. Can I get you one?' he asked, his jaw clenched.

Lauren's smile faltered for a moment. Poor woman. She was known for saying what she thought but she was usually much more sensitive about it. A few – make that several – birthday drinks had clearly numbed her filter and she'd probably just realised it. 'I've got three or four already linked up round the room but thank you. You're a good lad.' She smiled again. 'Did Sam tell you that we work together?'

'We were just about to have that conversation when you appeared,' I said.

Lauren squeezed Josh's arm. 'And did she tell you she's setting up a hedgehog rescue centre? You might be able to help her.' She nodded at me. 'He's a vet, you know.'

Josh smiled again but there was no twinkle in his eyes this time. 'Yes, Auntie Lauren, I know all about the hedgehogs and Sam knows I'm a vet.'

She clapped her hands together and grinned at us. 'Then my work here has already been done. You two kids enjoy yourself and don't forget to eat. Connie and I paid a fortune for that buffet and nobody's allowed to leave until it's all gone.'

Everything would probably have been fine and we could have laughed it off if she'd left it there but she had to take it further. She grabbed one of my hands and one of Josh's and squeezed. 'You look adorable together, you know. I can't tell you how much it warmed my heart to see you laughing earlier. I have such a good feeling about you two. Two troubled souls united at my birthday. The perfect birthday gift.' With a giggle, she let go and walked away.

Silence.

Ground swallow me up. Now. 'I might just...' I started.

'I think I'll...' he said at the same time.

We both stopped.

'You first,' Josh said.

'I was going to say I might just visit the ladies.'

'Yeah. Good. And I need to say hello to a few people.'

I glugged down my last few mouthfuls of wine, grabbed my clutch and slipped off the stool. 'Enjoy the rest of the party.'

'Yeah. You too. See you around.' His voice sounded light but the lack of smile and his stiff stance suggested discomfort.

In the ladies' toilets a few minutes later, I rested my hands on the sink unit and took deep breaths. Lauren meant well but that had been beyond awkward. It was abundantly clear that Josh wasn't interested in me and probably anyone else for that matter. And it was mutual. Yes, we'd laughed and perhaps even flirted a little but all that had done was move him out of the enemy camp. There'd been a moment of butterflies but I could put that down to the touch of a man's leg against mine. It had been a long time and it had stirred memories of being with James which, considering where I was, were rife again.

A toilet flushed then one of the cubicle doors behind me opened and one of my colleagues, Angie, stepped out. 'There you are! Lauren told us you were here but we couldn't see you.'

'I got chatting to someone at the bar,' I said, washing my hands.

'Are you free to join us now?' she asked. 'Lauren told us your friend couldn't make it so we were worried about you being on your own.'

'Yeah, he had to work. Joining you would be great, if you don't mind.'

'Of course not.'

We left the ladies together a few minutes later but, as grateful as I was to Angie for her kindness, I'd rather have called a taxi and headed home.

When we stepped back into The Arundel Room, there was no sign of Josh. Had he taken the opportunity to escape from Lauren's matchmaking? From me? My shoulders slumped at that thought. Was I really that bad a prospect? My track record with men and the look on his face would suggest I was. I looked down at Gwendoline's dress, my heart sinking. What had I been thinking? As I'd said to Thomas when he'd given me it, I couldn't pull off a stunning dress like that, and clearly Josh thought so too.

55

I tried so hard to enjoy the party; I really did. My colleagues couldn't have done more to make me feel like I was part of their group and very welcome to be there. I smiled and laughed and chatted but, the whole time, my throat felt tight and my eyes burned as I fought back an overwhelming urge to curl into a ball and sob. Mutton dressed as lamb; that's how I felt.

They were up and down to the dance floor and kept asking me to join them but I really wasn't in the mood. No way did I want to parade myself in front of everyone so they could all see I'd tried too hard. Angie had pulled a muscle in her calf and wasn't dancing and the men were propping up the bar so keeping her company gave me a good excuse not to dance.

Another couple of glasses of wine did nothing to relax me. If anything, it made me feel more tearful. Some food might help, but I'd left it too late to visit the buffet. *What a pity party!*

Josh had reappeared about half an hour after I joined my colleagues and I was aware of him working the room, but he never came close to our table.

Shortly after ten, I'd reached saturation point and had to get out of there. I bid goodnight to my colleagues and thanked them for entertaining me, then said goodbye to Lauren and thanked her for a lovely party. She nearly knocked me over as she lunged at me for a hug.

'Thank you for coming. I know how crap it can be when you don't know many people.'

'It was fine,' I said, when she let go, staggering a bit. I noticed she'd kicked off her heels, as predicted. 'It's been nice spending time with the team.'

'And with my nephew, Josh.' She wagged her finger and looked at me hopefully.

'We only spoke a bit at the start of the evening.'

Lauren frowned. 'I messed it up, didn't I?'

I shrugged. 'I don't think Josh is ready for any matchmaking just yet.' And in case she got the wrong idea, I quickly added, 'And neither am I.'

She hugged me again. 'Shame. Because I stand by what I said. You two would be perfect together.'

There was no response I could give so I squeezed her, wished her happy birthday, then left.

As I headed along the corridor towards the reception, I blinked back the tears that had been threatening all evening. *Hold on. It's nearly over.*

I'd booked a taxi for 11 p.m. The receptionist rang the company to see if there was a chance of anyone coming sooner but they were fully booked.

'Is there somewhere I can wait for my taxi where I won't be round people?' I asked her.

She smiled. 'Festivities a bit overpowering?'

'Something like that.'

'If you go past The Arundel Room and towards the back of the hotel, there's a corridor on your left. A little way along there, there are a couple of alcoves with comfy seats in them overlooking the gardens. Most guests don't know they exist.'

'Thank you. I'll be back here for eleven.'

'Would you like a drink bringing to you?' she asked.

I couldn't face any more wine but a spirit would be good to sip on while I waited. 'A large vodka and Coke if that's not too much trouble.'

'I'll ask someone to bring it to you.'

Thanking her, I set off following her directions and soon found the first alcove. A pair of high-backed chairs were positioned facing out towards the gardens. I moved towards one and was about to sit down when I realised the other was occupied. By Josh.

'Sorry.' I backed away. 'I didn't mean to disturb you.'

He looked up at me but didn't speak.

'I've got a taxi booked at eleven,' I babbled. 'And they can't come earlier so the receptionist said it was quiet round here to wait, but I didn't realise you were here.'

'It's fine. You can sit there.' He was slumped in his seat and his tone was weary, although I didn't get the impression the weariness was directed at me.

'No. I'll go to the next alcove. You continue doing whatever you're doing.' I clocked the tumbler of dark liquid in his hand.

'Change of plan,' he said, raising the glass. 'I'm coming back for my car in the morning.'

'I wasn't judging.'

'I know. I didn't think you were.' He sighed and nodded towards the empty chair encouragingly. 'I don't bite.'

Looking into his eyes was like looking into a mirror; so much hurt and confusion.

'Go on, then.' I sat down beside him.

'I'm sorry about my Auntie Lauren earlier. If you work with her, you'll already know she's not exactly backwards in coming forwards.'

I smiled. 'That's one way of putting it.'

'Has she blabbed about what happened to me?'

I shook my head. 'She said she had a nephew and... er... that you'd had a tough time.' Probably not a good idea to mention the word 'damaged'.

He swilled the drink round in his glass but didn't take a sip. 'I might as well tell you. Everyone knows everyone round here. They'll have seen us talking and tongues will start wagging.'

'You don't have to...'

'It's not a secret and I'd rather you hear it from me so you get the truth rather than the gossip.' He took a deep breath. 'Her name was Beth and she was a receptionist at the practice.'

Josh turned his gaze from me towards the gardens. It was pitch black out there except for a couple of trails of white lights illuminating what I imagined were pathways.

'She'd worked there for about three years before we got together. I really liked her from the start but I knew she was seeing someone so I never made a move. Then I found her crying at work. She told me she'd been seeing a married man who'd promised his marriage was over and was biding his time for the right moment to tell his wife. It never happened. Beth decided he wasn't serious about her or their relationship so had ended it. Alarm bells should have started ringing but they didn't. Beth played the victim card big time and I fell for it. She was adamant it was over and made it clear she was interested in me.' He shook his head. 'We were together for two years and I stupidly thought we were happy. Because her married man had hurt her, she wanted to take things slowly. We hadn't moved in together or anything but I thought we were heading somewhere. Very naïve of me.'

'She was still seeing the married man?' I asked when he fell silent.

He nodded. 'Never stopped.'

I winced. 'I'm sorry. How did—'

'A vodka and Coke?' The same barman who'd relieved Josh earlier appeared with two drinks on a tray.

'Yes, please.'

'And this must be yours, Joshy-boy,' he said handing over the other drink.

'Thanks, mate.' Josh handed him some money.

'You've got to let me get these,' I protested but he wouldn't hear of it.

'How did you find out?' I asked when the barman left.

'One of the other receptionists told me that Beth was crying in the ladies. She'd seemed down for a few weeks and I was getting worried about her. I went into the toilets to check on her and found her holding a pregnancy test. A positive one.'

'Not your baby?' I asked when he fell silent once more.

He shook his head slowly. 'But I assumed it was. It seemed like the obvious moment to ask her to marry me so there I was on bended knee when the door burst open and in he walked. He looked at me, then at the test in her hand, and it was like this huge epiphany. The baby wasn't mine; it was his. *He* was her married man. All this time, my girlfriend had been seeing my father.'

I gasped. 'Oh, Josh. That's awful. Your girlfriend and your dad? That's a bit...' Gross? Icky? Sick? I couldn't bring myself to say any of those words.

He shuddered. 'Yeah, I know! I can't bear to think about them being together when we...' He shuddered again. 'It was pretty horrendous and not just for me but for my mum too. They'd had their ups and downs but she never dreamed he could be seeing someone else.'

'How long had it been going on with Beth and your dad?'

'Seven years at that point.'

'Seven? Wow!'

'He'd met her on a night out in Hull, got her the job at the practice a couple of years later so he could see her all the time, and they were carrying on right under our noses.'

'That's cruel.'

He necked back the rest of his drink and picked up the fresh one. 'Isn't it? My mum threw him out and he moved in with Beth. They're still together playing happy families with a second baby on the way already. I know it sounds awful but I can't bring myself to think of them as my half-siblings after Beth and I... It's too...'

'How long did they stay working with you?' I asked when it was clear he wasn't going to finish his sentence.

'Not long. I own the controlling share of the practice so he had no choice but to leave.' He leaned forward and put his drink down on the carpet. 'You know that day we met when you asked me to move my car and I was rude to you? I was on the phone to Beth.'

'Oh. I could hear shouting.'

'She'd been phoning me constantly. Could I forgive Dad? Could I meet the baby? Could they move into the house at the practice because things were getting cramped at the flat? I snapped and completely lost it with her that day. The house at the practice was mine. I loved living there but I had to move out when I discovered that the pair of them had often used it for a quickie when I was in surgery.' He held his head in his hands and exhaled loudly. 'I'm sorry you heard me shouting. I've never shouted at anyone in my whole life but that day... I know it sounds harsh but, as far as I'm concerned, I don't have a dad and I certainly don't want anything to do with Beth.'

'I'm not surprised you think like that. I would too in that situation. And I'm guessing that's why you got all shouty when I came to see you at the practice that time.'

'I'm so sorry about that too. You said his name and it was like a red rag to a bull.'

'Yeah, I can see why.'

We both stared out into the darkness for a couple of minutes.

'Why was she seeing you?' I asked. 'Was it to make your dad jealous?'

'Supposedly. Beth told him she'd call it off with me the day he left my mum. Thing is, he couldn't afford to leave Mum because he knew she'd take him for every penny, rightly so. The pregnancy swung it. I'm an only child but not through choice. My parents wanted more kids but it never happened. Mum came to terms with it but, when Beth was able to offer Dad what he'd always wanted, he chose her.'

I'd cried myself to sleep after Dad told me Chloe and James were expecting their first child but Josh's circumstances were a million times worse than mine. He must have been in agony.

'There's no way the baby could have been...?' I bit my lip. Was that tactless?

'No. The dates couldn't have worked. I should have realised that when I saw her with the test. It had been so long since... It didn't register at the time, though. All I had in my head was that I should "do the right thing" as my granddad would have said.' He gave me a rueful smile. 'Bet you're really glad you sat down with me.'

'No, I am. I'm really sorry, Josh. A dad should be someone to look up to, not someone who betrays you like that.'

He clicked his fingers and pointed at me. 'Which reminds me. Your dad. I know you said he's going to help you set up the rescue centre but, if he's looking for a job in the area, we're still a vet short and, if he's as good as you say, there may even be a partnership going further down the line.'

'Oh my goodness! You mean that?'

He removed his wallet from his jeans and took out a business card. 'My direct email's on there. Tell him to email me an outline of his areas of expertise and we'll take it from there. No guarantees, mind.'

'Oh no. I get that. Thank you.' I put the card safely in my clutch. Dad would be thrilled. He could still help me with Project Prickles but I knew it wasn't going to be enough work or challenging enough for him in the long-run. Plus, he needed to start earning again.

'What about you, then?' Josh asked, adjusting his position to fully face me. 'Any stories of treachery and betrayal to share with me?'

'Not quite on the scale of yours.'

He looked at his watch. 'You've still got twenty minutes until your taxi and I'm a willing listener.' His eyes were twinkling again and those damn butterflies in my stomach took flight.

'Okay. Here goes. You know I said earlier that I saved Thomas's life when I got lost on my way to my cousin's wedding? Well, the person she was marrying was my ex-boyfriend and I've just discovered they got it together and I mean *fully* got it together while I was still seeing him...'

* * *

I sat back in the taxi half an hour later, my fingers intertwined with Josh's, my heart racing.

'North Emmerby please, Trev,' Josh instructed the driver, sending those butterflies soaring and swooping. What was I doing? What were *we* doing?

56

Trev was obviously one of Josh's customers. As they chatted about Trev's dogs, I couldn't concentrate on anything they were saying because Josh kept lightly stroking my wrist with his thumb, zipping electric pulses up and down my arm and throughout my body. *Oh my gosh! Is this really happening? I don't do things like this.* I'd never had a one-night-stand and I was under no illusion that this was anything more than that. Josh would not be ready for a relationship after what he'd been through.

I gave him a sideways glance and he winked at me, turning me to jelly.

After I'd shared my sorry tale, he'd looked at me with such sad eyes that those tears I'd just about managed to keep back all evening broke through the dam.

'Don't cry,' he'd whispered.

I wiped them away. 'I was determined not to, but I've been so close all evening.' More tears trickled.

'They're not worth it. None of them.'

'I know. And I thought I was completely over him but it's being back here that's doing it. I know it's not fair because it's a lovely hotel but I hate this place.'

'Me too.'

'But you used to work here.'

'I know. And I have a lifetime staff discount so guess where I brought Beth the first time we... you know. And guess who she used to come here with all the time?'

'Literally,' I quipped, then put my hand over my mouth. 'Too much?'

Josh's shoulders bounced and he started laughing long and hard. Infected by his mirth, I laughed with him.

'That's disgusting,' he said, finally gaining control. 'But I haven't laughed that much in months.'

'Same here. Not since...' And my laughter turned to tears again. 'Sorry. I shouldn't have drunk anything tonight. It's made me so emotional.'

'And it's made me melancholy but you've made me laugh properly and that's been a huge breakthrough.'

'You know what I think we should do?' I stood up and reached for his hand. 'I think we should both get out of here.'

He stood up, still holding my hand, and reached for my other one. We searched each other's eyes. My heart thumped and I held my breath for a moment.

'Together?' he whispered.

'It might be what we both need to help us move on.'

And that's how we'd ended up in the back of a taxi, heading to towards Josh's cottage, my mind racing as fast as my heart.

* * *

Standing on the path while Josh handed Trev a couple of notes through his open window and told him to keep the change, I felt like I was in a dream and would wake up at any moment in my bed back at Brook Cottage. I'd refused to turn and look at Hannah and Toby's cottage when Trev stopped outside it, not wanting to think what Hannah would say about the scenario. At least they were away for the weekend and wouldn't see me do the walk of shame in the morning. I bit my lip. Would it be the morning? Or would Josh call a taxi and send me packing after the deed was done? I had no idea how these things worked.

The taxi pulled away and Josh took my hand in his. In silence, we walked towards Wisteria Cottage. I stole a sideways glance at him and my heart thumped so fast that it felt like it was going to burst out of my chest and sprint down the lane.

The dim glow from a streetlamp a few cottages away cast shadows across his cheekbones, making him appear both mysterious and alluring. My head yelled: *Run! This isn't you. You don't do this!* But my heart and my body disagreed. I had never wanted Harry or James like I wanted Josh right now. Every nerve felt on fire. I thought about Chloe and James at Gramps's party and how I'd wondered what it must be like to be attracted to someone so strongly that you just had to have them there and then. Now I knew.

He took his key out of his pocket and unlocked the door, pushing it open a couple of inches, then he paused and turned to me.

'You're sure?' he whispered, cupping my face in his hand.

'Never been surer.'

And when he pressed his lips against mine, if there'd been even a slither of doubt, it evaporated as I melted against him. Oh my word, that kiss was everything I'd hoped for and so much more. Soft, tender, searching, passionate.

It was over too soon. He pulled away and I steeled myself for the immortal words: 'Sorry, but I can't do this.'

'I think we'd better take this inside,' he whispered.

I kicked off my shoes and dropped my clutch the moment I stepped into the lounge. Josh locked the door and was by my side instantly, kissing my lips, my ears, my neck. I ran my fingers through his hair and down his back then lifted his shirt up over his head, buttons still fastened. Running kisses down his chest and stomach, then back up to his neck, his heavy breathing made me want him even more.

'Come upstairs.' He took my hand and led me up to his bedroom.

He flicked on a bedside lamp then took me in his arms again, slipping off my shrug and unclipping my hair. It tumbled round my shoulders and he ran his fingers through it then pulled away and stepped back for a moment, as though drinking me in.

'You're so beautiful,' he whispered, searching my face.

My heart raced even faster. Nobody ever called me beautiful, yet the sincerity in his voice and in his eyes couldn't be mistaken. It wasn't a line; he genuinely meant it.

'Nobody's ever said that to me before,' I whispered back.

His eyes widened. 'Then they definitely didn't deserve you.' He kissed me so tenderly, tears rolled down my cheeks again and my heart melted as he kissed them away.

'And she was crazy to let you go,' I said, running my fingers down his bare chest.

'They're not worth it,' he agreed. 'None of them.'

'I know.'

As he unzipped my dress, I experienced a brief panic about my underwear. Was it even matching? Josh obviously approved as his breathing quickened and his kisses intensified.

He lowered me onto the bed, removed his jeans, then joined me, kissing, touching, teasing and making me feel like I really was the most beautiful and desirable woman in the world.

For the first time ever, I experienced what making love felt like. So Josh and I weren't in love but we were two troubled souls, as Lauren had called us, combined with desire and passion and a need to be one. With Harry and James, it had been fun, but it had been functional. Neither of them had loved me. Was that why it had never been great? But Josh didn't love me and it felt so different, so wonderful, so right.

When it was over, he cuddled me to his side under the duvet. He stroked my back and intermittently kissed the top of my head, but neither of us spoke. I felt... I searched for the right word... safe. Yes, I felt safe with him as though he would never intentionally hurt me and at that moment, I knew I'd somehow fallen in love with Josh Alderson.

I barely knew him yet I'd seen into his soul, he'd seen into mine, and we'd taken the first steps together towards healing.

If I was completely honest, he'd had me earlier at: 'So, tell me about the hedgehogs...'

57

Something was dazzling me. I tried to open my eyes but the light was too bright. I turned over and looked round the unfamiliar bedroom. Where was I? Then I smiled. Josh's place. We hadn't drawn the blinds last night – slightly distracted – and the daylight was flooding through the window.

Turning away from the light, I lay there for a moment, replaying last night. Wow! Some evening.

After ten minutes or so, with no sign of Josh, I padded to the door and looked out. The door to the bathroom was wide open so he clearly wasn't in there. I listened for noises from downstairs like a kettle boiling but there was absolute silence. Even though I felt certain I was alone, I grabbed a towel from the bathroom, wrapped it round me, and made my way downstairs.

'Josh?'

No answer.

My ballerina pumps were neatly placed near the door and I looked round for my clutch. It was on the dining table with a note.

Sam

Really sorry but had to run. Cow emergency!

Thanks so much for last night. It was just what I needed.
Beth who?
    I could be out for hours so there's no point sticking around. I've left you £20 in case you don't have cash for a taxi.
    Don't forget to get your dad to email me.
    Josh

He'd scribbled the numbers for a few taxi firms at the bottom. My stomach churned and I crumpled the note in my hand. *Right. Best be heading off, then.* I took a deep breath. It was fine. I'd known all along that it was only for the one night and that's all I'd wanted. At first. Careful what you wish for, eh?

Picking up my clutch, I grimaced as my fingers brushed the twenty-pound note. I knew it meant nothing and was simply Josh being kind, but it still made me feel wretched, like payment for services rendered.

The first taxi company he'd listed was the one we'd used last night and I didn't want to risk it being Trev again, so I called the second one and arranged for a driver to collect me in ten minutes' time. Back upstairs, I used the bathroom then sighed as I picked up Gwendoline's dress. Talk about the walk – or taxi ride – of shame. Surely Josh would have a pair of sweatpants and a hoodie I could borrow. I could drop them off at the practice so he didn't have to see me again which, given the tone of the note, appeared to be how he wanted to play things.

There was a chest of drawers next to a pine wardrobe which seemed to be as good a place to start as any. I opened the first drawer but it contained socks and pants, the second had T-shirts but bingo for the third. Removing a navy hoodie, I pulled it on over my bra then opened the fourth drawer down where I found a pair of grey sweatpants. I lifted them out, then suddenly stopped. They'd been covering a couple of photo frames and I was now faced with smiling images of Josh and an exceptionally pretty blonde woman. With ice-blue eyes and light blonde hair, she clearly came from the same sort of Scandinavian roots as Chloe. So that was his type? Nothing like me at all, then. *Don't be silly. Not everyone has a type and, even if they do, they sometimes stray from it. You fell for James and he was blond yet you prefer dark hair. Like Josh.* I shook my head as I stared at the photo, my stomach churning. *Josh said you were beautiful and you know he meant it. Ignore the photo. Ignore what Great-Aunt Agnes said. Ignore Mum.*

I should have closed the drawer and legged it but, stupidly, I moved aside the photo frames. There were more loose photos of the two of them together and a box containing an exquisite platinum and diamond engagement ring.

Sighing, I put the sweatpants back in the drawer and closed it. I pulled off the hoodie, put my dress on, then pulled the hoodie on again. It was long enough to take some of the bulk out of the petticoats and would have to do.

Two minutes later, I was in a taxi heading back to Brook Cottage, picturing the expression on Josh's face as he looked at Beth in those photos and picturing the ring. He wasn't about to get over a love like that any time soon and I should never have let myself imagine otherwise.

* * *

Rich was on his way upstairs after his night shift when I opened the door to Brook Cottage.

'Well, well, well,' he said, looking at my dress and sparkly bag. 'Who was the lucky guy?'

'Nobody.' And I crumbled again. What was wrong with me?

'Hey.' He rushed over and led me to the sofa. 'What's happened?'

It tumbled out between big sobs and I handed him the screwed-up note.

'Very *Pretty Woman*,' he observed, then slapped his wrist. 'Bad joke. Sorry. You know what I think?'

'That I'm stupid for letting another man hurt me?'

'I think he scribbled the note in a rush to attend to his... what was it? ... cow emergency. I honestly don't think you should read anything into it. Be grateful that you even got a note. And I know I joked about it but the money was a nice thing.' He yawned. 'I'm going to have to get to bed. Will you be okay?'

I nodded. 'I'm being overly sensitive. I'm not sure what's up with me at the moment.'

'Think how much emotional turmoil you've been through since I met you. I think it's all catching up with you. It was bound to at some point.'

'Perhaps.'

'I'd say definitely.' He smiled gently. 'I'll see you later.'

Rich headed upstairs and I lay back on the sofa, reflecting on what he'd said. He could be right. Life had been such a whirlwind since Thomas passed away and I'd never had the opportunity to properly grieve for him with the shock of the inheritance.

I read the note again.

Thanks so much for last night. It was just what I needed. Beth who?

What did that last part mean? Did it mean I'd helped him forget or – and my heart started racing at the thought – did it mean I'd just replaced her? I rolled off the sofa and headed up to the bathroom to take a shower. I could work myself into a state over-analysing every word when Rich was right: he'd scribbled it in a rush. And even if it did mean I'd been just what he needed for one night only, that had been the expectation right at the start. He'd never promised me anything more. It wasn't his fault that I'd let my guard down and let him in. It had been a one-night stand to get over our exes. We both knew that. I needed to get over it and get in the real world. As soon as I'd showered, I'd email Dad with a photo of Josh's business card, drop the hoodie off at the surgery and have a lazy afternoon reading through those letters from Hedgehog Hollow that I still hadn't looked at. There was nothing I could do to help Dave and the lads with Project Prickles and I was up to date with marking assignments so I might as well relax for once.

58

'What are you up to?' Rich asked, making his way back downstairs mid-afternoon. I was sitting on the floor, leaning against the sofa, with bundles of letters spread all round me.

'Reading the letters I found at the farm the other week.' I waved the one I was partway through.

Rich sat down in the armchair. 'Love letters?'

'This pile is.' I pointed to a bundle to my left. 'They're all from Thomas to Gwendoline but I haven't read them. I'd feel like I'm snooping. But all of these...' I swept my arm across the other piles. 'These are something else. And some of them go back as far as fifty years ago.'

He picked up one of the unfolded sheets closest to his feet and started reading. '"Dear Gwendoline. Who do you think you are ignoring my letters? You are not and never will be better than the rest of us..."' He widened his eyes. 'Someone's got a chip on their shoulder. Are they all like that?'

I nodded. 'From what I can gather, Gwendoline was the youngest of five. She's the only one who did well at school and they resented her for that. Thomas came from money and they resented that too, calling them both all sorts of nasty names. Then it seems there was a change of tune when she married. Somebody obviously befriended her, after which the money requests started. It seems she helped at first but, when the requests got bigger, she stopped and they turned on her again.'

'They sound like a delightful lot.'

'The things they say to her, Rich. The language too. I remember Thomas saying something about her family being users but I never imagined anything as bad as this.'

'I'll leave you to it. Coffee?'

'I've got one, thanks.'

While Rich pottered about in the kitchen, I finished reading the last few letters, tutting and shaking my head at regular intervals. They really were a horrible bunch of people. Her parents had passed away before Gwendoline, along with her eldest brother. From what I could work out, the other siblings had died at various points over the years but their kids had taken over the hate mail. It was always the same: name-calling and demands for money. What had possessed them to think it would work?

My heart broke at the thought of that wonderful couple being faced by such cruel words every few months and then, after Gwendoline died, them continuing to hound Thomas. Over recent years, the letters had diminished to once a year, usually around October, talking about how expensive Christmas could be. 'Get a job, then,' I'd muttered several times. Thomas owed them nothing. He never had when he was with Gwendoline and, after she'd gone, he wasn't even connected to their family yet the harassment had never ceased.

He was at peace now – they both were – and if another begging letter arrived in October, I'd get Mr Jeffreys to write an official letter to them telling them that Thomas had passed away and his estate had been given to the hedgehogs. Imagine their shock when they read that!

Dad rang shortly after I'd cleared the letters away, thanking me for Josh's details but wanting to check I was absolutely sure I didn't mind him getting in touch as a positive outcome would scupper our plans to have him help me set up Hedgehog Hollow.

'Don't be daft,' I assured him, trying to ignore the racing of my heart at the mention of Josh's name. 'Of course you should get in touch. You'll still be able to help me set things up and hopefully Josh will let you treat the hedgehogs at cost so you'll be doing me a huge favour if you work there.'

By 9.30 p.m. I couldn't keep my eyes open. Josh hadn't called or texted, not that I'd expected him to. It was only as I crawled under my duvet that I realised he couldn't have even if he'd wanted to; we hadn't exchanged numbers. The realisation that he wasn't ignoring me was comforting and I drifted off to sleep, smiling at last.

59

I picked up a voicemail from Dad at lunchtime on Monday: 'Hi Sammie. I wanted you to be the first to hear my news. I met with Josh this morning and he's offered me a job. I'm going in on Thursday and Friday this week to meet the team, find my way round and have some systems training, then I'll start seeing patients from Monday. Thanks so much for putting in a good word. Oh, and Josh said he'd misplaced your number so I gave him it. I hope that was the right thing. I figured you must know him well.'

A little too well, Dad! My heart thumped. Oh no. I'd been fine with zero contact all day yesterday after realising on Saturday night that he didn't know how to contact me, and discovering he wasn't on social media. But now...

I phoned Dad back to wish him congratulations but it went to voicemail so I texted him instead.

✉ To Dad
Just got your message. That's brilliant news! So pleased for you. Call me tonight to give me the full details xx

I hadn't seen Lauren all day but I spotted her in the car park at the end of the day, loading something into her boot.

'How was the head on Saturday?' I asked, making my way over to her.

'Saturday was a write-off and yesterday wasn't great either,' she said. 'I apologise right now for anything I said about you and Josh. Connie gave me several lectures over the weekend so I presume it must have been bad.'

'Forget about it. Josh and I are fine and he's offered my dad a job so he's right at the top of my Christmas card list at the moment.'

Lauren looked puzzled and I realised that I'd never mentioned that Dad was a vet which probably explained why I hadn't known her 'damaged' nephew was also a vet. I quickly filled her in on the situation at his work and his impending divorce.

'I'm worried about him doing the commute each day though,' I said. 'I'd hoped he could move in with me at the farm but it's nowhere near ready and Brook Cottage is too small.'

'Can he cook?' Lauren asked.

'He can, actually.'

'In that case, he's welcome to stay at mine. I've got two spare bedrooms and I hate cooking so your dad can stay for free in exchange for a few decent home-cooked meals a week.'

'Are you sure? It's a big ask.'

'I'll be glad of the company. And you can assure him I won't try any funny business. As I told you before, I'm done with men so he needn't fear for his newly-single status.'

'Thank you. I'll speak to him tonight and see what he thinks.'

She looked at her watch. 'Right. I've got to shoot. See you tomorrow.'

I sat in my car for a few minutes, staring at my mobile, willing it to ring. But, of course, it didn't. And why would it? Josh was likely still working. But he would call soon, wouldn't he? Why ask my dad for my number otherwise?

60

Wednesday evening arrived and Josh still hadn't called. I hated that I'd become one of *those women*. I'd never been the sort who'd stared at my phone, willing a man to call or text but I found myself longing to hear his voice and, more than that, to feel his touch. Argh!

'Nearly forgot to tell you,' Dave said, tucking into a stir-fry. 'There were a couple of blokes at the farm this afternoon asking questions.'

'From the council?'

'No. Not officials. They said they were relatives of Thomas's.'

My pulse raced and I exchanged looks with Rich.

'What did they want?' Rich asked.

'They were asking what had happened to Thomas and who owned the farm now.'

'What did you tell them?' I asked.

Dave put his fork down and looked from me to Rich then back to me. 'What am I missing?'

I filled him in about hate mail from Gwendoline's family.

'Crap,' Dave said. 'It was Pete who spoke to them. He said he didn't give them any details but he thought they seemed like decent blokes.'

'If they come back, can you make sure nobody tells them anything? I'll give Mr Jeffreys a call in the morning.'

I jumped when my mobile rang. Josh? But it was Dad. I'd spoken to him on Monday night to find out all about his first proper day and to let him know about Lauren's offer but I was too embarrassed to quiz him about Josh asking for my number.

'Hi, Dad.'

'Hi, poppet. I've been round to Lauren's. I like her and the room's great so I'm moving in on Saturday.'

'Wow! Fast mover.'

He sighed. 'There's no point prolonging it.' There was a sadness to his tone and I hated how much this was hurting him.

'You're doing the right thing, Dad,' I reassured him.

'I know. It feels like it took forever to get to this point and now everything's happening so quickly. It's a lot to process. Anyway, your mum and I accepted an offer on the house today. It's a family and they want to move in over the Easter holidays, which means a speedy completion. Your mum's house won't be ready but she'll stay with Louise so I might as well start my new life in the Wolds straightaway.'

'How's Mum doing?'

'She's like a different woman. She actually laughed at something I said the other day instead of growling at me.' I could hear the smile in his voice. 'We should have done this years ago.'

'I'd never have moved home if I'd thought it would cause so many problems for you.'

'Don't start blaming yourself, Sammie. This has been coming since way before that. I just didn't want to accept it was over. Anyway, I need to go as I'm meeting your Uncle Simon, but are you free tomorrow night for a celebratory dinner?'

'Sounds good.'

'Pick you up at seven. Avoid jeans if possible. We're not going to your local this time.'

'You mean wear a dress?'

'Do you have one?'

'Believe it or not, I have several, inherited from Gwendoline.'

'Then wear one of those, if you feel comfortable in it.'

After we'd said our goodbyes, I went up to my bedroom and looked at the dresses. Fingering the fabric of the one I'd worn on Friday, a zip of electricity shot through me. I'd felt very comfortable in it and even more comfortable out of it with Josh by my side. *Stop it! He hasn't called. He's not going to call. It was one night and one night only.*

I had more important things to worry about. If Gwendoline's horrible money-grabbing relatives had been to the farm, they'd probably heard through the grapevine that Thomas was dead. After reading their hate mail, there was no doubt in my mind that they'd contest the will. The last thing I needed right now was a legal fight but nothing and nobody was going to stop me from opening that rescue centre.

61

I phoned Mr Jeffreys at break the following morning and he assured me I had nothing to worry about. He said he couldn't go into details but he had legal paperwork disinheriting Gwendoline's family.

While feeling comforted that nobody was going to be able to stop me fulfilling Thomas and Gwendoline's legacy, I was appalled for them that they'd felt compelled to legally disinherit her family. There was no love lost between Mum and me but this was on a whole new level.

I dropped the letters off at Mr Jeffreys' office on my way home. He was between meetings and gave me the same reassurances in person. It didn't stop me being anxious about it all. Why couldn't something go smoothly for once?

* * *

'Aw, my little girl is all grown up,' Dad said when I answered the door that evening. 'That dress is stunning.'

'It's not too much?' I'd gone for another one of Gwendoline's vintage dresses but in a daring pillar-box red. It was like a fifties sleeveless prom dress but with a net blouse over the top to tone it down. Trying it on for Rich and Dave the night before, they'd showered me with compliments but insisted I had to wear heels with it so Hannah lent me a pair.

'It's perfect,' Dad said, smiling as I gave him a twirl.

'And look at you all smart in a suit.' I reached out and straightened his tie. 'How's work going?'

'Brilliant. I'll tell you all about it in the car.'

* * *

Twenty minutes later, we pulled into the car park of The Silver Birch in a village on my route to work. Lauren had highly recommended it but, with a pricey menu, she said it was for special occasions.

A buzz of chatter hit us as soon as we stepped through the door. Considering it was only a Thursday, there were a lot of customers. I loved the classy décor. The floors were wooden, the walls painted in muted shades of grey, green and purple, and the chairs and tables mismatched in an effortlessly stylish way.

'It's busy,' I said. 'Just as well you booked.'

'I need to nip to the gents,' Dad said. 'Do you want to go through to the restaurant? The table's booked in my name. You might as well sit down.'

The restaurant was decorated in the same colours as the bar but with subdued lighting.

'If you'd like to come this way,' the waitress said, smiling.

I followed her across the restaurant to a table in an alcove. But there was someone already sitting at it. My heart thumped.

'Sam!' he said, standing up. 'Wow! You look amazing.'

'Josh! What are you doing here?'

He laughed. 'Having a déjà vu moment. Didn't we have this conversation on Friday night?'

'Yes, but... I'm confused. You don't seem surprised to see me.'

'I'm not. I was expecting you.'

'There's only two chairs. My Dad's—'

'Taking my Auntie Lauren out for a meal in the next village. It's just the two of us, if that's okay with you.'

I opened my mouth but no words came out. What was going on? Did Dad know about what happened on Friday night? Was this a date?

'I'd invite you to sit down, but there's something I'd like to do first.'

'What?'

'This.' He cupped my face in his hands and gently kissed me. I was already unsteady on my feet thanks to the borrowed heels, but that kiss nearly made my legs give way.

'I've been dreaming of doing that all week,' he said, pulling my chair out.

I gratefully sank into it before I flopped onto the floor. 'I've dreamed of you doing it, but...'

Josh sat down beside me. 'But you didn't think I was interested because I haven't called.' He took hold of my hand and the butterflies went crazy. 'I wanted to. I picked up the phone so many times.'

'So what stopped you?'

'Over-thinking everything. I'm sorry. I didn't think I'd be ready to let anyone in again for a long time, yet there you were, this beautiful, passionate woman who saves a stranger's life and sets up a hedgehog rescue centre in his honour. Have you any idea how amazing that is? I wasn't sure I could ever be enough for you or if you'd even want me to be.'

'How could you think you wouldn't be enough?'

'I wasn't enough for Beth.'

I squeezed his hand and gave him a gentle smile. 'And I wasn't enough for James. But neither of them were enough for us either.'

He ran his fingers lightly across my wrist and electricity fizzed up my arm and through my body.

'I didn't think you were interested in anything more than the one night,' I admitted. 'That note you left?' I grimaced. 'I thought it was a brush-off.'

Josh groaned. 'I'm so sorry. I couldn't just abandon you but I had no idea what to write. What if I asked to see you again and you weren't interested? What if you woke up regretting what we'd done?'

'Definitely no regrets from that. Just worried about the note.'

'Would you believe me if I told you it was the best of a bad bunch?'

'You wrote more than one?'

'I wrote... Actually, they're probably still in my coat pocket. Hang on...' He disappeared then returned moments later and dumped several crumpled notes on the table. 'Aborted attempts. I thought they might be too intense.'

I picked up the first and smoothed it out:

Dear Samantha, Last night was amazing. I hadn't expected to

The second was crossed through but I could still read it:

Hi you, I wish I was still lying next to you right now but I've been called out. You looked so beautiful that I didn't like to

There were another two attempts, both in a similar vein.

'Oh, Josh.'

'I kicked myself later for leaving the money. I thought you might think I was trying to pay you for...' He lowered his head and shook it.

'It did cross my mind but my friend, Rich, told me not to read anything into it and to think myself lucky that you left anything, especially when you were dealing with an emergency.'

'You'd have shouted at me,' Josh said. 'I spent so long trying to write a decent note for you that I had to speed again.'

I feigned a shocked expression. 'Tut tut. But did you save the cows?'

He smiled and nodded. 'I am pleased to report that disaster was averted.'

'Glad to hear it.'

'For the cows anyway,' he added. 'My attempts at note-writing and any sort of follow-through were clearly an unmitigated disaster. I'm sorry, Sam. I should have phoned you but I just wanted to be sure. I mean, I was sure. I was sure how I felt the moment we kissed, but there was this teeny-weeny doubt that it might have been because it was new and exciting and the first time since Beth. I stopped being worried about getting hurt and started worrying about hurting you. Thing is, I couldn't stop thinking about you and hoping you were thinking about me too.'

'I was. All the time. So why the elaborate set-up tonight?'

'I made the decision to go for it but discovered your dad had plans to be with you. I admitted that I really liked you and was worried I'd blown it by not getting in touch. I asked him if he could put in a good word but he suggested I swap places with him instead. I think he's a bit of an old romantic.'

'He is. Unfortunately my mum never appreciated him but maybe he'll find someone who does when he settles here.'

'Like my Auntie Lauren?'

I laughed at the thought. 'She'd eat him alive. Plus she's adamant that she's sworn off men.'

'She's not as tough as she likes to make out. She's a romantic softie really. She's just been unlucky in love but even she keeps hoping that, one day, the right person will come along and the past will be in the past.'

'Is your past in the past?' I asked. 'Is that what you meant when you put "Beth who?" in your note?'

He nodded. 'It was meant to be, but I'm not sure it quite worked. But, yes, the past is definitely in the past. And yours?'

'Also in the past.'

Josh leaned across and gently kissed me again. 'And the future?' he whispered.

'Ours for the taking.'

'We'd better toast to that, then.' Josh inclined his head towards one of the waiters who came over and took our drinks orders, followed shortly after by food.

We chatted non-stop over our meal and, as I listened to Josh raving about the impact my dad had made on the team on his first day and how excited he was to have recruited him, I felt myself bursting with pride.

'And I have big some news for you,' Josh said when our plates had been cleared away. 'The practice supports a charity each tax year and we're pleased to announce that the charity for the forthcoming year will be... drum roll ... Hedgehog Hollow.'

My jaw dropped. 'You mean it? Oh my gosh! That's fantastic news.'

'It was unanimous after everyone met your dad and he told them about your plans. Sadie, one of our reception team, adores hedgehogs and she remembered you coming in so she was very vocal about wanting to support you.'

'Bless her. She was lovely.'

'And she's a million times better at her job than her predecessor.' He rolled his eyes at me and I felt encouraged that he could joke about Beth. 'As our charity of the year, there'll be a collection jar in reception, we'll run raffles and fundraisers throughout the year, and a small percentage of profits will be presented at the end of the financial year.'

'That's so generous. Thank you so much.'

'It's a pleasure. And, on top of that, we'll provide all medication and labour for free.'

I felt quite choked up. 'You'd do all that for me?'

'Yes. But you need to know something. Even if nothing had happened between us on Friday or if Friday had happened and you wanted to leave it at one night, I'd still be doing this. I hated myself that day you came to the practice. I've never spoken to anyone like that and it was a big wake-up call that I was turning into an angry and bitter person who could easily let the past destroy my life, so I was determined to sort things out with you and get my life back on track. That's why I came to the farm but that didn't go as planned. I was going to try one more time and then you turned up at Auntie Lauren's party and I did it again.'

'You've more than made up for it now.' I bit my lip. 'I think we should get the bill.'

'You don't want dessert?'

'I do, but I have a different kind of dessert in mind.'

62

Dave and a couple of his team were working on the barn when I arrived at Hedgehog Hollow on Saturday morning. I made them a round of drinks then headed across to the farmhouse.

As soon as I unlocked the door, a chill ran through me at the sight of the handwritten envelope lying on the doormat. No stamp. Which meant they'd been on my property when nobody was around, likely snooping. At least there was nothing to steal. Or was there?

I grabbed the letter and, slamming the door closed, sprinted round to the garden and breathed a sigh of relief. The bench was still there. I didn't want an unsightly chain and padlock attached to it but maybe it could be bolted to the ground. It was far too precious to lose.

I didn't want to read the letter on that special bench, soiling the beautiful memories with what were bound to be cruel words and threats, so I made my way back into the farmhouse and into the kitchen.

'Let's get this over with,' I muttered, ripping open the envelope.

To Miss Wishaw

There's been a big mistake. Our great-aunt and great-uncle owned this farm and it should have gone to their family when they

died. We don't know why you think it's yours but it isn't cos you
aren't family and you need to give it back.

    We want to give you a chance to do the right thing and return
what belongs to us without doing legal stuff. Our mobile numbers
are at the bottom. You can keep the farm and pay us the money for it
or you can sell it and pay us. Don't care. Just care about getting
what we're owed.

    If you don't phone today, we'll be back to have a word.
NOT YOURS! GET OUT!
Brynn & Cody Grimes

There was a knock on the front door, then it opened, swiftly followed by a shout of 'hello'.

'In here, Dad,' I called.

'Good morning. Oh. What's happened?'

I handed him the letter and watched his jaw tighten as he read it, shaking his head and tutting.

'I'm going to call Mr Jeffreys,' I said. 'I should catch him before his first appointment.'

Mr Jeffreys asked me to email him a photo of the letter. He'd be delighted to call the Grimes boys and advise them that they had no legal claim and, if they appeared that afternoon, they would be trespassing on private property and action would be taken.

'I don't imagine they're the sort to pay attention,' he said, 'so do keep your guard up and make sure you're not alone this afternoon.'

'Thanks. My dad's here and so are the builders.'

'This is all you need, eh?' Dad said when I hung up and he handed me a mug of tea. 'Especially when everything else is going so well for you right now.'

I knew exactly what he was referring to and couldn't help grinning. 'I still can't believe you ditched me like that but thank you. Josh and I had a brilliant evening.'

'I think you've picked a winner there.'

'It's early days. We've both been hurt so we're taking things one day at a time.'

'Sounds sensible. He's a good lad, though. Much better for you than James.'

'I agree.'

'I think he's dying to be part of the project but recognises, like I do, that it's your baby and neither of us want to push you aside.'

'I don't think either of you would,' I said. 'But I appreciate you saying it.' I've never been the sort of person who has to be in charge or push themselves forward as the leader, but I wanted to be in control of this one to show Thomas that he was right to have picked me. I needed a team to help but I had to be the driving force. If it worked, we could all bask in the glory. If it didn't, then that was down to me.

'Weren't you meant to be going back to Whitsborough Bay to pack up your stuff?' I asked as Dad finished his tea and took the mug over to the sink.

'I was. I only popped in to say hello and to say thank you again for getting me the job...'

'All I did was mention to Josh that you were a vet and you'd lost your job. You're the one who turned it into a job offer.'

'But it wouldn't have happened without you.' He pointed to the letter. 'I'm not so sure about leaving you alone now.'

I stood up and gave him a hug. 'Have you seen how many strapping builders there are at the barn? I'll be fine. Go home and get packed. Your new life awaits.'

'If you're sure? I'm going out with Simon tonight but I'll be back tomorrow. Let me know if anything happens.'

'I will. There's no need to worry about me.'

'It's my prerogative as a dad to worry about you.'

I waved him off a few minutes later then went to the barn to ask Dave to warn the others that there could be trouble and not to engage with any visiting strangers.

The interior of the barn was almost ready. Dave reckoned they'd need today and possibly Monday for the final fix then they'd be ready to fully focus on the farmhouse. Work on it had already started. During the past fortnight, the two floors upstairs had been gutted – bathrooms ripped out, carpets removed, wallpaper stripped, electrics sorted and walls freshly plastered. They'd start on the kitchen as a separate project once the bathrooms were fitted. Hopefully Dad and I would be able to move in by the end of April. I'd set 2nd May as the official opening day of the rescue centre because it would have been Gwendoline's birthday. It would fall on a Saturday so the idea was to do an official small-scale launch for press, friends and family, then a big community launch the day after.

The only potential spanner in the works was Brynn and Cody Grimes. If we started a load of legal wrangling, it could delay everything. Fingers crossed that Mr Jeffreys would be able to convince them to walk away and accept that their family had been cut off long ago.

63

Josh and I went to York the following day and it was lovely. Holding hands, we walked along the castle walls before enjoying a pub lunch. We talked non-stop, laughed and kissed. I'd never expected to feel so comfortable so soon, yet it felt as though we'd known each other for years instead of for weeks.

After wandering round The Shambles and various other side streets filled with fascinating gift shops, we drove to a retail park on the outskirts and I picked up some soft furnishings and accessories. I'd already chosen and ordered furniture.

There was no point taking my purchases back to Brook Cottage so we drove straight to Hedgehog Hollow. It was nearly half five as I pulled onto the farm track – gloomy but not yet dark – and, as I parked in the farmyard, something felt wrong, out of place.

'What's up?' Josh asked, obviously picking up on my sharp intake of breath.

'Hopefully nothing,' I said, trying to keep my voice bright. 'Probably just me being on edge after that letter.'

I took a torch out of the boot then led Josh towards the barn.

'No!' The padlock from the door lay on the ground with the

severed chain. I pushed open the wooden door and flicked on the lights. 'Oh no!'

The plastic crates that I'd painstakingly cleaned after getting a new hose installed had been smashed to smithereens. Shards of plastic from them were scattered all over the floor intermingled with broken pieces of the plant-pot holders I was going to use for food and water. It looked like a sledgehammer had been taken to the Belfast sink as it was missing large chunks although the water supply remained intact so at least we didn't have a flood to contend with. Teabags, coffee, sugar and milk had been poured all over the floor and several pouches of cat food emptied in dollops, the various flavours intermingling to create a horrible stench. The door to the fridge had been ripped off and smashed, and the words 'NOT YOURS' and 'GET OUT' were spray-painted on several of the wooden pillars.

My eyes flicked round the barn, barely able to comprehend what I was seeing. I couldn't cry, I couldn't shout, I couldn't move.

'I'm so sorry.' Josh pulled me close to him and I buried my head in his chest. 'We'll get it cleared up and fixed. We can buy some new crates.'

'But they were all I had left,' I cried, my voice sharp with anger and frustration. 'Gwendoline bought them before she got cancer. The crates and the pots were hers. They were important.'

Josh kissed my forehead. 'You still have the farm and that was much more important to the Micklebys than anything those thugs have destroyed. And you have one more thing from them that nobody can ever take away.'

'What's that?'

'Their vision. Hedgehog Hollow is about the belief and passion in doing something good for a potentially endangered species. The Grimes family can think they've won by trashing the place like this, but they'll never win because they'll never break you. Will they?'

I wrapped my arms round his waist. 'You're right. Thank you. I'm so glad you're here.'

'I'll always be here,' he whispered.

As he kissed the pain away in that barn full of carnage, I knew he was right, but I wasn't naïve enough to think that this was over. It was just the start of it but, whatever they threw at me, they wouldn't break me. Not when I was surrounded by people who cared about the farm and the Micklebys' vision. We would *not* be defeated.

'I'd better call the police,' I said, taking my phone out of my pocket. While I couldn't prove it was the Grimes boys, the graffiti was the exact wording they'd written in their letter. They obviously weren't the brightest tools in the box and, if they'd messed up like that, they'd hopefully messed up in their smashing-up party by not wearing gloves.

A week passed with no further incidents. The police came and I handed over the letter although I'd watched enough TV crime dramas to know it was only circumstantial evidence. There'd been no prints but they found blood on a fragment of broken crate. Unfortunately, there was no match to anyone in the system. I was told not to give up hope but, without prints, I knew the chances of them pinning it on the Grimes boys were pretty much non-existent.

I replaced Gwendoline's plastic crates and plant-pot holders; Josh's words giving me the strength not to let it break me. I also ordered a couple of large wheeled crates for Josh's reception area. One would collect newspapers for lining the crates while the hedgehogs were hibernating or healing. The other was for donations of food or cleaning materials – wet and dry kitten or cat food, dog food, binbags, washing powder, disinfectant, antibacterial wipes and kitchen roll. Pauline from Redcliffe Rescue had told me that she was indebted to the donations from the public and I should aim to get collecting bins in several places. The veterinary practice was the logical place to start but, as we grew, I was sure I'd find other willing outlets. I'd also put a couple of bins at the end of the farm track so that people could drop and go without driving all the way up to the farm.

Dave and I had a re-think on security, ordering a new door with an extra security shutter. His team installed motion-activated security lights and CCTV round the farm and in the barn.

Thanks to the extra work needed on the barn, the timescales to finish the house were going to be challenging so it was all hands on deck with painting the top two floors. On the Saturday, Dad drove Lauren over and Hannah and Toby left Amelia with his parents for the day so they could help. Josh would join us after work.

'Do you think there's something going on with your dad and Lauren?' Hannah asked as we painted the walls in the master bedroom a soft duck-egg-blue.

I glanced across the landing to where Dad and Lauren were meant to be painting the bedroom at the end. Instead, they were in the hall, laughing hysterically, facing each other with rollers held aloft. I suspected Lauren had started the paint fight because Dad was sporting a stripe of 'sandy calico' paint across his face and Lauren appeared to be paint-free... so far.

'I don't think so but who knows? Two single people living together with bad past relationships? Anything could happen.'

'Does it bother you?' Hannah asked.

'Dad and Lauren?'

'Your dad and anyone. I mean, he's only just separated.'

I shook my head. 'You've met Mum. You know what she's like. Do you really think that's been any sort of marriage since... well, since I came along?'

'Fair point,' she said.

I dipped my roller in the paint and completed another patch. 'In an ideal world, I'd prefer it if my boss didn't date my dad because it could get awkward but, ultimately, I want him to be happy. If that happens with Lauren, it happens with Lauren. Plus, I'm dating *his* boss so I can't have double standards.'

We continued painting in silence for a few minutes.

'How are you going to manage teaching and running this place?' Hannah asked.

I put my roller down on the tray and sat down cross-legged on the floor. 'I honestly don't know. It would be easier if I could teach part-time but I've already discussed it with Lauren and it's not an option. It just wouldn't work. So it's full-time or resign and I don't think I can afford to resign.'

'What about your inheritance from your gramps? You don't need it for a house deposit anymore. Can't you use that for food and bills?'

'It's not going to last forever, though.' I shrugged. 'I'll just have to see how it goes. I have no idea how many hogs I'll have. I might only have one or two and easily balance them alongside work. I might have hundreds.'

I picked up the roller and resumed painting. Finding time to work and run the centre was a big unknown but everything else was coming together nicely. The vandalism in the barn had been awful but Josh had been right; it could be mended. The farmhouse was starting to look like a home and it now felt like mine instead of Thomas's. The partnership with Josh's practice was exciting and was going to be financially rewarding, and my partnership with Josh was both unexpected and thrilling. Dad was happier than I'd ever seen him and, whether the thing with Lauren turned out to be a friendship, a fling, or a long-term relationship, it would do them both the world of good.

But thinking about Dad made me think about my family in Whitsborough Bay. I hadn't been back there since Chloe first came home from hospital with Samuel. Even though I was dying to have baby cuddles, I wasn't sure how welcome I'd be.

Chloe and I had spoken on the phone, she'd unblocked me on social media and we'd texted and messaged. It was all very civil and, if an outsider had heard us chatting, they'd be forgiven for thinking we were the best of friends. Things weren't the same, though. The conversation was superficial and I hadn't told her about Josh. I kept picturing those photos of Beth in his drawer and her striking resemblance to Chloe. The trust had gone and I wanted to keep Chloe away from Josh. Even though I knew it was irrational, that she loved James, and she'd never abandon Samuel and him, I couldn't help my niggles. Josh and Chloe were going to have to meet at some point and I'd have to pray that history wouldn't repeat itself.

And there was Mum to worry about too. I'd had no contact with her since the ugly scene at the hospital which was three weeks ago. Should I have reached out to her to say I was sorry about the divorce? I wasn't sorry, though, so how would that conversation go? *Hi Mum, just calling to say sorry not sorry. You deserved it after treating my dad like crap for thirty years. But I'm here for you if you want to talk about it... as long as you don't say anything nasty about Dad because he's the best parent in the world and you're the worst.* Hmm. Maybe not.

'Drinks are ready,' Toby announced, appearing in the doorway with a tray. 'And I've got Hobnobs.'

We swarmed round him, grabbing drinks and ripping open the packet of biscuits as though we hadn't eaten in days.

'This was on the mat.' He handed me an envelope he'd tucked under his arm.

I immediately clocked the legal branding on the envelope. 'I can guess what this is.' Sure enough, the Grimes boys had sought legal representation and were contesting the will.

'Another Saturday morning call to Mr Jeffreys,' I muttered.

'Stay strong,' Dad said. 'You know they don't have a leg to stand on.'

'I know. Doesn't make it any less unpleasant.'

No longer in the mood for biscuits, I took my coffee downstairs so I could phone Mr Jeffreys in peace. Why was it that, every time I felt my life was on track, something had to happen to disrupt it all?

65

The following day, Josh and I were painting one of the first floor bedrooms at the front of the house when I spotted a car I didn't recognise meandering along the track. The Grimes boys? Surely they weren't daft enough to pay a visit and would wait for news back from their solicitor first.

Josh followed me downstairs and we made our way across the farmyard. My racing heart didn't steady until a woman got out and opened the back door to let out a girl of about six or seven.

'Are you the hedgehog lady?' the little girl asked, running up to me.

I had a flashback to me calling Gwendoline that when I was little. I was her now! 'Er, yes, I suppose I am.'

'We've got a poorly hedgehog.' She ran back to the car and we followed.

The woman had removed a cardboard box from the back seat. 'Sorry, I know you're not open yet but we found a hedgehog in our garden and I read somewhere that, if they're out in broad daylight, it usually means they're ill.'

I looked at Josh in panic. *Argh! Customer!* But he nodded reassuringly and I took a deep breath. 'Yes, at this time of year, that's what it would usually mean. At certain times of year, a mother hedgehog could be looking for items for a nest, but mid-March is when they're just starting to come out of hibernation so there probably is something wrong. Can I look?'

'Mummy picked him up with gardening gloves and we gave him a drink,' said the girl.

I peeled back the towel. The hedgehog nestled below it looked quite small although that wasn't unexpected post-hibernation. There were a few patches where his spines had fallen out and there appeared to be a cut on one of the bald patches which would need cleaning up.

'What's your name?' I asked the girl, bending down beside her.

'I'm Molly Benson and I'm six years old and I have a cat called Willow.'

I smiled at the information dump. 'Thank you for bringing him here, Molly. I think you and your mummy are right and he is a bit poorly so we'll make sure he's better. Are you happy to leave him with us while we do that?'

Molly nodded, wide-eyed. 'He will get better, won't he?'

'I'm sure he'll be fine.' I stood up and addressed her mum. 'Can I just check what you gave him to drink?'

'I wanted to give him some milk,' Molly declared. 'Mummy wouldn't let me. She says milk makes hedgehogs poorly.'

'It was just water,' Mrs Benson said.

I smiled. 'That's good. Milk can be very dangerous for them so thank you. Have you given him any food?'

'No. We weren't sure whether you might need to give him some medicine first so we didn't like to feed him. They eat cat food, don't they?'

'Yes. Dog or cat food is great but not fish varieties.'

'We brought you these.' Molly reached into her pocket and removed two pouches of cat food. 'Willow won't mind.'

'I'm sorry it's not much,' Mrs Benson said, 'but we're down to our last few pouches and I didn't think Willow would appreciate us leaving none for her.'

'Every little helps. Thank you.'

'When he's better, can he come back to our garden?' Molly asked.

'We've got a big garden and there's a field at the bottom,' Mrs Benson added.

'In that case, it sounds perfect. If you can give me your mobile number, I can text you when Spike here is better.'

Molly giggled. 'I like that name.'

'I might discover we need to change it to Spikette if I discover he's really a she,' I said, which elicited more giggles.

Mrs Benson gave me her details and I tapped them into my phone, then they both said goodbye to Spike before driving off.

I turned to Josh. 'My first customer. And we're not even open yet. How do you think they knew?'

'Word spreads fast round here. I suspect Spike will be the first of many.'

'Just as well I've got those new crates. Do you mind taking him into the barn and I'll grab what we need from the house?'

I returned five minutes later with a notepad and pen, crate, a couple of dishes, a jug filled with water, a newspaper, fleecy blanket, antiseptic wipes, flea powder and some weighing scales. Fortunately, most of my new purchases had been kept in the farmhouse away from the building works so they'd not fallen victim to the vandalism.

It was scary yet thrilling treating my first patient. Spike did turn out to be Spikette and she was certainly hungry and thirsty.

'It's really happening,' I said to Josh as we walked back to the farmhouse once Spikette was cleaned up and settled in her new bed.

'And you're the one who made it happen. I'm so proud of you.'

In that fleeting moment before he took me in his arms and kissed me, I could have sworn I saw Thomas and Gwendoline standing outside the farmhouse, smiling at me.

66

Feeling emotionally drained after the vandalism and physically aching after a weekend of painting, I stayed at Brook Cottage on Monday evening. A long soak in the bath eased my muscles, after which I put the TV on low, lay on the sofa and flicked through my Facebook feed. I'd barely glanced at it since starting Project Prickles so it was good to catch up on what my old Whitsborough Bay colleagues had been doing. One of them, who was known for attention-seeking posts, had obviously had yet another dramatic falling-out and had shared a series of memes about negative relationships:

> The less you respond to negative people, the more peaceful your life will become. Find your peace

> The only way to win with a toxic person is not to play the game

> My biggest mistake: letting people stay in my life for much longer than they deserved to

> If they frequently do it, it isn't a mistake; it's how they are

I'd normally have flicked past posts like that, refusing to fall into the trap of asking what was wrong and getting embroiled in a drama about people I didn't know, but I found myself carefully reading and contemplating each message, thinking about my relationship with Mum. Each day, I still hoped she'd get in touch with me and hated the guilt I felt for never phoning or visiting her, even though I suspected she was glad I didn't.

I'd wondered if she'd reach out, even if only by text, after hearing about the barn attack. Auntie Louise, Uncle Simon, Chloe and even James had been in touch to express their shock, give sympathy and ask if they could do anything, but there hadn't been a peep from my own mother. And that hurt. Then I wondered if the silence was her revenge for me not getting in touch following her separation from Dad, which made me feel guilty all over again. The whole situation made me feel constantly anxious. Something had to be done.

As I was heading up to bed, another meme appeared:

Cutting people out of your life isn't about hating them. It's about you having respect for yourself. Not everyone in your life is meant to stay in your life

Lying in bed, I couldn't stop thinking about it. Was it time to sever ties completely? Could I do that to my own mother?

* * *

I phoned Mum several times on Tuesday and Wednesday evening but she didn't answer and she didn't call me back so I sent her a text asking if there was a good time to speak or, even better, to visit. Her speedy reply was like a slap across the face:

✉ From Mum
No. I'm not interested, Samantha

That was me told. That was me crushed. Those five words pretty much summed up our relationship.

As I curled up on the sofa wondering what to do next, a text arrived:

✉ From Chloe
HOT TIP! The Child That Came Back by E J Parnaby.
Edge of the seat stuff. You'll love it xx

I smiled as I read the message. I'd missed our 'HOT TIP' texts. Was this another step in our recovering relationship?

Looking online, I read the blurb and it sounded like my type of read. I ordered the eBook and was about to text Chloe to thank her but decided to call instead. Small talk about Samuel would be a good distraction from fretting about Mum, but Chloe must have heard a weariness in my voice because she suddenly stopped mid-update.

'Something's wrong, isn't it?' she asked.

'I'm fine. It's nothing.'

'I'm not getting off this phone until you tell me what's bothering you.'

So I did. I hadn't meant to spill it out but I couldn't help it. I told her about all the arguments I'd had with Mum post-wedding, how she'd reacted to me moving out, the way she was at the hospital after Samuel was born, how hurt I'd been by her lack of contact and how she'd refused to speak to me just now.

'I can't keep going on like this. If I could understand what I'd done to make her hate me so much, maybe I could fix it. Maybe we could draw a line in the sand and move on or decide that there's no relationship and call it a day. But how can I do either of those things if she won't speak to me?'

Chloe was silent for a moment. 'I might have an idea. Leave it with me. I need to speak to Mum first.'

'Can you give me a clue?'

'I don't want to give you false hope if Mum thinks it's stupid, but I know I haven't helped things between the two of you so I'll do what I can to put it right. Hang in there, Sammie, and speak soon, yeah?'

'Thanks, Chloe. It was good to talk.'

'Right back at you. I've missed this.'

'Me too.'

* * *

I hated being devious but I felt my hand had been forced. My stomach was on spin cycle as I drove over to Whitsborough Bay on Thursday evening.

As agreed, I rang the doorbell at 7.45 p.m. Uncle Simon and James had gone out to play pool and Chloe had invited Mum and Auntie Louise round for a Chinese takeaway.

Chloe answered and declared loudly, 'Sammie! Fancy seeing you here.'

'I came over to see one of my old colleagues but she came down with a migraine. I thought I'd call round here rather than waste the journey.' I rolled my eyes at Chloe and she winked back at me.

'Come in. We've got a house-full.'

I followed her into the lounge.

'Look who's here,' she announced.

Auntie Louise stood up. 'Sam! How lovely to see you.' She hugged me and whispered. 'Be strong.' When Chloe had told her the plan, she'd agreed that anything was worth a try.

'Hi, Mum,' I said. 'You look lovely.' Instead of her usual dark colours, she wore a beautiful floaty cream top with a colourful floral print on it. She'd had her hair cut into a layered style that took years off her.

'I wasn't expecting to see you this evening.' Her tone was flat. I hadn't expected her to sound pleased but at least she didn't sound hostile.

'Surprise!' Goodness knows why I felt the need to add jazz hands to that. Damn nerves. 'I can leave if you want.'

'You'll do no such thing,' Auntie Louise said, sitting down on the sofa beside Mum. 'We can all have a good old catch-up.'

'You'll have to excuse me,' Chloe said, patting Samuel's back. 'I need to get this one to bed but I'll be down soon.'

I gave his soft cheek a kiss, wishing I could have a cuddle with him, but he wasn't the reason for my visit. Cuddles would have to wait for another time.

I sat down on one of the armchairs. Probably best to start with small talk. 'I hear you're buying a new place round the corner.'

'That's right.' She fiddled with the edging on the cushion next to her, not looking at me.

Silence.

'Two-bed? Three?' Dad had already told me but it gave me something to talk about.

'Three,' she said.

'Detached?'

'Semi.'

Not a great start, but pretty much as expected. 'I'm sorry about you and Dad.'

She looked up, eyebrows raised. 'I very much doubt that,' she said, her voice dripping with bitterness. 'You were probably the one who put the idea in his head.'

'Debs! That's not fair,' Auntie Louise cried. 'You can't blame Sam for your marital problems.'

Mum folded her arms. 'Says who?'

Be strong! You can do this. 'I know we've not exactly been close over the years but I was hoping we could find a way to change that.'

'Oh, you were, were you?'

I ignored her sarcasm and pressed on. 'I know it wasn't ideal me moving back in after things ended with Harry and I'm really sorry for the disruption and inconvenience that caused but we had a difficult relationship long before that and...' I looked towards Auntie Louise who nodded reassuringly. 'And I thought that, now that I've properly moved away, it might be a good time to explore why things have been so fraught. If I knew what I'd done wrong, perhaps I could make it right.' My hands were shaking so I sat on them. My voice was shaking too but there was nothing I could do about that. Hopefully it wasn't as obvious to Mum as it was to me.

'Is this why you've been bombarding me with phone calls all week?' she snapped. 'Because *you've* suddenly decided that *you* want to talk? What about what *I* want?'

'Don't be like that,' Auntie Louise said. 'You wouldn't take her calls so what do you expect? I think it's a good idea.'

Mum turned to her, eyes flashing with anger. 'You and Chloe planned this?'

She started to rise but Auntie Louise pulled her back down. 'You're not leaving this house until you talk. I'm not saying you'll get it all resolved tonight but what do you think about making a start?'

'How am I supposed to have any thoughts when she's ambushed me like this?'

Auntie Louise squeezed her arm. 'Nobody's ambushed you. Sam just wants to address something that's been festering for decades and I'm fully in support of that. You can't go on like this. This hostility isn't healthy for either of you.'

She emitted some sort of dismissive snort. 'Says the woman who refused to speak to her for months after the wedding.'

'Yes, well, that was a big mistake that we all regret now. I've said sorry and we've put it behind us.'

'How very big of you. So I'm the bad guy now?'

'Debs! Nobody's saying that. Sam just wants to talk, don't you Sam?'

I nodded. 'As I said, if we talk about why things are difficult, we could—'

'Why?' Mum shouted, giving an exaggerated shrug. 'What's the obsession with talking? Why does everything need to be analysed and dissected? Plenty of kids don't get on with their parents. Can't you just accept that we have one of those relationships and leave it alone?'

'Because I don't want to have "one of those relationships". I want my mum.'

'Oh, grow up, Samantha. You're twenty-nine years old, not five. It's a bit late to try and play happy families now.'

'Why? Why is it too late?' My voice came out shrill and I swallowed hard to calm the rising panic. I hadn't imagined it going well but this was far worse than I'd anticipated. Her aggression towards me had stepped up a notch and my whole body was now trembling.

'Because it is,' she cried.

'Why?'

'Because too much has happened and we can't recover from it.'

'Like what?'

'You really want to know?' She leaned forward, thrust her hand out and started counting off her fingers. 'Because you moved back in without asking and stayed far too long, because you turned my dad against me, because you turned my mum against me, because you were always so needy, demanding my attention all the time, and because you took my husband away from me.'

Auntie Louise gasped, but I couldn't form any words. Was that what she really thought of me? Bile rose in my throat and I thought for a moment that I was going to be sick. I closed my eyes to gather myself but Mum was on a roll.

'Father of the year. Role model extraordinaire. The pair of you were thick as thieves. There was never any room for me. You broke up my marriage.'

There was no way I was going to take the blame for that. I fought to keep my voice calm as I narrowed my eyes at her. 'You go and convince yourself of that if it makes you feel better but we both know that's not the case. Dad *had* to be there for me because *you* never were but I wanted you to be. It's all I ever wanted. When I was little, you were my hero. Did you know that?'

'No, Samantha, your dad was and still is your hero.'

'But when I was little, so were you. You were so clever and I wanted to be just like you. You went to work, you looked after the house, you made the garden look beautiful, you could sew and cook and paint. I remember looking at you and wondering how you managed to fit it all in.'

'And your point is...?'

'And my point is that, one day, I realised that the reason why the house was immaculate and the garden was beautiful and you had so many other talents was because you devoted all your spare time to those things. And none of it to me.'

She rolled her eyes and clenched her jaw but didn't speak.

I continued in the same matter-of-fact tone, determined to remain factual but not emotional. 'The only time I ever got your attention was when Chloe was at our house and, when I say I got your attention, I mean you were in the vicinity. Chloe was the one that you focused on and I never understood why you adored her and not me. I wasn't a naughty child and I kept my room tidy so I thought it was because Chloe was beautiful and I wasn't. I thought you were ashamed of me.'

'Don't be ridiculous,' Mum snapped.

'Let her finish,' Auntie Louise said. 'You need to hear this.' She gave me an encouraging smile and mouthed, 'Go on.'

'I couldn't change how I looked but I thought that you might notice me if I worked even harder at school but it backfired on me. You'd accuse me of showing Chloe up by getting better grades than her, or you'd make a big fuss about Chloe getting a B-minus and ask me what I'd done wrong if I got an A instead of an A-plus. All I wanted was for you to say, "well done, Samantha, I'm proud of you, Samantha," but you never had a kind word for me. Ever. So if I was needy, it's because you made me that way. And if I was close to Dad and Nanna and Gramps, it was because they were all I had. I never did anything to turn anyone against you and I wasn't even aware that any of them *had* turned on you. They all loved you.'

'They hated me.'

'No, they didn't.' Auntie Louise reached for Mum's hand but she snatched it away. 'Debs! I'm telling you the truth and you know it. Mum and Dad always loved you. They just didn't love the way you treated Sam. And do you really think Jonathan would have stuck around as long as he did if he didn't love you too?'

Mum leapt to her feet. 'And now she's turned you against me too. I should have known it was only a matter of time.'

'Debbie!' Auntie Louise stood up and tried to hug Mum but was shrugged off. 'I'd never turn against you.'

'But you just have.' Mum grabbed her bag and stormed towards the door.

Shock rooted me to the spot. What the hell had just happened? I'd come to make peace with Mum yet had managed to start a new war instead.

Mum yanked open the lounge door, then paused and looked at me with such hate in her eyes and then she spoke with venom. 'I didn't want to keep you, you know, but your precious dad made me and now look what's happened. I said you'd destroy us and you have. You've destroyed everything.'

With a slam of the door, she was gone.

I couldn't speak. I could barely think. I rocked back and forth in the chair, the catch of each shocked breath piercing the heavy silence.

I became aware of Auntie Louise lowering herself onto the sofa, her hands in her hair, and Chloe drifting down the stairs, her hand across her mouth.

Had that really just happened? Had she really said that?

'She didn't mean it.' Auntie Louise's voice was barely audible.

'We both know she did.'

Chloe dropped onto the sofa beside her mum. 'Sammie. I'm so sorry.'

I nodded slowly. 'I can't... I've got to go. I'm sorry.'

Then I fled.

I'd only made it a little way down the main road before my eyes were too blurred to see the road. Turning into a pub car park, I pulled into the furthest, darkest point and screamed. Years of pent-up anger and frustration towards that cold, bitter woman raged through my veins as I beat the steering wheel with my fists, stamped my feet, yelled, swore and screeched. I didn't care who could hear me or see me. I had to have my release.

I stopped the car three times to vomit on the way home that night, and crawled into bed at Brook Cottage, shaking and sweating. Shock. It could do nasty things to people.

67

The following morning, I phoned in sick; something I couldn't remember doing for years.

Chloe and Auntie Louise both rang, in tears, devastated by the evening's outcome. Auntie Louise promised to keep talking to Mum and try to bring her round but I told her not to bother. I'd wanted the truth and that was exactly what I'd got. Brutally dished out.

Dad visited straight from work. The expression on his face when I relayed the conversation was heart-breaking. I begged him to tell me the whole truth and was astonished to discover that, before I was born, Mum had been pregnant with a baby girl who they lost at seven months.

'She had a bit of a breakdown after that,' Dad said. 'She was convinced it was something she'd done wrong like not eating the right foods or trying to do too much, even though the doctor told us it was just one of those unfortunate, unexplained things.' He slumped back in his chair and shook his head. 'She wasn't coping at all and I should have pushed her to get some professional help or even just talk to me about it but she got upset every time I broached the subject so I left it. I got home from work one day to find everything we'd bought for the baby piled up in the front garden. It would have been the baby's due date and I hadn't even registered.'

'Oh no.'

'Oh yes. She yelled at me and threw things and, when she finally calmed down, I asked about the stuff in the garden. She told me there was no way she could go through that sort of pain and loss again so she didn't want to try for another baby and was going to burn everything. I should have seen it coming but that completely threw me. We'd both wanted two or three kids and losing your sister had been awful but I assumed we'd come to terms with it together and eventually try again. She point blank refused but it turned out she was already pregnant with you.'

For the first time ever, I saw him cry. 'I'm so sorry, Sammie. I kept thinking that, one day, she'd realise what a precious gift you were, but she never did. I couldn't make it better. I let you both down.'

'You weren't to blame.' I hugged him tightly. 'You did everything you could for her and for me. Everything. Don't ever think you let either of us down because you absolutely didn't.'

* * *

Josh came round after Dad left and we talked into the small hours; something I'd never done with James or Harry.

'Painful as the truth was,' I said to him as we snuggled up on the sofa, 'I do at least now understand why Mum was so detached throughout my life. I'd always thought it was my fault, that I'd done something wrong, that I'd been a let-down. All I'd done wrong was not be my sister and there was nothing anybody could have done about that. Odd as it might sound, that brings me some comfort.'

'I can understand that,' he said, hugging me close to his side. 'I'm so sorry things have been so tough for you. I wish I could say or do something to take the hurt away.'

'You're already doing it by being here,' I assured him. And he was. My relationship with Josh was a revelation. He hadn't told me he loved me and I hadn't said those words either, but I felt it through every look, every touch, every word and every caring action. I'd loved James but it seemed like a schoolgirl crush compared to the depth of my feelings for Josh. I hadn't loved Harry, though, and I found myself questioning why I'd stayed with him for three years. And then it hit me: Mum. When I graduated from university and secured a job back in Whitsborough Bay, she made her feelings about me moving back in very clear. She also constantly belittled me for being single and dowdy while my stunning cousin had a string of gorgeous boyfriends. I hadn't started seeing Harry because I fancied him; I'd started seeing him because he was the first man to show me a bit of attention and I grasped at it and clung on. And I hadn't moved in with Harry because I loved him; I'd moved in with him to escape from Mum. It scared me how much control she'd had over my life and the decisions I made. It was all over now. She had no more influence over me.

* * *

Driving to the farmhouse on Saturday morning, I felt much brighter and the arrival of a second hedgehog moments after I parked cheered me up no end. The man dropping it off said he'd found it on the road near his house and suspected it had been clipped by a bicycle rather than a car as it had a 'gammy leg' but no other damage. A check-over in the barn revealed him to be our first male resident and I christened him Mr Snuffles. His leg was broken so I administered painkillers and applied a splint then bandaged him up before leaving him to rest in the crate next to Spikette.

I was keen to explore progress in the farmhouse. The old kitchen had been ripped out at the start of the week, first fix electrics put in, and the walls plastered. I felt quite emotional standing in the empty room; the last place I'd seen Thomas alive. I pictured him wearing his six paper hats with that stupid mouthguard in, giggling helplessly. If it hadn't been for my difficult relationship with Mum, I wouldn't have spent that day with him. Some things were meant to be because I wouldn't have traded those last hours with that wonderful old man for the world. Tears stung my eyes but I blinked them back. *No. Happy thoughts from now on.*

The bedrooms were ready for furniture and my en-suite was complete. The main bathroom needed a few more days' work and the kitchen would take about a week after that. There were another couple of rooms still to be tackled downstairs but they could wait until later. Dave was pretty certain everything would be ready for a fortnight's time which nicely coincided with the start of the Easter holidays.

Making myself a mug of tea, I took it round to Thomas and Gwendoline's bench, taking advantage of the peace before the builders arrived. The wildflowers had painted the meadow with an explosion of yellow and gold as buttercups, primrose, celandines and wild daffodils swayed in the spring breeze. Tall daisies and wood anemones added a splash of white, like clouds among the sunshine, and there were sparser spatters of purple and pink, although I'd yet to identify the names of those flowers.

Birds chirped and I picked out the sound of the blackbird, song thrush and wren – Gramps would have been impressed – among the gentle buzz of bees in the meadow. I breathed in deeply, the gentle fragrance of wildflowers and grass filling me with energy and excitement for the future.

'I hope you like what we've done,' I said, raising my mug towards the meadow in a toast. I like to think they were smiling and nodding.

68

A fortnight later, the farmhouse was ready. I woke up on the Saturday morning with a big smile on my face. *This is it! Moving day!* I'd already taken most of my belongings across. I could have slept there last night but I wanted to make a meal to say thank you to Rich and Dave for providing me with a home and friendship and helping me fulfil Thomas and Gwendoline's legacy.

Dad had decided not to move in, telling me he felt settled at Lauren's and didn't want to crowd me. I protested but I could see it made sense. He needed his space and so did I.

Mr Jeffreys had phoned me at work yesterday with the great news that the Grimes boys' solicitor had acknowledged they had no legal claim and would be dropping the case. It was therefore lovely to unlock my new front door that morning to find a letter on the mat from Mr Jeffreys confirming it was all over. Completely fresh start.

* * *

The first day in my new home was wonderful, unpacking crockery, cutlery and accessories for the kitchen and finding homes for every-thing, then doing the same with the bathrooms and my bedroom.

And, of course, checking on the five hedgehogs I was now looking after.

For an office, I'd chosen a bedroom overlooking the meadow. For now, I'd only furnished that room, the master bedroom at the front of the house, and what would have been Dad's room. I wanted to spend some time living in the farmhouse before deciding how to use the other bedrooms.

When I'd finished unpacking my clothes, I went downstairs, removed the meadow canvas from the lounge wall and hung it on the bedroom wall opposite the bed. I could see the actual meadow from the lounge and my office and I wanted to be able to see it from my bedroom too.

Unpacking Mickleby, the soft hedgehog Thomas had given me at Christmas, I took him into the office and sat him on my empty bookcase. I added three very special framed photos – one of Thomas from Christmas Day wearing his six paper hats, a selfie of Gramps and me from before his party started, and one of Nanna, Gwendoline and a six-year-old me in the back garden of Meadowcroft, all holding hedgehogs in our hands.

I lightly ran my fingers across the final photo. 'Thomas said you wished for me to stay at the farm and help you with the hedgehogs and here I am. Bit later than planned but your wish has come true, hedgehog lady, and I promise I won't let you down.' I moved my gaze across to the photo of Thomas. 'Or you. I miss you so much but you're not far away, are you? I can feel you both right beside me.'

* * *

Josh turned up early that evening with a couple of bouquets of flowers, some bubbly, a box of chocolates and an Indian takeaway. I was dying to take him on a tour but we didn't get much further than the bedroom.

The takeaway was cold by the time we padded back downstairs, stomachs growling, so we blasted it in the microwave. Josh went to open the bubbly for me but I stopped him.

'You're on call tonight so let's have it tomorrow night when we can share it.'

'I wish I wasn't on call tonight,' he said, kissing my neck. 'I'd rather be here with you all night.'

We were settling down to sleep when his mobile rang shortly after midnight.

'Labrador labour problems,' he said, pulling on his clothes after he'd taken the call. He leaned over and gently kissed me. 'You get some sleep.'

I lay back on my pillows, listening to the sound of his jeep pulling away. My arms ached from lugging boxes and my eyelids felt so heavy that I couldn't stay awake and wait for him even if I tried.

* * *

I walked through the meadow, my fingers lightly brushing the tops of the buttercups, poppies, and cornflowers. Wispy clouds floated across a baby-blue sky and the sun smiled at me, warming my hair and the side of my face. A woman walked beside me wearing a yellow and grey fifties-style dress. Gwendoline. A wicker picnic basket rested in the crook of her arm, covered with a red and white gingham cloth. She peeled back the cloth but, instead of a picnic, the basket contained five hedgehogs.

'Aren't they the most adorable creatures?' she asked, beaming at them.

'They are,' I agreed. 'We've got five hedgehogs in the barn now and we aren't even open yet.'

'I know. Thank you for rescuing them.' Then her smile slipped as the whole meadow darkened. The gentle breeze turned into a vicious wind, whipping my hair across my face. 'They need you, Sammie. They need you now.'

And someone was calling my name. Thomas?

I woke up alone in the bed, panting, drenched in sweat. Something was wrong. Running to the window, I caught the taillights of a vehicle on the track. *The Grimes boys? No! The barn!*

Sprinting down the stairs, I grabbed the keys from the kitchen and shoved my feet into my wellies. The movement-activated lights illuminated the farmyard and the barn and that's when I smelt it. Smoke.

'I'm coming!' I cried, fumbling with the keys in the new padlock. Pushing the door open, I reeled back from the heat. The amber flames were at the far end of the barn and way too big for me to tackle with an extinguisher.

Must save the hogs.

I pulled my nightshirt over my mouth and nose as I ran towards the crates. Stacking the first three on top of each other, barely able to see round them, I ran outside, and placed them by the side of the farmhouse. There was no time to check they were okay but I sent up a prayer to Gwendoline and Thomas to save my spiky babies. As I sprinted back towards the barn, I was vaguely aware of approaching headlights on the track – hopefully Josh returning. I ran inside, holding my arms up against the heat and coughing as I grabbed the final two crates.

'Shit! Sam!' Josh cried, running towards me as I exited the barn.

'Call the fire brigade,' I yelled, barely glancing at him as I placed the next two crates down. 'I've got the hogs.'

Flames were now bursting out of the roof, amber and gold, dancing into the blackness. I slumped against the side of the house, eyes streaming, heart thumping, listening to Josh relaying details to the emergency operator. *My barn. My beautiful barn.*

Panting, I flicked open the lid on the first crate and peeled back the fleecy blanket with shaking hands to reveal Spikette curled up. She was still breathing. Thank goodness. The combination of the fleece and her protective ball had likely protected her from any smoke. I repeated the same for the next three boxes. Mr Snuffles, Mrs Tiggy Winkle and Sonic were all breathing too. I lifted the lid on Quilly's crate, moved back the fleece, and I swear my heart stopped for a moment. Empty. My mind whizzed back to earlier that day. He'd spilled his water dish so I'd transferred him to another crate but got distracted by Mr Jeffreys phoning to check I'd received his letter. *I didn't transfer him back*. I felt sick.

Josh was still on the phone with his back to me. It was now or never. I sprinted across the yard again.

'Sam! No!'

'Quilly's still in there.'

All I remember after that point was the heat. Such intense heat. And the sound, like a waterfall roaring.

Then nothing.

69

I could hear Hannah's voice. Was she reading a story? It sounded like *The Hungry Caterpillar.* I loved that book when I was a child. I'd bought it for Amelia recently...

Music drifted to me. I recognised the artists. Favourites of mine. I tried to sing along but it seemed like too much effort. Sleep. I just wanted to sleep...

Dad and Uncle Simon were talking. What were they saying? Something about the barn? The fire! Quilly! I had to tell them to save him. Maybe when I woke up...

Josh was holding my hand and lightly stroking my wrist, like he'd done that first night in the taxi. I loved him doing that. I loved him. I should tell him. But it was so relaxing. Just a bit more sleep...

My hair was being stroked back from my face. 'You're going to be fine,' whispered a woman. 'Thank you for saving my hedgehogs.' Gwendoline? ...

'You brought joy to my life again,' Thomas said. My eyes flickered open. He sat on the edge of the bed. 'Your time for joy is coming. The bad times are gone. I promise.'...

People were moving around me. Bright lights. Something beeping. Low-volume murmuring. Why couldn't they speak more coherently? I wanted to shout at them to turn up the volume, but my mouth felt dry, and my eyelids heavy.

'Samantha? Can you hear me, Samantha? Can you open your eyes?'

I licked my lips. So dry. Where was my lip salve?

'Samantha? Are you able to open your eyes for me?'

Yes, yes, give me a minute. I've only just woken up. It seemed to take an enormous amount of effort to open them, as though they were taped shut.

'Samantha?'

Oh my gosh! Keep your hair on! I'm trying my best.

There were faces, peering over me, all a bit blurred. *Why are all these people in my bedroom? Where am I? This isn't my duvet.*

'You're doing great, Samantha. My name is Dr Javid. You're in Hull Royal Infirmary.'

'Why?' I could barely hear the word.

'It's probably best if you don't try to talk just yet. Your throat's going to be sore and dry. We'll get you some water in a moment. You were in an accident.'

Dr Javid came into focus. He had a round, friendly face with a shock of jet-black hair.

'Do you remember anything about the fire?' he asked. 'No need to speak. Just a nod or shake of the head.'

The fire. Yes. My barn. Gone. And my hedgehogs. Are they safe? I slowly nodded but my eyes were heavy again.

'She'll probably drift in and out of sleep,' Dr Javid said. 'That was good, though. She's going to be fine.'

Of course I am. Thomas and Gwendoline said so.

70

The following day, I felt like I'd awoken from the most refreshing and satisfying of sleeps. Despite feeling shaky, I was alert, hungry, and eager to find out what had happened. Over the course of the day, I heard from medical professionals about my head trauma, my score on the Glasgow Coma Scale and the treatment I'd received on ICU. It seemed that part of the barn had collapsed when I'd gone back in that second time, knocking me unconscious, but Josh had pulled me out. I'd broken my left arm, had some minor burns on both arms, was covered in cuts and bruises – most of which had now healed – and had minor smoke inhalation. I was very lucky.

When Hannah and I got our degree results, we hit the student bar then went into Liverpool and celebrated a little too hard. When I woke up the morning after, the back of my right hand was stamped for entry to a club neither of us could remember visiting. Losing an entire evening and knowing that the memory would probably never return was the weirdest sensation and I'd never wanted to repeat it. Yet now, without a drop of alcohol inside me, I'd lost nine days of my life. Nine.

The whole experience had been surreal, like swimming underwater at a busy public pool when you can still hear the talking, the laughter, the shouts, but it's all muffled. In my coma, I'd heard snippets of conversation, felt the touch of my loved ones, but I'd been unable to surface. I couldn't tell them I was there. I couldn't respond to their touch.

Hannah dropped by that afternoon with Amelia. She told me she'd visited several times.

'This might seem like a silly question, but did you read *The Hungry Caterpillar* to me?' I asked.

Her eyes widened. 'You could hear me?'

'Drifting in and out. I could hear my favourite music too.'

'Also me.'

I smiled. 'Thanks for doing that.'

Hannah nodded as she squeezed my hand. 'I'm so glad you're okay. You had me worried for a moment.'

Josh arrived in the evening, his face unshaven and dark shadows below his eyes.

'Aren't I meant to be the one who looks rough?' I joked as he lowered himself onto the bed, taking care not to knock my broken arm.

'I might have struggled to sleep recently.'

'I've slept for nine days solid. I highly recommend it.'

'I thought I'd lost you.' He gently stroked my face, his eyes full of concern. 'I've never been so scared in my whole life.'

'I'm sorry. I know it was stupid but I couldn't leave Quilly.'

Josh bit his lip.

'He didn't make it, did he?'

'I'm so sorry.'

A tear slid down my cheek and I swallowed hard on the lump in my throat. 'And the others?'

'All made it, thanks to you. Spikette was up to a good weight so she went back to the Bensons last week and they released her. Sonic should be ready for release this week too.'

'I need to know about the barn.' I shook my head. 'I'm imagining the worst so you might as well hit me with it.'

'The beams burned so the walls collapsed. All the fire brigade could do was stop it spreading to other buildings.'

I slumped back into my pillows and stared at the ceiling, tears pooling in my eyes again. No! I wasn't going to let them win. I took a deep breath and sat forward again.

'Did I tell you what my favourite film is?'

'*The Greatest Showman*?'

I nodded. 'When Barnum's circus burns down, it feels like it's hopeless. He's lost everything but he realises he still has the people he loves right beside him. The circus was just a building and buildings can be replaced. They sing about building it back up and that's what we're going to do. I know there's no chance of it opening for Gwendoline's birthday but it *will* happen. Hedgehog Hollow will rise again, bigger and better than before. I'm insured. It's just a setback and what building project doesn't have setbacks?'

He smiled and kissed me. 'I've got something to show you.' He took his phone out of his pocket and started playing a video.

'Oh my goodness, Josh! Who are all those people?'

'Builders, farmers, labourers and anyone who hated what happened to you and wanted to pitch in. Dave sent me it.'

I watched in astonishment at the hive of activity at the farm, from clearing the charred remains to starting over again with the salvaged stones. Short recordings had been made over several days, showing phenomenal progress rebuilding the barn.

'There were so many helpers, they've even managed to take down that dilapidated wooden barn,' he said. 'I think you might be open for Gwendoline's birthday after all.'

'I can't believe all those people doing that. All those strangers. So much kindness.'

'This community looks out for each other. There was bad feeling about the earlier vandalism, but this was something nobody could stomach, especially as you nearly...' His voice broke and I stroked his hand.

'I'm here. I came through it, and I've got you to thank for that. You saved my life.'

Josh gently stroked my hair away from my face. 'You saved mine first. Before I met you, I was existing but not living.' He kissed me tenderly. 'I have to say something. I know it's not the most romantic of settings but, if this tragedy has taught me anything, it's that you have to grab each day as it comes. I know we haven't been together for long but I don't think time matters when you meet the right person. You inspire me. You make me feel like I can achieve anything with you by my side and I want to be there for you while you save the world one hedgehog at a time.'

I laughed and squeezed his hand, waiting for him to continue.

'I was going to say this before I got called out and I can't tell you how many times I've beaten myself up since then for not telling you how I really feel. I love you, Sam. I love you so very much.'

At last! Those three little words I'd longed to hear and spoken with such passion from someone who so clearly meant them.

'I love you too, Josh. More than I could imagine was possible. I could feel you, you know. When I was asleep, I could feel your touch and hear your voice and my biggest goal was to get back to you.'

He leaned over and gently kissed me again.

'I don't know how many hours I must have sat here, staring at you, willing you to open those beautiful eyes. And I wasn't the only one. You've had lots of visitors.'

'Who came?' *Please say Mum.*

'Your dad's been here loads. Chloe's been a few times with her mum and the baby. Rich and Dave, James, Hannah and Toby, your Uncle Simon, my Auntie Lauren...'

I had to ask, even though I knew the answer. 'But not Mum?'

He shook his head slowly. 'Sorry.'

I smiled gently. That was that, then. I could have died and she never came. My relationship with Mum really, truly was completely over. Not that there'd ever been a relationship in the first place.

71

'Happy opening day!' Josh gathered me in his arms and showered me with kisses. 'Are you excited?'

'Very. I still can't believe what everyone did to get the barn ready. The kindness of strangers, eh?' I'd invited everyone to the family day tomorrow to say thank you and, although I hadn't had the time or energy to execute all my original plans, it still promised to be a big day. Today's event would be much cosier.

'I've got some opening day gifts for you.' Josh rolled out of bed and returned with three packages.

'There might be a recurring theme,' he said, handing over the first small, soft parcel wrapped in hedgehog-covered wrapping paper.

'Hmm. Let me guess what that theme might be...' I ripped open the wrapping and took out a pair of grey socks covered in hedgehogs. 'Cute.'

'And I know you've already got a hedgehog necklace and bracelet but I thought these might complete the set.'

I removed a pair of silver hedgehog earrings. 'They're gorgeous. Thank you.'

'And I've taken a chance with these.' He handed me the final package which was large and soft.

Inside were three tunic dresses in different styles and colours, all with small hedgehogs printed on them. 'You said you like wearing dresses now and I thought that Gwendoline's probably weren't ideal for mucking out the hogs but maybe these will be.'

'You have amazing taste,' I said, holding up one dress at a time. 'And you've just solved my what-to-wear dilemma for today and tomorrow.'

'You really like them?'

'I love them. But not as much as I love you.'

* * *

The official grand opening was planned for 4 p.m. to give us plenty of time to prepare. I was therefore surprised to glance out of the barn window and see a vehicle coming up the newly laid smooth farm track around mid-morning. As it got closer, I realised it was a police car.

Josh was up a ladder, hanging some hedgehog bunting across the front of the barn. 'Josh! Police are here.'

We met the two constables in the farmyard and invited them into the kitchen for drinks. I recognised the female, PC Griegson, from the vandalism but hadn't met the male, PC Sunning, before. They asked how I was and if I was all set for opening day while Josh made mugs of tea, then it was down to business.

'We have news,' PC Griegson said. 'Good news.'

I took hold of Josh's hand under the table.

'As you're aware, the CCTV from the fire was inconclusive...' I'd been gutted about that. It had picked up the two arsonists but they'd been wearing hoodies and there were no clear images of their faces. Watching one of them lob a brick through a window at the back of the barn then seeing the other throw in a flaming torch had made me feel sick. The registration number of their car had been clear but had been reported as stolen earlier that evening. They'd been caught on various

CCTV systems speeding through Hull but, again, none of the visuals were clear enough to show their faces.

'However, I did another system check on the blood on those plastic shards,' she continued. 'It pulled a match for Brynn Grimes, newly entered into the system following an assault.'

PC Sunning nodded. 'When we questioned him, he claimed the plan was only to smash some windows but his cousin, Cody Grimes, took it further and was the fire starter.'

I pressed my fingers to my lips, scarcely able to believe what I was hearing. 'So you've got them both?'

'They've both been charged for the crimes of vandalism, the theft of a motor vehicle, harassment and arson,' PC Griegson confirmed.

I jumped up and shook her hand, then his. 'Thank you so much. I can't tell you what a relief that is.'

'It's a pleasure,' she said. 'We'll let you get on with your opening day preparations. Good luck.'

'Thank you again and thanks to everyone who's worked on the case. If you're not working tomorrow, please come to the official opening barbeque. Bring your friends. Bring your family. There'll be a bouncy castle, a hog roast, craft stalls and Josh might even be dressing up as a hedgehog.' I glanced at his shocked face. 'We'll chat about that one later.'

72

'Thank you for all coming today,' I said to the small crowd that afternoon. 'It gives me enormous pleasure to welcome you to a project that started more than two decades ago when a wonderful man called Thomas Mickleby bought this farm for his wife, Gwendoline, to fulfil a lifelong dream of running a hedgehog rescue centre. Sadly, Gwendoline fell ill and passed away before it could happen. Thomas and I were stunned to discover that I knew Gwendoline from when I was a little girl and she used to release hedgehogs in my grandparents' garden. We became great friends and he decided that I could be the one to finally make their dream come true.'

I paused for a moment to gather myself. *Must not cry.* 'It's been a tough old journey and, a few weeks ago, we lost the barn, supplies and equipment. We also lost our third patient, Quilly, and I nearly lost my life.'

Deep breath. You can do this. 'But thanks to the hard work and generosity of my friend for life, Dave Williams, and his team, and the incredible support of this community, we built it back up and it's even better than the original. I've been overwhelmed by the donations we've had. There are so many other people to thank – my good friends Hannah, Toby, and Rich, my boss Lauren, and my colleagues for holding the fort at work while I decided to have a nine-day kip. To my wonderful dad and my amazing boyfriend, Josh, I couldn't have done this without your support or your belief in me. And a massive thank you to everyone at Alderson and Son Veterinary Practice for making us their charity of the year and already being so generous with their support. So, without any more wittering from me, on what would have been Gwendoline Mickleby's seventy-ninth birthday, I'm delighted to declare Hedgehog Hollow Rescue Centre officially—' I cut the bright yellow ribbon strung across the door '—OPEN!'

There were cheers and applause and someone gave a loud whistle. My heart swelled with pride as I beamed at everyone, the desire to cry replaced by a feeling of elation. I'd done it. With the help of family, friends and strangers, I'd made Thomas and Gwendoline's dreams come true.

I posed for photographs with the Mayor and various local businesspeople who'd provided labour, materials or sponsorship, then took them for a tour inside, introducing them to some of our twelve patients. The loss of a fortnight through hospital and bedrest at home meant I hadn't managed to set up social media or do any advertising, yet word had spread.

The press left an hour later, full of tea, cream scones and cake. The good news about the Grimes boys being caught and charged would probably result in the centre being front page news. The more coverage the better as hopefully that would make readers more aware of the plight of our beautiful indigenous creatures. I handed each reporter a fact sheet covering what to do if anyone found a sick or injured hedgehog and guidance on how to make gardens hedgehog-friendly. They all promised to include some of the information in their write-ups.

With my official duties now over, Auntie Louise, Uncle Simon and Chloe appeared by my side with hugs and congratulations. James hovered nearby, holding Samuel, and there was an awkward couple of seconds.

'For goodness' sake, give her a hug,' Chloe demanded, taking

Samuel from him. 'I've learned my lesson. I'm not going to have a hissy fit.'

James put his arms round me and kissed me on the cheek. 'Sorry and thank you again for everything,' he whispered.

'That's okay. Look after her and tell her the truth. Always.'

'I will.'

Chloe had told me that James had been for a couple of hospital appointments and everything was looking good. The cancer hadn't spread.

'Thank you for all coming today,' I said. 'It means a lot.' I bit my lip as I glanced back towards the barn entrance.

Auntie Louise slipped her hand into mine. 'Sorry. She wouldn't come.'

'I wasn't expecting her to. I just...'

Auntie Louise hugged me again. 'I know. I hoped too. We all tried.'

I pulled away and smiled a little too brightly. 'It is what it is. So, who wants to meet the hogs?'

* * *

Sitting on the edge of Thomas and Gwendoline's bench twenty minutes later, I gulped in deep breaths of fresh air. Misty-Blue was stretched out on the lawn, enjoying the warmth on her tummy. The meadow was now a full explosion of all the colours of the rainbow and, as I gazed at its beauty and listened to the birds chirping, a calmness settled over me.

The emotions of the day – and particularly the inevitable disappointment of a no-show from Mum – had suddenly become too much and I'd rushed out of the barn before they welled over. Why had I even imagined she'd turn up? Why had I clung to that sliver of hope? I needed to put Mum out of my thoughts once and for all because I was clearly not in hers.

'Happy birthday, Gwendoline,' I said, 'and happy opening day. We did it. We made your dream come true. Thank you for sending Josh to me. I know that was you and probably Nanna and Gramps.'

Closing my eyes, I rested my head on my hands.

'Are you okay, poppet?' Dad asked a few minutes later.

I looked up and smiled. 'There was a teeny tiny part of me that thought... hoped... Mum might come. It was stupid really. If she wasn't going to visit me in hospital, she wasn't going to turn up today.'

He sat down and put his arm round me and kissed the top of my head. 'You're not the only one who hoped. Was that why you ran out of the barn?'

I nodded. 'It suddenly got a bit much for me and I didn't want to start crying in front of everyone.' I was keen to refocus on something less emotional. 'So, how's it going with Lauren?'

'She's great fun. I haven't laughed so much in years. You might have introduced me to a friend for life there.'

'Just friends?'

Dad laughed. 'We knew you and Josh had been speculating. Yes, just friends. She's been good for me and I've managed to prove to her that not all men are idiots.'

'No. Some are heroes.'

'Like Josh, saving you from a burning barn.'

'Yes. And like you, saving me from Mum's wrath for all of these years.'

'I wish I could have done more.'

'You did loads.'

We sat in silence for a few minutes, the occasional burst of laughter reaching us from the barn.

'I never thought I'd call anywhere home other than Whitsborough Bay,' Dad said, 'but there's something about this place that's so...' He breathed in as though searching for the right word on the spring breeze.

'Magical?' I suggested.

'You know what? I think it is.' He stood up and gave my shoulder a squeeze. 'Don't sit out here too long. It's getting chilly now.' Such a Dad thing to say!

Ten minutes later, Josh appeared with one of my cardigans.

'Your family have gone into the house,' he said, draping the cardigan round my shoulders.

'I'll be in shortly.'

'Can I sit with you or would you rather be alone?'

'I'd rather be with you. Always.'

'Same here.' He sat beside me and put his arm round me. I snuggled into his shoulder as we sat back against the plaque.

'What are you thinking about? he asked.

'Something Gramps said to me the day before he died. He said "the fragrance always stays in the hand that gives the rose".'

'What does it mean?'

'It's about acts of kindness ultimately coming round and benefiting the giver. He was referring to me letting go of James so he could be with Chloe. At the time, I struggled to see how that could ever benefit me yet here I am today with you and with all of this.' I swept my hand round to emphasise my point. 'If James and Chloe hadn't married, I'd never have met Thomas and I'd never have moved away. I'd never have made friends with him, inherited the farm, set up the rescue centre or met you.'

Misty-Blue leapt up onto my knee and I smiled. 'And I'd never have met you, little one. One act of kindness and look how much it delivered back to me. Gramps was right. The fragrance definitely stayed in my hand.'

Josh stroked the cat. 'I wish I'd met your Gramps and Thomas.'

'So do I. They'd have loved you.'

He released a contented sigh. 'It's so beautiful and peaceful out here.'

'I know. It's my favourite place on the whole farm, sitting here on their special bench, looking at the meadow that Thomas and Gwendoline created. I can feel them both here.'

We sat in silence for a few minutes until the wind picked up and I shivered. Misty-Blue jumped down and ran along the side of the house, presumably feeling the cold too.

Josh took my hand in his. 'Your hands are like ice. Are you ready to go back inside and continue building those bridges with your family?'

'Some of my family,' I said.

'Some is better than none and don't forget that sometimes the chasm is too wide to build a bridge, no matter how much it hurts to accept that.' I knew he was thinking about his own irreparable situation with his dad but it definitely applied to Mum and me. The chasm was definitely too wide between us and I needed to accept that and move on with my life – my wonderful new life with Josh and the hedgehogs.

He gently pulled me to my feet, wrapped his arms round me, and kissed me. As I melted against him, I thought about what Thomas had told me about his love for Gwendoline: 'She was the best of the best... She was my everything... That woman brought me so much joy every day.' I'd wondered how that felt and now I knew because I'd found the same with Josh. I'd found my forever. I'd fulfilled my final promise to Gramps.

'Thank you,' I said.

'What for?'

'For understanding about Mum, for giving Dad a job, for everything you've done to help fulfil Thomas and Gwendoline's dreams, and for showing me what love really is.'

He kissed me slowly and tenderly. 'I'll keep showing you that for the rest of our lives. I love you so much and I'm so proud of you. I'm sure Thomas and Gwendoline would have been too.'

I looked back across to the meadow to where Thomas and Gwendoline were standing, hand in hand, waving to me. I placed my fingertips to my lips and blew them a kiss.

'Oh, they are. They're very proud of me.'

ACKNOWLEDGMENTS

Thank you so much for reading *Finding Love at Hedgehog Hollow*. This is my tenth novel. Can't believe I'm into double figures!

So many people have helped me with this story, particularly checking out information around nursing, Social Services, and cremations in order to ensure that the story, although fictional, does feel real. My cousin, Nikki Richardson, is a community staff nurse for the NHS and provided me with invaluable insight into the typical working day of a district or community nurse. My cousin, Amanda Miller, is a lecturer and was able to set me straight on whether Sam could tutor at a TEC without a teaching qualification. Claire Potter, a friend of mine, works for a funeral director and provided guidance on cremations and how soon ashes could be collected. And an extra enormous thank you has to go to my sister-in-law, Linda Fisher. Linda works for Social Services and I spoke to her regarding a plot point around Samantha potentially referring Thomas to them for help if he wasn't eating. While on that call, I discovered that a major plot point was unfeasible and, as a result, I had to significantly rewrite parts of the book. Frustratingly, I'd had my doubts early on but thought I'd found a workaround. Valuable lesson: don't wait until the end to check out major issues! So, Linda, I am extremely grateful for the time you spent brainstorming a way round this.

I've dedicated this book to my Auntie Gwen who is a real-life 'hedgehog lady'. For years, her garage has provided sanctuary for rescued hogs. She's on the call list for local vets and has looked after hundreds of hogs over the years, nursing them back to health and/or fattening them up for hibernation. My parents have a bungalow in a village which backs onto open fields – the inspiration for Meadowcroft – and she sometimes releases them there. I don't see Auntie Gwen nearly as often as I'd like as we don't live very close but I have very fond memories of staying with her during school holidays when I was little. It wasn't always possible because she worked shifts but, occasionally, I'd spend a few nights there without my brothers and it was lovely having my auntie all to myself. Auntie Gwen – I had hoped to see you this month but, as I write these acknowledgements, we are in a COVID-19 lockdown so I send my love virtually instead and hope to see you and Uncle Stan really soon xx

As well as the valuable input from my Auntie Gwen, I've learned so much about hedgehogs through membership of The British Hedgehog Preservation Society (BHPS) who do an amazing job in raising awareness and in campaigning for protection for hedgehogs. The Channel 5 documentary *Saving Britain's Hedgehogs* was also a great source of research into how a busy rescue centre operates.

I always thank my husband for being so supportive with my writing but this time I also have to thank him for a plot point. I don't normally run my stories by him because he's not a reader and, if he was, my books wouldn't be his cup of tea. However, when I had my re-writing disaster, he asked me to explain the problem then delighted me by coming up with a new idea of Samantha having met Gwendoline as a child. I love how that has pulled together. Now he keeps joking that I'm his ghost writer. The cheek!

Huge thanks to my team of beta readers – my mum, Joyce Williams, super talented fellow-writer and good friend, Sharon Booth, and my good friend, Liz Berry – for your skilled observations. You are fabulous x

And, of course, I cannot thank enough the team at Boldwood Books. This is my sixth release with them and every single book has been a joy to work on. Nia Beynon, my editor, is nothing short of amazing. She immediately responded to my re-writing crisis with reassuring words and an extended deadline. Thank you to Dushi Horti and Sue Lamprell for their fabulous work on the copy editing and proofreading stages, and to Debbie Clement, the designer of this stunning cover.

Finally, thank you to you, the reader, for your support. The lovely reviews and messages I receive touch me and keep me going – much needed when the plot goes horribly wrong and the author goes into meltdown! If you've loved Samantha's story, I'd be so grateful if you could leave a review and pass on the recommendation to friends and family.

Love and hugs

Jessica xx

HEDGEHOG TRUE/FALSE

Hedgehogs are born with spines

FALSE - Imagine poor mum giving birth if they had spines! Ouch! When hoglets are born, their skin is covered in fluid and, after a few hours, this is reabsorbed and soft white spines erupt from the skin

Hedgehogs are good swimmers

TRUE - They're really good swimmers and, perhaps even more surprisingly, can climb trees. They do sometimes drown, though. It's not the swimming that's the problem; it's the getting out again

Baby hedgehogs are called hoglets

TRUE - Isn't it cute? They're sometimes known as piglets, pups or kittens but the official term is hoglets

Hedgehogs are nocturnal

TRUE - They are nocturnal although. It's not unknown for them to be out and about during the day but this is often a sign that something's wrong

Hedgehogs can run in short bursts at speeds of up to 3mph

FALSE - They're even faster than that. They are surprisingly nippy and can reach top speeds of 5.5mph in short bursts. Go hedgehogs!

Hedgehogs lose half their body weight during hibernation

FALSE - It's actually just over a third but that's still a significant amount and hedgehogs fresh from hibernation are going to need some major feasts to build up their strength quickly

Hedgehogs got their name in the Middle Ages from the word 'hyge-hoge' which translates today as 'hedge' and 'pig' combined

TRUE - The name does what it says on the tin! They snuffle round hedges for their foot and this snuffling/grunting is just like a pig

Hedgehogs have good eyesight

TRUE - It's often believed that their eyesight is poor but it's not the case. They simply don't use their eyes because they don't need to. They have a keen sense of smell, taste and hearing and it's these senses they will use far more than their eyesight

Hedgehogs are quiet eaters

FALSE - They're very noisy when they eat. They love their food and will slurp, crunch and lip-smack with their mouths open. Not the ideal dinner guest!

HEDGEHOG DOS AND DONT'S

Food and Drink

DO NOT give hedgehogs milk to drink. They are lactose intolerant. Dairy products will give them diarrhoea which will dehydrate them and can kill them

DO give hedgehogs water but please have this in a shallow dish. If it's in a deep dish, the risk is that they'll fall in and be unable to get out again

DO give hedgehogs dog or cat food - tin, pouch or biscuit format - but not fishy varieties

DO try to create a feeding station for a hedgehog so that other garden visitors (including cats) don't beat the hedgehog to it. You don't need to buy anything expensive. There are loads of tutorials and factsheets online around creating your own simple station

Your Garden

DO avoid having fences with no gaps under them. Hedgehogs can travel a long way in an evening and they rely on being able to move from one garden to the next. Or you can create a hedgehog highway in your fence

DO place a ramp by a pond so that, if a hedgehog falls, it can easily get out

DO NOT let your dog out into your garden during babies season (May/June and Sept/Oct) without checking there are no hoglets out there first

DO build a bug hotel and DO plant bug-friendly plants. It will attract all sorts of delicious food for your hedgehogs

DO NOT use slug pellets. Hedgehogs love to eat slugs so pellets reduce their food supply and/or poison hedgehogs

DO have a compost heap or a messy part in your garden. If you can have some sticks/wood piled up in a safe corner, this makes a perfect habitat for hibernating

DO check your garden before strimming or mowing. Garden machinery can cause horrific accidents or fatalities

DO NOT leave netting out as hedgehogs can become trapped in it. If you have football goals in your garden, lift the netting up overnight and secure it safely to avoid injury or fatalities

DO always check bonfires before lighting as there may well be hogs nestling in there

Finding Hogs

DON'T assume that a hedgehog out in the daylight is in danger. They usually are but watch first. It could be a mum nesting. If it's moving quickly and appears to be gathering food or nesting materials, leave it alone. If this isn't the case, then something is likely to wrong. Seek help

DO handle hedgehogs with gardening glove - those spines are there to protect the hogs and hurt predators - but keep handling to a minimum. Stay calm and quiet and be gentle with them. Transfer them into a high-sided box or crate with a towel, fleecy blanket or shredded newspaper (and a thick layer of paper on the bottom to soak up their many toilet visits). This will help keep them warm and give them somewhere to hide. Make sure there are plenty of air holes

DON'T move hoglets if you accidentally uncover a nest but, if mum isn't there, do keep an eye on the nest and seek help if mum doesn't return. Hoglets won't survive long without their mother's milk. Put some water and food nearby so mum (assuming she returns) doesn't have far to travel for sustenance. If the hoglets are squeaking, this means they are hungry and you may need to call help if this continues and there's no sign of mum

MORE FROM JESSICA REDLAND

We hope you enjoyed reading *Finding Love at Hedgehog Hollow*. If you did, please leave a review.

If you'd like to gift a copy, this book is also available as an ebook, digital audio download and audiobook CD.

Sign up to Jessica Redland's mailing list for news, competitions and updates on future books.

http://bit.ly/JessicaRedlandNewsletter

ABOUT THE AUTHOR

Jessica Redland is the author of nine novels which are all set around the fictional location of Whitsborough Bay. Inspired by her hometown of Scarborough she writes uplifting women's fiction which has garnered many devoted fans.

Visit Jessica's website: https://www.jessicaredland.com/

Follow Jessica on social media:

facebook.com/JessicaRedlandWriter
twitter.com/JessicaRedland
instagram.com/JessicaRedlandWriter
bookbub.com/authors/jessica-redland

ALSO BY JESSICA REDLAND

Standalone Novels

The Secret To Happiness

Christmas at Carly's Cupcakes

Starry Skies Over The Chocolate Pot Café

Welcome To Whitsborough Bay Series

Making Wishes At Bay View

New Beginnings at Seaside Blooms

Finding Hope at Lighthouse Cove

Coming Home To Seashell Cottage

Hedgehog Hollow Series

Finding Love at Hedgehog Hollow

ABOUT BOLDWOOD BOOKS

Boldwood Books is a fiction publishing company seeking out the best stories from around the world.

Find out more at www.boldwoodbooks.com

Sign up to the Book and Tonic newsletter for news, offers and competitions from Boldwood Books!

http://www.bit.ly/bookandtonic

We'd love to hear from you, follow us on social media:

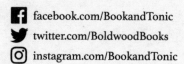

facebook.com/BookandTonic

twitter.com/BoldwoodBooks

instagram.com/BookandTonic